ENTER, KNIGHT ✕ HEL'S STORM

A Duology by
K. A. Keith

ENTER KNIGHT

K. A. KEITH

ENTER, KNIGHT

iUniverse books may be ordered through booksellers or by contacting:

iUniverse
1663 Liberty Drive
Bloomington, IN 47403
www.iuniverse.com
1-800-Authors (1-800-288-4677)

ISBN: 978-1-4917-6908-9 (sc)
ISBN: 978-1-4917-6909-6 (e)

Library of Congress Control Number: 2015912857

Print information available on the last page.

iUniverse rev. date: 01/25/2016

Dramatis Personae

Adestes Malgrim, known as **Malesh**. He shares the Star Burn with Apieron.

Apieron Farsinger, son of Xistus, is a veteran, husband, and father of three small children. He is also the secret vessel of the Star Burn.

Eirec is jarl of Amber Hall, no lowlander is his better.

Gault Candor is eighteen when his father, King Belagund of Ilycrium, is slain by a flying imp of Kör.

Gilead Galdarion, a gold elf warrior-mage. He awaits Kör's Malgrind.

Henlee, the black dwarf, is Apieron's childhood guardian. He wields a fearsome maul and rides the irascible **Bump.**

Isolde, warrior priestess of Gray-Eyed Wisdom. She is betrothed to Xephard.

Rudolph Mellor, who is called Jamello, a rakish troubadour of sunny Bestrand.

Tallux, the emerald-eyed archer, has kin amongst the wood elves of the Greenwolde. His war dog is **Sut.**

Xephard Brighthelm is Wisdom's perfect warrior.

Acknowledgments

I wish to thank Clement Blaise and Rita Shirley and the plethora of gamers, comic fans, outdoorsmen, and boon companions who endured decades of talk about a medieval action epic that, until now, seemed as mythical as unicorns.

The iUniverse team was outstanding: Sarah Disbrow of editing and perseverance, Yvonne Doane of Custom Illustrations, Traci Anderson the quarterback, and Julie Lyon, whose enthusiasm led me to the iUniverse doors.

Lori Paradise was indispensable as a copy editor and advisor and has my profound gratitude, as does Gieselle E. Estes for her encouragement and expert advice.

And my eternal indebtedness to those who followed the genesis of *Enter, Knight* and *Hel's Storm* at K. A. Keith.com, under the working titles, *Leviathan Stirs* and *Hel's Flyting*.

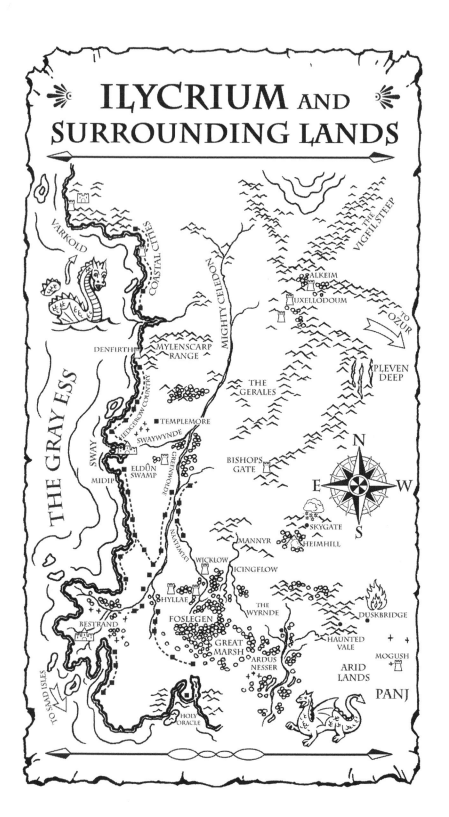

Book I

My name is Xephard, and I am dead.

The veil is lifted. My eyes see. Thus I say to each man and woman, you must choose for evil or the good. How long had It lingered? How long had It crept, fearing light and loathing laughter? No one knew.

My mistress, our Lady of Thought, has lent wings to this poor soldier's words that I might sing of my friend Apieron—who made a choice. For he was afflicted by a Hate most ancient. The margins of time blur, and my mind is small in its knowing. Forgive me, but in such a telling, it is best to hazard a beginning …

Prologue

The Ninth Heaven

The graceful dance of the Quas began. Colossal beings of radiant light, together the Quas joined in a creative energy that would become a most auspicious event. The birth of a new star. This little star would be a thing of matchless beauty, growing from a stellar embryo to join in the timeless journey of the heavens, perhaps in turn to bring the light of life and guidance to beings on some world illuminated by his youthful radiance.

The spell song of the Quas progressed, and their glow grew dim as the focus of their joining drew every energy into itself. All heads were raised in singing climax as a burst of luminescence marked the birth of the new sun. *Agelos* became aware, and felt unquenchable powers within his fiery heart. The Quas sang salutations to his advent and the beauty of his form, to welcome him into their care, to grow and learn the wisdom of the heavens.

Agelos had a capricious whim and wondered if he could break onto a path of his own. He did! Surging forward, he rejoiced in his speed and strength, and the open vault of space. Quas called to him, yet he heard a new beckoning, at once subtle and seductive.

Exactly where this hidden Other was, he could not discern, yet sensed the direction of *Her* presence.

Agelos sundered his final bonds, and the laments of the Quas were lost in the joyous notion that no other might control him. At the end of his journey would lay a wondrous thing, promised the new voice, a world already created and grown complex, a thing of boundless intricacy that he might rule without delay. With Her, if only he would.

Agelos hurtled across the lightless void, ecstatically trailing a streamer of living fire a thousand miles behind. He heedlessly tore through planar barriers and left untold chaos in his wake, ever drawn to the hidden entity. He spied a blue-and-brown sphere, marveling at its variety of creation, and perceived the winsome call of living beings who dwelt thereon, and whose natures he could vaguely sense. Agelos sought to adjust his approach that he might orbit this living jewel.

He could not!

His plummet accelerated, leaving a great burning in the airs of the blue world.

Agelos felt the nigh overwhelming presence of the Other, but She did not answer his frantic entreaties as, at last, Her dark abode was revealed. She meant to drive him straight through the orb!

Agelos conceived a desperate plan. As his mass pierced the crust of the planet and exploded a mighty swamp into blasted ruin, he poured his spirit into two naked infants he felt birthed at that instant. The black weight of Her immortal prison closed around Agelos, and the dark essence opened Her maw, consuming the embryo star. The massive influx of his energies surged through Her even as She perceived his deception. After countless millennia, the Beast raised Its seven heads and roared Its reawakened fury.

LAND'S END

The Sybil of Ilycrium felt the disturbance long before it found the sky. She perceived the confusion of the little sun and felt its desperate but futile struggle against the sentient force that captured it. Briesis hurried from the warmth of her cave to stand at her mountain's edge and behold the unfolding spectacle.

The infant Quas looped across the heavens and down in meteoric ruin, appearing as an enormous fireball that turned nighted sky into scarlet day. Briesis's eyes were seared as she strove to pierce its blazing shell, and she felt its shriek as it rent Blessed Earth and was lost within. Briesis sensed the *Presence* below, and a nauseating image came to her of a dark and horrifying deity. Her gods were those of cyclic endings and creation, such that the sorrows of death were ever balanced with the joy of new life. This new vision represented what could only be a destroyer—who, if It created aught, would only whelp new forces bent on chaos. Briesis contemplated the powers of a mighty goddess, awakened and combined with the aspect of a ravening beast. The Sybil swayed where she stood, unmindful of the cold or the precipice beneath her as an ancient and evil name came unbidden to her shuddering lips:

"*Tiamat.*"

Still in her trance, the prophetess was driven to her knees and cast upon her side, her scorched eyes unable to see the return of night to the mountain, and yet a kaleidoscope of images continued to assault her. To the North she beheld armies of Kör that marched under a fell banner as a strong prince gained ascendancy. Across civilized lands, hidden idols awakened, fueled by the return of their unforgotten goddess, while the dragon sons of earth blinked and stretched to send forth their malevolent thought at the behest of their imprisoned matron.

Briesis wept for the bright young kingdom that stretched away westward. Ilycrium, so filled with hope and enlightenment after a long age of barbarism. The starfall's howling wind whipped away blood-streaked tears and choked her cries of anguish as she fell into darkness.

SKYTOP

With words of comfort and love, Xistus Farsinger took the babe from Astir's arms. His wife had done well. A son! The birthing had been difficult, and he shook his head at the great pain she endured with stoic grace. Five children were already his by a deceased wife, all arriving with ease and as healthy as any parent could hope. This tiny infant, puling and weak, had inflicted three days of labor as if reluctant to greet the world. Then the baby had come with a mighty rush as a cataclysmic fit seized his wife. Master of spell and sword, Xistus had sensed an influx of arcane energies that focused within her womb at the very climax of the birthing, and his normally calm demeanor clouded with worries of losing her, the child, or both.

Not a few of his friends and advisors spoke against the bringing of a mystic into his home as wife. His elder children resented their new mother and no doubt in turn would resent their half brother. All that would be dealt with in time! As long as child and mother were hale. Xistus regarded the newborn, surprisingly quiet in his father's callused hands. He was wetly warm and soft, and *alive*.

Inspecting his son from crown to heel, Xistus found no flaw in form or reflex, and met his wife's liquid eyes, nodding with a smile. "You have birthed a fine son, my love. He shall be named Apieron, child of light."

A sense of wonderment came to Astir. Though handsome from childhood, too deep in the necromantic arts had she delved—her spirit assaulted, all notions of beauty lost. From whence came this man with his mighty song and the green light of wholesome creation in his eye? The phantoms of darkness had fled before the power of the Farsinger, never to return. Xistus held his son upon his shoulder, his lips pressed close as he whispered a father's words to the infant. Never had she inquired of Xistus's age. Kindly wrinkles lent experience to the corners of his eyes, and there was gray in his wavy brown hair, yet his muscles flowed and rippled when his robe swirled aside. Fatigued from her long struggles, Astir lay back and surrendered to a welling contentment that stole the strength from her limbs and lulled her to dreamless sleep.

Xistus bore his son onto a greensward under the stars. How incredible was the heaven's dance this night! A glowing star had appeared the eve Astir began her woman's pain. Soon it grew until it burst the sky as a brilliant meteor, then fell beneath the horizon, which continued to glow as if lit by a beacon fire of the Sea Kings. Those who lived below surely were smitten with grave fear or worse. Then the babe had come.

The celestial vault appeared quiescent, whether from exhaustion or silent expectation, he could not say. His stone palace behind lay hushed and dark, although a single light glowed whitely from Astir's quarters and turned the falling rush of a nearby watercourse into a sparkling curtain. Xistus thrust the infant towards the heavens and circled slowly such that every star shined upon his son. Thrice he made the naming before the powers of air and sky, mountain and earth, and finally, of water and fire. Xistus turned his back to the wild, cradling the child, Apieron, and strode into his palace.

Moments later a nighted essence threw itself with all force against stone portals, and was hurled back in consternation. *Never had any builded work of man restrained it*!

Probing forward with caution, it found the way barred by a subtle weave of power. It moaned enchantments of unbinding, needing only the slightest gap to slip within. The barrier held and even managed to lash out—stinging its undead form. Ulfelion considered a word of power but reasoned the adepts inside would sense the casting and whisk the child away before the threshold could be breeched.

With an impatient swirl, the dark spirit whipped around the fortress and again found no defect in the spell knit that enveloped this keep in the clouds. Ulfelion keened aloud his frustrated rage and shot from the tor like a bolt of black lightning.

LAND'S END

The Sybil woke on the mountainside. Blinded, battered, and nearly frozen, she struggled feebly to her knees. She felt the meager warmth of a bitter day upon her face and reasoned she had lain thus the night entire. She began to crawl. The prophetess had traversed this ledge path for a long lifetime of men, now in grim irony her abraded hands and knees more than once nearly took her off the edge.

In Briesis's dazed mind, stark images of the preceding night replayed themselves without reprieve. Grasping a stone, she attempted to pull herself upright. Twice she failed. To stand and walk was to further risk a tumble from the mountain, yet to crawl blindly was to die just as surely from exposure. She clasped the stone, and with bone-cracking effort managed to gain her feet. Buffeted by waves of vertigo, she began to shuffle, seeking some clue to the entrance of her shrine.

A small noise lifted above the sigh of wind over stone. It was a pitiful whimpering, and distant, as if from within a chasm. Or a cave! She turned and hobbled towards the sound, hoping it would not cease. There was no danger of that, for it was a man, sobbing with fear.

Briesis came gratefully into her holy sanctum. Fumbling until she found the source of the lament, she discovered the shuddering frame of a man curled upon the stone. His back seemed deformed under a patchwork of castoff rags and weathered skins. At her touch, he became aware and gazed upon her. Together they made fire and shared a stale loaf, the week-old offering of a peasant. In the weeks that followed, Briesis's body mended, and the broken man stayed with her. Oft he prattled and cackled, although he did not shy from the strange trances that at times incapacitated her. He guided her steps when needed and worked as a menial, thereby earning the right to dwell about the grotto. Never did she demand from whence he came, knowing he was somehow sent to serve.

The Sybil relearned her powers of communion. Some of the living dreams came but once, others with regularity. She beheld a brown-haired son of her people, complex of spirit and troubled within. Evil priests rose and walked the land, mouthing names of abomination as poisonous politics weakened the kingdoms of the West. To their defense, a gleaming blade and argent shield blazed the very pits of Helheim, yet the greatest nightmare vision was of a black-clad warrior burst from the Dragon Marches, his sword stained red, and in his eyes dancing a many-headed beast.

THE NORTHERN WILDS

Durmfere felt the labor pains again. She welcomed them, for she well knew the secret of woman's travail. By various fathers she had birthed several daughters, quick of mind and body, who would grow to serve perfectly the arcane rite. Yet the sum of their birthings was as naught compared to the hardship of this son's advent. Durmfere had scanned the darkling heavens and read by celestial signs that this would be the night. Thus before the merest contraction came, she had retreated to her prepared place.

Another gripping spasm seized her womb, sending its rippling fingers into her back. She panted and sweated, inhaling great draughts of the birthing chamber's air. Blazing ceramic braziers warmed the low-roofed room, and enchanted signs tattooed every surface of wall, ceiling, and floor. Here Durmfere, Runemaid of Nar, had commanded her most potent items brought, not least of which was the ensorcelled bone knife placed near at hand, should the child prove unworthy. Durmfere now knew it was a useless precaution, for she felt the power within the infant.

A wracking contraction took her, and she gritted her teeth. The three virgin novices who attended her stirred not and watched with kohl-shadowed eyes, no soothing words or cool compresses for the enchantress. The father's absence she had also commanded, and no doubt Uthos paced restlessly nearby, eager for word of the son she had assured him this was. He she had chosen for his strength of body and wit, and the savage reaver had willingly submitted to her charms. Indeed, after the initial glance, it might have been called rape had she not planned so well. Once his lust was sated, she had taken of his body small totems to bind him to her. In the time that passed, he ceased his roving to attend the dark-eyed witch woman as well as any man might, but this son would not be a comfort to Uthos in feeble old age. Once the boy reached manhood, he would eclipse the father as surely as lady moon outstrips the stars. *She had foreseen it.*

She did not hear the cries of alarm outside as Uthos's men beheld a falling star that filled the night sky with fiery ruin. Durmfere regarded her rippling belly, and felt the sudden influx of arcane energy. Her womb could not contain it and was torn asunder as the baby was expelled from her body. Durmfere's wail of anguish became a wild laugh of exultation, and her waiting women stirred to life to gather the infant with utmost care.

Seeing her weak gesture, one of the devotees held forth the

boy. Durmfere grasped his face with one taloned hand and turned him roughly, inspecting every inch. The boy regarded her with solemn eyes, nor did he cringe or whimper. The rune maid evinced a wan smile, for he was perfectly formed and robust, with a face that would lend itself well to nobility. She fell back in relief, her bone knife clattering to the floor.

Durmfere rejected a wooden cup filled with water and gathered her thoughts. That she was dying was obvious. Her womb was ruptured, and the bleeding would not cease. Just as this baby would never suckle her breast, so she would not be distracted from her last task. Nor would hope-filled Uthos know his son. What the sorceress intended called for blood. It also required a life sacrifice. That she would supply as well, to quicken her mightiest casting.

She gathered a dappling and inscribed a sign in the air. Crying a spell song of high, weird notes, she spattered crimson over her face and the newborn. "Adestes Malgrim, I name you, for the doom you bring." Her women covered their ears and cringed.

Uthos was joined by six of his stoutest retainers. Battle scarred and hardened they were, yet each was thrown into consternation by the enormous comet, and eerie wailing that emanated from the shut house. Uthos raged his impotence. His orders shouted in the direction of the enclosure had gone unanswered by those damnable witchy women, but he dared not cross the shallow trench they had dug. Although only a foot-span wide and inches deep, it nonetheless marked a boundary that no man, or work of man, might pass.

The enchantress and her silent women had selected and cut the timber, dressed it where it lay with sharp stones, and dragged it hither without the aid of forged yoke or bridle. They had constructed the shut house without so much as a by-your-leave. Now came the event that eclipsed any other this strange night. The meteor was scarcely faded when an indistinct shape of darkness descended with great speed upon the wood house, masking all light from within. The men drew steel at the sight of this new apparition and thronged to the boundary, waiting for some new sign.

As the last chanting echoes left numbed lips, Durmfere felt her life's ending. The shadows within the room grew deeper, and the confused, sweat-lined faces of her novices faded even as they watched her with apprehensive horror. Unheeded, the child lay quiet on her breast. Red and yellow flickerings of braziers suddenly flared and were quenched into a smoky reek as a form of darkling terror sank from the ceiling. A fell spirit of blackness it was, shot through with scintillant lights.

The women leapt back with cries of dismay, working futile symbols of holding. Durmfere felt Ulfelion's thought as it descended with majestic grace to enfold her. *Thy sacrifice is moot. On thee shall I feed, and thy child take.* On straining neck, she beheld her son a last time and nodded.

Before the first echoes of the women's screaming faded, Uthos led a roaring charge across the warding line. As his men surged across the threshold of the birth house, its walls were riven into splinters, and the spirit rose before them, swollen and malignant. Uthos's reavers cast themselves onto their faces, gibbering with fear. Fighting back madness and terror, Uthos gazed upon the undead spirit and beheld the tiny figure of his son held close to its intangible breast. Uthos screamed in rage and leaped to attack. If he could not slay the lich, at least he would deprive it of its prize.

Ulfelion laughed as it rose above the slashing mortal and

struck him down with a thought. As the sight grayed in Uthos's eyes, his last vision was of the apparition with his son, wending its way in the gloom … southeast, where lay the crypts of earth-chained dragons, and the dark realm of Kör.

Chapter 1

Windhover: Ilycrium's Outpost in Foslegen

Apieron, son of Xistus Farsinger, kicked a silken pillow across his bedchamber. Wheeling to a muffled exclamation, he glimpsed a retreating female figure. *Hypmine, one of Melónie's girls.* His bride of six years came from eastern lands to the stone keep, lonely outpost of a cold north kingdom, and had done her best to fill it with bright and sumptuous comforts. As with all she did, Apieron had been pleasantly surprised. Now it seemed he lived in a velvet prison. *Curse this restlessness.*

A short interval later found him hurrying down a wild forest path, great bow in hand and girt with sword and dagger. He cared not where his feet took him, although he was not equipped for any long journey. A mat of shed pine needles, slowly compressed by moisture and their own weight, lined the way and echoed like a low drum when trod upon. Tree roots twisted out of the red-brown layer like swarming eels, and conifers of all types, interspersed with white-garbed poplar, robbed the new sun such that there was little undergrowth to obscure ranks of solemn trunks that marched into shade. Lucky shafts of light pierced the arbor to reveal spreading ferns turned to gold. All this Apieron heeded little. Lesser son of a noble house, he took nothing of his father's save his natural gifts and a dwarven comrade who chose to pay debts to Xistus by looking after the son. Apieron's wanderings had led to the court of the Candor king to serve as his father before him.

"Ten years," he muttered, "and the scars to prove it." Now there were fiefdom and friends, and a gentle wife who had birthed their third child. *The gods punish the ungrateful.*

Apieron heard a cascade of water and knew at last where he hied. The stream was fat with spring rain, yet perhaps its subtle voice would soothe him as it ever had. He thought of those other falls, mighty Auroch of the Holy Vale. Though much lesser, he had named this little one Findlán. Better yet, it was *his*. Apieron lifted his head. He was nearly upon the stag before knowing it.

Its horns were velvet sprouts, nonetheless it fixed him with a disdainful look. Apieron's bow came up as the agitated beast tossed in preparation for a charge. The animal leapt forward. In the same instant, an arrow penetrated its mighty chest. The buck took two steps and fell. Apieron rushed to grant the deer a merciful stroke but saw it was unnecessary. He did not regret taking the stag, for by evidence of worn teeth and the many scars that crisscrossed its hide, the animal had lived a full life and no doubt passed on its seed many times.

He gutted and quartered the carcass, bundling meat to the riverbank for a final cleansing and butchering. He lit a small blaze and tasted a portion, offering a prayer of thanks to the spirit of the animal and forest, and to the Huntress. As he worked he listened to the unceasing rhythm of the water's rushing. His first exploration of Windhover yielded discovery of this foaming cascade and clear pool beneath. His mother had taught him place magic, thus for him, splashing falls harbored voices of wisdom. If he opened to the spell song, the spirit of Findlán would whisper gentle meanings. No mighty oracle as was the Auroch, nonetheless Findlán sang her song, and only for him.

Apieron lay back. He would cart the venison later. The day was young and cool, and it had been long weeks since he had taken leisure so. As Apieron fell into sleep, the river urged him on to something elsewhere …

Apieron was a boy. He ran alone through the forest. Off exploring again—welcome respite from the constant training and intrigue of Skytop. A pacing shadow glided to his left.

"Nagwolfe!"

Trees thinned, bringing his adversary into view. He deemed it was an old outcast by its grizzled muzzle and streak of white on its head. Apieron did not alter his pace, and the animal kept its distance. He listened as he ran, grateful not to hear the piping sounds of a hunting pack. He touched the signal horn at his waist but feared to fumble with it lest he drop his javelin or stumble, thus bringing the beast upon him. Nor would he stop to face it, miles from safety; he would wait until the animal charged. Perhaps he might out-stamina this older beast.

A nagwolfe was seven foot snout to tail, some said as smart as a human child. Apieron had faith in his weapons and training, and by house orders, his siblings and he went armed with sword and long knife whenever they ventured abroad. Moreover, he carried a fine javelin, his favorite weapon.

The animal edged closer. Even so, Apieron's confidence grew. He had run a mile and still no sign of a pack. Ahead he saw an excellent place to make a stand where a narrow defile ran onto a stone outcrop against which he could place his back. Apieron angled toward the prominence. The hunting beast immediately altered its course to cut him off.

'Intelligent indeed!' Apieron picked up speed and readied the

javelin. Streaking silhouettes of many nagwolves streamed in from the sides.

Apieron flicked his dart, striking the flanks of the older beast, and did not pause, bursting past the creature that wheeled and snapped at the painful barb. Apieron climbed the escarpment with two nagwolves slathering at his heels.

No thought of turning now! He leapt to a handhold just below the upper lip. Swaying, he gathered himself to swing over and onto the ledge. A foul-breathed maw shot down and champed where his leg would have been. With a painful wrench of his shoulder, Apieron fell back to dangle from his handhold to regard the nagwolfe above him. Queen of the pack, he saw the evil guile in her eyes.

'They herded him as they would have a goat!'

Apieron looked down. Eight nagwolves milled below. One gathered itself for a snapping leap, and Apieron curled up as best he could lest the crushing jaw seize his foot and drag him into the murderous circle. The queen yipped and laughed at him with mocking eyes.

'Nagwolfe!' It was said no evil could come to Skytop. It seemed he would give his life to prove that untrue.

Apieron's arms burned, and he could not feel his fingers. He stared at them, willing them not to slip. Horn useless at his belt, Apieron shouted. It was lost in the wild clamor of the pack below. The queen cackled above him and kicked dust into his face. Her weird piping laugh sounded when he choked and coughed. Apieron felt his fingers fail.

His left hand lost its grip. With it he fumbled for his sword, readying for the inevitable slide down the cliff face. To ascend was impossible. The queen would grasp his throat or rip his face before he could roll clear of the edge. Apieron was eleven. He stifled a sob and began to ease his handhold.

A flash of silver took a leaping nagwolfe in the base of the skull, slamming it against the rock. A second was transfixed in the spine. Howling in agony, it dragged itself away by the forelegs. Apieron tumbled and rolled. His eldest brother and Xistus rounded the escarpment, firing steel-tipped shafts on the run. Nagwolves peeled free to charge the newcomers but were slain ere they covered half the distance. Apieron closed his eyes and breathed a silent prayer to the goddess of mercy. He heard a sound, and looking up, he beheld the hate-filled eyes of the queen. So malevolent was her gaze, he knew she would never forget and would ever seek to avenge herself on him.

Xistus bent his bow but a chance shaft of sunlight blinded him before he could release. She gave a yelp and was gone. If Xistus was displeased with his son this day, he did not reveal it then or ever, yet within months a strange boisterous dwarf arrived to accompany Apieron whensoever he ventured afield. Soon Henlee became Apieron's true friend. Years passed. To Apieron's surprise the dwarf mumbled something about old debts the day Apieron left Skytop, and ventured west with his pupil.

… Apieron woke. The sun had shifted, and the air was still. He reclosed his eyes and dreamed of the Auroch. Singing Findlán blended with the deeper roar. No longer soothing, the water's rush grew, tumbling his thoughts. Xephard appeared—War Goddess's impeccable warrior who found the water's echo nothing but peaceful, discerning no particular voice or message. Apieron beheld the Donna, wise mistress of the Lampus. Xephard and others were pledged to serve her till death. Apieron wondered. Perhaps he would journey thither.

The distant call of wolves came to him. Apieron sat up. "Red wolves."

His encounter with the nagwolfe had burned all fear of pack hunters from him. Yet sleep left him apprehensive. He searched the river glade. This place no longer seemed his, or friendly. It was as if the land itself was shifting, like a serpent sliding in coils. A thought of the Holy Oracle came unbidden.

He remembered Xistus's words, '*The soothe man knowest he is not wise in himself, but only in unity with the spirit of the World. In the Oracle dwells wisdom beyond men.*'

"I know, Father."

Apieron shook his head. He would be desperate indeed to seek that lonely place. The wolves called again, and he remembered the nagwolfe queen's burning gaze. Apieron shouldered his deer and strode for Windhover.

A work crew of seventy heaved stones and carted barrels of earth to be packed behind the bulwark. Their labor was eased by the sight of their master who toiled alongside. Apieron's bare chest and breeks were as begrimed with sweat and dust as any man's. The season was not yet hot, but afternoon's sun was bright and the work heavy. Apieron felt an urgency that quickened his stomach, and his gray eyes searched the horizon above the trees of Foslegen. Somewhere out there lurked a storm.

"Well done, Telnus!" he called. A mule had started, tugging loose a scaffold brace. The quick-thinking armsman sliced the mule's traces and called down the men to safety until the piling could be reset.

Apieron smiled broadly. They labored well. Windhover's retaining wall was near complete. They strove also to expand the wall's fronting trench. Evacuated earth and stone were hauled to buttress a revetment. His housetroop had swelled. Veterans of his old regiment whose enlistment passed came as bachelors or with families. All were made welcome, now some five score soldiers served under the walls of Windhover.

Apieron joined venerable Duner, master of the garrison when its lord was absent. The men wiped their chests and ladled deep draughts from a water bucket. A pattering step turned them to find a bright-faced lass with lustrous red hair. Hypmine sketched a brief bow.

"Sir, the Lady Melónie says your board is set." Apieron acknowledged her with a courteous nod as the twain watched the girl retreat. Freshly sensuous, she laughed and returned good-natured jests with the men.

"A husband she'll be wantin'," mused Duner.

"Speaking of wives," said Apieron, "I recall my father once said: 'Whatever the task, when you are summoned to dinner, go immediately. If you are so blessed to have a woman prepare a meal, respect the labor she makes on your behalf.'"

"Wise, milord," grinned Duner, himself a widower and father of three children grown. "I'll finish up here."

Apieron shook his head. "Not wisdom, experience. I've been married six years."

"Aye, that is always better." The men laughed.

"'Twill soon be too dark to continue. Join me in the morning, we'll take a working breakfast while we complete the berm."

At a whistle and a wave from the steel-haired castellan, labor crews set aside tools and gathered what could not be left outdoors until dawn. Apieron paused. Duner's seamed face held a look. "In the ten or so years I've known you … eight for the Sea Kings and two since you settled here, I never heard you relate such a tale. Are there many? About Xistus, I mean."

Apieron's face grew pensive. "Regrettably no. I do not know what made me remember that little bit. Until tomorrow, my friend."

"An' may it be as fine a day as this."

As he walked, Apieron thought it odd that dormant memories

quickened within; there had always been few. Too few. Of course Duner was curious about Xistus. Hells below! *He* was curious. It seemed Xistus sired him three decades ago only to please his second wife, Astir.

Strong-willed sons and fine daughters he had in plenty by his first union. Xistus the warrior had laughed, not unkindly, to see his youngest son's unique interests whilst elder siblings strove only to emulate their father. *"And how's my little gardener today?"* Apieron shook his head, dispelling the memory. He sighed. It was an old proverb that sons were never as great as their sires, and in his case, it would ever be true!

That night, Apieron could not sleep. Muscles were sore and stomach full, yet he could not relax. *What rest promised sleep?* Oft reoccurring, his dream was a kaleidoscope ride through a land where twisted faces leered from smoky lairs and bestial yells echoed over blasted rocks. Blades flashed, stars fell like rain, and beyond all was a brooding presence, unrevealed, yet more real than he. Then his dream self would veer away to soar back over familiar landscapes. Far below he would see his home of Windhover or the royal palace of the Candor kings near Sway's harbor, and many other places flitted beneath like a drunken compendium of his life.

Apieron tossed coverlets aside and strode to gather travel gear suitable for ranging far and swift. He drew near Melónie ... softly, so as not to awaken her. Wise women said a woman near the birthing time needed twice the food and three times her normal rest. Little Jilly was already two months old, yet apparently those axioms still applied. *Gods above*, his wife was beautiful. One olive shoulder protruded from the coverlet. He kissed it.

Melónie mumbled something indiscernible. He closed and bolted the bedchamber door with a clever dwarven key lock Bagwart had fashioned. Apieron exited the keep's outer bailey, nodding briefly to the guardsman, but did not invite conversation. Crossing the courtyard swiftly, Apieron saluted a man at the castle wall, and some hundred yards beyond, he descended from the palisade where morning's work waited. He swiftly traversed long grasses to find the nighted tree line.

Apieron stole into the glade, glanced up to reacquire his bearing, and glided again amongst shadowed trees, silent in his tread. There it was again! A flickering glow, elusive behind dark trees. It came from a small, forest-enclosed valley. Too far to smell the burning or discern any smudge of gray above the tree line, yet the distant light of fire was unmistakable. No little campfire this, but such a pyre as men make when they signal others to a gathering, and on *his* land.

Windhover was bequeathed in return for a decade's service as officer, then captain of the King's Scouts. Apieron led the King's Long Knife, and soon had the foes of the Candor kings grown to fear them. Few knew the exact nature of the tasks he performed like his father before him, yet all at Court knew that Apieron had been given title and fiefdom, although some chuckled at the perceived jest. Windhover was a neglected donjon amidst wild, lonely lands that were the farthest border of Ilycrium southeast. Apieron did not laugh. This land he would hold, for king and kin.

With stealth, Apieron worked his way onto an escarpment that would bring him past the rim of the vale. He did not want to be detected coming onto this dark forest meeting! His sword hung easily at his hip, but absent was the mighty bow for this night's work. In its place, a brace of honed javelins rode high on his back.

Once in the lee of the rocky bank, he went without as much concern for snapping a twig or kicking a rustling branch. There was a sentry at the top of the stone face. Arms folded over bare chest, he faced back the way Apieron had come. The figure, discernible in the red glow from the waist up, seemed a man of nigh supernatural size, with low-slung brows and a mane of unshorn hair. Apieron paused briefly, then followed shadows to the edge of the conclave.

A wide roasting pit had been scooped in the strand of a trickling stream. Fat hinds were spitted over the blaze. Their dripping fat popped and flared amongst the flames with a tantalizing aroma. In the glare, the true nature of the gathered creatures was revealed.

Broad chested and casually clad torsos rose above the mighty bodies of horses, as centaurs supped and drank and held converse in their deep sonorous voices. The mightiest of these faced the fire directly. His body was that of a mighty stallion. From this rose a frame of heroic proportion, topped with a noble head and long-swept hair that fell to the withers. Apieron grinned. Seldom could one brag that he stealthed Vergessen, king of the forest.

"Welcome, Spear Dancer!" boomed the centaur lord.

Apieron laughed and strode into the circle of light, clasping hands with the man-horse. In these modern times, Vergessen's tribe dwelled in the moist darkness of the deep forest. Initially wary of men returned to Windhover, they grew to respect the new lord's mastery of branch and glen. And his respect for their secrecy. Not many centaurs remained, and even Apieron never beheld such a gathering as now. The fire's heat was profound. Whole trees lay within its orange embrace.

"Why the burning, Vergessen? They say the spirit burns more feebly with age, thus the old man seeks the comfort of cloak and hearth."

"I know not how two-footers age. I am scarcely a year or three over one hundred, still in my prime." An enormous hand thunked a shaggy torso as wide as it was thick. "You at least, sir, I'll outlive."

"I hope so," laughed Apieron. "My place needs the fertilizer."

The man-horse harrumphed. "As for the fire, it is in your honor. Of course you prefer your meat scorched, and by this pyre, even a knight of Ilycrium could find his way hence."

Apieron eyed five more carcasses hung to the side. "My wife says I eat too much meat, but even I cannot consume eight entire hinds."

The centaur's bluff face grew serious. "Tonight we hold a Thing. Our principals are here to discuss the winter that comes. You have felt it?" Vergessen appeared grimly pleased by Apieron's nod. "Creatures of this land grow restless and know not why. Centaurs also, four feet are wiser than two.

We harken to Earth's song. This place is very ancient, our birthplace of old. The ground trembles with the tread of many that march to war. From whence we cannot say, so tonight we decide whether to bide awhile or flee. Perhaps into the far swamps, perhaps elsewhither."

Apieron's sense of foreboding returned full force, and he was relieved that here was another who felt it too. He did not know what to say.

"Enough of such talk," called Vergessen. "That is for later. For now, feast!"

Centaurs shed their solemn demeanor, producing wineskins and various foodstuffs to accompany the meat. The thrumming tones of a giant lyre filled the night, and the calls and laughs of the horse people filled the vale. As wine warmed his belly, Apieron felt privileged and strangely saddened with the knowledge that such a merry gathering was occasioned by threat of a sundering.

The reverie lasted late. Only when the most gluttonous appetite was sated and the fire burned to winking embers did the centaurs hold serious counsel. Some spoke of flight, as was their habitual way. Others, mostly young, of warlike deeds and even of fighting in comradeship with the iron men of Ilycrium. Most remained noncommittal to either course, and by so doing the decision was made that Vergessen's tribe would continue to bide at Windhover whilst preparing itself for rapid march, whether to flight or battle, none could say.

In the end, Apieron promised every assistance that he might offer, should need arise for either course. Centaurs for once seemed satisfied and at his words nodded sagely under heavy brows while sucking their teeth or picking at an odd bone. When pale predawn found the vale, Apieron clasped hands with each in turn, repeating their names before turning for home. They watched him retreat, but his thoughts were of Melónie—probably asleep, her fragrant hair flung over her face.

Finding her thus, Apieron slipped quietly into bed. Her breath rose and fell in slow rhythm, and facing away from him, the curve of her hip and smooth skin of her back were silhouetted by day's light that grew in the casement. Her face was hidden by sable tresses thrown up over a pillow, leaving her neck bare.

"How lovely you are." Apieron pressed gently against her and wrapped his arm under her narrow waist.

"I smell the forest. Is ought amiss, husband?"

"Sh, my love. I meant not to wake you."

"I have been awake the night entire whilst my lord walks the darkness. I feared for him and prayed to Cryse for his safe return."

"I met friends this eve. Mayhap they will aid us in times to come."

Melónie rolled to fix him with her bottomless gaze. "All say you are a peerless woodsman, but must you dare the nighted forest? Who would succor your babes should you take hurt or meet some foul beast?"

Apieron smiled. "I do not fear the darkness."

She turned away, pulling his arm about her, clasping his hand between her breasts. "I do."

Dawn and birdsong filled the room. Apieron rose. Duner would be waiting.

Chapter 2

Windhover

Henlee had enough of Apieron's tale. "Each time Bagwart's hammer strikes hot iron, you see a galaxy of such sparks."

Apieron saw this was true. With each blow of the dwarf's four-pound sledge, a swarm of white sparks stuck in Bagwart's beard and eyebrows or on his hairy arms to turn yellow-orange, winking out before the next swarm erupted. The only apparent effect on the dwarven forge-master seemed a deeper squint as he studied some fine detail in the steel invisible to Henlee and Apieron.

"Now, Bagwart, don't rework the entire blade, just the edge. War is coming."

"Ye always say that," groused the smith.

Apieron noted that, remarkably, the dwarven ironworker was as broad in the shoulders as Henlee. Of course he was slighter in overall stature by way of comparison to the massive mountain dwarf who stood in the darkness behind the forge. Apieron thought of Henlee's disregard for the star signs that grew ominous in the minds of men. It was said these troubled even the Oracle upon her windy divide. "What then think you is beyond those lights in the night sky?"

"The living steel of Dwarf Father's anvil. Those specks in the night at which you gaze and mumble over are merely sparks of his forge hammer, whence the weapons of gods are birthed in holy flame."

"I see," said Apieron, stroking his chin, a slight beard started there. It was perhaps unwise to rebut too strongly his friend's words with two such dwarves at hand.

"And never listen to elves, boy. They'll tell that those stars are magic gnats swarming above some talking frog who sits on a sky lily, reciting poetry and getting drunk on twinkle dust."

Apieron dug chin into chest to suppress a laugh.

"Or some such. Eh, Bagwart?" The master forger merely grunted and scowled a final time at Maul's repaired edge. Seemingly satisfied, he tossed his hammer aside to produce a file. He clamped the dwarf lord's weapon for the final touches.

Henlee felt loquacious. "How do you like living here, Bagwart? These menfolk not driving you to distraction with all their yapping and foolery?" If the other dwarf responded, it was lost in the rasping screech of the file he wielded two-handed across Maul's cutting surface.

"He's the best, boy. Sometimes I regret sending him to you."

"And you, Uncle? I am surprised and pleased that you journey so far from Uxellodoum. Surely King Bardhest desires his chiefs be close in troubled times."

"My home is Saemid, and you yourself sent for me! Well, you nearly did with that letter that said Melónie'd be birthing soon. I'd not miss the coming of your second son. If not for me, who would pick out a proper name? Like *Henlee*."

"You missed it," laughed Apieron. "She is a girl. Sujita, my Jilly."

The dwarf appeared not to have heard. "Besides, old Redhand is getting daft. In one of his moods, he declared no nondwarves in

Uxellodoum. And worser, no further trade with forest elves or with the low peoples. That's when I decided to visit my kin hereabouts," added Henlee, "and yourself too, since it was on the way."

Apieron knew full well Henlee, as large as his family was, had no relatives within a hundred miles. He bowed.

"Don't get me wrong. Redhand is king of eight thousand dwarves and a war leader without equal, but there's times I feel he's gone soft in the head." Little did Henlee know, at that very moment, the dwarven patriarch was stroking his gray, gem-plated beard and saying the same of him.

Changing the subject, Henlee continued, "I see you've decided to fortify those palisades of yours. 'Bout time."

"I seem to remember a saying an old mentor of mine was fond of."

Together they intoned, "*No man is without enemies, even if he knows them not.*"

"Now you're talking!" said Henlee, well pleased with the warrior his erstwhile pupil had become. "I was afraid Ilycrium's city folk and lisping courtiers had turned you soft as they, milk-boned and fatuous."

"Not to worry, they kept me well afield and away from their precious palaces for those ten years."

"An' that's for the best. You, Bagwart, are you sharpening it or trying to file it down to one of those skinny toothpicks these human dainties call swords?"

"I'll be finished when I'm finished," growled Bagwart. There was no pause in the screeching.

Henlee took Apieron's arm and said softly, "Best we be leaving him, boy. He gets touchy when you criticize his work."

"You're doing mighty fine there, Bagwart!" Henlee tossed over his shoulder as they stepped from the heat of the forge into the cool day without. "He *is* the best."

Henlee tugged his beard thoughtfully. "And there's a reason why he is here with you and not back at Dwarf Home, but no time for that. When's supper?"

A pack of hounds fell in to greet their master in a chaotic swirl of cheerful yelping and tail wagging. "Nice dogs," grunted Henlee.

"It is good to see you," laughed Apieron. "My thoughts have been dire of late."

"There is time for dire, and there is time for dinner. Let's eat!"

Melónie smiled as she heard the twain laugh in odd synchrony from her garden window. She liked Henlee. His gruff presence comforted her with his obvious concern for Apieron. So many troubles clouded her husband's mind. How childlike he seemed at times … and he with responsibilities for wife and fiefdom, and now a new daughter.

She kissed and cradled little Jillia. Her arts had spoken of the sex of the child long before she was born, yet she had not revealed it to Apieron nor had he inquired, seemingly content with boy or girl. She mouthed a silent prayer to Cryse in thanks for this wonderful man.

There came a squeal. Setie chased unsteady Ilacus through the kitchen and into the garden, a tufted frond unmercifully tickling the toddler. Melónie smiled, for the boy was growing fast. Was he not the son of Apieron Farsinger? The children's roles would soon be reversed. She was happy.

"This place of yours, it's a sight better than the last time I saw it."

Henlee and Apieron walked, inspecting the improvements Apieron made to Windhover's central keep, curtain wall, and the outer revetment. The castle's garrison was out again, pikes and swords set aside in favor of more humble tools. Late morning's sun was gay, and men called and jested with one another as they worked.

Other folk were there as well. Land workers and craftspeople came to repopulate the small village adjacent to the keep. Not a few of Apieron's soldiers relocated their families thence, and others took wives among the townspeople. Timber was cleared and farm roads built. At the castle itself, the prior lord had run a small stream into a dilapidated moat, which, unattended, filled with silt and overran its banks, turning the sloped land below into a swampy morass and flooding a corner of the keep's basement with slimy mud. Apieron turned the rich soil of the moat into a garden and diverted the stream to a merry waterfall that clattered by the outer gates and thence to a stone-lined course where it chuckled past bright plantings Melónie set there.

The dwarf turned to face Apieron, hands on hips, black eyes boring into Apieron's gray. "So what's your problem? Here you have good land, a strong place, your people are content. And your woman—"

They heard Melónie faintly singing, happy to be in her garden. "—is better than you deserve."

"I don't know what is wrong," faltered Apieron. "I *do* know I've been blessed by good fortune." His brown hair caught in the wind, and for once his eyes were weak. "I've not felt such unrest since leaving Skytop. There is a threat in the air, I can taste it. Did you see the star that men call X'fel last night? It rose in the north and was gone in an hour's time."

The black-skinned dwarf studied Apieron intensely. "Nay, I slept."

Apieron gestured southward where a haze marked the boundaries of his forest turned to swampland at the nether regions the rulers of Ilycrium named their own. "I have prepared our retreat."

"What of those greedy neighbors of yours? And the gossipers at Court who hated your father? Are *they* fretting you?"

"Yes, and no." Henlee arched an eyebrow.

"Always, but it is more. What paltry magic given me by Astir speaks of it. At times I feel a panic, as if enemies I cannot see are closing in." Apieron quickly related his unsettling night visions and detailed his conversation with the centaur chieftain.

"And your wife?"

"As you know, she is a skilled adept. Whether she senses these things and holds them from me, or thinks only of her new home and babes, I do not know."

Henlee furrowed his brow in concentration. Personally without magical abilities, he nonetheless held a healthy respect for occult castings when they gave intelligence of mighty deeds afoot. The dwarven shamans of Uxellodoum wielded much power amongst his people.

"That's an earful to be certain."

Encouraged, Apieron continued, "The oracle of Land's End has been much on my mind. I've bethought myself to seek her out. What think you?"

Henlee sucked his teeth. "I knew something was amiss by the tone of your letter. When do we leave?"

Apieron was overjoyed. "You will travel with me to the Sybil? I knew not dwarves heeded her words."

"Bullocks. That oracle was there before your king's great-grandsire was born, or even dwarven longbeards came to this land. Three hells! 'Tis probably the same old witchy woman as been there the whole time. I admit my people also grow uneasy. King Bardhest prepares for war in his own way, though the durned fool thinks we might hide in our holes and let it pass by."

Apieron could not imagine what that meant, the dwarves of Uxellodoum were always prepared for war. "Besides," winked

Henlee, "the old badger turned away trade caravans before the spring beer. I've decided to stretch my legs a bit and get a taste of it."

Preparations for their departure were made swiftly. The heavy repairs at Windhover were largely done, and those armsmen not set to toil under Duner's watchful eye were dispersed amongst the farms. These went with willing hearts, for the villagers welcomed extra hands with hearty meals and pots of brown ale. Apieron was further surprised when Melónie had no objection to his journey. She came to the bailey the next morn to bid the twain farewell.

"It would tempt an ill fate to disregard a call to the Holy Oracle. What wife needs a husband besotted? I miss my *old* Apieron, who was strong enough to cow my brothers, and clever enough to charm my mother and aunts. What choice then did my father have, save yield up his desert flower?"

Setie bounded into Apieron's leg, hugging him tightly. Ilacus ambled up to tug Henlee's beard. Hypmine placed Jilly in Melónie's arms. Apieron kissed them all. "There *he* is!" teased Melónie as she laughed and returned Apieron's kiss with passion.

Henlee stuck his hands in his belt and pursed his lips while looking away. Melónie did not let him escape so easily. "And you, Henlee, were ever a kind uncle. Be so now again and bring my husband back to me, hale and strong."

Henlee bowed. When his words came, they were thick in his mouth. "I will, Lady. I swear it."

Chapter 3

Sway: Capital of Ilycrium

Midday's sun brightened Sway's streets. The steady bustle of city life paused when the noon sun was warm, lunches were taken, and the lucky or indolent managed a siesta. Gault reined his horse at a shop front. Out well before the dawn, he had neatly escaped his nigh unavoidable escort and roamed far afield before returning to the capital. His favorite pastime had ever been to flee the palace grounds with only a friend or two on such a jaunt. Today his thoughts were troubled, and his was a solitary ride.

Since Gault's childhood adoption, the old King had encouraged his associations and friendships outside royal circles, and for some months, the most trusted of these brought to him growing murmurs of sundry disturbances afflicting the countryside. Tales such as ancient grapevines unaccountably withering, or of whole crops of wheat and rye blighted with black rust. The king's advising council, themselves unaffected, were quick to discount the reports and went so far as to insinuate that the Prince's friendships were a charming but silly foible on the part of a well-intentioned, although naïve young man.

Gault Candor smote his palm. He knew better. Even Sway,

seat of the kingdom, was not immune. Prices were rising as foreign goods grew scarce. Sea merchants grew timid, cautioned by tellings of pirates and contagion, and those few ships of which the Crown could boast increasingly braved the seas but oft returned with empty holds. Some not at all.

Gault greeted Raasa the shopkeeper with a smile. The stout Clvain returned in kind. "Greetings, my Prince. You honor this unworthy person." The bow, graceful for one so thick of girth, illustrated the man's completely bald pate. "As you can see, milord, all that I have is yours. Alone."

The merchant chuckled, sweeping the room with a gesture that revealed it devoid of other patrons. This was a fact unusual in itself; the haberdashery of Raasa the Clvain boasted one of the finest selections and clientele available anywhere on the coast. A son of sun-drenched southlands, the Clvain had well adapted to his new home, taking the dress and speech of his patrons, and by reports, a local woman to wife with four fine children to boast.

Gault stroked a trim beard, auburn like his head. "I thought to purchase a woolen riding cloak for the winter, something in green or brown, and with the usual alterations. I may be campaigning again."

The Clvain rubbed his ebony scalp with a nervous gesture. "There are scarce little of those to be had, and none of fine enough make for yourself. You know I've first pick at the dockside and arriving caravans." The man's tone was apologetic. Candor frowned; if a Clvain tradesman were deprived of a sale, shortages must be dire indeed.

"It's the sheep, lord."

Gault waited.

"Hill men claim the sheep won't fleece out this year. By reports, they've gone an' got some sort of sickness that also festers in the skin and the lungs of the herders, and there's no cure."

Candor recalled his dawn ride. The countryside prepared for harvest as was the norm for the time of year, but with less bustle than usual. Thinned-out, weedy crops were everywhere, and many a field was given over completely to grass or brush-weed. He had seen buzzards circling more than once, inevitably marking the site of a dead or dying goat or kine. No kind word or drink had been spared for a thirsty, nobly dressed traveler.

"Normally," continued Raasa, "I would discount any story coming from those smelly, neighbor-raiding hill humpers, but it does have a ring o' truth to it. A hillman may pass off stolen goods and lie again about the weight, but he won't spurn true coin. My runner muttered something of the hill folk going on 'bout the *Hand of Pestilence*, and them buggers retreatin' up to the high slopes."

"Thank you, friend." Gault was too preoccupied to offer more than a wan smile.

"If I acquire what you need, I'll send a man."

Candor left the shop. *The Hand of Pestilence!*

His memory returned to his morning's journey and to a sight given little thought at the time. A roadside shrine had been toppled, and three wall stones had been set side to side, upon which was a young foal tied to starve and rot. He had spurred away with no consideration except to escape the stench. Now he wondered.

While the country folk honored a variety of local deities, animal sacrifices were traditionally made only in feast where special portions were burnt as offerings, with reverence of thanks given to the animal chosen. Only the old dark gods of troubled earth and the storm-riven skies of elder days were worshipped with the tortured struggle of life's ending and death's rot.

Gault swung his mare's head toward Kings Gate. He would have a word with the so-called advisors who propelled the Council into perpetual bickering whilst suspicious happenings were afoot.

🚶 🚶

Dexius listened to his prince with a studious expression, for the young man was so painstakingly earnest in his description of the troubles besetting country serfs, and now the low folk of the city? In a way, he had to secretly congratulate the whelp. Of all the king's advisors, young Candor was the one most perceptive of forward events, yet even he would be fatefully slow to alter the course of the kingdom. It was not the peasantry that would be the target. They were but simple tools to stir into unrest, thereby undermining the ruling class of support when the blow came. With the populace paralyzed with fear, and minor barons isolated and suspicious (as was their instinctual habit), the Throne would be vulnerable to a telling thrust.

"Then you agree, Dexius, that these signs are not random chance?"

"Most assuredly, lord."

"And you will press my argument before the King's Council?"

"It will be as you say." Dexius bowed.

Candor clasped the slighter man warmly on the arm. "You have my thanks, Minister."

Dexius stood to regard the Prince's broad back as he retreated. It really was a shame, for if young Candor had been less brain-addled in his upbringings by his paladin-like instructors, a most valuable ally he could have been in days to come. As it were, his slavish devotion to the great unwashed and his inflexible principles made him simply another obstacle.

Dexius pondered again if Gault's traits might be turned to some benefit. One must not frivolously shed the blood royal. At the very least, they might become fine marionettes.

PLEVEN DEEP: THE DRAGON RIFT

The sun-darkened warrior rode leisurely into the cleft where stark red cliffs rose above the narrow defile. A wind lived there and grew until it shrieked. The nexus of weather magic produced siroccos of withering heat that might be shattered within seconds by onslaughts of pounding hail as dust devils vied with microbursts in the upper airs. In civilized lands, vague murmur spoke of the place, yet few were those who believed the tales. Nonetheless, it had a name, the Dragon Fells of Pleven Deep. The rider seemed oblivious to the tempest, nor did it affect his steed.

Adestes Malgrim was glad to be away from Körgüz, to lose himself on this final errand, for the intrigues of the capital grew tedious. He yawned in the face of the gale and whiled away the long hours of his journey with pleasant reflection …

Amber Khan sat in state. The mighty Ascapundi ruled a vast expanse of wild hinterland—a frozen plain that described Kör's northernmost borders. At his command were a score of widely scattered companies of Ascapundi berserkers totaling several thousands. The average Ascapundi stood nine feet tall with a barreled trunk above mighty thews, and enormous axes or glaives oft depended from knotted arms and ham-sized fists.

Amber Khan was a full two feet taller than the mightiest of his thanes, and outweighed any by half. He recked not of any southern prince, no matter what mouthings the scaled priests uttered.

The great warlord gazed over the gathering that filled his great hall. Its mighty timbers echoed to the clamor. Amber Khan gorged and guzzled and hurled rude banter to his cup companions who stood to pull apart the last of the screaming captives plundered from a merchant caravan that very day. The wains had unwisely chosen a course close upon the border, and the giants counted themselves doubly fortunate, for the merchant train bore casks of strong liquor destined for *Körgüz. It had been accompanied by some twenty human drovers, most of whom fought poorly, thus surviving the initial onslaught.*

From his position behind an arras to the rear of Amber Khan's cushioned seat, a man regarded the proceedings with dispassionate interest. Except for the smooth rise and fall of his chest, Adestes was motionless. His bribes to the caravan's scouts had been well spent. They had led their charges fatefully astray before disappearing into the tumbled lands in a spray of snow and dust. Adestes smiled and slowly drew sword, well pleased at the riot, for he doubted that but for the liquor and revelry, spell-cloaked though he was, he would not have gotten so near an Ascapundi lord of Amber Khan's power.

Adestes eyed the rounded expanse of lobster-red skin that stretched over the mound of muscle and gristle that composed Amber Khan's mountainous back. He wondered where he might place a blow for a quick, fatal strike.

Adestes' attention returned to the great hall. The screaming ceased as the pathetic wretch on the flags below finally succumbed to irresistible limbs that pulled his own asunder as easily as those of a boiled chicken. Apparently the Ascapundi took wagers on which would finish with the largest piece before selecting an appendage to seize. After each victim was summarily dismembered, the giants tossed the gruesome remains to the floor to begin anew with a fresh subject. There remained only a dripping pile, and the monsters tracked through a widening pool of crimson until the entire floor seemed awash in blood.

Gargantuan laughter and mocking calls erupted from Amber Khan whilst his house carles kicked or tossed the carcasses about. Adestes had chosen well. Ascapundi loved nothing so much as fire wine and the torture of helpless victims, especially when it meant an impending meal of man flesh. Adestes stepped to the stone dais, easily keeping his silhouette concealed from the length of the room by the bulk of Amber Khan, as tall as he sitting thus. Then a pair of dark eyes caught and held Adestes' own.

A hall scullion, the merest wisp of a human girl, regarded him solemnly from her post in a wall niche where she stood ready to hasten to one of the giant's needs. Adestes had spied several such during the ruckus, quietly serving their fierce masters and hoping to avoid unwanted attention lest a new player be selected for the game. Her skin was dark as chestnut, and the eyes that regarded him were not those of the other spirit-broken drabs who cringed about the room. Hers burned with inner fires. Adestes changed his plan.

Amber Khan turned as the flat of Adestes' blade tapped him on the shoulder. The Ascapundi lord had time to stare in shock and open his mouth to shout his outrage when the tip of Adestes' weapon pierced his bulging eye and punched through to the soft brain within.

The girl ran to him as Adestes kicked the weirdly twitching corpse off his blade. It rolled off the dais with a wet thud. Silence descended in the hall. Speeding her course, the girl struck Adestes' front to bury herself beneath his left shoulder, and he raised his vermillion blade to the holdfast.

Stunned Ascapundi regarded this mighty human with his black, cloth-of-steel mesh over heaving breast, and a uncanny bastard sword that dripped the blood of their king. So terrible was his aspect that they looked to one another uncertainly, as if he were some avenging devil sent to exact retribution for the slaughter of the wagoneers.

"Come on then, you blubbering cowards! Who's next?"

With a conjoined roar, they rushed the platform. Adestes withdrew a small item and dashed it to the floor. He dissolved from view as twenty tons of charging Ascapundi reached the dais, rematerializing in a small grove in which he had left his steed. He glanced to the raven-haired beauty cradled against his bosom. Giving back a pace, she returned him a look that bespoke nothing but wariness and pride.

He smiled, pleased with this unexpected twist to a successful errand for the prince of Kör. No doubt the giants would think his actions those of retribution. Kör's king gained removal of the rebellious Amber Khan, who was a salient obstacle to the subjugation of Ascapundi under his suzerainty. And he, Adestes Malgrim, got a fine wench as trophy; one not steeped in the intrigues of Tyrfang, and his to keep alone, or discard on a whim. He swung upon the horse, nodding to the girl. She did not move.

Adestes gestured impatiently to the rear of his saddle. She tensed her legs and looked from side to side but did not flee.

"If you do not recognize this copse, girl, know that it stands less than one-half league from the Holfstag—that's about five minutes for an enraged Ascapundi." She leapt onto the saddle behind him. Laughing, Adestes set in his spurs and shot from the trees.

It was a full hour before Ascapundi hunting parties found his spoor, another before they gave up the trail. By then Adestes had struck a worn path and set pace to ride through the night. A royal heliograph lay but ten leagues distant, and Iblis, Prince of Kör, would have news of the triumphant return of his prize subject, Adestes Malgrim, known in the dark land by name of Malesh, before the following moonrise.

Ignoring a spray of wind-whipped rain and debris, Adestes again pondered the dark-haired wench. It was perhaps regrettable to leave her in Körgüz. One could hardly say they had grown close; he did not even know her name, nor did he care to hear it. Even so, he could not deny that he would miss her presence. How those shadowed eyes drew him ever deeper into their wet depths.

Adestes shook his head and laughed. She could not follow where he hied. Pleven Deep, home of dragons, was not a place hospitable to the uninitiated. Here he had been schooled until his services were lent to Iblis of Kör, and for ten long years had wondered whether he had been apprentice, hostage, or spy. All and none, he mused. The Kör prince had found many uses for an adept of the dragon priests, one who conveniently possessed no corrupting connections to the lords of the demon court. Busy indeed! Well had he aided Iblis' ascendancy over the many realms of Kör. Untold numbers of men and monsters alike paid tribute and pledged fealty to Kör's king, and Adestes could not easily count the bloody heads and golden treasures he had piled before the Living Throne.

Adestes thought of the girl. No doubt she now graced the collection of one of Iblis' demon captains. He shrugged. She who escaped the dangerous holdfast of Amber Khan would survive the shadow-steeped corridors of Tyrfang. Or perhaps not.

Adestes laughed again. Many wenches would he bed on this journey. First a return to Dragon Home, then a new mission for Malesh—one that liked him well. A sojourn into the soft, fat lands of the West. New conquest and port on the open sea for Kör, a land called by the uncouth name *Ilycrium*.

Adestes stood before the fissure. A trickle of gray water felt its way down the cavern wall before him. A half mile under the torn hills of Dragonmarch, nothing stirred save the vapor of his breath. He felt rather than heard the presence speak.

"Your time of indenture to the Kör prince is over. You approach the Zenith of your power. I feel your thought. Hie if you will to foment this war for Iblis. It serves well the purpose of She Who Waits."

In his mind's eye, Adestes beheld a titanic form, serpentine and clothed with wings of death, twisting and thrashing at times in rage against its confines. It possessed an elemental power, conceived when its deity mother first spawned with darkness, only to be banished when She fell to ruination in the dim eons of lost time. Three short decades ago, Her will quickened this one, Grazmesnil the eldest and strongest, and no doubt similarly wakened his brethren. *Soon*, it promised, *soon Her three mighty sons would burst their prisons and herald Her glorious return.*

The dragon flexed his bulk, striving fiercely against the binding force of his gaol, and above, in the Dragon Fells, a lava swell exploded, blasting an orange molten geyser of rock that froze in midair into thunderous boulders of slag to pound the unhappy region in hellish bombardment. It availed him not.

Ensconced within the deep, Adestes endured the dragon lord's fury without changing expression. Had he not witnessed such oft enough since his first waking memories? Malesh smirked, that such as this one were what his infant self regarded as father! He felt the glare of its preternatural thought light upon him once again.

"Thou art troubled. I discern in thee a seething." Adestes stifled a guffaw at the irony. "What sayest, Dark Star, the king of Kör?"

Adestes was surprised by the words that came unbidden to his lips. "I have no illusion of a long life of glory and comfort under Kör's lash. The whims of such a prince are unfathomable to any man. Even should the unthinkable happen, and I remain in favor, how long will my strength last? Twenty years? Forty? Not much by way of reckoning for that spawn of demons."

Adestes' hand involuntarily sought his lodestone blade. "Nay! To the Everfire with Kör and his lick spittle generals and magelings."

Grazmesnil laughed. The sound was like boiling stone. "Foolish man, know thou not those touched by the energies of the fallen orb are not bound by the common frailties of men?"

Adestes pondered. A second notion came to him. "There are more?"

"Yes, one other."

A sudden eagerness seized Adestes. "Who? Where is he?"

"He comes anon. Can you not feel him? Thou moreso than I."

Adestes digested this in silence, sensing no further information would be forthcoming, and was surprised when the presence spoke again. "Go on thy errand for Kör. Remember, thou man, heed well my words. Soon there will be summons to a greater purpose, a nobler journey. One to which thou wast born."

The thought-bond was broken. Adestes nodded to the shadowed fissure, now empty, and took his way up the stair to the outer world, paying scant heed to monk-priests that abode the outer caves. It was a decade since he vanquished their best, when they bethought themselves to test a young scion of dragons before his errantry.

Only ten years … it seemed more. And still Adestes felt more kinship with the presence in the rock than any of the dour monks. That they attended to his infrequent needs for provisions and shelter was enough. Without a backward glance, he swung onto his stallion, turning its head west by south.

To the sea, to Ilycrium!

Chapter 4

Land's End

Apieron labored for breath as he ascended the difficult slope. Behind him, Henlee huffed with each crunching step of his heavy boots. They could hear the murmur of the restless sea brushing against the gravel strand where they left their mounts, Apieron's roan mare and Henlee's burro. The sloop that had taxied them across the narrows would wait. Above, Apieron caught the stray gleam of a freshet, no doubt fed by the heavy mist that shrouded the summit of the oracle. Where the stream found its way to the sea, the gray Ess, he did not know, but its presence reassured him. "We walk the correct path."

Henlee's response was unenthusiastic.

"How lonely this place is," said Apieron. They followed a steep trail, nearly invisible, toward the crest of a low mountain that bestrode the sea to brush an unquiet sky—a gloomy place where the raw elements of earth, air, and water were thrown together in opposition.

"Perhaps as it was when the gods first raised this land," spoke Apieron. "The site was originally a place of worship to Earth Mother, sacred to my people. Wise men say Sky God came and slew the guardian of the old order." Henlee only grunted.

Another hour's toil brought them to the banks of the stream. It was twenty feet in breadth, and swift. The vapor above it was cold on their faces. Beyond rose a steep bank, nigh vertical, in which crude steps were cut. There was no way to make the final approach to the oracle without getting wet.

"Here I wait for you. Do not tarry!" said the dwarf. "Afternoon passes, and I have no desire to stumble down this goat trail in the dark."

Apieron laughed and tossed his clothes and boots to the other side. He entered the rushing water, sword held clear of the icy current. In this spot the sun shined brightly, and the freshet's swift surface danced and sparkled, clean as the first water running.

"It *is* cold!" shouted Apieron when he reached waist deep. Henlee laughed and splashed a handful of frigid water on his dark face. Apieron strode, swift as he might, to the far side. He rubbed dry with his cloak and donned breeches and boots.

"Apieron, ware!"

Down the stair capered a wild, unkempt figure clothed in patchwork rags. A man leapt dangerously close to Apieron and then crouched, swaying. A tattered vest of wolf's hair partially covered the man's chest, and the wolf's head topped his own. From his waist depended the mottled skin of a snake, and he cackled and tittered under his breath, eyes gleaming bright under shaggy brows.

Apieron could hear Henlee scramble aside to angle for a throw of the deadly maul he bore. The man stood his full height, and Apieron saw that his back would forever remain hunched under the outworn fur. Apieron fixed those wild eyes with a stern glare, which took on the color of the sea and the mountain and the mist. Staring down at the man's dirty face, he grasped his sword's hilt.

"Keep you back!" said Apieron. The man's mouthings ceased, and he searched about, clearing his throat many times as if recalling the ability to speak.

"Your stone-walker may not pass." The man's rolling eye caressed Henlee for a moment. "The god within knows him not." He withdrew his gaze to Apieron. "And you, lesser son of a greater father, have not earned the right of passage." A singsong cackle escaped the man's lips. "You wish to draw your weapon and smite me, eh? Cleanse the unclean with clever, man-bright steel?"

Apieron gave back a step, unnerved that the wilding might read his thoughts. Henlee glared as if by stare alone he could drive the figure into the rock. Instead, he withdrew his hands from the temptation of his weapon's grip and shoved them into his belt.

Wholly unconcerned, the man continued, "You wou' na' be the first to spill blood on hallowed ground, you know. P'raps blood is what made it hallow! There *was* another … far, far greater than you, who slew the serpent."

The shaggy figure fingered the hanging skin at his waist. He flourished it accusingly at Apieron. "Will you obey *your* summons? Dare you step within?" He leapt up and gesticulated wildly, falling into an obsequious bow. Crouching thus, he backed up the steps, beckoning Apieron forward as might a courtier. Soon he disappeared over the crest and all sound from him ceased.

"Like I said," said Henlee, "I wait here." Apieron tossed back a forlorn smile and followed the way thus prepared.

There was an ordinary grove of stone pine and a single laurel. The shrine itself lay beyond a peaking arch where two mighty slabs of rock had mated when the mountain's top rose from the sea.

Inside was cool and dark. Apieron could no longer hear the wind that stirred the airy pines, nor the clamor of birds gathering against coming nightfall. Small tapers burned in random niches along wax-shrouded walls. Apieron could discern an occasional tree limb nestled within the stonework where the natural construction of the place had been augmented by the hand of man. A crooning melody beckoned from a darkened recess, flanked by narrowing buttresses.

Ducking, Apieron stepped forward to find a shallow passage that gave immediately onto an earth-floored cavern not much bigger than a peasant's hovel. A low brazier stood near the far wall, its guttering flames yellow against the black iron of the bowl. Its smoke added to the already close feel of the place, yet from somewhere above Apieron smelled the tang of sea salt and the cloying mists that perpetually cloaked the mountain's summit.

The Sybil sat a tripod stool. In the uncertain light she appeared old but erect. Her voice echoed eerily in the close space. "What befalls, young Apieron? Did my servant startle you?"

"If he flirts with the dwarf, he may find the death he seems to seek."

"The dwarf concerns him not. It is *your* coming that has unsettled his mind."

Apieron frowned in consternation. Briesis rocked forward, and he beheld that her eyes were filmed, opaque as the whites of an egg. "It was your patron, the Archer God, who slew the serpent of the ancient rite. Blood always lingers; old and new are thus mingled in this place. Just so, in the time before reckoning, the elder oracle stood upon the very halls of earth giants who lived before the gods."

"I am not ignorant of my heritage." *Why was he here? Had this witch somehow summoned him from her mountain cell?* "It is also said the Archer paid atonement for his deeds."

"And so he did. Are *you* willing to spill the blood of the serpent? P'raps pay the tithe with your own?"

Apieron's anger fled like water out of a bag, and now he felt only trepidation. He looked for something on which to sit, but there was nowhere to do so.

"What is happening?"

The Pythia said nothing. They waited in silence. The gray light of the cave's entrance waned, and the air became chill, the cavern's rough ceiling receding into insubstantiality. It seemed to Apieron they looked upon a dark sky illuminated by faint lights.

The stars grew bright. He beheld many constellations in greater detail than ever before, and there were others he did not know. There was a frowning titan who held a glowing hammer before a beard that flowed to his knees, and a high-breasted maiden bestrode a winged horse. Yet disturbingly prominent was the red star called X'fel. Apieron saw that it glowed at the heart of a many-headed dragon, its coiled tail poised to sweep half the lights from the sky. On the facing surface rose the amphithere of Kör, its head a black absence of starshine that formed a gaping mouth and questing tongue. The sinuous neck stretched forward such that its eye was also the red star.

"The power of the gods of light grows corrupt," murmured the old woman. As she spoke, the glow of Hammer and Maiden faded against the encroaching darkness of Kör and the sickly essence of the red star. "A king withers. His legions languish whilst citizens murmur against the banner that liberated the fathers of their grandsires."

"Where does my path lead? Shall I serve the son as I have the father?"

"Nay, you will hie to another place … *beyond*." With her scrawny arms, Briesis described a flat circle. Star glow vanished, leaving only the leaping glare of the tripod. "There is a road over the abyss, to a recess in the earth. A place of fire."

The brazier surged, and a sulphurous reek filled the room. Apieron's watering eyes were drawn to his sword as, untouched, it inched from his scabbard to fall clanging to the floor. He reached for it and beheld on its polished surface fantastic scenes not present in the cave, or any other place of the world. Demonic faces leered and flitted across an orange-lit landscape where titanic upheavals of the ground met fiery ruin from a riven sky.

The Pythia spoke in sepulchral tones. "The doom that threatens to whelm this land comes not from the gods, but of an abomination risen in Helheim. There my vision fails. It is *there* you must go."

Apieron stared at the hungry-featured crone. The forebodings he had felt were as nothing in comparison to the reality of this terrible woman's words. What dark entity could be so monstrous?

"Expand your mind," whispered she. "There were many that were before the gods of the new order. Vaster. Unsubtle. Whence came this very fane?"

Apieron gathered his sword, snapping it into its scabbard. He straightened. "I will go, but to the wars, should my king ask it."

"You have letters. Bring me that slate."

Apieron squinted in the gloom and gathered for her a piece of shattered pottery and a splinter of charcoal. "There is an ancient word, too potent to mouth in this place." The blind woman scratched an intricate symbol. She turned its face to Apieron, her milky eyes searching his as he took the shard. Comprehension dawned on Apieron's features.

"Speak not the name."

"But this?" The ceramic shattered on the floor. "It is said this Thing of evil died in holocaust, its carcass becoming the pillars of the world." Apieron's head shook with distaste. "An unclean legend spawned by a race depraved." He straightened his shoulders, standing tall. "My ancestors swept the land clean of their taint with fire and the blood of many good men."

"Know you, man, any myth that is wholly true or merely fancy? The serpent coils, dragons of earth stir." She indicated the broken pottery. "The soul of darkness only sleeps."

"Why tell me this?" An image of gentle Melónie came unbidden to Apieron's mind. She stood in her garden, in sunshine, and at her skirt crouched Setie, the miniature of her mother. Ilacus tottered after butterflies.

"Your father came to the vale of Ilycrium, uttering a strange tongue and wielding song and sword, true to the will of his gods. Your line remains uncorrupt. Your feet shall wend their way to the fire. You were summoned the instant you were born."

"There must be another—" faltered Apieron.

The Sybil remained seated, but her shadow loomed over him, and her features were less tangible. When she spoke, her voice vibrated from the stone such that Apieron feared the cave's collapse. "Many that are as dirt shall be raised up. Many who are great shall be cast down! Forget you the defeat of titans of sky and earth? Forget you the gift of fire to lowly man, weak and naked?"

Apieron recoiled before the Oracle, and all retorts fled his brain. His legs bade him run, his mind that he kneel in deference. His frame stirred not an inch. Chin upheld, his gray eyes smoldered the yellow light of the brazier.

The shadow dissipated. Briesis gasped in pain, her body trembling as did her voice. "Earth Mother weeps for the nidus of evil grown within Her." The prophetess struggled. "Seek you such might of arms as you have at hand, for trust weighs heavier than numbers! Delay brooks doom."

Apieron found his voice despite the anguish in his breast. "Seek you to break my life? Who will walk with me? … Who will I condemn to the fire?"

"The vision," she gasped, "—the vision is given only to those who reverence the golden-haired god of the oracle. Trust in your faith, trust in the faith of thy friends."

Briesis shrank into her withered body. "To speak thusly spends my life, and I would see this land live a bit more. Go now … go!"

Apieron stumbled into the clean air of deepening dusk. He heard her crooning in the dark. The gloomy cliff over slated seas seemed now like a sunny edge. The wild slave of the fain was nowhere to be seen. Wooden legged, Apieron found the trail where the dwarf would be waiting.

🚶 🚶

"Bah! I know what you think, Son. He smokes twinkle dust."

"*Galor?*" Apieron considered his friend, Galor Galdarion, deliverer and prince of Amor, the most powerful creature he knew.

"Crazy as they come," the dwarf slyly touched his nose, "and I've heard (from reliable sources) he has tree mold growing under those fancy robes. Mayhap he's more plant than not."

The dignified golden elf, centuries wise, struck Apieron as anything but deranged. Yet if Galor could be persuaded to attend a dilemma not pertaining to elves, a great weight would be lifted. The mere notion lightened Apieron's dragging steps.

"Let us to your temple. For the price of all those offerings, the least those bead-tellers can do is conjure up one skinny elf."

Apieron looked up. "The Donna serves both Wisdom and He of the Harp. Will *she* dispute the Sybil? But Melónie waits—"

"Posh the distance. We've done half already." Henlee waved away Apieron's objections. "Never thought I'd wish to visit a human cloister. Pease and spring water no doubt. Here is Bump!"

They neared the path's end where their mounts waited. Apieron's graceful mare nibbled at thready grass amongst rocks while Henlee's enormous donkey stared up the trail, ears cocked as if he followed their conversation. At the dwarf's approach, Bump flared his lips to reveal long teeth while flattening his ears. Henlee dodged a vicious bite and swung up. "Put the words of that mountain-perched crone from your mind. Night gathers on the water, and this place chills my bones. Yon lazy ferryman had best be awake."

Apieron chuckled. "You are afraid to camp here? Never mind. Cynthia's table is wide, and her monks drink better droughts than spring water."

"Why do we tarry?" The dwarf spurred Bump to a jouncy trot.

Chapter 5

Ilycrium: Eldûn Forest

Sun's setting cast lengthening shadows on the hamlet of Cynegils. Here a handful of woodcutters and trappers gleaned a hard living from the fickle bounty of the swamp-ridden Eldûn. Dressed lumber and tanned hides were sent via wain northwest to Sway and to other towns in exchange for wagonloads of metal goods, flour, and weavings. The people of Cynegils were loosely knit, preferring to homestead isolated acreages to better access the provender of the forest.

"Gart, you go on out to the woodpile afore supper and git more sticks. An' wash yer hands after," called Fregga.

"Don't let the shaggy man git ya!" echoed Lil, his younger sister.

"Shush now, youngling," said the stout farm wife. She seized the culprit's ear. "Where'd you 'ear such talk?"

Gart's face flushed, but the boy mustered his nerve and stamped out. "If'n 'e does," he called over his shoulder, "I'll be sure an' tell 'im where to find ya." The door bounced behind him on its straps.

Mother Fregga brandished a wooden spoon. "You kin finish a snappin' those beans whilst you answer my questions, snoopy."

"Neighbor Tiina told me," squawked the child.

"That Tiina's always runnin' her mouth."

Encouraged by this opportunity to deflect the blame (and hopefully the ensuing switching) the girl gushed, "Tiina told me that she t'overheard her pa and t'other menfolk talkin' 'bout the shaggy man when they didna know she was a' listenin'."

Fregga looked to her husband, who returned the glance from his whittling stool. In his work-hardened hands an axe handle slowly took shape. The cured hickory blunted his knife incessantly and would require a few more evenings' effort. Mother Fregga regarded her daughter, now industriously slicing the stems from a pile of beans, snapping the large ones once before her small hands scooped the pile into a bowl to soak.

"Like as not them menfolk filled her ears with rubbish to teach naughty little snips not to eavesdrop."

"Likely some scared farmer's son saw a dog gone feral and taken to livin' in the swamp," added the man. "Or the dogs 'ave gone and stirred somethin' out o' the fen tha' shoulda been let be. Either way, I'd best talk to Tiina's pa an' his boys tomorrow. Meanwhile, I'll see what's keepin' Gart." He set the small whittling knife aside but kept the stave as he walked out into the gathering dusk.

"An' you, young missy—"

Five miles distant resided old man Compton and his wife, Gerti, on the last parcel of dry land nigh the fen. Although not blessed with children, the aging couple had held one another in lifelong bond for five decades. They enjoyed the quiet of the evening, supper done and the door locked as was habit for any who lived so near the Eldûn. A hearth fire crackled merrily, built more for its sweet smoke than for any expected chill during the mild spring night. The farm wife sat humming, cracking nuts in her brown, weathered hands. Compton dozed in his low chair, piled with cloth pillows stuffed full with aromatic rushes and soft down. Their orange tabby of respectable age had perfected the art of sitting as close to the little blaze as possible without actually getting singed. His ears perked.

Gerti smiled. "What is it, kitty? Hear a mouse?"

With a spray of dust and splinters and shattered plaster, the door and frame burst inward. A looming shadow stepped into the yellow light. Nuts bounced and scattered across the floor, and the cat was no longer to be seen. A whoosh of air doused the fire. Compton leapt up with a belligerent yell. He raised a small mattock unsteadily against the towering form.

"Pa!" shouted Malesh. His mailed fist smashed down onto the old man's bare head, crumpling him loosely to the floor. "What's for dinner, Ma?" He stood in the middle of the room, hands on hips to survey his surroundings. The farm wife was on her knees, swooning in shock.

"Why, this is a cozy place you have here, Mother," said Malesh, looking about. He fixed the horrified woman with a level stare. "But there *is* a bit of a draft." He nodded to the fireplace before fixing the horrified woman with an exaggerated wink.

SWAYMEET

"What, so few?" asked Gault.

"Harvest," replied Dexius apologetically. The thin minister, Regent of Swaymeet—King's Palace of Ilycrium, rapped his knuckles. "Gentlemen, first a report from Mincon, a worthy who serves as breed master of the Royal stables."

The hubbub of voices ceased with the apparent opening of official business. The king's council chamber was dominated by a table of richly worked mahogany at which were seated such principals as white-bearded Tertullion, seer advisor to the king. And Exeter, the King's distant cousin and seneschal of the realm.

A frowning representative of the far-flung country lords, Exeter was March Warden, commonly known as Hawk for his brown cloak and creamy doublet. Fat Lysander was also there, who was spokesman for the powerful shipping and merchant guilds of Sway. Other seats at table there were for servants of the courts, noble guests from the clergy or military, as well as those placed against the paneled walls for invited observers and witnesses called to summons. These were vacant at present save for two occupied by sons of country barons who where there to listen but not speak.

Gault sat his father's chair, his hair burnished copper in the yellow light of a massive candelabra dependent over the center of the table. Tall, thin windows set with thick glass offered a wan illumination through a thick outer wall to the harbor sky.

The man Mincon cleared his throat twice. "For some months I've tallied a dearth of healthy born foals, and some that appear well-formed oft as not are shunned by their dams. I've bought what I could from our own rural estates," Mincon favored Exeter with a polite nod, "yet such are few and expensive."

"And the cause?" asked Tertullion.

Dexius shrugged. "We do not know."

"And the solution?" asked Lysander, his many heavy rings glinting with gold.

The man Mincon looked to his employer. Dexius spoke, "We must purchase replacement stock abroad before the cavalry generals are taken with panic."

"The traders of Prebanks?" asked Exeter suspiciously.

"If necessary."

"I smell a tax increase." Lysander yawned.

Dexius favored him with a sour look. "When have you heard of a government council enacting a tax *decrease*?"

"Even so," replied Lysander, his thick fingers twiddling, "it is always we tradesmen who bear such burdens, and our losses at sea are much increased from times aforenow."

"We shall need the horses," broke in Gault. "Blight does indeed walk the countryside. I have seen it. The peasantry bespeak themselves of the *Hand of Pestilence*."

Around the table an uneasy muttering arose. "Foul words from a fair mouth, my prince," said Dexius.

"Nonetheless, I speak them. Not merely horses are whelmed; much is amiss! There are tales of slayings in the rurals, and yestermorn I saw a blood altar after the manner of the Black Druids."

"The Earth Mother has always been given an occasional warm offering," countered Exeter. "In sooth, many of them are at least *partially* willing."

"Aye Seneschal, a sort of rustic crop insurance," said Lysander with a grin.

A smattering of laughter rose, yet it was as quickly abated by the Prince's glare. While several of those present commented in private over Gault's unseemly passions for matters outside the normal purview of a royal heir, none dared front him openly, for the blood of Wgend conquerors ran true in his veins, and such were quick to take umbrage at any perceived challenge of honor. Reinforcing this notion stood rows of blackened bronze and stone figures, set in wall niches in likeness of the elder King and his sires, those who had ventured from northland homes to claim the rich valleys and uplands of Ilycrium. Each was clad as a warrior and glowered with stern mien under tall helms.

"Take heart, my prince," said Lysander. "We are not at war. Our land has known the long peace of a generation, and our peoples grow prosperous whilst wild beasts and monsters alike are driven to the lonely places, there to starve or consume themselves. And number-wise, we are strong should a true emergency arise."

The ring-heavy finger wagged with slow wisdom. "If you seek a single cause for our troubles, you may look long indeed."

"Yet the words of our prince seem true to me," said Dexius.

"Then what, Minister?" queried Exeter, glad to have a target other than Gault for his remarks. "What think you the causation of so many disparate events? What can storms at sea, horse dams gone barren, and a yokel throat-cutter or two have aught to do with the other? I deemed your mind more subtle than that."

"We have enemies," replied Gault evenly, not missing the true target of Exeter's remarks. He had no wish to directly antagonize the voice of the barons, without whose support no mobilization of Ilycrium's resources could occur in strength.

"My lord," Exeter nodded to Gault, "think you *Kör* to blame? Or mayhap those crazy cults of younglings who worship the full moon, or the red star, or gods know what?"

Tertullion cleared his raspy throat. "Just as the Cannia tree gives off a poisonous substance from its branching roots such that the ground around it grows barren, so does Kör. The tree at least possesses a beauty within itself that some good is born of its habits, yet no good ever came from that place of foulest blackness. There is no dearth of monsters and fell peoples alike in those lands, gentlemen, and those within our own borders are more numerous than you reckon. Ever they heed the call of the Kör king."

"Is there one prince of that realm, Seer?" asked Exeter. "I think it more likely to be a broad land beset with many warring tribes of orc and human alike. I even hear tale of dwarven fiefdoms, not unlike those that take squatters' rights on our own northern passes. Are we to fear these plot to smite us as well?"

"At least the children of elves and dwarves do not embrace heretical sects or call for the destruction of what their fathers have earned," grumbled Tertullion. His piece said, the old mage sank back and groused to himself in his weedy beard.

"Peace, Seer. Wish us no ill wind," said Lysander. "My guild captains will have difficulties enough negotiating with the Saad Isles without scattering our sailors' resolve with tales of invasion from Kör."

"Then we are decided," said Dexius. "Let us proceed to the meat of this council. We must mark which trade goods shall be surcharged and to what degree."

"My prince?" said Dexius, turning to regard Gault's incredulous expression.

"What of the protection owed our people?"

"What do you propose?" replied Dexius patiently.

"Action against the criminals or monsters who slay in the countryside!"

"A committee? A most excellent idea."

"A royal commission?" added Exeter doubtfully. "More officials to hound country lords with requests for lodging and assistance? Harvest beckons."

"I shall lead it myself," snapped Gault. He stood rapidly, gave a curt bow, and exited before others finished scraping their chairs. When the chamber doors shut behind him and the guard without resumed his station, as evidenced by the thump of his halberd, a welling of general conversation ensued.

"Impetuous," said Lysander, shaking his head ponderously.

"I would that the King sired a son of his own body," added Exeter. "Gault's birth father, Gor du Roc, was no friend to the Crown."

Tertullion stood to leave. "An old man grows tired, and I have learned all that I may, but know that the Duke was a great man, and his wife was in no way lesser by reason of blood or wit. When Belagund married her, he named young Gault heir. There can be no doubt who will be the next king of Ilycrium."

The venerable seer departed. There was a moment's silence

broken by Lysander's almost mirthful tone. "Without doubt, the King's beloved Candice was quick witted indeed to bed a duke, next a king, then place her son by the former, a sworn enemy to the second, in line for the throne of the mightiest kingdom of the West, all without losing the inheritance of the first!"

Exeter added nothing but shared a long look with the two nobles seated against the wall, sons of his peers sent to observe the Council as guests and make report to their fathers.

"Gentleman," interjected Dexius, "may we please return to the true business of this session? With only three voting members present, surely we can decide the monies issue today."

"We have a crisis brewing, and those dusters won't see." Gault jerked his head angrily towards the council chamber.

The stone-faced guard before its doors appeared as deaf and mute as the lintel beside which he stood. Tallux had happened by, only to find his friend exiting the meeting chamber of Swaymeet in a foul mood. Tertullion followed, bowing to the forest-clad elf and greeting Sut the hound. He begged leave for a nap.

"If they got off their soft arses to see the countryside for themselves, they might notice the bear gazing through the trees. But no, Lysander's idea of visiting the rurals is a coach ride surrounded by partygoers to hie straight behind the walls of his villa for a fete or three before returning, too hung-over to notice aught."

Tallux nodded appreciatively. The elvin archer was girt with sword and knife, and was never without his famous longbow despite his presence in the polished halls of Swaymeet. His war dog stood sentinel, back placed to his master and feet firmly planted. The dog swung a heavy head to eye closely any worker or courtsman who passed into view. None interrupted or approached, although each was tracked carefully by the great hound.

"And Dexius keeps the Council busy counting tax levies, enacting writs for tradesmen and nobles!" Candor attempted at the minister's oiled tones: "My dear prince, the business of running the kingdom requires more than simply riding about waving that silly sword of yours. It demands hard, tedious work of this sort, and attention to the smallest detail must be paid lest we go broke, or the barons and burghers gain serious grievance, or the petty folk starve over-much."

"Fah, I could spit. If Kör and the demons of earth swallow us up, there will be no bank to bother over."

Tallux surrendered a rare grin. "Your imitations are getting better down the years, but why speak you of banished earth spirits whose names we say not?"

Gault forced a strained laugh. Tallux regarded him closely. To his keen emerald eyes, the young prince had aged muchly in the short months since he had last seen him. Gault spoke again. "I don't know. Just the other day Tertullion whispered dire warnings to my father. He had a priest of Sky in tow, Turpin, Archbishop of Sway. There's more. The King spoke of ordering the resurrection of his Long Knives." Tallux stirred. "Royal scouts return with odd, contradictory reports. You who are their advisor and live amongst them know this better than I."

When Tallux did not respond, Gault continued, "Kör is sleeping, say some. That our troubles are rooted in the rebirth of cults that revere ancient wyrms and devils that once beset this land. Others say the forces of Kör gather from many far lands, that a new god-king has arisen who is strong and filled with fell intent. My father the King did not forbid my telling you this. I deem it well you know his mind."

Candor paused, facing Tallux with an expression so earnest

that the wood elf would never doubt his words. "There are few in Sway whom I trust. You are one of them, and of course mighty Sut here." He bent to pat the hound's thick neck. The dog remained intent on his self-appointed task.

"It is well that you confide in me thus," ventured Tallux at last. "Of the team, you know as well as I the principals are scattered like storm drift. Xephard has returned to the shrine of his goddess. Eirec took offense with your father years ago and left us for Amber Hall, where I'm sure he is enjoying the life of a northern jarl. Rudolph Mellor has no doubt lost himself in the sewers and alleys of this or some other large town, but I deem not here, because I have at times searched for him."

Candor smiled. "If the tales are true, perhaps he has already met his fate at the hands of some jealous husband." Tallux nodded as if he regarded this last a serious possibility.

"And Apieron?" asked Candor quietly.

"The Spear Runner, who sometimes led us, took his reward of Windhover. He longs for a quiet retirement as a country lord to raise his children in peace."

"You have word of him."

Tallux eyed the Prince speculatively. "Yes. He is not idle, and tries his hand at farming. How many times when the Knife was abroad did he speak his dreams of just that?" They were silent a moment. A pageboy clattered around the corner and, spying the unusual trio, mumbled some unintelligible honorific before redoubling his pace to disappear from view.

"You are a good friend to protect your comrades so. My father has issued no decree for his recall. Or yours, but I fear it may come soon—and if Apieron is unwilling, it will be *you* we hope who leads again the Scouts."

"And well it were your father did not." Tallux laughed lightly, easily deflating the slight imperious air Gault affected. "My master is lord of the Malave, our Greenwolde. He recks little of draft notices for his soldiers by foreign kings, allies or no! I'm here to counsel and to observe, and to further communications between our peoples."

Gault laughed and shrugged. "I told him I would try. I know all you say is true, and your worth is invaluable to us, however it may be you are here."

"Your views are not shared by many who hold power."

"Alas, half the Council forget the Malave provides an anchoring strength to our center, and that the fortresses of dwarf folk and free northmen shield the marches to Kör. To my noble peers, Sway *is* Ilycrium. In their minds, the bloody battles to win this land, when Apieron's sire (the mighty Xistus) called down the hill peoples to aid my father's father, are naught but distasteful trivia of ruder times."

The stocky wood elf shook his head in disgust. "Humans have an amazing ability to go from passion to apathy in a season."

"Not all the kingdom is asleep," answered Gault, "and perhaps I can illuminate you on the whereabouts of your friend, Xephard." He handed Tallux a weather-stained scroll bound with a silk ribbon. Its wax seal was broken. Tallux opened the letter and beheld its elegant script.

"It is perfumed!"

"That is from the lord Count Malchar, who is also a major of infantry assigned to the watch battalion at Denfirth."

Tallux cocked an eyebrow and read quietly:

> Salutations and fondest regards to his Highness, Gault Candor, Prince of the Realm.
>
> I enclose for your perusal the following interview with an enlisted soldier of the coastal at Denfirth. In my position as procurement officer, it

is a simple affair to request escorts from the garrison commander for valuable perishables en route to the battalion. In the present case, Lady Fortune smiled, and I was lucky enough to encounter a grizzled sergeant of the line who saw combat at the recent skirmish of Manzikert. I am told that error-ridden rumors abound at Capital as to the exact nature of that action. Herein I have reconstructed his tale unabridged, though I daresay my childhood tutors would faint if they beheld this text.

"Oh, no sir. Thankee. Such is not for the likes o' me. But I'll take a spot o' that liquor on yonder little table."

The man obviously possessed a soldier's unswerving intuition for quality spirits. I set aside the new beer I offered and fetched the decanter. He poured the Dididion from my mother's crystal into his tin cup and gulped it like common grog! Little did he know that one bottle was worth half my wine stock. Perhaps he did, gods bless him. Its worth was proved as you shall see.

"Ye gods, it was a slaughter, sir. They'un kept a comin' like every mother's son o' them was there that night. Who, ye ask me? Twas the Körlings, sir, come alandin' on our beach. We killed and killed, and they jes kept on." Here the man paused to take a pull directly from my decanter, then ran his tongue over his teeth and smacked like a baby. "An' they was no slaggards t'either, lordship. Ye know them Kör marines, them's the same outfit as done for our boys at Salamas. Not a man t'under six foot and each 'un armed to the nines.

"Well, your Cap'n Sturm had all the landings presighted by archers that morn. Gods below, there wad no lack o' good targets t'either, and those Kör bastards went down in windrows. Our boys ran short o' shafts and them marines kept a comin', jes marchin' o'er the dead like it was a parade. An' so we commenced to tearin' down wall stones and tossin' 'em over, though by then those bastards was in our teeth and snarlin' like scalded tigers." As he spoke, the man's eyes shined with that inner light, which, as my lord well knows, marks the true remembrance of a man reliving a moment as if he were in that place and not the present.

"But our boys was steady on account that our wains had been sent off that afternoon an' the land bridge behind us cut by the engineers on Cap'n Sturm's orders. That'll put a bit o' steel in your spine, sir. No way out!" The sergeant laughed drunkenly and took another pull, wiping my Dididion from his lips with his filthy sleeve.

"We fought brave enough, our boys give back as good as we got, but them Kör marines ain't got no quit in 'em. You know, sir, tha' hand to hand those buggers are nigh invincible. Each can fight jes as well wi' blade or bare hands. Then two score o' them dastards gained the parapet behind us, an' was a kickin' us back onto their friends awaitin' below. Not a one that made that tumble lived, I can tell ye!"

The man sighed, then slammed down his mug, which he recovered on finding the lips of the decanter overly difficult to navigate. "An' tha' was when the Lord Xephard showed up. Dawn was abreakin' in the east as he and a few o' them temple knights came ridin' in on their big warhorses, right through the foam o' the surf.

"How'd I know, ye ask? How'd ye know your own name this morn? All an' every one knew 'twas he."

The sergeant's countenance was flushed with the brandy, more so the fires of his spirit, as if he burned with the memory. "If'n the din was bad 'afore, it was somethin' fiercer then. Those Körlings set up a howl and charged him. See, they knew! But it didna do 'em no good. 'E was like a damn windmill an' cut down those marines like they was paper men. I seen it all, though it didna take as long t'happen as it do to tell it.

"The cap'n o' them Kör men, a giant, iron-cased bugger with a helm like a grinnin' mask and horns like a demon, bounded right up to Lord Xephard who was then afightin' on foot. They swore and hewed a t'other till the sparks flew and lo! Xephard kicks the Körlin's blade aflyin', but tha' slave o' demons pulled out 'is long dirk quick as water runnin' an' stuck it full into Xephard's chest—right through that pretty suit o' mail!

"Sea Father strike me blind if I'm lyin', I seen it all! Well, the blade was hilt deep in 'is left breast, an' here's tha' marine hangin' on like some damn leech tryin' to work it in a bit more. Tha's about when ol' Xephard had enough, an' knocked off 'is fancy headpiece. He grabbed that bugger by the hair and chopped off 'is head as easy as killin' chickens.

"After tha', the fightin' was about done. We was standin' there dazed-like an' wonderin' if'n it was truly over when Xephard calls his troop, remounts, and rides off wi' tha' dirk still in his chest! 'E's strong, tha' one, an' mighty thick, and maybe tha' long pig-sticker didna reach 'is vitals. Who's ta say? But who's ta say it didn't?"

The sergeant bethought himself a moment and added, "Where an' how those marines avoided our sloops and landed on Sea Wall, no one was to say. Mayhap one of the boys saw it. If'n he did, he ne'er lived to tell." The old salty completed his tale and would add no more. I discerned a brown-stained bandage on his sword arm and knew he had been forward in the fray. Despite this, he had neglected to aggrandize himself.

He swayed a bit as he stood to go. I thanked him and inquired if there was aught of use I could provide him before his departure. He simply smiled his stub-toothed grin and did an about-face, marching from my drawing room as crisp as any academy cadet, with my Dididion! The decanter belonged to my grandmother. She once met your father. I am certain Your Highness now understands the depths of my servitude to him.

Trivialities aside, the man's tale correlates exactly with others I have interviewed in one fashion or the other. As you know, I am strictly forbidden to command combat troops, nonetheless the line captain of that company is an astute fellow who fortunately paid swift heed to my missive the morn prior stating that Yarm, my hire-mage, spied a darkened drommond bearing down the Denfirth. As for your friend Xephard, his Templars must have smelled the battle a ten-day beforehand to arrive as they did.

Another oddity, the sergeant mentioned Salamis. I had to research this. That battle was nigh two decades ago when Kör marines razed Cardeus to ashes in retaliation for the loss of a merchantman in their sponsor. I deem it passing strange that now the same unit should probe our coastals in a night attack. Practice? Or perhaps my imagination has grown mischievous from lack of happy tasks. My general is content only when I retire to my family lands and assure him that victuals and wine will arrive as scheduled.

I am told there are tales in Sway that the dire attack at Manzikert was actually by Ess pirates, passing as enemies, or a military exercise gone foul. I wonder sometimes if our foolish country will survive these times—there can be no doubt this was a probing attack, nearly successful, by a reinforced company of Kör's Royal Marines! Though many here would multiply that number tenfold.

Your loyal servant,
Malchar of Denfirth.

Tallux carefully rolled the scroll and returned it to Gault. "Can you not take this before the Council? Surely this is proof enough that the long peace is over?"

Gault sighed. "The Lord Count's letter cannot be presented. His, er, romantic leanings are well known, and any words of his would be deemed of little worth. Besides, what would the Council do, form a committee?"

Tallux shook his head. "The longer I live among your kind, the less I understand. Is this not the same Count Malchar who is reckoned the deadliest blade of North Ilycrium, whose father is Castellan of Denfirth?"

"Indeed," Gault's chuckle was soft with irony, "and he but a major who regularly earns his general's stern censure. Yet perhaps the more valuable to us for all that. Tell me again about Apieron of Windhover. Will he answer a summons?"

Tallux sighed. "He will. His father was gifted with the power of great vision, and I have seen the same in him, though he deems himself a simpler person. Events stir around him even as we speak."

"You mean the warnings of the Sybil? Our religious repeat them oft of late, but the Council has heard them before. They say her seat rests on some sea-scraped crag, far removed from knowledge of men. A backcountry witch they name her, good for muttering portents for the gods of bumpkins and wild woods-folk."

No one was near, but Tallux pulled the Prince close. Sut pricked his ears at the subtle change yet did not alter his watchful stance. It was Gault's turn to be impressed by the earnest undertones in the elf's voice.

"These troubles you speak of are tremors felt by every wise people, and they go beyond the unrest of any one kingdom. Trust in such warnings. Apieron is a country landholder, underlord to your father, yet he is also son to Xistus Farsinger and hears the summons of his oracle. That he will act accordingly I do not doubt." Tallux gripped Gault's sleeve. "Have faith, and lend your support to any plan he proposes."

"You ask much. A king in troubled times normally gathers his knights to him."

Gault raised his hand to continue. "Yet I feel you speak rightly in this, and I will echo your words to my father and to the Council. Although I have little hope for that body! Besides," he grinned at the serious scout, "whenever has dour Tallux spoken so much at one time? Surely then his words must be heeded."

Gault drew Tallux with him as they began to walk. "Tell me of two hundreds scouts. What are their needs?" As the twain rejoined the ebb of foot traffic, Sut fell in behind, and all gave them wide berth.

Chapter 6

Ilycrium

Apieron and Henlee journeyed in comfort. The southern belly of Ilycrium was at its core yet bounteous, and once clear of the wind and sea-scoured rock of the oracle, they rode rather than walked, dawn to dusk. The jouncing pace of Henlee's mount made for a leisurely walk for Apieron's graceful racer. Despite this, they made good time.

Dome-like stacks of piled hay dwindled as new grass grew long and green in fields. Farm folk with room to spare were not adverse to a silver penny for a night's board and mat. Roast pig and fowl were graced by coarse breads. Dark winter ales were still to be had, and spring's new beers were light and fresh enough for any road-weary man or dwarf.

Pushing back from table after one such meal, Apieron settled comfortably into a low chair, legs outstretched. A small fire lent the room merry cheer as darkness came. The farmer's daughter brushed against him as she bustled dishes whilst her mother set the guest room aright.

Apieron guessed the girl's age to be sixteen. Buxom of chest, her teeth shined in a sunburned face when she favored him with frequent smiles. Henlee smacked contentedly over a last ale jack.

Apieron gave over a small, leathern sack that the farmer's wife packed with victuals meant for the next day's travel. They would be off before light, for Apieron begrudged the delay of even a hot breakfast. The property owner saw to the final comfort of the animals while Apieron and Henlee were led to a spacious room with two low beds piled high with comfortable flax cloths and woolens.

The dwarf fell instantly asleep. Apieron stared as shadows encroached along walls and ceiling from the shuttered window. It felt good to stretch and sink into the bed, although sleep did not come. His thoughts returned to Windhover. Like her mother, Setie had grown quick of mind and figure. Ilacus explored and ambled like a bear cub, and Jilly was *beautiful*. He felt almost perverse that the unrest came when he should have been most settled. The soul-yearning, ever present, only beckoned to dangerous unknowns. The Oracle bespoke herself of fate. *His* fate. The dwarf sensed it and would doggedly follow him to the depths of any pit, yet how he could he be sure of himself?

The door's hide latch was lifted. It glided open. A rustling figure, whose hair now smelled of rosewater, bent over Apieron. The girl smiled in the low light when she saw he was awake.

"Yes, lass?"

"Does my lord desire aught before he sleeps?" She glanced quickly at the dwarf, whose thunderous snores continued unabated. The soft illumination of moon and stars filtered into the room, highlighting her hair. Taut breasts were high and quivered under a thin shift. Though only three hands her senior, Apieron felt the great gulf of experience that separated their worlds.

"You are kind. I seek only to rest."

The girl cupped his face in her cool grasp. Her breath smelled of mint, and her hair cascaded about him, veiling the wan light. "Millicent can massage muscles that ache." She touched his bare chest and broad shoulder. "A man cannot rest with so much tension in him."

He enveloped her hand in his large, warm grip. He pulled her face to him and then lightly kissed her forehead. She simply stared.

"Again lass, you are most kind, but I will sleep. Long is the road ahead."

The girl's face was unreadable. She cast a second glance at the dwarf and exited in a swish less silent than her approach. Apieron lay back with a sigh. The dwarf, undisturbed, continued to rattle the night.

They departed before sunrise, after the husbandman fetched their mounts and bade them fare safely. Apieron's mare and Bump appeared well rested and eager. The girl and her mother were absent. The companions struck an easy pace into the cool morning. Dew glistened from every blade of grass and tree, and the packed dirt of their road, here little more than a cart path, glowed like wet silver. Cloaks were doffed as man and steed warmed to the pace.

Apieron's mind drifted. Soon they would enter the sacred vale. Memories of the shrine comforted him. His sword brother Xephard dwelled there, as did Isolde—more sister to him than his father's daughters had ever been. If Cynthia, Perpetua of the vale, would hear his dilemma and lend her wisdom, his choice would perhaps grow clear, mayhap back to Windhover. To stay. *Could the Auroch cure his unquiet?*

"Well, my boy, perhaps you are lost in contemplation of that lovely less-than-maiden you spurned last eve?"

Apieron saw the dwarf grin up at him from his bushy moustaches. "I should have known you were awake."

"Your sigh would have roused a drunken boar orc."

"Sooth, my sigh was for Melónie, who I missed sore when the girl came to me."

The dwarf ceased his jesting tone. "This I know, or I would not have mentioned it. But to less important and more immediate matters: If your temple matron is less than friendly, are we to ride all the way to Amor to fetch the elf? Five days on this ass is bad enough, and the extra religion I'm sure is good for you, but I'll become an atheist if I have to ride numberless miles to summon one silken elf-wizard."

Apieron was thoughtful. When no response was forthcoming, the dwarf continued, "There *is* another way to Amor, or anywhere else for that matter. A dwarven way."

"You speak of the White One?" Apieron had heard of the dwarven shaman aforetime and wasn't sure which was more frightening, the gods-touched mountain dwarf or the spell whereby he might transport others untold leagues at rapid speed via magical conduits in the very earth.

"Aye, Ohm could whisk us on errand to Fairie and not miss a meal. Although after the ride, I'm guessin' we might not want one."

Apieron shook his head. "The Donna can spell-touch the mage, or at least his family priestesses. And should they desire, I daresay any of Galor's kin can reach us more easily than we can find them."

The dwarf shrugged nonchalantly. "Your mission, your problem." As the dwarf spoke, Apieron thought he discerned a brief picture of relief on Henlee's features.

"Uncle, I think we would do well to bide a while and plan carefully whilst in the vale. Perpetua wields great wisdom."

Henlee shrugged again. "Let's hope she speaks with less riddle than that mountain crone … of course, she should. All reports say that tongue of hers cuts quicker than Dangbad's thrice-enchanted axe."

Apieron laughed. Rustic and unpretentious, the shrine and clerics of the Warrior Goddess would suite the dwarf well. "Besides, Uncle, I hope friends await."

Henlee grunted noncommittally.

"Xephard and Isolde, and perhaps news of Tallux and Rudolph Mellor. Maybe even Eirec."

"I can see you've been thinking, and none too well. The others I know, and your paladin will never let us drag his beloved cleric-woman on your questing." Henlee chuckled darkly. "Of course I owe Eirec a debt he'll not be glad to receive. As for the tree elf, who cares? As long as that bow of his is not pointed my way. Same goes for his dog.

"And Jamello?" continued Henlee. "Why drag a sneaky, thievin' city rat along with us?"

"I'm afraid we may not have time to secure him, much less convince the man to risk his life on a journey without profit of coin."

Henlee looked optimistic.

"It's not a question of want, we need the thief."

"We do?"

"Can you leap over spiked walls? Pick locks? Or climb through sewer pipes?"

Henlee tugged at his beard. "Well, if you are talking about bets …"

Apieron frowned.

"Couldn't we just nab one on the way? I don't see trudging all the way to Bestrand and searching every dingy alley for one throat-slitter," grunted Henlee with irritation.

Apieron sympathized with the dwarf's impatience. Hell's below! *He* did not know what they were doing. "What is the saying? Dwarves are patient only in matters of craft, gold, and revenge?"

Henlee chortled. "That is the short of it."

They passed three land workers who stared dully at the unusual twain before returning to their work, eyes downcast.

Henlee stroked his pleated beard, absently checking that every gem and silver clasp was in place. "The people hereabouts are awful glum for farmers with a bright day and a field full of rye."

"Aye," agreed Apieron softly, "those closest to the land know first when the earth trembles." Henlee swiveled quickly as if the field behind them was soon to erupt in fire and ruin.

"Come," urged Apieron, "let us haste to the Holy Valley."

"An' so much for a leisurely ride, eh, Bump?" The dwarf patted his donkey's face, only to be nipped hard on the finger by the surly creature. Henlee's yell startled Apieron's mare to a trot, and poor Bump was forced to double his stride to keep pace.

"Your fault," scolded Henlee.

In this wise, they made good progress. Hazy rays of midmorning sun cast a warm gleaming over woodcot and farmland bourn as they neared the temple environ. By noon, Apieron and Henlee walked, leading the steeds. Apieron's mare was coated with a sheen of sweat. Bump cast Henlee a look of absolute fury. The dwarf ignored it, his thick hand hard on the halter.

A valley flanked by low hills lay open before them. On either side, where free-croppers' fields of grain and hay grass rustled, dove warbled as they raced low over waving millet. Piled stone lined the lots, in some places man-high, with plow-breaking rocks unearthed each year and carefully set aside. Small dwellings littered the vale, for people were in abundance here. Apieron knew the temple grounds lay at the apex of the vale, nestled in the arms of the Auroch. It was the highest tor thereabouts, whence a brisk white stream flowed. They would find the enclave well before day's end.

"At least folk here are less close-lipped than those surly rascals we passed this morn." Henlee wiped a splash of water off his beard. They stood before a shaded well at a roadside dwelling, humble but neat. A girl child proffered a pail to the fearsome dwarf with an open smile and a twirl of pigtails. Henlee grunted in appreciation of her bravery.

They resumed their walk, and were oft as not waved to by farmers and tradesmen. "I hope yon prayer-folk haven't forgotten how to make beer an' gone over to drinking well water and eating parsley snips."

Apieron laughed. The temple ales were famous in this part of the kingdom, having been brewed in the same way and place for generations. The clever clerics did not export their wares, consequently pilgrims by the hundreds flocked to the Lampus to seek wisdom, or at least relief of thirst. The shrine was situated astride key roads linking the center of the land with less settled southern marches and so had become a way station for trade caravans and a gathering place for intelligences of the world beyond.

"The druids of my father's country claim that clean water purifies one's body of the pollutions of impure foods and drink … and thoughts."

"That may be true." Henlee sucked his teeth. "Sprout-eating elves live nigh forever. But I never saw a druid who could flourish a hammer with any bit o' weight to it. Or split an ogre's skull with a single blow."

"For years I've wanted to bring you here. I think we can be reasonably certain that if the monks and priestesses have given over strong food and drink, special dispensation will be made for such a daughty trencherman as Henlee, lord of Saemid."

"Then stop talking and walk faster. Eh, Bump? Evenin' meal will be on soon … and we don't want to miss it." For once the burro seemed to agree with his master and followed eagerly, sensing an end to their journey.

Chapter 7

Bestrand: Port City on the Gray Ess

The thief heard the echo of men's voices as they approached with stealth. Unfortunately for him, a trick in the curve of the decrepit passage allowed his pursuers to draw nigh before detection. He had only seconds. Squeezing his narrow frame behind the scant shelter offered by an out-thrust corner of a rotting crate, he set down his burden with great care and fingered a brace of throwing knives slung at his waist.

Flight was impossible, for the low-ceilinged corridor ended in the next room, wherein lay the boarded window he had pried open to enter and replaced that his intrusion might not be detected. Rudolph Mellor cursed to be cornered like a rabbit. In less than a minute, he could be through the casement and amongst the collapsed brick of the abandoned service entry and onto an ascending stairwell overgrown with vines, never to return to the fort-like manor house of Procrius, patron of the largest shipping clan in Bestrand and her wealthiest citizen, notwithstanding the Regent himself.

Jamello stifled an imprecation that would do a sailing man proud. One breath later, puddles of light found the musty passageway.

Two well-equipped men-at-arms bore smoking torches. They were followed by an officer of enormous stature and a scarred continence. Jamello stood. Two flicks of his wrist missiled a quirt into the leg of each torchbearer where the knee fossa was protected by only straps of their chain leggings. The guards spun away and cried out in pained alarm, their fagots flying to bounce and spark on pave stones.

Jamello drew his jewel-hilted smallsword in a flash and leapt to meet the bull rush of the captain. A mistake! He barely managed to counter the rain of blows from the man's heavy saber, giving back before the hammer-like strikes of his foe. The sinews of his wrists were strong from a life of swordplay, yet the thunderous attacks numbed his hands and sent little shocks up his arm. Within the flurry, Jamello eyed the man closely as his assailant attempted to drive him into the vengeful grasp of the men on the floor, but a few well-placed kicks rendered one unconscious and mashed the sword hand of the other.

"Nowhere to run, eh, dog?"

The thief was cautious. Normally he would let such an aggressive opponent tire himself in the initial frenzy and counter with his lighter blade, yet his antagonist breathed slow and easy. He recognized the sneering fighter! Tacitus the Cruel had a wide and most dangerous reputation.

"Where's the cask? Tell me, little worm, and I'll slay you clean and quick."

Rudolph Mellor loosed his black burnoose to reveal the small, peaked cap of weasel that denoted a master thief.

"Ah, p'raps not." Tacitus gave a short, mocking bow. "The scum of the street spoke truth when they said you were about. Know you not? His Grace and I well guessed you would come for the trove."

Jamello assumed a classic fighter's stance, right leg forward and weight poised gracefully on the balls of the feet. His blade was cocked forward but not extended. Procrius's mercenary captain laughed and produced a thick poniard that he held in his left. His saber's tip, angled at the thief's face, circled menacingly as he spoke. "You Bestrand boy-shaggers are all alike. Pretty dancers all, useless in the clench. You'll howl to tell me of every dram you've ever earned before I'm done carving you."

As he finished his taunting, the warrior made a sudden lunge, deceptively fast for his muscle-bound frame. Saber held high in an open jab, he cocked his wicked poniard low for a passing thrust as he expected the slighter man to sidestep the menacing saber. Jamello did indeed leap aside, his out-thrusting smallsword only inches longer than the captain's fighting knife, but enough to lightly deflect it from his own flesh and sting the larger man as they rushed past and wheeled. Tacitus shrugged aside the touch, impatient and frustrated that the thief's blood did not stain his saber. He took in a breath to throw another taunt and felt a burning pain in his chest.

"Maybe I won't kill you today," spoke the captain. "You might last a week with the sport I've in mind."

Again Tacitus charged, again his blows were deflected shy of his target. His breath now came in ragged gasps. His left side below the wound grew numb, the knife hand falling nervelessly to his side. The thief initiated no attacks, preferring only to defend.

The giant warrior continuously launched wild blows that grew progressively more feeble as the slow realization of defeat crawled onto his features and an unfamiliar fear found his eyes. Jamello would let Tacitus suffer the full agony of the lung death and the knowledge that the smaller man could end the struggle at any time. The two sentries lay quiet, hoping to avoid the attentions of the slender thief who had bested their master.

Jamello turned to go. Tacitus lay supine, propped against the crate, chest heaving and covered with sweat. A trickle of pink froth blew in and out of a thumbnail-sized wound below his nipple. Jamello imagined he heard a faint wheeze emanate from the puncture site.

Jamello smiled and crawled back through the window, carefully resealing the entry lest the mercenary managed to cry out, thereby alerting a passing sentry. The night had grown old. Jamello chose a course that would take him rapidly through the grounds to the perimeter wall and the safety of the city. As he waited for a cloud to obscure the waxing moon, he thought of his fight with Tacitus. He hoped that one took a long while in dying. None of the many men Tacitus had mutilated and broken, or the young girls he raped and strangled would feel the benefit of the deed, but he, Rudolph Mellor, master thief of Bestrand, would.

Jamello dropped lightly from the palace wall and moved carefully but swiftly along uneven cobbles between shuttered houses and shops. He maintained a quick trot, keeping to shadows when possible and loping along wet alleys. Continuously altering his course, he purposefully strayed from the path of his initial approach. The rapidity at which Tacitus had responded to the theft of the item, now slung in a bag from his left shoulder, had taken him by surprise.

Ahead Jamello noted the pearl-gray sheen of the paved road that, after a quick dash, would bear him to a culvert beneath the city's wall and thence to scrub dunes and mazed waterways where the elusive thief would be nigh untraceable. As he jogged close, he noted that the intervening ground appeared to be of loose, ornamental gravel. Without breaking stride, Jamello continued across, preferring the brief noise to any delay. He cleared the area and leapt a low wooden barricade to the road beyond, swiftly seeking shadows of overhanging eaves along its boundaries.

Jamello heard the crunching of quick steps behind. He spun and backpedaled, seeing nothing. Without losing his forward momentum, he turned and picked up speed, now seeking the center of the street to avoid ambush from garden walls and vine-heavy trestles.

Three steps … damn!

Too many for a random fall of unbalanced stones, too loud to be the weight of a small animal, and not enough to be the step of a man. Jamello smelled a wet stench on the air, reminiscent of soiled fur and leather.

Sadôk. Jamello gripped his precious burden and lengthened his stride.

Jamello had heard dark rumor that Procrius secretly kept the forbidden beasts to sate his curiosities, but to release the subhuman creatures in numbers enough to track a man into Bestrand's streets? The contents of the cask must be valuable indeed! Jamello strained his eyes to pierce arbor shadows, no longer his friend. The lane narrowed, and the broad eaves of tropical trees completely overhung the way. Jamello ran.

A prickle on the nape of his neck spun him round. A Sadôk grinned from a trestle suspended across the way. In its hand it bore a throwing iron, which it pumped at him, searching for an opening.

Jamello flipped his right hand back over his shoulder as he resumed his previous course, triggering a small crossbow. Not really hoping to strike the creature, he wished only to slow it until he gained sufficient range to outdistance its own weapon.

The Sadôk squawked and cringed as the quarrel flashed through the leaves, inches short of its head. The man-ape hung there, paralyzed by the thought of the wicked barb speeding through its brain en route through the wires and vines of the trestle.

Jamello dropped the spent bow and burst through a tight turn, tumbling into a roll that would protect the casket. A half-dozen clubs and rude javelins clattered against a wall behind him. He sprang up to see a dozen Sadôk milling before him. He scattered a bag of blackened caltrops onto the road and wheeled to race back the way he had come. While short and muscular, Sadôk moved rapidly with the aid of long arms and knuckled hands, yet Jamello doubted they could catch him in a flat-out foot race. He grinned when their howls announced the caltrops. He breathed easily and without panic. If he could only find his back path clear, the master thief was confident he could dodge an encirclement and slay any stray Sadôk he might encounter in single combat. After all, he was Rudolph Mellor, jongleur and Edshu, and still bore the cask of Procrius worth thrice its weight in gems to those who desired it!

Jamello sped past the arbor where he had abandoned the little bow. It was gone. No doubt the creature had scooped it up and made off with its supposed booty. Jamello grinned again. Simply a magical creation, the intricate bow would dissolve into the air to further the consternation in his wake. If only an exploding incantation had been placed on the thing as well! It was always this way … the discarded weapon or tool became evidence once discovered, and when later found missing, produced suspicion of theft and incompetence amongst his enemies.

Four of the beast-men loomed from the height of a fence. Shielding the cask sack, Jamello burst into a flashing sprint. Howls and ill-aimed darts chased him as he pounded down the wet pave. How many of these things were there?

Any thought of surrender was ludicrous. The vicious demi-humans would show no mercy to any prey whether of their ilk or not. Old tales and whisperings of their ghastly rituals came to mind.

Jamello halted. Fifty paces ahead lay the cutoff he had hoped to take. Thronging it from side to side was a mass of at least two score Sadôk, stamping their feet and working their frothing mouths into frenzy. He did not need to turn to know of the equal number gathered behind. The bullet heads and hairy, gibbon-like arms of many others clambered the avenue's walls. For the first time in his tumultuous career, Rudolph Mellor felt the complete weight of hopelessness descend upon his slumped shoulders. A patrol of guardsmen would be welcome. Trial and execution by the governor? Preferable!

Jamello unslung his prize and placed it at his feet. He drew his thin blade, its hilt jewels flashing subtly in the light of the pallid moon. He produced an exquisitely worked dagger in his left, the forge-twin of the sword. He regarded them.

"Well, my children, let us weave a path to glory! At least you shall live past this day, though I can but hope you will find a worthier hand than that of a filthy Sadôk." The thought seemed to inflame the thief, and it was a stern and deadly face he bore into the closing ring.

ILYCRIUM

Townsfolk gave wide berth to the tall warrior who sat a magnificent black charger. Both man and horse were well muscled but not brutishly so. His kit and the harness of the beast were of the best quality yet lacked any badge or adornment that would give clue to lord or land of origin.

A boy scurried aside, spilling an onion basket. Those that fell near the destrier he let be. Better a beating than the attentions of the dark one. The man's sun-browned hand rested comfortably near a waist scabbard even as he swung from the stallion, who remained untethered where he was, stamping and eyeing other beasts. And other steeds there were aplenty; Dexius had chosen the day of Springfair in the hamlet of Midip for his appointment with Adestes Malgrim, Kör's Malesh.

Dexius was proud of his disguise. Again he adjusted his silken robes. Although he could not pass for a tradesman or landworker, his skin far too fair and his hands uncalloused, he knew it would never do for the First Steward of Swaymeet to be seen in this backwater burg without fanfare and escort. From the shadow of an open window, Dexius discerned the warrior's approach.

He had correctly chosen the taproom of the Owl's Nest, Midip's largest and busiest inn, for the encounter. Never had he met this one in person, but there was little mistaking the man who advanced on the hostel's door. Dark sun-burnished hair fell onto broad shoulders, and a trim beard adorned the face. The man entered the common room and stepped around a happily idle cluster of stable hands and sundry laborers already well into their cups, to settle into the alcove Dexius had prepared. He fixed the steward with a wry smile.

"A perfumer, Dexius? Not bad garb for one whose honeyed words daily besot king and Council, eh?"

Startled by the effrontery, Dexius took a moment to analyze his speech. Deep and rich as his appearance, the man spoke the common tongue of the West fluently, with a hint of accent, not unpleasant but with hard undertones.

"A word of caution. That we be safe enough here does not mean that every agent of the King's Council is a fool."

Adestes sank comfortably into his seat. He began to skin a citrus with a belt knife after sending a serving girl scuttling off for a drink. "And these counselors, Dexius? Do those slaves of merchants and near-extinct soldiers suspect aught is behind the killings?"

"The violence is random, as you commanded." Dexius's

hushed, urgent tones revealed his discomfort with his brazen companion.

"Be at ease," reassured Adestes. "None shall overhear."

Dexius beheld a peculiar motion of Adestes' hand and knew that some sort of dweomer had been cast. The minister allowed himself to be mollified ... somewhat. "Indeed, these *acts* you proscribe take a life of their own. But two nights past, some fool painted a likeness of the sleeping dragon on the front stone of the very temple of Sky! By happy chance I learned of it and had it cleansed before the city woke."

"Let them play." Adestes laughed. "The roots of that cult are as deep as the earth itself. Mayhap deeper. Besides," he said with a wink, "*She* sleeps no more."

He casually accepted a foaming tankard from the bar maid, her lithe waist and swinging hips lifting his gaze beyond the table. Adestes drank deeply. "Ahh. I have heard that your country boasts the best brewers in all the realms." He paused for effect. "In all of Kör, there is none so fine. A barrel of this would be worth a horse. Well, maybe yours, but not mine."

Studiously ignoring Dexius's aghast expression, Adestes continued in blasé tones. "In fact, I fear that in Körguz, my tastes are regarded as rather unusual. Most of the ruling elite prefer blood wines, some of which are pressed in your own land." Adestes nodded briefly at Dexius, "Iblis, however, favors a fiery vintage obtained from the hidden realms. A rare wine indeed, men have died for it."

Dexius felt like he might faint, for every fifth word spoken would be evidence enough to have him dishonored and impaled. Now the nonchalant rogue was, if anything, warming up for more. Dexius suddenly felt he would rather be anywhere else than in the common room of the Owl's Nest.

"Ahem, milord. You desire to know of the King's intelligences?"

Adestes frowned slightly at the interruption, yet ceased his discourse to assume an air of bored attentiveness.

"Not all of the royal court are complete jackanapes. The King takes report directly from his favorite scouts, and the Prince has grown into a man of his own mind."

A raucous ditty broke forth from the celebrants at the bar, punctuated by shouts and cheers and much banging of mugs and calls for ale. Adestes raised his voice to be heard over the din. "What, Dexius? You have guided the whelp's steps for years and have not yet managed to divert him with lotus wine or young boys?"

"Be not so flippant!" Dexius's voice shook with offended pride. "The Prince, while unblooded, is an able knight. Many of his companions are veterans. Some would say *heroes*."

"And who are these notables?"

Dexius sat back, pleased to turn the tables on this cocky warrior. He managed to grin himself at Adestes' sarcasm. Let the mighty son of dragons experience some trepidation. "Their chief is Xephard, a knight peer in Hyllae—Vale of the War Goddess." Adestes merely grunted and waved his tankard, but his curiosity was clearly piqued. Dexius continued, "His second is one Apieron of Windhover. That estate was bequeathed to him by Belagund personally."

"And the deeds that earned him such esteem?"

"I know them only by rumor. The King and our Prince closely guard the secrets of their private little strike force."

Adestes snorted derisively although leaned forward to miss nothing. The courtier was pleased. "I do know that Apieron of Windhover names himself scion of Xistus Farsinger. One would be wise to avoid any of that ilk."

The dark warrior contemplated before snorting. "Another Oisin of the Isles, no doubt."

"If you knew ought of Farsinger's clan of slayers, you would not jest so."

Adestes saluted with his tankard. "Future kings all, I am sure." But he leaned back to replace the jack untouched and stroke his beard pensively.

Dexius was uncertain if his diatribe had been altogether wise, yet he would not retreat. Certainly he had uncharacteristically volunteered information for free, as if the Kör agent had drawn out his anger deliberately. But he did not feel it so. Belagund's Long Knife almost never entered into his thoughts, as he was not participant to their dealings with the Throne. He could see that news of their existence certainly struck some resonance, possibly unsettling the man. *No*, Dexius decided, as he always did, *he had been correct in directing the flow of conversation as he had. To show fear before this one invited the lion to dinner.*

Adestes tapped his chin. "You appear to be in earnest, so I must take your news seriously." He raised his fingers to silence any interjection. "You will increase your activities, and spare none of the gold we have sent, even of your own. There will be loot enough when Sway falls."

Dexius nodded cooperatively while silently reproaching himself for goading the Kör-man too far. "And you, milord? What is your course?"

Adestes relaxed into his seat once again. "I have deeply enjoyed the hospitality of your country but am soon off. And yet, in the time allowed, much may be done."

The understatement of the millennium, Dexius doubted not. There was little else for him to do but play his role to the nines. There would be no turning back, especially with this one. He imagined Malesh would smile just as wide as he caught and exquisitely punished anyone who he thought betrayed him.

The man regarded him as if he could read his thoughts. Dexius shuddered at the notion. Adestes dispelled these reflections with a gesture. "And now, dear Steward, if you have nothing further, I have other business to attend."

Dexius followed the line of Adestes' gaze to a lissome beauty holding forth over a small gaggle near the bar top. Dexius guessed her local by her rich but rustic garb, and she was obviously well known, judging by her circle of girlfriends and admirers. Overtly ignoring Adestes' intent expression, she simultaneously presented him with her best facial angles amidst various assorted chest heavings and hair flipping. Dexius was incredulous. The man was simply outrageous! He deliberately flaunted every principle of subterfuge. Obviously he intended to bed her in this very inn!

"Yes, my dear Dexius, I fear your disguise is not subtle enough for this astute and sophisticated gathering. You had best be leaving."

Adestes' remarks were punctuated by a course of bawdy jests from the hostler's corner as one of their number approached the young maiden only to be resoundingly slapped. Red-faced, Dexius gave a seated half bow and pushed through to the exit. His pony was soon clipping down the road to Sway. Adestes chuckled at the little man's hastily retreating form and reclined again to enjoy his game of visual fencing with the haughty wench.

He cast an obvious look at her that she caught from the corner of her eye, glanced back, then pointedly turned her head away in mock rejection, all within a span of a long second. 'Ah, this one had a confi dence born of a life of conceit—and incredible ignorance of anything outside of her carefully constructed world. Enlightenment was in order.'

"*Nilonda*," whispered he.

Chapter 8

Midip

Nilonda lay back on the tousled bed to watch the tall warrior busy himself with his clothing and gear. She could not recall in her twenty years an encounter as bold, or feeling so very deeply satisfied as she did now. She had met this stranger at the Owl's Nest whilst enjoying a cool sip to counter the heat of the Spring Fair, and vaguely listening to her brother who endlessly argued politics with his pub cronies. She could never see how grown men got so worked up over such remote events. The latest troubles from the country and Sway itself had merely given them more cud to chew, although she knew that if it wasn't for the present crisis, they would but find another thing to yammer over—how excited they became over such utter nonsense! *Kör!* She wasn't even sure where it was. How could it be important?

The man paused his activities to favor her with his quirky grin. Delighted, she blew him a kiss and reclined to arrange her tresses for maximum effect. He donned the dark and well-cut garments she had first seen him in. He packed others into saddlebags. "Going somewhere, my lord?"

Again, that smile. She knew he would be back, no man left

her voluntarily. They were either driven off by her jealous brother or summarily dismissed on a whim. Silly Hnaf was a failure as a chaperone, barely noticing when she told him she'd grown weary and would wend her own way home. How he would rage if he knew that the man whose eyes she met and shared secret smiles across the crowd, whispered an invitation to meet that sounded magically in her ear. Such a delightful cantrip! She had seduced a magician once, yet that one had been dull and plain to look upon.

She regarded the stranger with a smoldering look. Obviously a man of taste and breeding, evidenced by the quality of his clothes and grooming, his erect bearing, and most tellingly, his profound interest in her. He was also sun-bronzed and strong, how unlike the pampered nobles' sons she grew so weary of.

Nilonda gave vent to a sound that was a blend of a sigh and a purr. When she had knocked softly at his door, she felt as timorous as a schoolgirl and as wanton as a street whore. He spake not a word but swept her into his arms with a hunger and strength that no man had ever matched. She gave their torrid lovemaking her best; now her silly mysterious prince thought to take himself on errands elsewhither.

His gear assembled, Adestes set saddlebags by the door and turned to face her. *Ah ha*, she nearly said aloud. *They can never leave without anguish, and then not for long.* She sat up to receive her due.

Nilonda frowned in confusion at the curiously shaped blade in his hand. It flew across the room to embed its point in the center of her forehead. Rocking against the headboard and slumping, her eyes rolled in death, and the long blade depended obscenely over her face.

Malesh shook his head. "Ignorant to the last, now you get my point." He shrugged. "P'raps in the next life." He eyed her curiously but did not retrieve the blade, noting the odd angle of her head and wondering as he exited if she died from the head wound or from the broken neck. He shrugged again as he slung his bags onto the stallion. *Just another of life's little mysteries.*

Adestes turned his destrier's head, kicking it into a trot. The spirited beast reared in protest. Adestes wrenched the bit until blood started from the animal's sensitive mouth. It screamed its fury but made no further defiance.

So far he was untrackable. None had taken note of him at the tavern—his spell cloak had seen to that. It would not do for authorities to link the seemingly random events to a dark foreigner. *Authorities.* Soon these nitherings would learn the true meaning of the word!

He whistled a merry tune, well pleased with his adventures to date. Another, more important journey loomed ahead. One that would define his very existence. One that would either kill or elevate him to a position beyond the comprehension of normal men. But first, he had a letter to write.

BESTRAND

Jamello woke to an oath punctuated by a kick. He peeled one eye to regard the ugly form leering over him. The man bore a wooden bucket in his filth-crusted hands. Jamello closed his eye against the painful light of a small aperture high on the cell wall, wan though it was. He could hear the ocean. The jailer cursed and kicked him repeatedly. These blows bothered him less than the intense throbbing behind his ears and a welling nausea that accompanied his swimming vision.

"Wakey, wakey! His Grace is 'ere to see ye ... you'd best be bathed and fresh!"

The gnomish creature proceeded to dump the contents of the bucket over him. Jamello spat cold seawater as the turnkey pulled open the door to admit a stately figure garbed in resplendent silks and bedecked with many jewels. The man's flesh jiggled with his careful tread over the greasy floor, but the eyes were black and soulless under a beetling, hairless brow line. Fat gemstones were pinned into the flesh there. Jamello groaned inwardly. Procrius himself was come.

"Rudolph Mellor, do you deem yourself more clever than I? Did it not occur to you to wonder why, in this city of thieves, one so long absent would be hired?" With utmost care, Jamello leaned back against the cool stone, hoping to steady his vision.

"Think you I withheld the Sadôk out of mercy? You will name he or they that hired you."

"Can't," Jamello slurred weakly.

"You cannot?" inquired Procrius in a soft, dangerous voice.

Jamello tried to rise and fell back. Head bobbing, he fought against his heaving stomach and squinted his eyes against the lancing sunlight to regard his captor. His tongue, apparently lacerated when the Sadôk beat him, was too large for his mouth.

"Can't—because no one hired me."

"You dared this on your own? Outrageous!"

"Liar!" seconded the leering servant.

That one planted a heavy kick into Jamello's small ribs. The thief ignored it as best he could. In a fit of anger, the Doce stretched forth a velvet-gloved hand and grasped Jamello's chin to violently shake the thief's head until his arm grew tired. Nothing Jamello had endured so far was as bad as this new agony. His bruised brain felt like a loose pebble in his skull. Released, he curled into a pain-wracked ball. His suffering seemed to calm the master somewhat. The misshapen jailer capered up and down in sadistic glee.

Procrius resumed a dignified stance, flicking away several invisible offending particles that had lit upon his immaculate dress. "I grant you one day to recollect the names of your conspirators." The man gave a stately pause as if addressing an assembly of senators. "And try to imagine your future, that you might be more pleasant to me when I return." Procrius nodded imperiously to the turnkey, who preceded him from the cell after aiming a final kick at Jamello's prostrate form.

Suddenly the shipmaster turned and spoke in nonchalant tones. "Tacitus named you, of course. His associates are missing." Jamello strove to listen and managed to crack a single lid at the jewels sewn into Procrius's skin. They seemed like the glittering eyes of a spider.

"He was found dead of your little sting, although managed to scratch your identity into the dust with his poniard. As his last act was to my benefit, I denied the Sadôk his body. How they howled! I gather he played amongst them often."

Procrius's slightly amused face grew grim. "You shall not be quite dead when they receive *you* unless your memory improves … Rudolph Mellor, your career ends here." With a commanding gesture to his servant and a swish of robes, Procrius was gone.

The misshapen jailer sneered, "Sadôk chow!" and banged the door closed, then shot home the bolt with a clanking that struck the thief like a punch to the head.

Jamello sank down with a moan. As his consciousness dimmed, he only hoped he would wake before Procrius returned. The man had the casket and his blades, and no doubt a handsome fee could be earned from magistrates for the capture of Jamello Edshu. It would not be enough. Jamello would need a plausible lie to intrigue the fiend's cupidity enough to prolong his life.

Through his battered lips, Jamello sighed. *Why would Procrius allow any witness to live to tell of a thousand Sadôk living beneath Bestrand's very shops and homes?*

Morning brought a thin light to the cell. Jamello looked up. A figure was there, garbed as a soldier of the guard. He regarded the thief with a look that was neither sympathetic nor cruel. Of the vicious turnkey there was no sign. "Do not resist," said the man before unfettering him from the wall and resecuring his shaking limbs with manacles and a toe chain. Jamello's head was draped in a leather hood, tightly cinched at the neck with binding fiber.

A quick ride through the sleeping streets of Bestrand nearly made him retch and found him again underground, this time in a more spacious cell. Once hood, handcuffs, and chain were removed, Jamello discovered a cot, a glory hole in the outer wall, and a clay water jug. The soldier said nothing as he withdrew. Jamello respected his silence, afraid to wake from what might be only a marvelous dream. The man departed without looking at the thief. Jamello never saw him again.

One day stretched to three, then to ten. Bit by bit, the searing headaches receded, and Jamello found himself able again to ponder his future. From the occasional banter of guards, he gathered that Procrius was not high in the favor of the Regent. He speculated that he had been removed to his current prison ostensibly for trial and execution—mayhap it amused magistrates to keep him a while, perhaps secretly pleased to thwart the difficult merchant prince.

One night a man walked into his cell.

Expecting an assassin, Jamello wheeled from his cot with a curse and brandished the half-filled jug. His eyes grew wide when he beheld that the cell door remained closed. The man had simply walked through the iron-banded oak. He was clothed in the white garb of an acolyte, and wore a black curly beard. Jamello was certain he had never seen him before.

The stranger proffered a steady hand, palm up. After a moment, Jamello took it and soon found himself riding through the prison courtyard and out valves that were opened by silent guardsmen.

Once beyond the canaled city, a second mount waited, and the man guided his horse to a path that would lead them north and east. Jamello guessed the destination.

Ilycrium! And the vale of the Donna.

He reined back and spoke softly. "Why should I, jongleur and master thief, follow one such as he?" Jamello's gelding tugged and nibbled at the low grass between sandy cart tracks of the road. Turning the beast, he could be gone in darkness to where he willed in a trice. Jamello sighed and regarded the gracefully erect, receding figure of the acolyte. The gelding began to walk.

Perhaps he was not in a mood for the dodging of spell-casting priests or warrior monks. Or mayhap he was simply too tired to scheme effectively. With a second, more pronounced sigh, Rudolph Mellor ended these reflections and prodded his rouncy to rejoin the young priest.

Jamello studied Cynthia with suspicion. He stood in the brightness that filled the outer courtyard of the temple of the goddess. His silent, priestly companion of the last ten-day had departed with the steeds when the temple matron came in person to greet her guest. Mindful of the honor bestowed, Jamello returned his most grandiose bow and flourish. He felt the effort wasted on the hard-eyed woman.

"Most benevolent Perpetua, please accept my eternal gratitude for your interventions on my behalf." She inclined her head a fraction.

"I beg your indulgence, Radiant Mother. Let me digress to matters dross."

Again that unrevealing nod; this was going poorly. The old witch wasn't going to show her hand for free. Perhaps the direct approach … "What are the terms of my parole?"

"None."

The thief pulled his goatee and thought hard. High clerics of Ilycrium did not rescue such as he from the dungeons of lawful allies for mere amusement. Jamello decided he did not wish to be in her debt. Religious tended to be fanatics, and fanatics oft had dreams of martyrdom—not unattractive, except that one invariably had to die to accomplish it … not something high on his priority list. "And my ransom? At the present, I am without means, albeit if you will but allow me a steed and affix me a reasonable rate of interest, I can—"

"You cost nothing."

Jamello was shocked. This was worse than he thought. *"Nothing?"* The Matron regarded him without revealing aught behind her unwavering gaze.

Jamello gave pause. He was flummoxed, used to dealing in the currencies of greed, lust, fear … and more greed. Moreover he was not sure he liked the fact that his liberty cost her nothing. *Nothing indeed. Next time he would steal from the Protector himself!*

Jamello glowered at the Donna. Was that a hint of amusement in the many wrinkles around her eyes? An uncomfortable yet distinct feeling grew in him that she could read his thoughts as easily as he could the scales of a Farseppian gem merchant.

She spread her hands in a gesture of welcome. "You may remain here to recover. Thoughtful Onus has brought your weapons, they will be returned. Of course you will have free roam of the temple." Jamello could scarcely imagine anywhere that he would less like to explore, but smoothed his thin moustache and swept into another bow.

"I thank you, gracious lady!"

She chuckled and moved to go, then turned back. "I think you may find old friends nearby. And more coming soon."

Jamello regarded the dignified walk of the temple mistress back to her stone house. He cast his eye about to regard the gardens and the work areas of the temple compound where columned walks gave onto shaded porticos that fronted buildings of the shrine proper. Built of carefully cut, ton-weight blocks of white marble and limestone, there was no need for mortar or buttress. They would endure in perfect alignment for thousands of years after he was dead and buried. The occupants moved without undue haste, but also without distraction. Horses and fowl were attended to, acolytes sparred and wrestled in the practice yard. Smells of bread baking and roasting meats emanated from low kitchens, and a quiet bustle of goods coursed to and from the patchwork farmlands that surrounded the temple grounds. Property lines were marked by groves of trees or planted vine, chuckling brooks, or centuries-old rows of stones extracted, one at a time, from growing fields. All together the scene was one of quiescent, idyllic harmony between man and nature.

Jamello sighed in despair.

Chapter 9

The Lampus of Hyllae

Xephard regarded the sun. He stood on the sparkling sand of the temple's arena. White horsehair plumes crested his helm, and an argent cloak draped the burnished steel of his chest plate. The full battle armor sat easily on his great frame. Ranged around him were five Mgesh tribesmen who eagerly fingered weapons and licked dry lips. Such as these were known amongst all peoples as merciless killers who spared not even the weak amongst their own kind. Their women were but chattels, dispensed as with all tribal possessions by powerful warlords. The clans of the Mgesh neither tilled the soil nor practiced any craft, taking in trade or pillage all they desired.

Zaddik spoke. "Wise Donna, I'm sure yon holy warrior is most excellent."

"*Areté,*" breathed Xeopolus, a temple helper of long years who liked none too well the look of this oily Capacian trader. The serving man clamped his mouth shut at a small glance from Cynthia.

"Whatever," continued Zaddik, "yet would you honor contract set on wager against such slender chance of victory?"

"Have you not ever received fair payment of us?"

The Capacian touched his silken breast with affected innocence, and added an ingratiating smile.

"Ilycrium needs your wares if war comes, as you well know. Not many caravans run east in these troubled times."

Zaddik grinned inwardly, having himself arranged for the destruction of several competing wagon trains. "And this bet? Five trained Mgesh assassins to your one acolyte? You will employ no magic?"

The Donna's voice was strong in the clean light. "No sorcery shall be allowed by either side." She fixed him with a meaningful stare.

The unctuous merchant stroked his chin pensively, as if in reluctant agreement, yet he was mightily pleased. The only trump he feared was the old matron's divine influence in this, her place of power. No single man, no matter what his repute, could stand before five Mgesh—raised from infancy to a life of rapine and slaughter. Moreover, these handpicked rogues of his were worse than their fellows, if that could be imagined. Exiled from their clans for psychopathic cruelty or murder, they formed the core of his retainers whose mere rumor dissuaded all would-be bandits. They made him rich.

"Xephard, discard your sword."

The Capacian shot Cynthia a suspicious glance. The Donna's seamed face cracked a disarming smile. "Not merely a wager. Rather, demonstration of the quiet power that resides in this land." The trader nodded eagerly, scarcely believing his luck for the mad whim that seized the old crone.

Xephard silently regarded the Reverend Mother. He nodded his plumed helm and strode to the side of the palisade where he turned his scabbarded sword over to a young attendant, who received it like an offering. As Zaddik turned to greet with effusion some random temple notable, Xeopolus whispered earnestly,

"Mistress, I like this not. We can convince this eastern profiteer by t'another way."

She placed a hand reassuringly on his shoulder, but her eyes were cool. "Xephard, remove your iron."

No expression was visible behind the dark eyelets of the bright helm. The plumes dipped again. The temple knight proceeded to remove his armament with the help of two burly male attendants and an equally athletic female whose red hair was bound by a blue cloth band. The matron's face was inscrutable.

Zaddik nearly goggled. With their cursed Captain of Areté (or whatever it was) gone, he would double the fees already half-paid for goods as yet undelivered to the central provinces of the country, then take profit of Kör and deliver to the doomed Western lowlanders only those damaged or inferior. When this was over, he would make sacrifice to their Gray-Eyed Goddess of the Lampus who surely robbed her own priestess of any last wit.

"Xephard," called Cynthia a third time, more softly, "today you will fight naked of all garments, weapons, and protections."

The paladin spoke for the first time. "As you will, Lady."

His deep, slow voice revealed neither doubt nor anxiety. He removed his padded jupon and light tunic underneath, and last his laced sandals. Scores of temple folk and locals thronged around the wooden rails of the fighting pit. The caravan master's servants and spare guards stood apart. The fat Capacian chatted happily, supremely at ease in the midst of those he would openly betray. Henlee and Apieron arrived, the dwarf sniggering at the unclothed Templar. Apieron could only turn helplessly to his friend and shrug, incredulous as he in witness to the unfolding spectacle.

Isolde stood across the arena from the Donna and gnawed her knuckles red while the Mgesh slapped one another in congratulations and jeered the disrobing peer of the temple. Xephard finished stripping the last of his garments with perfect calm and then strode to the center of the fighting pit. The five Mgesh closed in. Titters and the crowd's chatter faded.

The fierce steppesmen no longer jibed the massive man who stood without fear in their midst. Their eyes squinted, and they chewed moustaches, fists clenched tight on weapons. Two held long javelins and small bucklers, the third a hand axe, its heavy head backed by a pointed adz, ideal for punching through armor, but the man kept it, thinking it would do nicely for the temple knight's thick chest. The last two gripped steel scimitars. These were fine kilij with silver mounting along graceful three-foot sweeps of watered steel, and hilted with ornately scrolled ivory. The sword wielders held cruel-looking kindjals in their weak hands. The others also wore scimitars or knives at their belts over skirts of lacquered leather. The spearmen drifted apart. These killers were not novices to any kind of fighting, spectacle or otherwise, and did not give into their murderous first impulse to instantly rush and hack this impudent man to crimson tatters. Instead they circled like fierce hyenas, waiting some unknown stimulus to rend their prey.

Isolde could not suppress a groan. Her knuckles were bleeding. She looked frantically to the wizened matron who incredibly yet conversed with Zaddik. The Mgesh looked as if they would gladly tear Xephard with their teeth if given the chance.

Henlee said to Apieron, "If your friend can survive this, he's hired." Apieron "Actually," the dwarf continued, "the smell down there probably—"

His remark was cut short by a flurry of activity in the arena. One of the javeliners, a pock-faced criminal, kicked a distracting spray of sand at Xephard and yelled as if to throw. At this signal, his counterpart behind the paladin cast his spear while the three

Mgesh with hand weapons charged. What followed was quick and violent.

At the first flicker of sand, Xephard wheeled and flung himself forward to catch the hurled javelin. With a lightning-fast twist, he buried its iron counterweight in the belly of the shocked Mgesh, who fell backward, doubled over the shaft. The running axe-bearer outstripped his comrades by two paces and promptly had his throat cleaved by a slash of the downed javeliner's kindjal. Leaving the curved blade wedged in the gawking man's vertebrae, Xephard hoisted the body and dashed it upon the swordsmen who frantically tried to halt their momentum. One leapt aside as the other was smashed to the ground. The first sprang at Xephard. His maddened charge, topknot flying, spoiled an opening for the second spearman. The sword-wielder gave two feints and then a straight thrust at Xephard's naked stomach.

Isolde screamed. Xephard stepped inside the blow, gripping the sword arm so that the blade thrust harmlessly beyond his left flank. He allowed the compact warrior's momentum to carry the twain to the ground, thus spoiling a second attempt by the waiting spearman who held up a fraction short, nearly skewering his friend.

The tribesman fell on Xephard with a breath-whooshing grunt and then proceeded to grind his ridged armor along Xephard's front, drawing a score of cuts along the knight's bare skin. Xephard placed his right hand next to his left on the Mgesh's forearm. The frustrated spearman called for his comrade to roll free as his upraised dart flickered impatiently over his shoulder. Laughing through blackened teeth, the Mgesh on Xephard dove his left hand for his belt knife while making a token effort to regain control of his sword arm.

The Mgesh's arm bore the thickened muscle of a practiced swordsman, corded with bulging, iron-hard sinews. Xephard snapped it like driftwood. The Mgesh screamed and cleared his knife just before his own sword hilt crushed the tender bones above his nose and his eyes filled with blood. Xephard heaved the man off him with a leg-thrust up into the spearman. Xephard stood over the writhing Mgesh as the downed swordsman finished extricating himself from the body of the dead axe-man and was attempting to stand on a shattered knee. He yet bore his weapon, and his scimitar tip quivered with pain and fury. The javeliner kicked the face-smashed man from him, took a step, and let fly. Xephard sidestepped the dart and casually switched hands to backhand the long blade out at the knee-smashed swordsman, sweeping away his sword hand. The man staggered to the ground in anguish. Xephard finished him. A townsman, standing along the light wood palisade, turned white when he saw the javelin quiver in the arena's low wall a foot from his chest.

The thrice-frustrated spearman yelled and drew a kindjal from his waist. It had a curved, weighted tip for hacking and a keen point for the thrust above eighteen inches of killing edge. The paladin met him before he got three steps. The kindjal was long for a belt weapon but was no match for the reach of the scimitar Xephard bore. One graceful blow and the Mgesh's angry head went flying aside, trailing a red streamer.

The first spearman finally regained his feet behind Xephard and charged with a maddened bellow, his weapon held at the waist, tip leading like a pike. The temple peer drove an upward, two-handed strike that sheared through the lance into the Mgesh's belly to the hilt. He left the blade protruding a foot from the man's back. The Mgesh voided himself and sank open-mouthed to the red-splashed sand.

The remaining Mgesh again regained his feet, mazed with the pain of broken forearm and battered face, notwithstanding the loss of his companions. Seeing no hostile move, Xephard nodded and faced the old priestess. They shared a smile. She turned it onto the darkening face of the Capacian. His appalled retainers looked about fearfully and backed slowly towards their wagons. Isolde screamed again.

The Mgesh had cocked his left arm for a cast with a throwing knife. Xephard wheeled but was too far away to intercept the strike with a lunge. Those assembled caught a streaking glimpse of a throwing axe that buried itself in the tribesman chest, dashing him to the earth and sending the knife hurtling straight up.

Xephard stood caked with dirt and blood, staring in surprise at his unnoticed friend and the dwarf. "Hmm, balance seems a tad off," said the dwarf. The twain leapt over the short wall. "I meant only to take his throwing arm."

The priestess turned wrathfully on Zaddik, who shrugged. "Mgesh do not surrender. One of the javeliners was his brother. He would have a taken a blood oath. Better to end this way than to live with ignominy." The aged cleric continued to stare, and sweat gathered on the swarthy merchant's face. He wheedled, "It was thou, Mistress, who proposed the challenge."

"Indeed, and I expect you to honor it. The goods shall be priced as before and of acceptable quality. We will hold your present train as pledge of good faith." She stifled his quick protest with an upraised hand. "Else I shall send *him* to inquire why you break troth—"

Zaddik regarded the gore-spattered warrior who stood above his shattered foes like some barbaric, northern battle god. The paladin's chest heaved with great, slow breaths. The man fixed him with those too-bright, ugly blue eyes. Zaddik felt as if he were the one who was naked.

"You misjudge me, Lady. All will be as you say!"

Cynthia smiled thinly. She turned her attention to Xephard and his two companions, gesturing subtly for them to follow as she walked in her erect manner towards the portico of the temple, a chastened Zaddik in tow.

Isolde rushed across the sand to drape a cloak over Xephard. She pressed her lips to his hand before stepping back to slap his face with a resounding clap. Xephard stared stupidly as Apieron politely looked away. Before Xephard could utter a word, Isolde wheeled and stalked off to her own apartments. The crowd drifted off, excepting the acolytes who saw to the mangled corpses. One of them brought Henlee's axe after wiping it clean.

"Whew," whistled Henlee, eyeing the edge of the weapon suspiciously, then Xephard. "You're bad enough, but I'd hate to have to fight *her*." He gestured toward Isolde's retreating back.

Xephard turned helplessly to Apieron, who gave up and laughed aloud. "A great victory! Let me introduce you to a most worthy dwarf, the very Henlee I've oft told you of."

"Twice well met, friend," said Xephard. "I am in your debt."

"Oh, for that … Apieron might have a remedy."

Xephard raised his eyebrows, and the three shared a laugh. A short while later, Apieron and Xephard were refreshed with cold well water while the dwarf assuaged his own concerns of the temple's current management. His beard was soon flecked with foam. They passed the Capacian caravan master as he exited the Perpetua's private chambers. Face suffused with shame, he muttered and chewed his lip before noticing the trio. He shot Xephard one frightened glance before brushing past with redoubled speed to the outer court where he cursed his slaves and shouted for a hasty departure.

"Enter, gentlemen," the voice of Xeopolus carried to them.

Apieron parted hangings and ducked his head to enter, followed by Henlee and Xephard. The temple matron's chambers were cool and spacious, well lit by wall apertures and many fragrant sconces. A low table and floor cushions were set, where the Donna was flanked by her trusted Xeopolus and Isolde. After gauging her mood, Xephard sat next to his beloved while Apieron bent one knee to take Cynthia's hand in his. Henlee plopped down and looked about for refreshment.

"It has been long, too long, my son. You have aged since last I saw you."

"And you, Reverend Mother, look no different than ever."

"See here, Xeopolus, a graduate from the court of Xistus Silver-Tongue can well give a course in flattery." Yet behind the jest, Cynthia's eyes were serious. She cupped Apieron's face. "Times have grown strange."

"Aye, Your Wisdom," said Apieron, finding a seat betwixt Xeopolus and the dwarf. "And worse, we are come directly from the Oracle."

"And at an auspicious moment," beamed Xeopolus at the dwarf.

"At least *I* think so," chuckled Xephard's baritone.

"Aye, now that sow's offspring of a merchant will wait until he's off your lands to cheat you, rather than before," growled the dwarf.

"Zaddik is loyal to his one true god," answered the Donna. "Money. Where there is war, there is profit. He'll be back."

Henlee grunted unintelligibly before turning to a heavy tray carried by a serving girl. Of black glazed wood, its rim was inlaid with many circling male and female athletes in bright reds and yellows, but the dwarf's eyes were only for the contents. There were briny olives and crusted bread. Fresh-caught fish from the valley stream were set next to pungent goat's cheese. White glazed dishes held warmed oils of varying flavors. Pistachios, figs, and dates were piled into bowls, and there were honey-sweetened sesame cakes for dessert. A great tankard of spring beer was set before the dwarf whilst others sipped water or the resiny wine of the valley decanted from an ornate prochous. The hungry travelers conversed as they feasted.

"Why have you come, young Apieron?" queried Xeopolus. "To steal our captain away to serve with your company of scouts, these forest-runners of the Candor king?"

"Is it true, my friend?" asked Xephard, who appeared to have one hand short to fulfill his three desires for eating, drinking, and touching his beloved. "If so, I accept."

"What spoke the Sybil?" asked Cynthia.

Apieron had rehearsed this conversation a hundred times. Now that he was here, the words would not come, as if speaking them would evoke their doom. It would certainly doom their joyous gathering.

"Did she speak of the inevitability of war? The fall of the house of Candor?" It was Apieron's turn to stare. "Perhaps the rise of a foul beast fueled by the blood of war, who seeks to bring the end of days as we know them." The Matron laughed long and low.

Xeopolus grunted. "Be not so astonished, the Donna's sight is clear. Long has she seen strife in the heavens, and much is revealed to her by many who pass hither or send word."

Henlee cleared his throat and mumbled, "Shamans of my people have noted many unsettling earth signs as well. Evil resides not only in the sky."

"Well spoken, noble dwarf," said Cynthia. "P'raps all wise people of this continent feel the tremors of change." Cynthia fixed Apieron with her bird-bright stare. "A blight is come to this land that no lord of Kör or crazed sorcerer could effect alone. The gates of Tartarus are creaking open, and the Sybil has spoken your fate, for by the strange power that dwells in you are you to close those gates again."

Apieron bowed his head. His gray eyes lost focus as the child of fire stirred in him. The room grew still save for the faint sounds of the day without.

"*Doom* and fear," Apieron said at last. He straightened and regarded the Perpetua with unswerving gaze. "If it is my fate to walk this madness, what of my family? What of my servants and fighting men who look to me as provider? What of my oath to king who has need as ne'er before?"

Isolde cast about. "The words of the Sybil are oft tangled webs. Men cannot fully know their meaning. What did she say, exactly?" Isolde faltered, "Perhaps we are wrong." She sobbed once.

At this, all eyes were cast down in pause until Xephard's low, strong voice spoke, "If you go into darkness, Apieron, so too go I." He shared a look with the dwarf. Both nodded in silent agreement. Isolde pulled away from him to seek the Donna's face.

Cynthia rose to leave but motioned for the meal to continue. "Tomorrow we will take counsel. Turpin of Sky comes hither."

At her departure, the business of eating and the inquiries of old friends resumed. Henlee and Xephard were in deep converse when Apieron saw Isolde rise quietly to follow her matron, who paused to await her in an inner courtyard. The curving alcove held a statue of a green ocean god. Water spewed from his lips to splash merrily down his nude form before collecting in a myriad of stone shelves and the upraised hands of nereids who cavorted about his scaled torso. His serene eyes were of lapis lazuli. The breasts of the nymphs were tipped with blushing garnet. The shaded colonnade and pave were without blemish, and a breeze wafted a pleasing scent, borne from the sweet hay of the Hyllae.

Yet the gentle architecture of the hemicyclium did nothing to assuage the heat that rose in Isolde's breast. Aswirl in a sea of conflicting emotions the entire morn, she could contain her passions no longer. "And the deaths of those men? Was Zaddik's humiliation worth the cost of their lives?"

"Nonsense, the merchant sought to betray us. His Mgesh were certainly nothing loathe."

"You put Xephard in mortal danger to barter a contract?"

"Wake up, girl. Soon the raven of war will spread her wings over this land. The paths of the ocean are grown perilous, from whence shall we get foreign goods if the southern caravans shun our door?" The Matron's tones were hard but not unkind.

"Xephard might have died."

"Each of those tribesmen were named villains who flaunted their crimes. Xephard saw this in them."

Isolde had not worked up her courage to be so easily defeated. "Now you would send him to the *Pit?*" Her voice was close to breaking.

Cynthia eyed her speculatively. "*I* could not hold him from it. It is you alone that holds power over him. It is time for you to decide your purpose in this." Isolde made to bite her knuckle, then thrust it from her. "We who walk the way of the warrior cannot falter when the path grows hard."

Isolde, spear-maiden of her goddess, allowed the tide of her feelings of fear and doubt to wash over her. She staggered to sit on a low bench, and when she spoke, her voice was that of a little girl. Unbrushed tears shined on her cheek. "I never dreamt I would find love, now that I touch it, it pulls away."

"My child, this is not about some knight's quest for honor. This is about survival."

The old woman placed a comforting arm about her favorite. "Xephard goes to the gravest of perils with the face of good cheer. Hinder him not, lest you unman him at a critical moment—for go he will. It is simply whether you will aid or thwart him."

Each of Isolde's words dripped a full measure of her grief and loss. "He will die there. Won't he?"

"The future is known only to the gods."

"But you are the eyes and voice of the Goddess!"

"I am not the Sybil, say rather the arm of the Goddess, and it grows frail. I am tired. My hope is for such as you and Xephard to succor us in my waning, but I fear your trial has come too soon."

"Am I to go with him?"

"No!" The fierceness of the Matron's reply set Isolde back.

The woman softened again. "No," the old hand waved, "press me not in this, I am resolute. It is oft harder to sit and bide whilst those you love march to peril. You remain a priestess of the Lampus. I will brook no argument."

Isolde did not at the moment feel capable of presenting any true resistance, so much had happened.

"I have a task for you. You will place all in readiness for their journey, and here is a second duty: Tomorrow comes Turpin, High Priest of Father Sky. You will receive him."

Isolde drew herself up, dashed away her tears, and pulled her hair back. "Madam, as he is Patriarch of Sway, would it not be more fitting that *you* greet him? Such would convey more respect to His Eminence."

"You resent me and so grow formal." Cynthia touched Isolde's face and chuckled. "Long have you been at temple, my little flower is becoming political. What you meant to say is that you'd rather be with Xephard and Apieron. There will be time enough for that. Today I shall send them off to gather the thief."

"Oh." If a single word could convey a world of disgust, the young woman was successful.

"In the morn, whilst you welcome His Grace, I shall prepare for a lunch conclave. It were well the principals be formally introduced and pledge themselves to their task."

"As you say, Mistress." Isolde was ashamed yet could not keep the relapsing sorrow from welling in her eyes.

"Turpin and I have said long ago all that we would to one another, and I've no doubt he would rather you to greet him. The years are piled high since I looked my best in the light of cruel dawn." The Matron squeezed Isolde's shoulder to lend her strength. "I assign you this task, not as a chore but that I desire your eyes. You will tell me what you learn."

"Me? Judge such as he?"

"Of course."

"But a high cleric of Sky?"

"Men are men. Now we needs must set all in order for the morrow. There are forces at work that will undo us if we delay!"

The Matron dwindled into the shadows of the colonnade, and Isolde took thought of all that had transpired. As the green god spewed his foamy offering and water nymphs gathered his bounty, Isolde's mind wandered. How many men had knelt to woo her? And yet Xephard was one who knelt only in meditation. He prayed standing, arms outspread with utter frankness, incapable of guile or guilt or doubt. Isolde smiled, warming to her first memories of him, a tow-headed barbarian boy of thirteen summers, although already a fighter and an athlete. How many times had she been repelled by the primeval that lurked under his surface? How she longed to tame him! and at the same time be dominated by him. Isolde gazed at the nereids and touched her breasts, as Xephard had not. She wondered.

Chapter 10

Hyllae: Valley of Wisdom

Jamello Edshu, jongleur and master thief, lowered his head upon folded hands to continue his languorous recline on the meadow grass of Hyllae. Of course he had marked the approach of the three heavy persons. By their gaits he easily discerned each identity, and yet the bright sun and blue sky, painted with lazy clouds, made his eyes heavy.

"Explain to me again why we need him," asked Henlee of Apieron as the dwarf spied Jamello's supine figure amongst the wildflowers.

"Lower your voice," Apieron urged, although their target was yet a hundred paces' distant. "That one's ears can hear two coppers jingle in the next town."

Henlee frowned at this allusion to thievery and reflexively touched the purse at his belt.

"Once again I am impressed by the wisdom of my order's vow of poverty," said Xephard innocently. The dwarf eyed the paladin with distaste.

"He has a nose that can scent danger better than the best boarhound," continued Apieron.

"Only when 'tis his own hide that's at stake," growled the dwarf.

Apieron chuckled. "And so we shall ensure that it is!" Henlee joined in the laughter, although his tones were more sinister than the ranger's.

"Quiet now," Henlee whispered perhaps louder than their speech, and nudged his friends.

"We approach the rapscallion," agreed Xephard, who glided forward, his large body rustling the grass.

Apieron shook his head, incredulous, and as they neared the sleeping figure's feet, he observed the elegantly tooled and silver-piped boots of supple maroon leather. These disappeared under corded black breeches bloused over the boots and tightly cinched at the man's slim waist. A white silk shirt billowed open to reveal the man's smooth, olive-skinned chest. The cap of weasel slipped to reveal the dark, aquiline face with its proud nose and manicured goatee. Beside the dreaming figure lay a skin of wine and the shells of a dozen green lamas. An industrious column of ants plundered their sticky interiors. Stuck in the turf within arm's reach was a jewel-hilted longsword of superb craftsmanship, a twin poniard dangled from a belt loop.

A jumble of emotions played openly across Henlee's features as he analyzed the man at his comforts. Apieron knew Henlee was torn between finding the thief at hand without an arduous journey to the port cities, and vexation that the man looked as hale and hearty as he did. Apieron cleared his throat respectfully, but this only elicited a quiet snore from the reclining figure. Henlee kicked the sole of the thief's boot.

Jamello's eyes widened in surprise. "Bless me! Could it be the illustrious Xephard? Apieron, son of fabled Xistus? And the noble Henlee, dwarf of many riches?

"Welcome, noble sirs, to Jamello's cow pasture." His hands swept expansively, albeit lazily in the air. All this said, Henlee noticed the figure scarcely moved and certainly made no indication that he was on the verge of rising to proffer a traditional bow or even handshake of greeting.

"What do you here, rogue?"

"Where else should I be? I often abide in temples these days. It is so—" he glanced quickly at Xephard's frowning countenance, "—relaxing."

Apieron searched the man's features. Having been weaned on the intrigue in his father's court, he sensed a flicker of tribulation in the thief's deceptively light tone. He proffered a hand to Jamello, who heaved himself up to laugh and slap Apieron on the back, and also gave a short bow to Xephard and Henlee, all the while eyeing the gems dependent from the dwarf's plaited beard.

Henlee took a step back and harrumphed. "Let's off to supper, boys. Your good friend here left us naught but an empty skin and a pile of husks."

Jamello dipped into his famous bow and gave Apieron back his belt pouch. Henlee appeared mortified. "Lead on, good dwarf. I too look forward to dinner, if only for the hope that now you are here, the Donna will tell me why *I* am here."

Henlee took up a position that placed the others betwixt himself and Rudolph Mellor for the walk back to the temple. "Be careful what you ask for, thief. She may do just that."

Isolde stood in the temple's receiving yard. She awaited the arrival of Turpin, high cleric of Sway. Morning's sun topped the stone wall and felt wonderful on her back. She shifted her feet on the cold flags in attempt to drive out their chill. At last the Patriarch and his escorts approached. Turpin handled his destrier with surprising strength and grace for a man of his bulk and years.

No gentle pony for him! Isolde noted that his well-fitted travel garb was of the inevitable blood red, under an ermine collar. He reined in his stallion, tossing the straps to a stable boy.

"Thank you, my lord." The boy led off the stamping, sweating best.

"Welcome, Your Grace," said Isolde in her best court accent, although she had never visited one. She sketched a respectful bow. A quick glance took in the heavy ruby-and-gold ring and various jeweled accouterments tucked about his person, not gaudily displayed, but nevertheless revealed as a man does when long grown accustomed to station.

"And you, my dear," Turpin favored her with his rich baritone. "Well pleased am I to see that the famed flower of the Blessed Vale is no thistle."

She met his eyes briefly, seeing how bright and cunning they were despite his jowls and ruddy complexion, stigmata of years of hearty living. Isolde returned a bow for gratitude (quicker this time), half-embarrassed and half-irritated. Turpin chuckled dryly and took her by the elbow. Two armed acolytes of his escort maintained a respectful position behind, just out of earshot.

As the clerics walked and exchanged necessary pleasantries, Isolde learned his features and affect. The face was pensive, perhaps with the weight of office, one that in prior years might have laughed boisterously at a jest or bawdy song but now listened more than he spoke, and when he did, knew that men attended. She made to guide him to the guest wing, reopened and provisioned for his comforts, but the high priest seemed disposed to linger. Turpin steered her onto a walkway partially obscured by hanging vines that gave onto a small, shaded portico. Black-veined marble kept the little courtyard cool despite the bright sun. Sparkling gravel crunched under their feet. Turpin found a bench and pulled Isolde to sit by him. *He seems to know the temple better than do I.*

"Milord, we're to be summoned to table in one hour. The Donna wishes to hold council over our midday meal."

"Then I accept the gift of one portion of an hour to converse with you."

Isolde knew this was a man she could never best in any argument. As if knowing her sentiment, Turpin allowed a wry smile and made to speak when a large figure parted the vines and entered.

"Xephard!" Isolde exclaimed happily. Turpin's somber armsmen gave back to allow the broad-shouldered paladin access. Turpin surged to his feet and gripped Xephard on the upper arm.

Xephard inclined his head. "Well met, Eminence. We are fortunate to have such aid in the troubles that befall us."

"Nay, it is I who am fortunate to make the acquaintance of so doughty a peer. I see tales do not lie when they speak of you!"

Any relief Isolde felt at Xephard's intervention was quickly dispelled by the notion that Turpin appraised her beloved as a man might appraise a stallion he meant to race, or perhaps a purebred bullock he intends for sacrifice.

Xephard's eyes reflected the blue of the sky. "We gather for feast and to hear your words of wisdom, lord. Xeopolus has outdone himself. I do not think he slept."

"I am a man to appreciate a laden table." Turpin dropped an arm about each with a familiarity Isolde did not feel. "Lead on, my children. I would fain learn much of your lives here at the Lampus, particularly in that you both have the stamp of the wild North on you." As they strolled together, Isolde turned to regard Turpin's warrior monks. Their faces were as if cast from molded stone, and they made no sound upon the gravel path.

The company was ushered into a formal chamber where a meal was set. There were thick slabs of cured pork, sliced into slivers and set next to round loaves of bread while baked waterfowl dripped honeyed wine. Skewers of lamb were wrapped in grape leaves, and pickled eggs of quail and hen were strewn on every platter. Olives of various sizes and hues were mixed in glazed bowls. For a centerpiece, there was an enormous wheel of yellow-brown cheese. When the rind was broached, it exuded a nutty flavor. The dwarf was fascinated and brandished a heavy wedge. "This is not goat's cheese."

"No," said Xeopolus, "it is something unique, a specialty of our temple."

Henlee bit into the stuff then chased the treat down with a mighty pull on his tankard. "Better than any cheese I have ever had, or even heard tell of!"

Apieron laughed. "They have a cave full of the stuff. So much for the austere life of a devotee."

"One must find a few comforts where one may," answered Xeopolus.

"Here, here!" echoed Jamello.

"Besides," added Xephard, "the fighting men must be fed."

The dwarf adopted a mournful air. "Indeed, if I'd have known of such things, I would have invaded this valley myself long ago. Alas, now it is too late, you are my friends."

"You see, Xeopolus, your cheese is mightier than the sword," laughed Apieron.

Henlee leaned forward on his elbows and pitched the steward a serious look under thick eyebrows. "So what's your secret of the cheese?"

Xeopolus glanced at the Donna, who smiled and nodded. "In a special grotto, we bath it in sea water. Then grow mold on it."

"Bah. If you don't want to tell me, then do not. I'll not believe such a thing."

"Xeopolus never lies," laughed Xephard. "Just ask the Perpetua, or Isolde, or even good Turpin here."

The females said nothing, and Turpin seemed preoccupied. He glanced up surreptitiously and muttered, "I know him not."

The fighters ate with gusto, and yet the food was piled in such heaps that even the great appetites of Xephard and Henlee could not diminish them. Wine, beer, and spring water were also consumed in profusion. The clerics were more restrained and chewed contemplatively.

"I am conquered," said the dwarf. He pushed back. "I'll say one thing for you priestly types, you don't scrimp on the victuals. At this rate even the thief will get some meat on his skinny bones."

Jamello pointed a leg of fowl at the dwarf. "Ever heard of stuffing a goose before wringing its neck?"

"He's right," added Xephard as he happily consumed a loaf he stuffed with ham, cheese, and olive. "Who knows when we'll eat so well next?"

"I *was* conquered," Henlee corrected as a youth, clad in a simple shift, entered with a dessert tray of pears steeped in aromatic liquor and doused with clotted cream.

When the feasters were at last sated, the meal was cleared and drinks refilled a final time. At a look from Cynthia, servants withdrew. She studied each person in turn. "It is time to discuss our plans. No introductions are needed save for Turpin who arrived this morn. He is high cleric of our brother order. I sent message to him when I discerned Apieron's intent."

At a questioning look from Jamello, she explained, "Apieron is close to my heart. When his thought is bent hither, I sense him with ease."

Jamello looked aghast. "Can you do so with all those you know?" Henlee and Isolde snickered.

"Nay, thief. Should Apieron wish to shield his mind from me, he has more than enough skill to do so. I would not wish to view aught he would conceal!"

"Why does noble Turpin offer himself to share our peril?" asked Apieron. "The Temple of the Valley sends the monk warrior, Xephard, who is my friend."

"Hear! That should be sufficient," said Jamello. He fiddled with his slim, jeweled dirk. "With the dwarf, Xephard and Apieron should be enough for any dragon or evil wizard or whatever folly he intends."

"In your heart, Rudolph Mellor, you know that you are wrong," answered Cynthia. "There is more to this than simple quest. Else why are you here?"

"He is often wrong," said Isolde.

"Ah, what man could argue with such beauty?" quoth the thief with a lascivious wink to the young priestess.

"'Twere well to speak plainly of these issues," said Turpin. "None here should withhold any portion of his misgivings."

"In this holy place we are safe from betrayal," added Xeopolus. "Perpetua's chambers are shielded from any who might spy, near or far."

Turpin stood to address the small gathering. "That being said, I will address Sir Apieron's questions and perhaps answer others that have not been spoken.

"Our gods, and here I presume to include the gods of the dwarves," he looked to Henlee, who nodded for him to proceed, "first were those who resembled the ever-changing face of the natural world. Such are fearsome or kind, randomly just or tyrannical.

"Since, man has discovered gods more suited to certain of his moods. Gods of home, hearth, and family who smile upon those wise enough to cherish them."

The red-and-gold ring flashed on Turpin's hand. "Yet in the hidden souls of weathered stone and darkling forest lurks the memory of eldritch gods who once wielded titanic powers of destruction. Who slew without remorse. Civilized men name them demons, monsters of earth and sky. The world is a wide place of many uncouth lands where strange rituals are practiced and the eldest rights do not die. The land Kör is such a place." Turpin paused for a pull from his silvered cup.

"More close to home, it is said that in the darkest hours of night, ancient peoples of hill and fen creep from hidden places to worship their lost gods in forgotten ruins. Who can say what perforce occurs in those nighted heaps? We of the religious remember the lusts of the gods they revere, bestial desires for the blood of the innocent." The wine of Turpin's cup left a vermilion stain on the corners of the priest's mouth. "The taste of life's final agony ripped from helpless victims." As Turpin spoke, he lost his pedantic tones, and it seemed to Isolde that a light of dark animus found his eyes.

"You admire these gods!"

"These elementals are moved by the passion that quickens them, knowing no weakness spawned by guilt or consequence."

"Yet you would oppose them?"

"Nay, little thistle, that is too great a task for any one man, or group of men, no matter how heroic." Here he nodded the grimly attentive dwarf, troubled Apieron, and the steadfast Xephard. Nor did he exclude Jamello in his glance, who slumped low in his seat to avoid such attentions. "I mean only one such monster. One is enough!

"For *She* is the greatest and most evil of those whereof I speak. Long ago She was cast down by gods of light who were strong in their youth and yet needed their united strength to break Her carcass upon newborn earth. The weight of Her sin then sank Her to the world's center, where She lays imprisoned in Tartarus."

All was quiet in the room, and the sound of breathing was scarcely heard. Turpin continued, "Some new power hast She found, and the lock is broken.

"None may doubt the many signs that abound! Her slaves rush to do Her bidding, and they but prepare a way for Her ultimate resurrection."

Turpin looked to Isolde. "So my dear, oppose Her we must. Else we, who are the children of the new order, and all we have built, will be swept away. 'Tis not some foreign land She assails, nay, it is *this* one." Turpin's ham-like fist pounded the table, and his face was florid.

"The Sybil said that is so because this land is very ancient," spoke Apieron.

"Cradle of the gods," echoed Cynthia softly.

"You hath mentioned Kör," said Xephard. "I know the old tales speak of Ilycrium's wars with that fell land."

"This is true," replied the Donna as Turpin sat down, drained from his diatribe. "Kör exerted much influence upon this land. In the days when the Old Marshal, Baemund, came hither to unite it by his bright steel, he was aided by such powers as the enlightened religious commanded, as well as wise rural barons and others, among whom Xistus Farsinger was not least."

"So you hope to strike at the tyrant of Kör?" said Henlee. "I've heard it said he sits a throne that is both beautiful and terrible. It is alive but also worked of precious materials, a priceless artifact that projects his dark thought. The Throne that Dreams."

"Then let us hope we shall never see it!" added Apieron.

Jamello fiddled and squirmed. "Too true. Though such baubles normally make my palms itch, I also have no desire to see Kör's throne. He can keep his gems, I hope they are uncomfortable to sit upon!"

Turpin again waved his hand. "You need not worry yourselves about exploring the confines of the Tyrfang, where Kör's slaves build his dark mansions for him."

Jamello breathed an audible sigh of relief and looked to the others. Henlee and Xephard sat side by side, gazing at Turpin, unmoved by his words. Had they not been dwarf and man, Jamello would have thought them twins, so alike were their stern expressions. Isolde's flaxen hair had come unbound. "Cynthia—" she began.

"Let Turpin continue."

"His Grace said that we shall not tempt the wintry marches of Kör," said Apieron. "He did *not* say that our task would be any easier or less dangerous. In fact, it is vastly more so. Perhaps impossible."

"Oh, that!" said Jamello. His grin faded as he saw the faces around him. Isolde's normally expressive face had become a carefully guarded mask against the dooms being pronounced.

"We must journey to a land of death," intoned Turpin, "to wrest a power from Tiamat, Queen of Hel." Jamello rocked back, dumbstruck. Isolde looked to Cynthia to read the truth of the bishop's words in her sad eyes.

"It is foretold," boomed Turpin, "and can be no other way."

Jamello shook his long, straight hair as if he struggled to wake from a troubled sleep. "Surely this cannot be."

The others offered no support. Isolde silently implored Xephard with her now liquid eyes. He did not return her gaze but stared ahead as did the dwarf. Cynthia's hands trembled, but her face was resolute. Apieron seemed only tired, his head down.

"Who could lead us to such a place?" asked Jamello in a small voice.

"I will lead us, good thief," said Turpin. "Apieron is drawn to this, and *you* are destined to aid him."

The conversation paused, leaving each to his own thoughts. Drinks were sipped by most. Jamello downed his wine in a single toss and quickly poured another. His hands worked nervously, yet he seemed to regain a portion of his wit. He stood, smoothed his sleeves, and pulled his goatee. Straightening, he puffed out his silken blouse. "It is my official policy not to practice my art in the home fortresses of subterranean peoples whose customs and lingual vagaries are unknown to me, and who hoard their wealth with unmatched avarice. These have included mountain dwarves, pale-skinned gnomes, cave-dwelling trolls, and any barrow of undead drow, ghouls, or liches. After today's luncheon, I am certain that the keep of the Mistress of Hel most definitely applies. In short, my answer is no."

Henlee emitted a dour chuckle. Cynthia's expression was not unsympathetic as she flicked for the thief to resume his seat. "The hell of Tiamat's prison is not a place that you can find under the earth. It is one removed from the walkings of our world. What is proposed is uncommon and certainly extreme but not unheard of."

Xeopolus mused aloud, "Ah, were it so that my arms still retained the vigor of youth … when, in the temple of squat Turg, I bested their man-breaking wrestlers, three in a row. Then would I ride out with you to try my luck with the hellions!"

"You can have my place," said Jamello.

Xephard spoke with confidence. "Our small number can move rapidly, living off the land if needs be. Then we stab, quick as the serpent that one does not notice until it is too late. We front this demoness and leave." His massive shoulders shrugged as if to belittle the deed.

"Well put," added Cynthia. "Know all that to strike the heart of Tiamat's power is necessary, else the deadly atmosphere of her domain and her inexhaustible resources will gather. Even a great army would be withered. Moreover by the time such could be assembled (if ever) this bitch of destruction will come hither to destroy our land and reestablish her cults of old."

Turpin gave a shudder. "To force an army, a legion, or even a full company through the Hel Gate would call down the worst disaster on us."

The Donna continued, "Apieron holds some power that mayhap can reseal the bronze gates of Tartarus. A small, gallant team is necessary to deliver him there." Her voice assumed a powerful and majestic tone, her face stern. "Fate and the power of the gods of light have brought you five hence."

"And Galor Galdarion?" asked Isolde. "Apieron and Xephard and even Rudolph Mellor have oft told me that his knowledge is very great. He may have grown aware of whereof we speak, perhaps even considered other solutions."

"I would not place undue hope on succor from your allies amongst the elf lords," corrected Turpin. Henlee grunted an affirmation, and then remembered he had suggested just such a course to Apieron.

The Matron met Apieron's glance, who nodded in slow agreement. "I will contact him for you this evening during what I think will be our final gathering," said she. "I shall construct a fire mirror to his home in distant Amor." Cynthia's voice had grown tired, and after the many serious words spoken, none felt they could debate their future any further. She gestured to the doorway.

"The day is bright and fair. I bid you seek someplace hereabouts to find some portion of the peace that dwells in Our Lady's valley."

As the others filed out, Jamello sat brooding. He looked

up, startled to see that the Donna remained. She regarded him intently. He began to rise, but she motioned him stay. He beheld a strange, grim smile on her face and met her gaze as steadfastly as anyone ever had …

Chapter 11

Sway

"Now what were the circumstances again, Tyfir?"
The soldier shrugged his brawny neck. "Old swampfoot couple found slain, milord."
"Details, man! What were the exact details?"

The strain of recent weeks cracked Gault's tones. They were closeted in a neglected chamber within Swaymeet. Its sole furnishing was a small table at which sat the Prince with Brockhorst, prefect of Sway's police. Behind him stood Tertullion, whose unruly white locks were strewn upon his fringed mantle. The room's illumination was provided by a narrow loophole and an oil taper.

Tyfir dredged up his mental picture of the latest kill. The Prince had ordered a royal warden to investigate all suspicious deaths in the surrounding rurals. For this one, that lucky individual was he. Such occurrences were normally the purview of the nearest ranking knight, but the spate of seemingly random slayings apparently aroused young Candor's interest, and so now he stood before that one and the royal seer. Far beyond him were the motives of the powerful. No one had ever cared about swampfoot squatters before.

"The man was struck down. His neck broken, the old woman stuck up the flue, three days dead 'afore a neighbor thought to look in … five before we arrived."

Brockhorst joined in. "Was aught taken?"

Tyfir shrugged again. "Nothing to take."

Gault studied the warden's bluff face. The Prince's annoyance was palpable. "There is no reason to this riddle. Fifty deaths! Young and old. These killings virtually paralyze our inner provinces. Now precious little will be done about trade and blight. The King is ill whilst his barons wish to retreat behind their walls and be petty kings themselves."

Gault regarded Tertullion, but the venerable mage's bearded lips offered nothing, and he gave a slight shake of his head. Brockhorst met Gault's eyes, then nodded to Tyfir.

"Anything else, Warden?" continued Gault in a low, defeated voice.

"Begging Yur Highness's pardon, there was something that I reckoned a bit small to mention afore. The old couple was killed by havin' their bones broken, but there *was* some bloodletting. It was the cat."

"The cat?"

"Er, yes, milord. House cat, cut in twain."

Tertullion shot Gault a bright look. "That will be all," said he. "You have done well. Rest today."

"Me thanks, lord."

As soon as the bulky warden exited and the valve closed, Tertullion began to speak. "Oft by the trivial do the mighty reveal themselves."

"To hew a house cat?" asked Brockhorst.

"An act of murderous frenzy," declared Gault.

"Possibly, yet perhaps a fox's trick to confound the hounds. Think on this, our custom prohibits interview by necromancy, but the countryside boasts many a druid priest who might interrogate a live animal."

"The cat?"

Tertullion nodded enthusiastically, looking pleased for the first time in days. "This tells us that our slayer is a force or person who has knowledge of the arcane. Such a notable does not make shift to slay without purpose."

"I agree with your analysis, wise Tertullion, in all but this— say not a fox, rather a wolf!"

"Verily, Highness, and we know not his purpose."

Candor pushed his fists against his cheeks, elbows on the table. "Whilst we sit here like tree moss, this red-handed devil works his will on us. Why?"

Brockhorst and Tertullion shook their heads, expressions grim. There ensued a silence between the men as the lamp's flames sputtered softly in its bath of oil. Shafts of yellow sunlight from the window transected the small chamber, lighting motes of floating dust that drifted in random motion before sinking into the room's shadow. "I feel like a speck myself," said Candor, "circling at the whimsy of something I cannot see."

"Me too," said Brockhorst.

Tertullion smiled thinly. He placed his knobbed hand on Candor's shoulder.

On a peg, Dexius hung his coat of office. He admired its silk liniments, background for the crest of the Candor kings that stood so boldly on the surcoat's breast. For him the white horse of Ilycrium was crossed in dexter by a small rood of white wood. His eyes ached, a long day for the administrator of Swaymeet! Ironically he worked harder than ever at tasks he knew were futile in light of days to come. The sheer volume of proposals, analyses, and edicts that his overburdened secretaries generated, in no small way hindered the axle wheels of government while simultaneously erecting a facade of tireless effort on behalf of a troubled nation.

Dexius humbly acknowledged words of praise from court functionaries for his near-heroic performance. These same individuals would no doubt look to him for succor from the forces that came soon to assail their very doorsteps! Dexius's slender fingers caressed the garment's seal. Yes, his star was on the rise. Soon a new device would ride on his robes—*one of his own house.* For the nonce, however, proper forms must be obeyed. Long ago, he pledged oaths of binding to the body of the Candors. No direct harm, or knowledge thereof, must come to the old man or his adopted son from the office of the high minister of the realm.

"Well, Dexius, will you keep those pretty badges? Souvenirs of years of slavedom?"

Dexius wheeled to find Adestes Malgrim sprawled indolently on his settee. "The risks you take, man. Are you mad?"

Malesh did not reply, and Dexius fell silent before that dark continence. What alien thoughts filed through the brain of a man raised by an eldar Wyrm? Dexius repressed a shudder.

"To business, the children. You have arranged for their transport as I have directed?"

"Quite. Some hundreds younglings of cities and villages go missing. Rumor is rampant as you no doubt desire. But the cost …"

Adestes broke in impatiently, "You have been assigned enough gold to buy a dozen slavers."

Dexius bowed. "'Tis not the slavers, those scum come cheap, and the waifs are mostly alley mice or the get of rutting peasants. Even so, questions arise at higher levels. The Prince himself leads the investigation. Search spells have been cast, all this shuffling about and shielding magics to foil them cost me dear."

Adestes stood, letting fall a scattering of documents Dexius recognized as those safeguarded in his personal study. That the room was carefully locked by a single key worn round his neck apparently mattered not. Dexius regarded the warrior who stroked his goatee and stared back analytically. Dexius marked no weapon on Adestes' person, yet even so innocuous a gesture seemed fraught with menace. There was simply no predicting the man.

"Your lack of imagination disappoints me. Soon I depart this abode of servile fools. Send the children! And not merely guttersnipes. There must be some of this land's elite amongst them." Adestes' dark eyes glowered down at the slighter man. "I care not how you accomplish your task, or for the risks involved. Such are trifles before the will of the *Dragon.*"

Adestes Malgrim, Kör's Malesh, stretched forth a hand to touch the seal on the hanging garment. The cendal of the Candors twisted into a figure of black and gold, wreathed in tiny tongues of crimson flame. Dexius gasped as he beheld a beast of many heads, quickly nodding his submission as the assassin withdrew his hand to stroll past, out of the door and into the street.

THE SAAD ISLES

With a light step, Valente approached the palazzo of Farseps, chief municipality of Prebanks in the Saad Isles. The shear bulk of wealth listed in the original contract with Kör was staggering, and thus for three months his cargo ships had bypassed Sway in favor of ports friendly to the prince of Kör. Pirates and sea raiders had yielded wide berth, and indeed occasionally provided an escort of honor!

Now dock masters sent bills to ascertain the accounting of payment in full. That landlocked Kör would offer to bribe his city, thwarting Sway's sea traffic, was expected. For her to pay such a kingly ransom to buy what was, in effect, a naval stranglehold was something completely novel. Yet ever Farseps had grown rich by dealing in compromise, and then, Valente mused pleasantly, what might the lords of Ilycrium bid in time, when war walked their very doorstep?

Normally of a sour visage, Valente could not suppress a giggle as he took the portico steps. He favored a lowly guard with his thin smile, the astounded soldier just managing to snap his short pike in proper salute. Valente noted the man's surprise. *Why not a bit of levity?*

With wealth enough to buy outright the barbarous colonies his merchants served, no longer need they scrape and bow for profit. The fleet would expand beyond those of any rival, and monopoly over ocean trade-ways would force each kingdom's prince to compete for his favor. Had not mighty Kör been first? Three hundred talents of refined gold! Twenty bales of gemstones and amber! This one transaction matched the entirety of coin that changed hands in the island state for a year. The fools of the Shipmasters' Congress who had gainsaid him would be smitten; Valente could scarce wait to deliver his usual address to their staid faces and watch their mouths go slack when the treasure was revealed.

Valente laughed again, this time aloud and from his belly. He had to see the treasure for himself. Though long inured to riches and preferring to deal in tidy lists of scribes' figures rather than base coinage, he could not help his curiosity. That the demonic hand of Iblis had very possibly stroked the costly relics, or caressed the exquisite jewels only piqued his interest. So now Valente's feet skimmed across inlaid marble and passed entryways manned by the guard detail he had ordered. After city alchemists verified the contents of the gray ships, scores of dockworkers had labored all morning to haul the trove to the Congress's own vault. Workmen were flanked by rows of guardsmen to prevent pilferage more than to secure against any external threat. No raider had tried Farseps' amply defended shores in more generations than Valente's family remembered. And for good reason. Who would anger the chief trading nation of the western sea, thereby facing embargo and public unrest at home when citizens must realize their foolish prince deprived them of precious commodities?

Valente entered the strong room's anteroom at last. Standing before the bivalved door was another armsman he had known for years but whose name he could not recall. Palace veterans knew each congressman by face and were chosen for these reward duties on basis of discretion and longitude of service. Valente doubted the man had ever used his halberd in anger, although it looked serviceable enough. He proffered the long key worn about his neck and waited as the chamber warden turned to unfasten a sturdy lock set within the doors, these fashioned of near-impervious ironwood from the jungles of Gonj and reinforced with metal bands.

Three hundred talents of gold, and twenty bushels of gemstones! The "kingdom" of Farseps? How sweet it sounded in his mind's ear, and with kingdoms came kings of course. Congress, hah! Rich merchants with an equal voice until one might buy enough votes for a limited term as Speaker—rather pathetic. Would this be his legacy to his family? Dynasty?

He stepped into the vault and heard the lock snick in keeping with routine. An enormous hand of gold, encrusted with gems, grasped him by the throat and raised him off the floor. Witchfire lit inhuman, black diamond eyes under lowered brows of vermillion. Valente frantically searched the impassive face for empathy, but the golem regarded him with the alien objectivity of a mantis clasping its prey. Valente knew his life was ended … yet could not help remarking in his mind on the sheer size of those diamonds— as wide as his palm and well cut!

The crushed body of the Speaker of Farseps was flung twice its own length to the flags with a broken crunch. Brains and blood spattered the fine silk and brocade waistcoat. A towering leg of fused coins and ingots smashed flat the inert form. The chamber's valves were crushed like matchwood. Ignoring the insignificant guard, the construct strode without hesitation toward its next destination.

Yambol pushed and punched into the Captain's Hall of the Ca' d' Oro. Magnificently arched, the airy chamber allowed the merchant princes of the Saad Isles to gaze out on the sea that brought them wealth. The place was in an uproar. Guardsmen were everywhere, babbling reports to an overwhelmed lieutenant while sailors and dockhands clambered and surged against door wardens. Lesser Congress members huddled in small groups like confused sheep. Even lazy Fuquit had arrived, hastily buttoning his voluminous waistcoat.

"Silence!" Yambol bellowed and rapped his cane thunderously on the floor, snapping its silver head. He reddened further.

"Silence for Messire Yambol," echoed fat Fuquit in a booming voice from his stance beneath a wall hanging that depicted three rotund nymphs on a fountained greensward. The room's sudden quiet was almost eerie. Now strangely calm, Yambol noted how similar Fuquit was to the tapestry nudes. *Perhaps they were related.* He glanced to Fuquit with a gesture that somehow conveyed gratitude and contempt simultaneously. Fuquit nodded seriously in return, apparently blithe to the insult.

"Excellencies—" the pale face officer addressed Yambol.

"You may report, Lieutenant."

"A golden giant assaults the docks!"

"Indeed, Lieutenant," Yambol's voice dripped with sarcasm, "from whence has this marvel come?"

"From this very palazzo, lord. It leaves passage a blind man could follow. Several of my men are dead. More give battle on the wharves where the creature attacks the fleet."

"Sir!" called the door warden. "This man has news." The vault guard, Asaro, approached the lieutenant and gave hurried report in a low voice as Fuquit hastened his bulk to Yambol.

"Yambol, what make you of this? It is greedy Valente's dealings with Kör I am sure."

"Uhmm," nodded Yambol. *Perhaps this cloud had a gilt lining after all, and here was foolish, forthright Fuquit willing to act the chief accuser when only he, Yambol of the Rose, stood to gain the high seat at Congress.* "Indeed. Where is our glorious leader, I wonder?"

"Excellencies ..." The officer turned to continue his report.

Yambol did not reveal his perturbation at being lumped together with Fuquit. "You may proceed, Lieutenant."

"This man has been vault warden for a decade and served with distinction. He has seen the creature."

Yambol scrutinized the man. *He did look passing familiar ... of course all these soldier types did after a time.* "Speak, man," blubbered Fuquit.

"Sires, I 'ad just admitted his lor'ship Valente to the bank chamber a half hour or so gone, when a great troll made o' gold kicked down the door as easy as you please. 'E's headed to t'exit facing wharfside."

Yambol's mood turned sour again. He did not like the sound of a gold anything *leaving* the vault. "Why did you not slay it?"

The guardsman stared as if Yambol suddenly sprouted a second head. "Enough of that," said Fuquit. "What of the treasure?"

The guardsman shook his head. "I came back when the creature left ... gone, lord. New *and* old, 'cepting paper."

Yambol leaned heavily on his broken walking stick. He felt faint. "And the Speaker?" The guardsman shook his head again, but his lieutenant prodded him. "Go on, man."

"I could only tell it was 'im by the crest on his doublet."

Six galleys slouched crookedly, their keels settling on the shallow bottom. The golem had staved their bows. A few, fortunate to have crews nearby, pushed off in a panic and looked on helplessly as the wharf battled raged. Others, who had been on the approach, lingered in the harbor mouth.

Ballistae snapped against the creature's aureate front, hardened by rare and strange gems. A spewing flume of tube-shot fire obscured it from view—this closely guarded recipe would have immolated any hostile ship foolish enough to approach the jetties. Through the burning, the golem hove into view, trailing wisps of flame as small beads of molten gold fell from its frame. It passed under five men on a defense crane who loosed arbalests and tramped its way to the tube crew. With great blows of its arms and shuffling kicks, it crushed men and machine. The flame tubes' tinder and flares set off an explosion that ripped a hole in the crested seawall. Defenders scattered like a field of nesting birds startled into flight as seawater cascaded over the broken levee into the streets. Half the waterfront was obscured by a wave of brown water.

Seemingly satisfied by the general destruction, the construct spied the five men quietly clinging to the crane. Wading over, it casually pulled free the thirty-foot timber and swatted the men until their struggles ceased. It scanned the town, noting the most prominent spires. Its seeming leisurely pace was such that even a fast runner might match only with difficulty.

In the city, the lumbering golem never slowed as it crashed through shimmering veils erected by hastily summoned wizards. These hire mages resided on the isle, retained by the Congress chiefly for maintenance of the fleet, although a provision for island defense was in their contract. They were not in the least unhappy with the current disaster, for in addition to the added repairs to ensue, a finder's fee for a portion of the construct would surely belong to he who subdued it. A hand or foot from the monster would be sufficient to maintain even a wizard's extravagances for a year.

The foremost spellcaster hurled a ball of sparkling light at the charging monolith, who snapped it up in its great maw and gave back an evil grin, thus revealing a row of uneven quartz tusks. The three noted how surprisingly quick it moved despite its nigh twenty-foot frame. The first spellmaster, undaunted and businesslike, prepared to loose a final spell before the monster was on him. He accurately gauged its stride, knowing he would be able to strike and vanish should the golem prove more resilient than any of which he had heard. And Arthus of Bejon had learned much in two hundred years.

Waves of negative energy cast by the two flanking conjurers bounded off the creature's shoulders as Arthus pointed an exquisite wand of pure jet. The golden construct, never breaking stride, reached a many-fingered hand into its torso to withdraw a rough ingot a full foot across and hurled it at its foe. The incredibly heavy missile blasted wand and man backward as a child might loft an insect with a stick. Arthus's comrades shared a quick glance before simultaneously disappearing into puffs of green-and-pink mist. The creation stooped to recover the ingot, then moved inexorably onto the tall merchant houses it had noted earlier. Each contained a strong room filled with many treasures.

Yambol and Fuquit sat, sweating and weary, at the Congress' table. Seven members of thirteen were missing. Four perhaps were killed, three had fled the island city. The remainder looked bedraggled and lost. Yambol occupied Valente's vacant chair, his goblet untouched. Fuquit's was empty. It had been refilled many times.

Yambol waved wearily. "Go on, Lieutenant." The man wore a sergeant's chevron on his tunic. He had been promoted to officer in command of the shattered harbor garrison by Fuquit after his former officer had been crushed whilst leading a charge on the rampaging behemoth.

"Sir, the houses of Crés, Salome, and Astor are no more. The beast has fed on their coin and grown in size."

Yambol seemed to shrink within himself. Those three exchange houses would have financed a general rebuild. Congress members murmured gravely, for thus three of their missing brethren were explained. Yambol pondered the destruction of his fair nation. Someone had known how to hurt them most. A strange notion, one never perceived by him, occurred … he pondered the taste of guilt.

"And the beast?" queried Fuquit—his voice still held strength.

"It disappeared under the waves after destroying the north docks."

Fuquit thundered his hand upon the polished table. "Back to Kör!"

Yambol did not respond. A few of the others nodded dumbly. Fuquit hammered his meaty fist again against the unmoving table. The lieutenant met Fuquit's eyes. The merchant rulers of Farseps were not known for generosity with those who bore ill tidings. The former sergeant was beyond caring. Many of his friends had died under the bright sun today. He had dangled more than a few of their babes on his knee. The duty that was to come was worse, and he dreaded to see the faces of their pitiful widows.

Fuquit looked around the room and saw no spark of authority. Yambol looked as if all life had left him. "Summon the fleet captains, Lieutenant, even those whose ships were holed."

"Sir?" queried the soldier.

"You heard me, *Captain*. Summon for me a council of war."

"Sir!" boomed the man. His heels drummed from the room.

Fuquit looked at the now expectant faces. All except Yambol, who remained focused on the grain of the wood before him. "Gentleman, I think our path is clear. Do we have a consensus?" Four voices added their vote of aye.

"Messire Yambol?"

Yambol slowly stirred himself as if surprised to discover where he was. "I think I must attend my household." In the invigorated session that followed, no one noticed his departure.

It had been a week. From his private quay, Yambol stood and regarded the Ess. It was peaceful here. The only sounds were the cry of gulls that wheeled and stooped, and the rhythm of small waves striking wooden pilings. Elsewhere, work ordered by the new congress proceeded at frantic pace. Yambol's villa had been spared. Better it had not, for then he could have been found missing as were others who also signed pacts with Kör. The time for honor was past, surrendered years ago in incremental measure. *Honor.* How odd that he had never noted its death, so subtle were the machinations of politics that had eroded it. Now his folly had exceeded his personal destruction to ruin even his beloved island.

He could stay, wielding power as he had ever done. But over

what? A nation beggared by avarice, deprived of allies? Soon any barbarian chiefling who boasted a fleet would plunder their shipping and these very shores. Kör had proved how easy it was to do. Let naïve Fuquit and his flock of sheep bleat in vain! Soon the wolves would ring the pen with greedy eyes. Yambol had lived as a prince; he would not face life as a lowly shepherd. This way was better, and honorable Fuquit would see to the protection of his family.

Honorable. Bitter sounded the word in his mind's ear. The last of his treasure weighting his pockets, Yambol of the Rose walked out into placid waters burnished by a leveling sun. There was no change in the sea's endless murmur as she closed over his head.

Uncounted miles to the north, a second figure stalked the waves. Night was upon the land, therefore no one was there to mark an immense automaton of gold that slashed through breakers of a darkling shore, and swung untiring steps north and east, to the hill gates of Kör.

Chapter 12

Hyllae

Isolde slipped into the men's wardroom. At this time of day, acolytes were about their tasks and absent, although quiet cells were set off the main barracks for those with night duties. These she bypassed, moving quickly toward the private chambers reserved for peers of the temple. Xephard held position of honor at the center of these. Isolde eased the latch. Like all the doors here, it had no lock. Isolde felt her heart skip. Should a squire discover her, even a priestess would be hard-pressed to make plausible excuse, and embarrassing rumors would follow her for weeks. She blew hair out of her face. Squires be damned, things were past that now.

The plain wooden door opened easily. Xephard's chamber was sparse. There were his soldier's cot and racks that sported various armor as well as personal weapons and trophies. A small desk bore an unlit taper and a neat stack of illustrated scrolls. In the years she had known him, he had ever shown great respect for writings of any sort, but never had she seen him pen aught but the simple pictographs and runes of his native people.

Isolde moved to Xephard's sleeping pallet, running her hands over its head. The clean fabric was stretched tight, and she silently cursed his tidiness. There! Her eyes lit as she found the object of her search. Isolde delicately raised a single strand of short blond hair and folded it into a pocket near her bosom. She almost made it across the narrow barracks to the far exit when she nearly ran into three soldiers returning from the outer yards. Their gear was stained, and they joked and laughed after their exercise.

"Xephard is not here, Mistress. He is with the knight Apieron."

"My thanks, Androppus." Isolde pushed past, scarce meeting the man's eyes.

"Shall I tell him you require aught when he returns?"

"Nay, I will do so myself."

"As you will, Lady."

Isolde smiled in triumph and hurried to her next errand. Her hand touched her chest where her treasure reposed.

"Know you she came from his sleeping chamber, Androppus?" asked one of the men.

"Aye, and it is no business of such as we. Besides, I'll wager 'tis not the first time."

The man laughed and nudged his friend. "He can have her, that one's full o' spit and vinegar. Strong as a mule! She nearly skewered poor Cretus here with a spear at practice."

"Bested by a woman!" snorted Androppus.

"Lief here is a scoundrel," said Cretus defensively, "picks only the winning side in any debate. She's a wild-assed Northron by blood, as well you know, and those are worth any man in a fight. I pity even Xephard should he try to tame her."

"Like unto like," shrugged Androppus with a smile. "Since Cretus here lost to a priestess, he shall have to clean our gear whilst we bathe."

Faint echoes of the men's laughter followed Isolde as she approached her second destination. The men's guest chambers were typically frequented only by male attendants as were the females' in kind. Isolde rapped softly at the door she had chosen.

A deep voice grunted, "Come."

She swung open the portal and let it shut behind. Isolde gave a short bow to the occupant. If he felt any surprise at the intrusion, his dark eyes revealed little as he rose to return an even more pronounced bow, traditional of his people's custom. Reassured, Isolde decided to forego her rehearsed explanations. "I need your help."

"Speak."

Isolde took a deep breath and withdrew the hair. The dwarf lord pursed his lips. "Xephard's?" He saw the flickering need in her eyes and frowned in contemplation. A long moment passed, then a smile broke the brown beard. "It can be done."

The smile faded. "Is there aught else?"

It was her turn, and Isolde's own smile lit the guestroom. She curtsied. "I am a woman, there is *always* something else."

Apieron sat on a smooth boulder next to cascading water. The foam-flecked rush down the Auroch produced a chorus unlike any stream or falls he had ever heard. Xephard had accompanied him and was on the rocky beach, humming broken snatches of marching songs as he saw to his travel kit.

Apieron smiled at the temple knight's unskilled attempt to carry a tune, and turned to stare into the ever-changing face of the water's flow. The Falls of Voices might speak to him, once his mind was cleared of clutter and his heart opened to the natural magic of this place, ensconced in a high ravine at the head of Hyllae, Valley of Wisdom.

Many times Apieron visited there, always returning with some feeling of guidance. Today though, the voices seem strident. Discordant. Try as he might, he could discern no clear missive over the murmuring chaos of the swirling current. With a sigh,

Apieron tossed a dried leaf into the flow and watched it bob and swirl as it rushed down the stream, powerless in the face of the cascade. Like the leaf, he knew he was swept helplessly along by events beyond his knowing.

Apieron returned his attention to his friend. Xephard was obviously pleased by the prospect of what the paladin no doubt perceived as an ultimate quest. Apieron's mood was buoyed.

Isolde found them thus, Apieron singing in his rich voice, another legacy of his father. He was seated at water's edge, applying a layer of wax to certain of his travel gear, sword sheath, bow and quiver, and javelins. Nearby was Xephard, who glided a whetstone up and down the length of his sword, filing down tiny nicks and burrs along the killing edge. Stripped to the waist, beads of sweat stood out on his neck and muscular chest. The argent blade gleamed softly in the westering light.

Isolde watched the two for a time and smiled at how much like brethren they seemed. Xephard the stronger, confident in his beliefs, ever forthright. Apieron perhaps then the elder, who listened before speaking and watched before acting, these traits possibly making him the more puissant, she mused.

Apieron's song was that of a soldier who leaves his family and marches off to war, finding himself in a land of which he has never heard. But he is also glad, for war is his profession and the rewards might be high. Xephard's tenor voice joined the simpler refrains. The paladin now oiled his sword with a soft cloth.

"My lord," said Isolde, stepping onto the strand. "Surely Leitus was honed many minutes ago. It seems you would caress her over much."

"Look, Xephard," said Apieron, "a lovely nereid has slipped her streambed to bring us pleasure."

Xephard laughed. "Truly, and better, a most wise and knowing nymph."

"That is apparent," agreed Apieron, "but methinks this one is of the jealous sort."

"I only know, sirs, what my own eyes tell me. It appears Xephard would rather stroke his silver maiden than me." Isolde warmed to the game she had begun. Her hair was bound and honey bright.

Xephard showed her the naked blade. "A warrior's first duty is to the perfection of his weapons and the order of his kit. In such he begins his excellence."

"The many attentions you lavish upon your sword seem those of love, not duty. Indeed I have never seen you shower one thousand caresses on, say, your bootstraps, or your saddlebags."

Xephard looked hopefully to Apieron, who merely laughed and shrugged, but no relief was forthcoming. "My friend, it was you who fell swoon for a priestess, not I."

Xephard stood apart and swept the great blade in a shining arc. "Woman! The time a warrior spends with his weapon means more than mere cleaning and simple practice. It is a time to share; she teaches me many things. She is firm and strong. She is deadly but balanced. She can bend to an obstacle stiffer than she, only to recover and find her way with the next stroke, or p'raps another."

Isolde folded her arms. "You said shared. What does Leitus get from you?"

"She works my will, and thereby is herself fulfilled. Be not jealous of Leitus, for my life and her existence are pledged to your defense. Forever. Always."

Isolde allowed her smile to blossom and moved to embrace her betrothed. "This is a first," said Apieron. "Xephard has won a contest of words."

Isolde replied sweetly from around Xephard's shoulder, "Surely you realize, Captain, that one battle does not a war make."

Apieron showed his palms, signaling "no contest." The friends gathered their gear and took the steep ascent from the river cliff. Apieron paused at the edge to listen one last time. To his chagrin, the water's rush remained oddly disjointed, depriving him of the confident harmony he hoped to find in the voice of the Falls. *One more hope failed.*

Apieron put on a light face before his friends, for tonight would be their last together at temple. Perpetua would summon her fire mirror and send forth a message to distant Amor, nigh a thousand miles northwest. Each and all anticipated the event, for Galor Galdarion was a scion of elvin royalty and the most powerful dweomorcaster they knew. More importantly, he named himself their friend.

And as they walked, the young cleric of the Lampus wondered what would be the outcome of her own schemes for the evening.

A long skewer was removed from the cooking fire. New fagots were heaped on coals, and bright flames licked up to fill the clearing with a merry glow. At a nod from Xeopolus, green boughs from a nearby cedar were added to the blaze. Shortly these produced a sweet, gray smoke that wended out over treetops outlined against the night sky.

From an amphora Cynthia poured a measure of undiluted wine as the others, save Isolde, stepped back a respectful distance. The Matron spoke words of prayer, invoking favor of the Messenger. Isolde tossed handfuls of fragrant sandalwood and precious ambergris onto the flames, which yielded billowing waves of purple smoke. Cynthia called out in the ancient tongue of the valley, old before came Baemund Candor and his Wgend liberators. She named Galor Galdarion and his elfin home of Amor, surrounded by uncounted acres of mysterious forest. In the coiling smoke, a fair visage took shape—a face of angular features and incredible beauty, the incense weaving graceful tendrils for hair.

Cynthia beamed with pleasure at the countenance above them. Isolde gasped, for here was not the archmage Galor they named, but his wife, Dorclai, high priestess of Amor, Lady of the Forest.

"Well met and welcome, fair Queen," said Cynthia. "Your arrival gives us unexpected pleasure."

"And to you, Perpetua." The radiant image swept the gathering side to side. "A noble gathering. I am honored by your sending."

The Matron sketched a polite bow, and Isolde followed suit. Apieron stepped to stand betwixt Isolde and Cynthia, and a kind smile found the beatific visage. "Well met, Apieron Forest Walker, I see that a troubling shadows you."

"My apologies for spoiling this happy meeting with urgent words, but our need is very great. Wherefore does Galor not answer our call?"

"My husband is not here. Nor is he roaming Amor's deep trails or the sunny glades as was his wont. Galor Galdarion has again taken himself to a secret place amongst the beeches he loves, and has transfixed himself to appear even as one to all but I. He speaks only to fertile Earth and whispering winds. Long ago his thoughts strayed from the trials of unhappy mortal-kind."

A silence filled the grove save for the wet fluttering of the fire. To the gathering, it seemed a great blow had been struck against their cause before it had even begun. Henlee surged forward to confront the floating queen, hands on hips and beard bristling.

"Can he not be summoned? Are you not his wife?"

The fair face grew stern as her gaze fell on the belligerent dwarf. Apieron intervened. "Lady, I am tempted to journey to shining Amor to plead with your husband, yet whether by horse or spell, I fear we have not the leisure."

"Should you travel hither, I will make you welcome, as well as Henlee of the bearded folk. But my lord will not answer you."

"Noble Dorclai—" said Apieron in elvish, interrupting the dwarf's muttering. "I do not hesitate to speak your name in the eldest tongue so that my words sound pleasing to your ears."

The floating visage focused intensely on the tall ranger, and to those that heard, whether they understood the elvish tongue or not, it seemed he spoke with great dignity and the deep confidence of a man who knows his words are true. He explained the unrest in his country and of the gathering of the ravens of war. He spoke the dire predictions of the Oracle, and last, the crescendo of doubts that assaulted his very soul.

Dorclai's face was grave when he finished, and she addressed the gathering in the common tongue of men, "The words you speak fall heavily on my ears. We too have seen the fell star risen in the South. It is a portent of the unrest whereof you speak. Some name it *Serpent Fire*, the Dragon Star.

"I will summon the Ring of Six. Apieron, your father fought with us when Amor was a place of darkness. You yourself did so (with your mighty company) when the last Children of the Night were driven forth. Elves do not forget. We will aid you as we may."

Apieron moved again to speak, but the image lost focus. The last glimpse they had was of a slender hand as the smoky window into Amor was shut. The spell was broken, its energy dispersed on the soft wind as the fire sank to a winking bed of coals, surrounded by a ring of half-charred boughs.

Isolde asked, "The Ring of Six, what does that mean?"

Apieron spoke. "There are six elvin lords of Amor who advise Galor, or it appears, rule in his stead."

"When will this Ring meet?" asked Jamello. "How soon can we expect their aid? Perhaps we should await them," added the thief hopefully.

"We cannot," said Apieron, "and once we take the road, we shall be hard to find."

"Mayhaps their magic will seek us out," persisted Jamello.

Henlee's frustration with the thief was growing. "If forest witches can track us, then so can others who don't mean us well. Best to leave soon or not at all. Besides, I need to wrap this up and get back to Uxellodoum. With all this talk of war, old Redhand might need some advice."

Turpin, who had hitherto been silent, spoke. "I shall cloak us from ill-meaning eyes whilst we travel, and I agree with master Henlee, to delay brooks disaster." The sturdy cleric shrugged his heavy shoulders. "If elves find us not, so be it."

"Perhaps they will send their war master Drust, or Galen Trazequintil—Galor's son the cavalier," added Xephard. "Ever have I desired to meet them." Henlee snorted, but Xephard laughed. "With the strongest knights in elvindom and mighty Henlee, and my moody friend Apieron, none shall stand before us."

Jamello sniffed. "Hard to find? We might as well bring a marching band."

"Who? When? How much?" said Henlee. "You can ask till you've gone blue in the face and go on wondering. Bah! You shall never get a straight-up answer (or a fight) from elves."

The Perpetua raised a withered hand. "We know only this, the lords of Amor do not make idle promises, aid they will send. Whether it be in a fashion that will succor us now we cannot know."

Turpin met her gaze. "Very well. Us mortals must struggle on as we may. Are we agreed upon departure in the morn?"

"We are," answered the Donna with a meaningful glance to Isolde. "This debate is ended."

"I have one thing further," said Isolde. Each face regarded hers as she strode to Xephard, encircling his thick arm in hers. "Tonight we are to be married."

Xephard shouted with laughter and lifted her up to kiss before shaking hands all around. "I did not expect such a guerdon prior to our journey."

Cynthia shared a long look with Isolde, and her face filled with sad comprehension as she gave her nod of consent. Jamello produced a small lyre, Henlee two strands of delicate, ornately twisted wire. One of platinum, the other of yellow gold. The thief struck a bawdy air that he quickly mellowed after a frozen glare from Isolde. She accepted the shining strands from the dwarf with a beaming smile and turned to hold them up.

"You see … wedding gifts of exchange, platinum for Xephard contains my hair twined within, and gold for me, encircling one of Xephard's." Embarrassed, Henlee muttered something unintelligible and stepped back to gather fresh kindling for the fire. Apieron chuckled. "I see this was a conspiracy of everyone, excepting me."

"And me," echoed Xephard happily.

"Not so, Apieron, bard's son." Isolde's tones brimmed with laughter. "You shall supply the voice to Rudolph's tune."

"Ah, but whence came the ingots for the bridal gifts?" asked Jamello. "I did not know that priestesses of the Lampus kept any store of such."

"As we do not, at least for ourselves," answered the Matron. A crash sounded from where the dwarf threw an armload of wood onto the fire pit and stomped off. A general laugh ensued while Cynthia came forward to handle the precious ropes. "The work is fine. I shall strengthen it by words of blessing."

She held the gleaming twines in a hand upstretched to the heavens and mouthed a silent prayer, then turned in slow circle to pause before each person present that they might add their goodwill to the strength of the links. Turpin was last and came forward when the benediction was done to kiss Isolde lightly on the cheek.

"So, the thistle blooms. Long may it flourish before withering."

Isolde smiled thinly. She gestured to Jamello, who began a lilting tune to which Apieron added his voice. Isolde waved to acolytes in the background who attended to the details of the feast. These came forward grinning to proffer their good wishes, and soon a circle of dance was formed around the couple, who held each other close by the fire.

Isolde secured the platinum twine about Xephard's corded neck. "So may I remain near your heart."

In turn, he affixed the gold wire around her waist. "So may our union be fruitful and pleasing to the Goddess."

They kissed, and all stopped to cheer and clap. The notes of Apieron's song changed as the new couple danced the steps of the marriage rite before their friends. In the long shadows behind them, tears lined Cynthia's cheeks, although her lips were lifted in a smile.

The face of Turpin was somber. Ruddy firelight leapt and flickered on his pale eyes, and in the distance, thunder rumbled and a high wind moaned over treetops.

Morning came clear and fine. Night's rain showers were scattered and a fresh breeze invigorated the animals. The group was provided with horses for the journey. Xephard would ride his mighty charger, Axylus, whilst his second mount would bear the bulk of his knights' equipage. Bump was there, and despite his extra burden of enriched grain for the other mounts, he seemed in good fettle. A small crowd gathered to bid the five travelers good-bye. Isolde and Cynthia stood side by side in identical voluminous cloaks, appearing like mother and daughter, and there were many servants and townspeople as well as most of the temple garrison who stood about informally to converse in low tones. These were mostly commoners of ability who had pledged themselves to the Twin Gods and in turn were given food and board, education, and training until the valley of the Warrior Goddess could boast an extended company of soldiers as elite as any in the kingdom.

Rudolph Mellor looked on glumly. Somewhere he had acquired an orange pomander. He sniffed it often, but it did not cheer him. At length he was forced to steer his bay from Henlee's burro that had developed a taste for his fine leather boots. The dwarf's expression was unreadable as he stood nigh, muttering and picking his teeth. Jamello looked to Turpin for diversion, but the cleric sat his horse quietly, frowning as if in difficult thought. Jamello saw he now wore a thin but weighty mace on an ornate weapon's girdle around his waist. The mace was near three feet in length yet seemed of normal size against his bulky frame. Soon Turpin, apparently suppressing his inner debate, spurred his chestnut stallion toward the gate where he meant to await the others. Henlee and Jamello drifted after.

Isolde asked Cynthia, "Did you share counsel with Turpin? Were you able to give him guidance?"

"He asked for none, I gave him none."

To Isolde's quizzical look, she added, "He has ever shielded his thoughts."

"But does not the Goddess reveal his intent to you?"

"Turpin's god is almighty Sky, whose high clerics need not heed the will of goddesses."

"*Men*, men of pride!"

"Look yonder to your gallant. Surely he is one such."

Xephard had left Apieron's side and mounted Axylus to begin a brilliant series of maneuvers, as he did to celebrate the start of every martial errand. His white cloak swirled and danced as if with a life of its own. Townsfolk chattered excitedly amongst themselves as turnout for Xephard's antics had become local tradition and a carnival atmosphere oft accompanied the paladin's departures. They loved him for his unmatched victories and for his blind generosity, but most importantly for the unashamed gifts of faith and hope that he represented. Isolde filled her eyes with the sight of Xephard at his cavorting, so handsome to her and skillful, like a bold, young god.

Cynthia said, "Nay, my dear, I only spake thus in jest. Your Xephard's thoughts sing out to me. There is not a morsel of duplicity in him. It is true our respected Turpin is of a secretive nature, and his mind is a well that cannot be plumbed. Whether this be for good or ill, I cannot say. It is too late for such meanderings."

"I care not if he hoards a dragon's trove of secrets … as long as he has the power to bring my love back to me."

"Pray it is so. This wind gives me the ague." Cynthia snugged her cloak about her.

Apieron drew near and clasped Isolde to him in farewell. She could find nothing to say and was pulled aside gently by the Donna, who smiled and bade her prepare a final blessing. "I will walk a moment with Apieron."

As they watched her move to a simple stone altar under a vined trellis where many of the crowd gathered, Apieron searched Cynthia's face. "How can you smile so when all we have stands in jeopardy?"

"I smile because this may be one of my last days to do so."

Apieron looked at the temple grounds. "I place you in great danger."

"Because you acquired our captain and our blessing? You fear we are weakened before the onslaught of Kör?"

"I fear rather the depredations of Exeter's wardens once they've discovered this little expedition."

"On the contrary, I dispatched missives to Tertullion, who is trustworthy and has the King's ear. He sends word of Belagund's private approval of our course and his regret that he cannot aid us in more direct fashion. Of course I sweetened the deal by offering to the Throne our entire company, warriors and warrioresses alike, to serve in any capacity he desires."

Apieron was shocked. "And leave fair Lampus undefended?"

"If Kör has allied himself to the black bitch of *uncreation*, no force of mine could protect this or any other place."

"And Isolde?"

The twain regarded her, singing a low prayer that many joined. She was herself a favorite in the valley, and an equal number of the folk attended her benedictions as did throng to Xephard and the companions. "She pressed me hard to accompany us. Xephard did not help me at all."

Cynthia chuckled dryly. "A good husband yourself, and no worse for wear. Xephard is wiser than you! Nay, there must be only one cleric to guide the party. Turpin has asserted himself. In this I agree, it is not yet Isolde's time."

"Experience over beauty?" Apieron chuckled.

"Quite so. Like you, Isolde walks her own fate, and none of us know what that is to be. She will remain, though in this I earn the enmity of one dearest to me."

Apieron inclined his head. "As you say, Matron. The many sacrifices you make on my behalf do not escape me."

"My unhappy child—" The priestess extended a thin arm to touch Apieron's face with more warmth than words could convey. He searched her eyes for a moment, smiled and turned away.

Cynthia watched Apieron go to his fellows. She stared at her hand in amazement. Where she touched him, her palm was covered in blood, and she shivered violently. Unnoticed, she sought her way back to her quarters. The benedictions of departure she would leave to Isolde. With faltering steps, she bethought herself of another orison, a prayer for the dying.

The score knights who were peers of the temple openly cheered as Xephard walked Axylus backward before their ranks and nodded his plumed helm to each among them. Isolde saw Apieron mount his horse. She began the final invocation, casting raw barley grains upon the earth and pouring wine from a sacred vessel. She named the Hunter and the Gray-Eyed Goddess and other friendly gods before finally calling upon the very hopes of the souls gathered in the yard.

When she concluded, the people seemed pleased. Isolde felt muchly drained and looked for Xephard among the press at the gate. She and he had shared tender good-byes before daybreak, yet she yearned for one last glimpse. It seemed as if all her desires, however humble, were to be denied.

Xephard's shout rang. She saw him there, astride brave Axylus. He reared and gave an amazing salute, Lcitus flashing in the sun. "Isolde!" he boomed. "Your love gives me strength." With that, he fell in at the head of the little troop and they moved off at a fair pace. The crowd dispersed as she watched the adventurers fade from view. The morning now seemed dreary and cheerless, its light faded. She let the tears stand on her cheeks before turning to follow Cynthia indoors.

Chapter 13

Sway

The Council of Swaymeet was bedlam. Table and wall seats were occupied by the principals of Ilycrium while less important personages stood where they might amongst the statues on the periphery. Lysander was there, surrounded by a gaggle of merchants and guild masters who bickered and shouted. He fingered a chain of gold links and swung his jowled chin to and fro as each speaker vied for his attention. A delegation of rural lords was also present, and with serious faces spoke amongst themselves and with Exeter, who with his quick glance and predatory nose, resembled more than ever a hunting falcon. Gault suspected that the dour demeanor and untrusting airs of the provincial lords were aimed as much at one another as elseward.

The Prince's gaze swept over seats along the walls. Military officers of the infantry and Ilycrium's small navy he recognized. He marked Tallux who held high rank amongst the King's scouts but who deferred taking the seat at table reserved by tradition for guest lords of the Malave. The wood elf sat alone save for the fierce war dog at his feet.

"Plague and murder!" shouted a burgher, leveling a thick

finger at Brockhorst. "Why do your men stand idly by?" The lieutenant's reply was lost in the hubbub.

There were also court functionaries, summoned by their masters. These nervously clutched scrolls of figures for everything from treasury balances to countings of military commodities. The din was uproarious as each party voiced their particular theories as to why sudden chaos had descended into their area of province. "Please, please," shouted Dexius. He banged his rod of office repeatedly on a stone trivet. His efforts were unheeded.

Perhaps at long last the sleepers waken! Gault regarded the glowering faces of the sires of house Candor cast in stone and bronze. Flanking the chamber, they gazed on the gathering with stern disapproval. "At last I know how you feel."

"To order!" shrilled Dexius.

His thin arm beat an unending tattoo on the table with his short ivory rod. One of the country lords pointed at him and nudged his companion to laugh. The man had a heavy, low-slung brow and a lantern jaw that thrust truculently over his barrel-like torso. His name was Buthard. His partner was a man of similar lineaments, save taller and less massive. Stamped on the latter's face was a sour look. Gault recognized them and as son and father, the elder being the warden of Wicklow by name of Wulfstane and holding broad properties of rich farmlands and spreading woods.

Gault recollected Wulfstane's neighbor southward was Apieron of Windhover. How he wished that knight were here.

It had been a long year since Apieron visited the capital. To Gault, the courteous, smiling warrior would always be a friend. Many were the times as a wistful youth had he been regaled by the tales of that far-ranging soldier of the Scouts. *If I could trade places with anyone in the kingdom, it would be he.*

"Peace!" boomed Tertullion in a thunderous voice that belied his age. Silence descended on the chamber. He bowed to Dexius, who returned a curt nod of thanks.

"You are come to council to discuss the import and interrelations, if any, of the myriad troubles that beset our fair land," said Dexius.

A welter of complaints arose and was as quickly stifled when Tertullion half-rose, black eyes glinting under wintry brows. "Scribe of the treasury," called Dexius. "A report, sirrah."

A handsome youth, albeit sallow of face, stood from his seat and began to recite in a clear voice. He held before him a parchment, dark with tallies, although he did not appear to require its presence, save perhaps as reassurance. The youth emitted a squawk of protest as he was buffeted aside by Buthard.

"Good Dexius, are we to listen to every one of your pretty pageboys before we hold a discourse of equals?"

It seemed that if Dexius could have incinerated the Baron's son with a mere glance, Buthard would at that moment been reduced to smoldering ruin. As it was, a chorus of shouts erupted in agreement with the bellicose country lord. His father stood behind him, scowling at any who did not voice their support. Dexius knew that if he did not ride the emotional wave of the assembly, he would be rolled over by it. After an impatient flick of his hand, court functionaries and servitors filed out. When the oaken valves were closed behind the last of these, he leaned over the table.

"Well, Buthard, what now?"

"What else? You cannot fool us with flowery words forever. We have reports of military officers wearing the paves thin to and from the King's chambers. Why does he not speak to us? Does this ill wind blow from Kör?"

Gault smiled thinly from his seat on Tertullion's right. That it took a swaggering boor like Buthard to discern the muddy truth was indeed high irony.

"The King is ill disposed," returned Dexius, "but needs no excuse to avoid the likes of you."

Wulfstane gripped his sword hilt, but his son displayed a toothy grin at the gibe, well pleased to thus draw out the normally evasive minister. "Were you of more pure blood, I would challenge you to a trial of arms. Do you have a noble champion in your stable of simpering whisperers?"

Dexius's face turned white. He shook. Exeter rose quickly. "Come, gentleman, let us be reasonable." He passed a knowing look at Wulfstane and Buthard.

"You sirs have gained your desire for a conference removed from the dross of the Court. And you, Dexius, have our respectful attention. Buthard speaks unjustly. However that may be, his point is well taken. We have listened for months to endless reports and calculations whilst our situation worsens. What befalls? Does some foreign prince plot our ruin?"

Gault glanced at Dexius, who was somewhat more composed, although not yet able to speak. Instead Tertullion gathered his robes and stood. "You speak of Kör, Exeter, but what do we truly know of that land's rulership?"

"In bygone days, great lords therein would at times grow restless and engage us in conflict, both subtle and direct—yet were inevitably drawn away by internal struggles in that vast and chaotic realm. My fear is that a singular prince has risen, one of monstrous strength who might establish overlordship over all its peoples. One to whom the conventions of war and trade are nil—who revels in dangerous displays of raw power. If such a one has come, his erstwhile sires would be as naught."

"What of our spies and border-runners?" asked Lysander. His busy hands and flashing rings gave evidence to his anxiety. An ominous pattern was beginning to emerge, for who knew better than he the difficulties of late besetting commerce by land and sea? He felt nauseated.

"What spies?" queried Dexius, once again affecting his customary mien of a patient yet disdainful professor before ignorant students. "As for the King's scouts, you have one of their chiefs before you." He gestured to Tallux.

"An elf," pronounced Wulfstane, scarcely masking his contempt. "Why does the woodland lord, our *ally*, not send a *royal* emissary to sit at the high table?"

Tallux's voice was even, but his face grim. "I do not recall an invitation having been sent. As for the doings of the King's rangers, your words reveal that you knew of their intelligences afore now." He shrugged. "Kör has a dozen Snakes, reinforced, to send against us. Will he? And when? For that, ask another."

The offhand tone in which Tallux delivered this last did more to stupefy them than any dramatic oratory. Dexius swallowed hard, disguising it with a sip from his cup.

"But our harvest will be a poor one!" protested a sun-reddened landman who owned lowland tracts of grain crops. "What say our merchantmen and sea captains? Will they trade for goods we lack with the cities of Prebanks?"

Eyes turned to Lysander and the tradesman of rank who flanked him. Some of these were masters of merchant vessels, experienced sea captains themselves, and individually they were no less bold than any veteran soldier or warlike noble's son. Now they looked to Lysander for guidance. His ring-bedecked fingers cupped his face as he studied the mahogany grain of the table. When he raised his eyes to meet those around him, his face was grave. "No help will come from the Saad Isles. The Farsepians refuse to approach our shores, and their harbor has been closed to trade vessels for a month."

"I have never heard tell of the merchants of that ship-faring city refusing to take contract," protested Exeter. "Little have they to fear behind their sea fence."

A craggy-faced seaman spoke forth. The gold epaulets of a merchant officer adorned his shoulder, and he addressed the gathering by right of a small family crest on his doublet. "Aye, always have our doings in the Prebanks been profitable. Of course," he mused, "one had best remember to bring one's own scales to the adding table." The patter of laughter that ensued seemed to Gault rather strained.

"Unfortunately, I rather disagree," Lysander replied slowly. "Perhaps the Farsepians have *not* refused any contract. Mayhap ours was the second, and the less worthy bid?"

A low murmur ensued as the assembled counselors' suspicions were kindled. Exeter burst out incredulously, "Say you that men, even the gold-loving captains of Farseps, would ally with beast-men 'gainst their own kind?"

Wulfstane seconded him. "Oh aye, p'raps the island folk of Farseps are tired of our bulky shiploads of timbers and wool. Mayhap they grow weary of salted meat and forged goods," he added sarcastically.

"The lords of Kör are by far more rich than we," answered Tertullion cooly. "It is said they possess vast mines of precious stones and rare minerals as yet unknown in type to those of the West."

Lysander's next words were as heavy as his body. "Let me put it plainly. If we have been played for fools, it may be the Farsepians take Kör's bid … then, when we are broken and desperate, they will renegotiate for our base needs. An' the price dear when we can least afford it."

Gault surveyed the perplexed and angry faces of his countrymen. He was somewhat mollified that these men finally acknowledged the danger besetting the realm. He was sad that it took such dire tidings to achieve even modest unity. Of habit the provincial barons would pay little heed to troubles besetting the capital, particularly the merchant class, who, with their new money and disregard for bloodlines, were at best an irritation. Yet herein was a crisis that outweighed such concerns, for none of the rural lords doubted but that outlying settlements would be first to feel the wrath of any invading army.

Dexius spoke above the diffuse mumbling, "There is another matter. The Sybil at Seabridge has answered the delegation sent at the behest of our prince with only these cryptic words." He rattled a parchment and read from it in a dry voice:

"Like shadows, Ilycrium's doom falls from sky-born wings. The eye that kens truth, victory favors. From heaven's wings, hope returns."

Dexius let the paper fall to the table. "Who in this noble assembly has the wit to cipher this riddle? If he can, speak, for I myself cannot."

"Nor can I," answered Tertullion "Even so, our friends among the religious tell me that Apieron of Windhover betakes himself a journey on her behalf to Duskbridge. With him go a handful of stalwarts, not the least of which is Xephard of the Lampus." After a moment of stunned silence, a heated discussion ensued. Tallux stirred, following the conversation closely, but only his lambent green eyes revealed the intensity of his concern.

Gault despaired. Tertullion's words came a shock to him as well. He took note of Tallux. *How he longed to venture with men such as those!* Men who were long on action and short of words.

"This is a sore jest, Seer," said Exeter. "Will you have young Apieron chart out the underworld for us? Does he reck that someday we can settle these lands, or perhaps negotiate trade?"

"Aye, Lysander," added Buthard, "send in your merchants if they be idle … the hellions will have no chance!" A smattering of rough laughter followed.

Tertullion rapped his knuckles upon the table. "The ways of that fell place are not unknown amongst certain of the wise."

Dexius rose, and the passion of his speech surprised them. "Here your wisdom surely fails, Seer. The ways to that place were lost long ago—the better for all men! It is a forbidden realm."

"And I, who am young, remember my cleric's lessons of childhood," said Gault. "What of dragons that sleep in the earth? What of their ancient cults that once befouled this land before my grandsire's time?"

Dexius' slender hands worked. "Has anyone here ever seen such a beast? Or better, heard tale of one who has seen such a beast? I thought not. Let us worry more for the soldier of Kör who walks the waking world than the dreams of dragons!"

Tertullion nodded to Gault. "As always, Dexius, you speak wisely from the store of knowledge that you hold. But what of the Sybil? You advise caution, yet one sees others of great names who fear p'raps the stirring of an ancient evil into this fair land. Look about you, I say the evil they fear hast already found us."

Dexius turned to Candor. "I like this not, my Prince. Why were the Sybil's words not spoken onto royal ears? Or perhaps unto a trusted advisor?"

"Rubbish," said Tertullion. "Would you have a blind prophetess hobble hence from her holy mountain to stand in your waiting chambers? Her ways are a mystery, not in plain speech, but by verse or riddle does the godhead move her. Never one meaning, always two or more, the words designed to bloom one year, or a hundred past the prophecy.

"Nay, 'twere folly to seek to contain all the wisdom of God within the small box of our thought." Tertullion tapped his head for emphasis.

"As always," said Candor, "your words ring truth like a silver bell." Tertullion stood and bowed to the Prince.

Dexius continued, "Whose knowledge can sound the depths of the Pit, Seer? *Yours?* I say nay, none of this land. Let us please consider the real issues that confront us. I suggest another delegation to Prebanks, perhaps headed by one of royal blood?"

Tertullion was not done. "Certainly no man of this gathering has such knowledge, for I myself do not. Yet within the endless tracts of Amor such knowledge lives, and therein lies a kingdom proper, with white shores and leagues of sweet swelling meads. The slender ships of Amor are well known to the tribesmen of the far north where they ply their trade."

"Bales of moonstones and bushels of elvin glass, no doubt!" laughed Wulfstane.

"My lord Prince," said Dexius, "be not cozened by these tales for children."

Tallux stood. Both he and Sut surveyed the gathering, sweeping it with their glance. "You speak of my distant kin. The high lord of Amor can hurl many thousands spears against his foes, and the magecraft of golden elves knows no equal. My people of old had dealings with them." He gave a short bow and reseated himself, placing a hand on Sut's massive head.

Exeter also stood and scowled at the war hound and his master. "Be that as it may, I have yet to see any carrack of elves or magical warriors near to our shores, unless they masqueraded as waterfowl, and the ship a spouting whale. As for elvin knights on winged steeds, 'twould take better than a year's time ere any kingdom so distant could aid us. By then this palace may be a smoking ruin, and we ourselves twittering ghosts."

"I feel like one already," muttered Gault.

"Speak no such words, my Prince," said Tertullion.

"Kör is our true foe as he has ever been," said Exeter. "The Dream Throne laughs while we cast about after red-eyed witchmen from beyond the iron gate. Let us march now over White Throat after first making our city strong. We cannot rely on hill men and mountain dwarves to hold our northern borders."

"Who will protect our sea flanks?" asked the weathered naval captain. "If the ambassadors of Kör have made truce with Farseps, we cannot hope to defend our ports 'gainst such numbers combined. The unholy priests of Kör are said to call up monsters from the deep to aid them in battle. Only two days ago I saw a dam goose with her goslings dead on the shoreline, rocking in a tidal pool. An ill omen!" The man signed himself in warding.

"Nonsense," replied Exeter flatly. "The main thrust will come from the northern heights as it has before. Kör cannot bring large numbers of his creatures to the southern coast without great loss and discord."

"But what numbers?" demanded Wulfstane. "The King's borderers now instruct us to prepare to meet the assault of twelve Snakes when, as squire at his father's side, he himself nearly foundered against one such legion? Who can believe these impossible tales?"

"Do so we must. Or perish," replied Gault softly.

"I fear, gentlemen," said Tertullion, "that the true threat is something altogether different. I sense that Kör moves only to consolidate gains made against us from beyond our ken—an awakening of a more ancient and powerful evil than even he."

"So are we back to spellcastings and dweomorcraft?" asked Dexius as he gripped his head in studied exacerbation. "Sending a half-dozen troublemakers to their doom, deserved or not, cannot aid our cause. Would not their swords be best employed in defense of the realm? Can we not command them hence?"

"Brave swords to light dark places," whispered Gault.

"The clergy is behind this!" shouted Wulfstane.

"Why are *they* not here?" Buthard's bull neck swelled, and his voice grew thick. "Is sitting in some dark cell and telling prayer beads of more import than the safety of the kingdom?"

"My Prince," asked Dexius, "does not Apieron hold royal appointment? Bequeathed Windhover, I believe, in guardianship by your father?"

"Renegade ranger, son of a foreign barbarian. Given the most isolated place the Crown could dream up," cried Wulfstane. "I should know, his fief is nigh my own."

"He patrols darksome woods and befriends swamp demons," pronounced Buthard.

Gault shook his auburn hair. *How had it come to this?* "Come now, his father was a hero of this realm, and voice of his god."

Buthard was undeterred. "His wife is a fey of the East, perhaps she bewitched your noble father into granting favor to Apieron?"

"And my son's pledgemen spend as much time watching over this unwholesome neighbor as they do obeying the edicts of the King."

Gault searched their faces. Buthard's meaty visage was happily smug. He was chewing on something. Wulfstane's was fiercely intense, and Exeter's eyes were bright over his beak-like nose. "It is well that your clan holds the King's will in such high import, Wulfstane of Wicklow. The Crown may have need of these obedient bondsmen," said Gault dryly.

Dexius stood again and patted down the empty air with the skilled gestures of a master orator. "My Prince speaks the true feelings that fill his heart, for he is young and brave. However it were well he harken to men more experienced than he. Men who see that Apieron's wild-woods spirits have the power to corrupt the ears of the unwary. How much more so those who eagerly listen?"

"I agree and more." Wulfstane flung back his yellow cloak as if overheated in the cool chamber. "Apieron of Windhover keeps to his backcountry witches and fairy friends in defiance of his liege. Did not the summons bid him hither? If he heeds not the call to arms, you—Exeter, seneschal of the realm—must declare his land and title forfeit! He must present himself before the King, his sworn lord, for judgment."

Tertullion pointed at Wulfstane and his son. "Remember, there is wisdom in the lonely places. Men of the cities and walled estates were well to remember the voice of the gods. Who would deny the Sybil of the Holy Oracle?"

"The men of cities and these modern lords of the great estates have outgrown your peasant totems," declared Dexius. "Are we not masters of a great realm? Whilst the rustic folk guide a plowshare, we guide the destiny of the West. The King knows this and does not oppose us. Nay, *we* are Ilycrium. My liege, the wise prince pays heed to men of wisdom when some say his own succession is in doubt."

Gault rocked back. *What ate at the man so?* Gault suppressed his anger and tried to think. To chasten the minister before this gathering would serve little purpose, and he was certain that Dexius but voiced the sentiments of many.

Tertullion remained standing. His voice shook. "My ears ache from these insolent mouthings! Have you forgotten Apieron's noble father? Xistus Farsinger heard the summons of his god when he came down from the wilderness. It was not known if he was of lofty station, for when he came unto the vale of Ilycrium with the song of the *ever young* on his lips and beheld the cities of the West for the first time, he spoke not the common tongue of men. Even so, his song was mighty, and he is reckoned among the great bards of yore.

"His deeds were many, not least of which was to lead the forest peoples onto the snow plains to the succor of our king's mighty sire. I see faces here whose great grandsires and fathers' fathers fought in the battle as freshly bearded youths." When he had had his say, Tertullion sat down with a thump of his stave and glared about him.

"Ancient history, Seer," called Buthard. "Xistus Farsinger was just another foreign barbarian, and his son be no better."

Tallux restrained himself no longer and strode to the fore, Sut close behind, growling deep in his throat. "Aye and for that, know you that the fiefdom of Windhover was earned in the ranks. None of your scented furs or gentlemen's hunts for my lord Apieron. He was with the King's rangers when we froze on the bloody ice at White Throat, and boiled on the sands of Agge in service to the King. I hope what this gathering lacks in wit, they gain in luck, for I can abide here no longer." With a nod to Gault and Tertullion, the elf swept from the room.

"Very impressive testimonials, my Prince," said Exeter. "There remains the law of the land."

"I say again," said Wulfstane, "he who answers not the summons to arms, forfeits lands and title."

"I may be young and merely prince, not king, yet *I* say to Dexius and to you, Exeter, Seneschal of the Realm, no royal summons has been made. Apieron is not gainsaid."

"If not now, when?" shouted Buthard. He was echoed by not a few others.

Gault looked from face to face, then said heavily, "By the authority of my father, King of Ilycrium, all barons and nobles have thirty days from this day to present themselves and evidences of armed retainers for disposal as suits the Crown."

"So be it," said Exeter gravely.

Gault stood, and stony faced, strode from the chamber, eyes straight ahead. Tertullion also departed, leaning heavily on his stick and muttering into his beard. Others followed, not quite certain of what they had learned but filled with apprehension. In a matter of minutes, the room was empty save Dexius, who remained at table with Wulfstane and his son. The latter propped his feet upon the table and reclined with a grin, picking at his horse-like teeth. The two warlords raised silver flagons in tandem.

"And so, Dexius, with one sweep of your adroit brush, we are rid of clan Farsinger, the mummeries of the toothless mountain hag at Sea Bridge, and a gaggle of renegade elf-lovers. We salute you." Father and son drank deeply, red wine staining their mouths, lending them the aspect of red-muzzled wolves. Dexuis's dark eyes were lit with strange lights as he raised his jeweled goblet in silence.

Tallux approached the barracks of the Royal Scouts. The pennant bearing their ensign hung limp in the humidity. From this place he could see the harbor of Sway, where the river Swaywynde grew sluggish as it entered the bay and abutted against the never-ending surf of the western ocean. Two buttressing hills of stone flanked either side of the port. Sisters they were called, standing as faithful sentinels in the mist-gray light of late afternoon. Each rose precipitously from the water and was, in effect, an island. Their landward sides and tops were graced with a covering of olive-drab scrub that resisted salt-laden gusts by virtue of fibrous roots, strong as steel cables and anchored deep within the rock. On their seaward faces, beetling cliffs rose shear and black to battle the weight of the crashing surf. Long rollers of the ponderous Ess, born many leagues out to sea, would have rendered this section of coast untenable to any deep-drafted vessels were it not for the Sisters. Thus men fondly named them Haskald the Bounteous, and Idvil—Maiden Protectress.

A rain-filled cloud, dark and low laden, was scudding into the harbor, and already the farthest of the harbor twins was covered by its veil. Soon the air would grow cool, and a gentle shower cleanse the buildings of the capital. Tallux knew that by the time the rain wrack broke over land, day would have westered upon the sea, but he would not be present to see, having traversed miles on a mission that spoke plainly to him.

He, Tallux of Greenwolde, was not given to rash impulse. When his course was chosen, however, he acted swift and sure. It was evident that his friend Apieron Farsinger had need for news of the forces arrayed against him. And more so, allies in the trials he took upon himself.

Tallux considered his options. He might follow his old comrade by the path that led to Windhover and Melónie, who by her gentle magics might be able to contact her husband. But he feared the gamble, for any delay would render Apieron's party uncatchable. Nay! He and Sut would strike a direct course. A mighty journey for the finest ranger of the West, across fen and forest and the nigh impassable cliffs and ravines of the Gorganj that lie above Duskbridge.

He entered the barracks. Previously a stable, it was a low-slung structure nestled inauspiciously into the leeward side of the hill upon which stood the palace Swaymeet, and hidden from the canals and streets of the capital city. The barracks' current occupants were well pleased with its isolation from the governing complex. Such conveniences were worth the occasional jests of garrison soldiers and regular infantry about the tendency of horse scouts to be found in the company of their mounts rather than that of their fellow armsmen. Moreover, such jibes were seldom directed to the face of a border runner, for they were a grim lot, sun-scarred and shriven of the petty distractions of common soldiery by lives of hard toil and dire risks oft faced alone. They looked to themselves and recked not of higher authority, civilian or military, save the king to which each had sworn oath of the body.

It took Tallux only minutes to gather his gear and find Windstrong, his favorite mount. The gelding nuzzled him warmly in greeting and nickered with impatience to be off on any venture with the elf ranger and Sut, who was an ever-vigilant guardian to him.

"Go you now to find him?" asked a voice.

Tallux wheeled and beheld Gault, a look of grave concern writ on the young man's features. Tallux swung onto the gelding's back. "If not I, who else?" He swung the gelding's head and urged him to a cantor across the bailey and to a sheltered trail that would skirt the city into greenlands away from prying eyes.

"Go with the blessing of the Goddess of Fortune, my friend," spoke Gault to the retreating form.

The Prince sat heavily on a farrier's bench and stared into slanting beams of sunlight that lit gaps in wooden slats and crisscrossed the straw dust of the stable's interior. Again he envied Apieron, fortunate in the steadfast friends he had made, all so very different, yet much the same for the light of honor that lit each face as he remembered. Who would be *his* beacon in days of darkness? It seemed they departed him, one by one.

The Narrows were a ramshackle part of the city Sway, where every dwelling was an extension of a prior structure expanded ever upward in years of piled-on growth, like a snake that never sheds its skin. For all this, it was no slum but a neighborhood in which street vendors cried their wares by day and merry taverns spilled forth light and song to cheer cool evenings. Skilled laborers of every sort lived here, and the people of the Narrows felt they were the true heart of Sway.

It was three hours past midnight's bell. The last bar lamps dimmed and shutters bolted as even the heartiest revelers wended their way home. Adestes entered an alleyway and eyed the close-packed buildings appreciatively. Coarse-dressed woodwork, buttressed with rotting stonework, supplied most of their structure. Swathed in black, Adestes had enacted his strongest spell-cloak for this night's work in the very capital of the enemy. His footfalls were silent as he gathered his tools, an old bucket heavy with a dark liquid, flint, and tinder. Had anyone cared to peer into the narrow back way, they would have seen and heard nothing, although a keen nose might have discerned acrid fumes as he thoroughly doused the dwellings on either side. The tinder kindled in his cupped hand, illuminating his palm with a shell-like glow, much like a votive. Malesh pondered. With this gifting he would transform ordinary peasants, senseless and unheeding, into holy sleepers, sent by his offering on a journey into sacred Evernight. How fortunate they were!

The flame took to the sides of the buildings as if it belonged. Soon its hungry whisper became a crackling roar. Malesh gave a shout and a wind whipped the blaze, blowing the leaping inferno across the alley to engulf the entire block. The night was lit with a crimson glare shot with bursts of green and yellow as various combustibles were hurled aloft to fall like living flares.

Malesh stumbled into a large byway as his alley exploded behind. He ignored the few dazed stragglers who crawled to lie gasping upon their stomachs. He cocked his head, hand to ear, and was rewarded by a welter of screaming that rose and fell, lacing the bellowing cacophony of the fire in hideous symphony. He fell to his knees with arms uplifted and head thrown back, dark locks flowing. His face was lit by the garish light, and a rapture welled in him. Malesh vented a choked scream of ecstasy …

After a time, Adestes recovered his senses, and looked around. The fire had moved mostly beyond his area, leaving small burnings scattered amongst the blackened skeletons of the neighborhood. He heard the distant tumult of the holocaust's expanding front. Gathering himself, Adestes Malgrim, Körs Malesh, slipped into the night.

Chapter 14

Amor: South Gate

"Hoy, hold there!"

Several hands reached up to grasp the halter of the rather peevish horse and the legs of its rider, who was an elf of many years and clad in drab garb, a wearied cast to his face. "Is it customary for the small-folk of Amor to detain a messenger of the Ring of Six?" The rider had made as of to ride without slowing through the mighty thorn gate of south Amor. Two sturdy gnome fighters detained him while a dozen more patrolled atop inner walls of the living palisade.

"Well, well. What have we here?" boomed a stocky gnome. An axe handle was visible above his back, and in his green hat was struck a yellow feather. "Telig Foesplitter, I be, but that's Telig Gate Warden to you."

"What we have," replied the elf testily, "—er, gnome lord, is one with urgent business southward and no time for silly, small-people antics."

The gravel-voiced gnome was quick to answer. "Yer time is now *my* time, Mr. Elf. I be responsible for what goes 'out' of Amor as much as what goes 'in', as well as the lives of four hundred gnome warriors and their kin. And *you* arrive without word from yer elvish masters."

At this, the gnomes atop the gate prepared to shut the thorn-covered valves. Once its gears were engaged, a dozen oxen could not have slowed it. Telig felt irately justified in his detention of this low-ranking elvin messenger. Something about him, however, intrigued the experienced clan leader.

The elf hunched his narrow shoulders in submission before responding in meek tones. "What would it take to clear up this matter? Payment of a toll, perhaps?"

Telig did not respond as the elf flipped him a largish green gem, but of altogether poor quality. Telig's expert gaze regarded it in his hand and then fixed the elf with a cocked eyebrow and a frown. The elf smiled in sympathetic acknowledgment of the inferior nature of the jewel. "It is the best I have."

That smirk triggered an odd suspicion in the gnome warden's mind. On an impulse he again held the green gem before his eye, and gasped when he beheld the rider. Through its foggy perspective, the transformation was astonishing, for the drab rider was replaced by a splendid golden elf in the prime of his youthful power. His silky tabor bore the crest of the lord of the forest, such as worn exclusively by Galor's household. Where the sleeves and skirt of his mail showed, they were of flowing scintillant silver, like the skin of a trout. The tired nag was now a magnificent gray mare, whose tack alone would shame even the jewel-hungry gnome kings of Bel-Nár.

In the eighty years Telig had held his post, never were his encounters with this one dull. With a disgusted wave, he motioned his soldiers aside, although they stared as if he had suddenly sprouted a dwarfen beard. The rider favored him with an elaborate flourish before spurring south like a zephyr destined for the lands of men.

"What?" Telig grated at the sentries as he pocketed the now worthless gem. He must remember to prepare something special for Giliad Galdarion the next time they met. Very special.

The girl mustered her best attempt at a smile for the glowering man who sat at table. His calloused hand bruised the soft skin of her upper arm.

"I said 'more ale', you!"

Bruhil nodded fearfully. She broke away to fill more jacks for the rough-looking men. By their garb, they looked to be some sort of soldier and appeared much traveled. How she wished Father were back! But he would be gone hours on his errands this long, long afternoon. "It won't be a bother," he had said. "Give them beer and don't burn the meat pie." Yet just last week he had run off a pack of beggars not much different from these, save for the soldier's gear. It seemed to her the only people to frequent the little hostel were ruffians and no-pay-ems. These three had arrived but an hour hence and had flashed coin enough, now she wished they would up and leave, pay or not. Bruhil walked from the table, her ears burning with their coarse jests. She could hear one of them poking the tabletop with his belt knife.

Her coworker, Gundli, a gangly youth of seventeen who was (as usual) too self-absorbed to note her plight as he drew the ales. The only other patrons in the Tossled Hop were two drovers and a silent figure who sat by the guttering hearth, completely swathed in his dark cloak, though the day was mild and the shutters opened. He had taken his meal with only a single draught and could well be asleep for all she knew.

"Horse piss, you little trollop!" said the man who had grabbed her, spraying her apron with beer spittle. He slammed down his mug.

"Like as not, she's 'a given us the cheap draw since we've 'ad a few," added his fellow, who sported only two lower teeth that protruded onto his upper lip like a yellow-tusked boar.

Bruhil searched their faces for any compassion as she blushed above her kirtle and nervously tucked back a reddish lock beneath her bonnet to keep from crying. The knife carver stopped his fiddling to eye her dangerously. "I didna mean to, sir … sirs! I mean, it's the same beer an' all—"

"You callin' me a liar?" demanded the spitter.

"No, sir, I—"

"Our silver's as good as yers, or theirs." The spitter pointed at the drovers who promptly set down a fistful of small coin and made swift exit. "Now whatayer goin' to do 'bout it?" The man was shouting. He stood.

"I dunna know, I—"

He grasped her by the shoulders and spun her face-first across the table. She felt her smock tear across the back, and the edge of the eating board knocked the breath from her. The knife man leapt up as tankards and victuals were tossed, further soiling her. The third ruffian, still seated, clapped his meaty paws on her forearms with a guffaw, smashing her breasts painfully against the rough wood. Bruhil turned her head to Gundli. The boy simply stared, astonished to find himself in the real world.

"Now, little bird, we'll be seein' whether ye can sing for us." The spitter kicked her legs apart. Bruhil wanted to reason with the men, but her mouth produced only a squeaky babble. The responding chortles were cruel.

The knife wielder suddenly cursed and threw his blade at a figure charging from the fire. A word was shouted, and the missile hurtled back into the thrower's face, who recoiled and flopped to the floorboards with the hilt protruding from his eye.

Bruhil glimpsed a silver swirl as a glittering blade buried itself into the tabletop before her, severing tusk-face's arms at the elbows. She screamed wildly and tore the disembodied hands from her own. After a paralyzing moment of shock, tusk-face screamed and cavorted wildly about the room, his waving stumps spurting blood like twin hoses before he collapsed over the doorway.

Beer-spitter released the girl at the first blow and backpedaled from the table, producing a wicked-looking saber and a small, spiked buckler. The other figure stood tall beside Bruhil. Cloak thrown back, his armor rippled like argent scales, and his hair was gold.

"Leave off, bugger!" snarled beer-spitter. "The wench is unharmed, an' them blokes is dead enough." Despite his bravado, the ruffian's face was pallid, and his sword tip trembled.

The tall warrior left his sword where it lay, gently pushing the girl aside. "But," said the melodious voice, "you are *not.*"

With a yell, beer-spitter charged and swung a mighty horizontal blow with his saber. The air in front of the warrior rippled. He reached up to grasp the handle of his own sword. It intersected the steel sabre with a screeching flash, breaking it in two. The mercenary threw his hilt at the warrior's face and spun to leap and tuck out of the open casement. His scrambling fall and footsteps receded quickly.

The warrior turned to the girl. "You let him go!" she sobbed, incredulous.

"I do not care to slay the man."

"Milord, he'll only come back to find me, or my pa."

The stranger regarded the frantic girl. Recently come into womanhood, she was no doubt at that awkward age when the world treated her as an adult, but who had yet the temperament of a child. He sighed and stooped to retrieve a shard from the mercenary's blade. He passed his hand over the fragment, speaking an arcane language. The jagged fragment flew out of the window like an arrow from the string. He turned back to study the girl. She was grooming herself as best she might. The bar boy had collapsed in a faint.

"It is done."

He placed a smallish gold coin of curious design on the table. Her hazel eyes met his depthless orbs with a pleading look that, without words, spoke of many things. "In all my life," she stammered, "never have I seen such horrible things, or, a man like you."

"Things have changed, for the worse. Stay close to your father."

"But you? —"

"Am no one." He departed.

Later that evening, a small but elaborately constructed tent was perched, nigh invisibly, under the eaves of a willow that topped a merry brook. The illumination of a censure lit its depths like that of a glowing coal. Within, the warrior reclined on pillows and costly fabrics and sipped wine to a wistful tinkling music without apparent source. He was melancholy, having been forced to unmake three lives for no reason other than sheer human stupidity. For all his valor, Giliad Galdarion knew that the gift of creation should never be undone without grave purpose. Though magnificently skilled at weapons and yet mightier mage-craft, he did not relish power for power's sake, which was not the tradition of elvin dweomer casters, nor was it the way of his master, Galor Galdarion, Lord of Amor.

Giliad sighed, shaking his golden locks. He clapped his hands— and lo! A spirit-woman of flawless perfection coalesced below the platinum censure. She flowed toward him as he leaned back and smiled. *Enough of the drollery of human settlements and rough tavern meals.* He would keep to himself, perhaps even ride the night through, knowing that Ingold would bear him swift beyond normal reckoning through the kingdom of Ilycrium, yet not *too* swiftly, for he needed time to readjust to the dreary world outside Elvinhome.

The elemental nymph came to him wearing only the smile of long recognition and desire … and dark, floor-length hair that shimmered and twisted with her moods, here concealing, there revealing, always enticing.

"Tomorrow," he said to no one in particular. The small light dimmed.

JOURNEY TO FOSLEGEN

The five companions were well rested and better fed at temple, and so made good time their first day. Long and heart wrenching the decision to undertake their dire mission was, yet once their course determined (Rudolph Mellor notwithstanding), they desired to proceed with as much expediency as possible. For Apieron, he deemed it true only as far as Windhover. He could nearly taste Melónie's lips, and it might be he would find reason to tarry there.

By afternoon the travelers were outside of the circle of hills that were sentry to the valley of the Spear Goddess, and a brisk canter took them cross-country past a series of low rolling meadows peopled by herd boys and flocks of goats. As the sun dropped westward, warm slanting rays marked singles, then clumps of hardwoods, outliers of an open forest. The companions slowed their mounts to a walk as the shadows of dusk lengthened.

Apieron was the first to spy the strange campsite. "Hsst, there is a peaked tent ahead that glows as if lit within."

Soon all were able to discern the ornate tent, decorated with silks of every color that wrapped it round in merry stripes. At its peak floated a thin pennant bearing devices indiscernible in the gathering darkness. A smell of rich meats and baked bread permeated the evening air, and a soft light emanated from the structure. Jamello thought he spied a fleeting feminine silhouette.

Henlee urged Bump forward, peering intensely at the structure, trying to pierce the near darkness. "What do you think, Apieron? It smells of magic."

"Perhaps it is a trap. Or illusion," said Jamello.

Xephard's stallion drifted in front of the others. "I know not what it portends, but there is no deception here."

"Perhaps they would like to share their provender," said Henlee, fingering the haft of Maul.

"Perhaps," answered Apieron. "Mayhap it is best to avoid it entirely—"

"Egads," sounded a melodious voice behind them. Jamello, who was closest, nearly jumped out of his skin. "This is more rare than a total alignment of every star in the heavens. All four of these sages are correct at once."

They rounded to regard a tall figure on the back trail. A voluminous mantle swathed its shoulders, and they dimly perceived a sheathed longsword, dependent from the slim waist, although a faint nimbus of gold obscured the being's exact features. The bright sheen of body armor flashed silver in the dying light.

Recognition crossed Henlee's features. He groaned. Dismounting, Apieron emitted a small gasp of astonishment and pleasure, and was joined by Xephard, who smiled broadly.

They now clearly perceived a resplendent elf clad in mail like a sparkling fish and girt with longsword in rich scabbard. "How fortuitous!" said he, bowing to Xephard and clasping Apieron's forearms warmly. The elf's face shined with the youthful beauty of his race, and if it held any age, it was perhaps around his laughing, cerulean eyes. His hair was gold and cascaded onto a cloth of silver mantle. Apieron remarked to himself again the similarity with Galor Galdarion, although this new elf was broader at the shoulder and garbed as a swordsman.

Apieron gestured to Jamello and Turpin. "Gentleman, I give you Giliad, warrior mage of Amor. He is kin to Galor and high in the counsels of that kingdom."

The elf sketched a graceful bow. "Pretty elves," muttered Henlee, none too softly, "it's always the pretty elves."

Giliad laughed again and included Henlee in a more eloquent flourish. "And again to you, Lord Henlee of the high hills, or famous mounds of orcin skulls, or what-have-you. Last time we met, you were teaching young Apieron to fight like a dwarf. I see that he carries a bow of yew, javelins, and a sword. Have dwarven tactics changed so much in one short decade?"

"He can throw an axe, elf," growled Henlee, looking Giliad up and down. "If he's got a good target."

"Indeed he can," added Xephard, still grinning. "I for one, however, would rather stand behind him."

"The training was, er, difficult," replied the dwarf while stroking his beard thoughtfully. "I'm afraid our friend is by blood a runner and spearman, but he at least knows not to cut himself with the axe." All joined in easy laughter as they repaired to Giliad's clearing once Turpin and Giliad exchanged greetings, as well as Jamello. The golden elf set before them a feast more suited to a fine eatery than a campsite, and the mage's elfin wine soon had saddle-sore muscles relaxed and tongues loosened. The dwarf alone drank from a skin that had been filled with the temple's finest.

"Porcelain plates?" mouthed Jamello quietly to Apieron, who merely smiled and shrugged.

Turpin cleared his throat. "When the fire mirror was closed, I thought of saying 'Help that arrives too late is no help at all.'"

"Aye, if your lady knew of your coming to meet us," added Henlee, "why not say so? Ahh," he touched his temple as if in sudden comprehension, "the mystery of the magical forest."

Giliad regarded him with small favor. "Firstly, Dorclai of Amor does not dissemble, hairy dog. What lies in her mind I know not. Secondly, spell links are not always secure from prying mages, and third, who says I came to aid *you*?"

"You came all this way to feed us?" snickered Henlee.

"I told you the food was an illusion!" shouted Jamello, causing the dwarf to choke on a dainty he was nibbling.

"Silence, fool," said Turpin. "It is a very great journey hence from Amor, even for a mage. Shall we not see what our host came hither to say?"

Giliad nodded to the cleric, appearing somewhat mollified. "Despite my present misgivings on the level of intelligence of the members of this expedition," he shot the dwarf and Jamello a pointed look, "I do intend to aid you on your quest. You need my help more than one might have guessed!"

"Of course I am delighted," said Apieron, "as are we all. By intercepting us here, I presume you've garnered our intent to proceed to Windhover and thereby directly into the Wyrnde."

Giliad nodded in affirmation. "The gateway there is as good as any other. Long ago I pondered these things with Galor, who had special interests in such … *windows*."

"Then why is *he* not here?" queried the dwarf.

"Did you not ask that of Dorclai? Whatever answer she has given you is better than any surmise of mine. Indeed, I was en route hither when I gather your fire mirror was summoned."

"Slippier than a Farsepian money lender," muttered the dwarf.

"I know a little of the Lord Galor," said Jamello, "and if you are his friend or pupil, perhaps you can say what we might expect beyond the Hel Gate."

Xephard stirred at the thief's open speech but was reassured by Turpin. "Rest easy, my son. We remain near to your matron's valley, and I do not sense we are spied upon."

"We have ridden eight leagues from the center of the valley," cautioned Apieron.

"Yet the knave's question is moot," countered Turpin. "I would fain hear what an elvin sage says on the subject."

"Thank you," said Jamello.

"I am no sage, but a warrior and a wielder of certain magics," replied Giliad. "To Jamello, I say that I am both friend and pupil to Galor Galdarion, and will answer you as best I can."

Giliad took a long draught of a burgundy-hued wine from his crystal goblet. "It is the *athelos*, the hidden way, for which we search. Once there, we will enter an abscess within Mother Earth where an ancient evil, once banished, contrives to reform. The keys to Her release walk our earth. The oracles of the wise have seen Her aspect. It is terrible!"

"If She is so powerful, why do not the gods again assemble to do battle?" asked Jamello.

"The gods of light do not act so. Once creation was made, they do not remake it, and to oppose Her directly, they would be forced to do so. Their will is wrought by heroes; elves and mortals who shine briefly with the light of the Divine."

"I feel anything but divine," said Jamello.

"Aye," agreed Apieron softly.

"See yon paladin." Giliad raised his goblet at Xephard. "His sect is ancient; they are defenders of the land who predate king and country and therefore earn the distrust of the ruling castes. Such as they remember the time of darkness when man was but a flickering flame, weak before the winds of darkness."

The elf's words, more eloquent than Cynthia's and Turpin's, or even those of the Oracle, sounded with awful truth in Apieron's ear. He could not speak.

"What of your Lord Galor?" cried Jamello. "Surely he can better face Her than we."

Giliad stared a moment at Apieron before replying. "I wish that fate on none here (even the dwarf). It is my hope another way can be found. And Galor, perhaps in wielding principal powers would bring deadly attentions on us all, thus rendering stealth for naught."

"Oh," said Jamello quietly. Apieron was crestfallen.

"Knowledge is strength," said Turpin.

Sensing their mood, Xephard held his sword up to the light. "Leitus, then, must be very wise." The laughter that ensued seemed strained, but none voiced it.

"With that, I bid you good night." Giliad rose and escorted them from his tent. "Leave the dishes," he called before snapping shut the flaps. A light flared briefly within the silken walls before the interior went dark. "Always the pretty elves," said Henlee as they bedded down.

Though they were well within the King's borders, watches were chosen for the night, and the young thief was to have first shift. As the camp quieted into an easy rhythm of light snores and shiftings of the beasts, he would have sworn on his thief's tattoo, had any been awake to hear, that he discerned a lilting feminine laughter emanating from Giliad's silken pavilion. He sighed and turned back to the night and the mirror-bright stars overhead.

X'fel the demon star glimmered red as it rose over the world.

In the morning, the companions noted the magnificent tent had disappeared along with all evidences of their evening meal. They never saw that construction again. Under the shadow of the willow where the tent stood, they beheld a mare shimmering whitely in the shadows.

"Her name is Ingold," said Giliad.

She did not look up at their intrusion, her attentions fixed on a clump of tall clover. Her trappings were jeweled, and she was a large beast, yet fine-boned next to Axylus, with a long neck and prancing hooves that promised speed and maneuverability. The eyes of the horse were blue and gleamed with an unnatural intelligence. The party busied themselves in preparation for the day's travel as Jamello patted the elfin steed's hindquarters, wistfully eyeing her rich tack. He nearly fainted when coarse whiskers and a rough voice brushed his ear.

"He's a mage, boy," whispered Henlee. "Such do not take well to sneaky thieves fingering their precious baubles."

Jamello shot a look at the sparkling gems in the dwarf's beard and gave a sinister smile. Henlee's hand reflexively moved to touch the treasures woven therein. Triumphantly Jamello moved to join the others as the dwarf's dark stare followed him. Giliad's mare wheeled her proud neck to regard Henlee with a suspicious eye.

"Aw shut up," he said, stomping off to jerk at Bump's more humble gear. The burro shot him an unpleasant look.

"Sluggards, the day is getting older, and so am I! Besides, I tire of these dainty woods." He swung up and headed into the trees without glancing back. The others mounted quickly to follow. Soon their passing was obscured by the lush greenery of Foslegen in springtime.

The next day was spent in easy discourse, the six companions learning well the mannerisms of the other. The trail was not difficult and the weather mild, sunny although cool in the evenings, with grass and water aplenty for the mounts. By the third day from Hyllae, they struck the road to Windhover where a village without name had sprung up once a strong lord took the keep for his home.

As they rode, Apieron's mind returned time and again to Melónie, fervently clinging to each memory, cherishing its flavor against the dangers that lay ahead. He thought of his wife's garden, and while he preferred the surprises to be found among the untamed growths of forest and marsh on the fringes of his estate, Melónie delighted in her ordered plots of herbs and foodstuffs. He pictured her in the enclave planted on the banks of a small stream he had diverted for her pleasure. The brook splashed merrily around boulders, comfortable for stepping or sitting, and was shaded for half the day by water-loving dogwoods whose boughs were heavy with white blossoms in spring.

Oft he would be drawn to her private place by the sound of her singing, and she had placed soft bells in the trees. There he might find her on hands and knees, dirty to the elbows and blowing disobedient strands of her magnificent dark mane that would suffer no confinement by scarf or hat. He would simply stand to watch and listen, inhaling the scents of clinging jasmine and white clustered narcissus.

How happy she seemed. A small noise or perhaps a shadow would cause her to turn and smile in welcome. *And her eyes shined!* He would draw her into his arms, ignoring her protests that her hands were filthy or her hair awry. By the great Archer, he would return to her with love and honor. Devils and demon spawn be damned forever! They would not keep him from his love.

Chapter 15

Windhover

A pieron dismounted, giving over his reins to Henlee that he might walk a wheat field that lay betwixt thorp and the keep proper. The others kept to a worn track, avoiding the fragile growth. A light breeze tossed the supple blades a foot over the rich earth. After spring's kiss, the plants were growing rapidly and cattle had long since been fenced away from the tender shoots. In moist, low places, the crop was pale emerald, and on sunny ridges, a rich green blue. Apicron plucked a stem and sucked out the pith. No head of spiked kernels graced the maturing plants, but he could already taste the mildly acrid flavor of raw grain. He raised his eyes as a greater wind swept the wheat into waves of undulant unison.

"What a beautiful thing we have made in this place, she and I."

The party's sojourn at Windhover was brief. When Melónie saw the stern faces of the warriors who rode with Apieron, she burst into tears that were warm against his neck, yet gracious welcome she made for them, treating each with honor. To Xephard and Henlee, who Melónie knew well, she cast many searching looks, although in her moist, brown eyes they beheld a sorrow more poignant than words might frame. Despite this, she buoyed Apieron, knowing he was in some way chosen, that his road back to her lay beyond the darkness.

What few possessions the companions consumed during their swift journey from Lampus were restocked. In addition, each was given a supply of iron rations consisting of cakes of marrow rolled with dried meat. There were also hardtack biscuits, meat jerked with berries, skins of wine and water, and strings of salted eels. Henlee procured a small but heavy cask of beer that Bump eyed dubiously. He also spent some hours sequestered with Bagwart, though he did not reveal what they were about.

Apieron thought to delay their departure, perhaps to await news of events in the capital. He wished to walk his forest in secret to seek out Vergessen and perhaps try his luck again with a second sojourn at Findlán. Turpin vigorously opposed any repose beyond a single night.

"We stand astride a nexus of doom that is both vast and fragile." The cleric's tenor was painfully authoritarian. "It trembles with tension, the slightest nudge might send events roiling away in one direction or the other in uncontrollable cascade. We must away 'ere some mishap undue all we intend!"

No argument was forthcoming, and so a rather solemn meal was taken before guests were led to their lodgings for a final evening in the comfort of a bed. Once alone, Apieron and Melónie spoke the night through of small things and quaint memories they cherished. When at last their desire for converse fled, Melónie bestrode Apieron's hips and leaned forward. Her sable hair cascaded over him like the fabric of whispering nightfall. Her scent enveloped him, holding him in a place he never wanted to leave.

"Sweet, gentle prison," he murmured.

Melónie moaned when his calloused hands found her. The

feel of her warm, yielding skin burned indelible images in his mind. Softly, with consummate feeling, he caressed her face and swollen lips. Again she moaned and kissed fervently at his fingers and inner wrist. She swayed above him, dragging her breasts against him.

Apieron grasped the back of her neck. Entwining a handful of tresses, he pulled her hard onto him. Melónie arched her back and cried out as they rocked back and forth. Apieron guided her movements with hands in hair and on hip. Slowly at first, then with gathering momentum, they thrust together and Apieron groaned aloud as their movements rode a wild crescendo, neither knowing where one body stopped and the other began. Melónie's yelping cries became one continuous undulant wail.

With a climactic heave Apieron shouted, and they fell together in triumph. Melónie collapsed upon her husband's sweat-beaded chest as his hands lovingly stroked her heaving back and flanks. He felt her limp form, overheated but too drained and too comfortable to roll away.

"So," she mused, "this is what my sisters meant by *woman's rapture*." Apieron had no words, choked with love and protectiveness towards her, and shame of the inner flaw that led him away. She kissed his cheek, tasting the salt of a tear amidst the sweat of their lovemaking.

Dawn found the others assembled before the gate. Apieron was last to come. Melónie's waterfall chattered, and they could see her standing high atop the gate tower, swathed against morning's chill next to Duner. The ever-buoyant Xephard called out, "I tell you this, milady, never will Xephard of the Valley leave the field without Apieron at my side."

Melónie's soft words of thanks were lost in the stamping and snorting of the beasts. Apieron met her eyes a long moment, then they were off through the palisade gate and across the clear cut

onto a forest trail bearing east that was more or less direct to what
Apieron hoped would be high ground through the Wyrnde. The
mournful clang of a bell followed their hoof beats into a cloaking
mist as they rode from sight.

SWAYMEET

Belagund Candor sat in his empty throne room as had been his
wont of late, to brood on the fortunes of house and kingdom.
From the angle of his seat he could see the ascent of a large, orange
moon, its gibbous light cut into myriad angles by the faceted
crystals of the room's tall windows. If he remained awake, he
knew he would see the rise of the new star that men named X'fel,
the Demon. His curse echoed softly.

Perhaps the common people were correct. Did not the roots of
wisdom spring from deep soil? And those of his realm's peasantry
were deep indeed. They had seen the ebb and flow of overlords,
good and bad, and new names had been put to old boundaries
for people who needed them not. Yet they toiled on, asking only
freedom to live without oppression or cruelty. Belagund hoped he
had provided at least that, mayhap a little more. He was old, but
his eyes could see, and his ears hear the growing tide of troubles
that rose to engulf his land.

How he longed to sink into bright memories of his days of
strength and glory, but they would not come. He was restless
against these rumblings of evil.

And so he had ordered spies sent forth and magics of knowing
wrought to no avail. No one source or culprit emerged that could
be dealt with in proper, upright fashion. The King felt tired, a soul
weariness that could not be assuaged by rest or comfort. Surely
an old warrior who had carved out a kingdom as a youth at his
father's side, who had spent a lifetime consolidating by spear and

Enter, Knight

pact, deserved a final peace? He had lived a life of honor, betraying not his wife or his subjects.

Belagund sighed aloud at the memory of her open, smiling face with its noble brow and wayward brown tresses. Oh, Candice! It was ten years gone since she was laid to rest, not living to see her son grown to manhood. Gault was a good boy, rapidly maturing into a strong man, although as yet unblooded.

Courtiers murmured when the King adopted to heir his wife's son by prior marriage, and that to a powerful duke, himself a rival who made claim to the throne. And Ilycrium under his yoke would not have been the enlightened land she was today. Nor would Sway be her gem, rather in its place a forbidding northern bastion that loomed atop its high mountain like some pitiless eagle. The *Roc*. Ye gods, what a battle that had been!

"By the gauge of one's enemies is one judged," murmured Candor. Who was his enemy now? Was it Kör? If so, why the unrest upon Ilycrium's western shores so far from the snow-swept passes onto Kör land? And so he came here often, when all was still, to wait alone with a sense of foreboding for he knew not what.

A faint scrabbling sounded in the corridor beyond the furthest arch. "Is that you, Edrain?" Silence. It was just as well the pageboy was not there; the stripling meant well, but his clumsy attentions only made the old king feel more frail. "And by the seven souls, I am worn thin."

Bel Candor pursed his lips as with a sour taste. It was bitter ill fortune to have his silver years tarnished by this malaise. "X'fel, what doom moves you?" His chin nodded, and his eyes began to close. The moon was in high ascent, smaller yet no less bright as the dog star crested the eastern horizon. Reddish light glinted through the window as if in mockery.

The King slept on. If he heard the weird piping in his dreams, he gave no sign of rousing. His breathing quickened then sank to the ebb of a deeper trance. A small figure approached the throne, cautiously and with absolute silence. Above the collar of the King's evening robes, Tizil reached a misshapen but dexterous hand to Belagund's exposed skin. His chanting came soft and close to the monarch's ear. The lisping words were lost in a subtler tempo that changed in time to match the pulse of Belagund's heart, visible in the veins of his thin neck. Slender claws delved slowly to grasp the thick blue vessel and pulled rhythmically. The hand sank deeper. Bel Candor did not stir from his coma.

Tizil beheld the vein's course onto greater vessels above the heart and down into the pumping chamber itself. His chant became a squeal of delight as he tugged mightily and ripped free the vena cava from its heart root. Blood boiled in Belagund's chest, and his eyes flew open for a single moment of horrified awareness. The imp's foul breath caressed his face. The King's eyes filled with blood, then he slumped into death.

Tizil shrieked with laughter and threw the clotted rope across the chamber. Greedy talons sought the King's soft belly and spread the fat across the floor in a grizzly blanket. Shouts and a stomping rush of feet sounded in the far corridor. Torches flared as spell wards roused the guard. Too late. The fluttering light revealed the bloody maw of the demonoid dripping over its obscene banquet.

Tizil screamed and leapt out of the nearest window, shattering crystal panes in a small explosion. Chamber guards gawked, staring in horror and dismay.

"What befalls?" shouted Tertullion, coming in great wrath. He beheld the King.

Two soldiers rushed to the window ledge and looked down and out. They saw nothing. Tizil's skin-like wings made the faintest rustling as they propelled him in gleeful arc over the slumbering city, out past the river and towards the Pleven Deep. Blacker than night, he was less than a shadow lost in darkness.

Whilst guards yelled and ran about in consternation, Tertullion stood and wept over what remained of his king and friend. He bent stiffly to gather Belagund's gold fillet from the bloody flags. He lifted it gently and spoke a word of cleansing before secreting it near his breast. The royal crown of Ilycrium would not serve as trophy for monster or rebel lord while he, Tertullion, Seer Magnus of Ilycrium, yet lived.

Chapter 16

The Wyrnde

Two settings of the sun found the adventurers far from Windhover yet still within the lands of which Apieron was nominally overload. The companions led their horses through dense strands of tall fir whose shaded boles never witnessed the full light of day. Strange mosses and fungi draped rotting logs and tumbledown boulders under the spreading fronds of deep forest ferns of every sort. Ever bearing south and east saw the tangled growth of ancient trees eventually give way to an open under-canopy whence the mounts might be ridden at times. Here were white-flowering cornel and dark-swathed alder, useful for tanning. Jamello was amazed to discover that his expensive boots likely acquired their black sheen from an extract of such a common growth.

"I paid twenty silver pennies for bark juice?"

"From whence did you think the color came?" inquired Henlee. "A maroon calf?"

"Your surprise is understandable," said Apieron. "See here are far more expensive growths." He indicated a yard-high plant topped with a crimson flower.

"Foxglove, whose bloom men call Dead Men's Bells. And there is branching hemlock that foresters name Kex."

"Many are the guild thieves of Bestrand who would pay true silver for such a garden as yours."

"Indeed?" Apieron pointed to a shadowed patch against a gnarled oak. "Then let them bring gold for deadly nightshade, blooming white with innocence. Its berries are green. Soon they will blacken as the poison fills them."

"Weapons of the coward … and treacherous women," intoned Xephard.

"Never mind that!" cried Jamello. "Through the trees, a menhir."

They gathered around a standing stone that stood alone in a grassy clearing. It was the only object that bore the hand of man since their departure. "Probably dragged from the shelf we just passed," said Henlee.

"Five hundred paces?" exclaimed Jamello. "To what purpose?"

"Let us read the writing," said Xephard as he traced the symbols with a thick finger. He gave up. "This slanted light is dim for me."

Coming to his side, Jamello looked at him quizzically. Although late afternoon, the sky was clear and held much light. He read the runes aloud, as they were cut in the common tongue of men and surprisingly fresh:

> *In the name of the Candor kings, here is set line*
> *of border of Ilycrium, Bride of the West.*
> *Apieron of Windhover*

"Nice rock," said Henlee sincerely.

Apieron laughed heartily. "I had help."

"I have heard it said," added Giliad, his clear voice brimming with mirth, "ever the clan of Farsinger owns more skill than they show." Apieron accepted the accolades but did not share aloud the image that came to mind of straining centaurs, strong as draft horses, setting the ten-foot cippus aright. The labor had not been free—the thirst of such creatures was not easily assuaged.

They camped under the stone. Despite his jest, Apieron was uneasy. Once their journey took them past the boundary, he left behind home and crown. How he wished a king's messenger would somehow arrive, bearing direct command from his liege to return. How much simpler a place in the coming war would be. What would he say to such a herald? Apieron asked himself this over and over as sleep took him.

Dawn of the third day from Windhover led the companions into new territory. The ground in spots grew soft, and they forced reluctant steeds past clumps of fragrant honeysuckle and acres of clover studded with wild strawberry. Soon they encountered standing water where dozens of noisy croakers splashed the water as the horses drew near. The pools grew larger and more numerous, and the riders oft had to dismount. In one such bog, they traversed a mat of bushy water plants with thick, flabby roots that oozed a white gum when crushed, coating their boots and the horses to the fetlock with a resin that dried orange. Apieron bade them stop once on the far bank to scrape the crust free.

"Touch it not, for it is water dropwort. It causes convulsions."

"Methinks I like your forest garden less by the day," spake Turpin who, being heavy, had soaked his leathers to the thighs. All agreed, for the day was hot and tiring, and before long Apieron called a well-received halt. "Under yonder stand of hardwood is a cache I built. A cool place for a rest and a snack, and nearby is clean water where we can refill our skins."

Jamello gazed at the smallish size of the trees, some barely taller than he could reach, though many had buds that would yield nut or fruit. "How is it that one who lives in a forest plants trees?"

Xephard and Henlee hoisted aside a fallen log that lay against a rocky spur, hidden amidst the hardwoods. "Obviously, he thusly marks his cache," said Xephard, eager to score a win against the thief after the reading incident.

"More wise than that," added Giliad, "here is hickory, straight ash, and tensile yew for weapons. Walnut and pecan, persimmon and chestnut for eating ... and the game they will attract in winter."

"Enough talk of trees." Henlee dropped into the rocky hole he had revealed. Soon all followed suit to discover a wide, shallow cave with circulating air and a floor of comfortably worn pebbles that indicated this was once a watercourse ten feet below the forest floor.

The companions unslung their gear while Apieron checked that all was undisturbed. Here he had placed a small store of weapons and provisions, and there was even a stone oven. He showed them the secret signs used by his old regiment of scouts to denote such a place, usually chosen near a clean water supply and coign of vantage for observation of the surrounding terrain. There were also two routes of escape.

"By Bardhest's red balls, how many of these do you have?" demanded Henlee.

"Between Tallux and I, we know of some hundreds across the kingdom. But I have had time to build only five or six since coming here."

"Great gods!" said Jamello. "You are such cheery fellows. What if there is no war?"

"See yon badge of horse over green that Apieron wears?" instructed Xephard. "To be scout for the king means to be ever vigilant. The man who sleeps light is not surprised in the night."

"We are on the edge of civilized lands," said Apieron. "My king charged me with improvement of this border. I have done my best."

"Of course these holes of Apieron's are naught compared to the mighty stores of Templars," stated Xephard. Turpin attended this closely but said nothing. "That aside," added the paladin between large bites of Apieron's hard tack and generous gulps of water, "there is *always* war with the enemies of man. The 'peace' folks speak of is merely a pause in the struggle."

Henlee wagged a thick finger in Jamello's direction. "Preparation, thief, is the mother of good fortune."

"An unhappy state of affairs," said Giliad. "However, too often true of your quarrelsome breeds."

"My good mage, fell things stir that lay for eons hidden," stated Turpin. "Even the long-lived elves of your line cannot hope to outlast the age of darkness should it come."

"What exactly that means, we are here to discover," Gilead replied.

"Exactly what *what* means?" asked Jamello.

Turpin answered, "Whether or not young Apieron here can influence events enough to avert a never-ending holocaust of war amongst our lands and homes."

"And what *that* means, boy," said Henlee, "is that we are heading for a fight. Are you ready?"

"I am ready to sleep tonight in this nice, dry cave."

Apieron smiled apologetically. "We cannot stay. The horses would leave enough spoor outside to mark the entrance for months to come."

"Oh, that's grand!" cried Jamello. "Why do we bother with them anyway?"

Henlee chuckled darkly. "Ask him in a hundred miles."

Apieron explained, "This forest does not go on forever. Even now we pass into the Wyrnde. Thence to a broken country heaved up out of the swamp that, with our burdens, would be well nigh impassible without the mounts."

Turpin made a sign. "Duskbridge, land of the Starfall."

"Oh," said Jamello.

They hoisted themselves and restored the area as well as possible before leading their steeds to a tidy-looking stream with rounded, mossy banks and a stone-lined course. Following it a mile downstream, they made an early camp. Whilst others busied themselves, Jamello and Xephard walked upstream of the watering horses to fill skins and bathe a bit in the cool water. It was pleasant there.

Golden-red longfoil and skunk cabbage edged the watercourse. The rill was cool and clear. Jamello watched as Xephard ladled a dipperful of water over his head and back. The number of crisscross scars borne by the warrior amazed him. One would normally expect a few marks on the sword arm, yet Xephard's covered both his extremities, neck and torso. Most were pale, faded etches, but several were raised and pink.

Xephard noted Jamello eyeing him as he rubbed his chest dry with a rag. He playfully flexed and rotated for his audience of one. The display only infused more color into his skin, making the pale lines more visible. "Are you admiring my physique, trickster? Perhaps you contemplate the life of a shield-man and are looking for a role model?"

"Nay," said Jamello, shaking his head, "double nay. It seems painful! Your wounds look like the tangled roots of a tree that I once saw white and fresh after the trunk was overturned by a gust."

Jamello sucked his teeth a bit before continuing, "Only the dwarf carries such marks as you, and his wrinkly hide probably came anew with such as a bonus. The ways of such folk are strange. But tell me, warrior, whence came that puckered sign on your midriff with the matching wound on the back? It is at least three fingers. Surely that was a killing thrust?"

"You forget to whom you speak," said Xephard, not at all

displeased. "You also forget the healing power of the Goddess and her wise women." Xephard gazed at Jamello thoughtfully. "The story of these marks can wait, let me see your hands." Confused, Jamello held them out to the holy warrior, who turned them palms up to note the callouses on the right and also the thickened wrist on that side. "Ah, a fencer. We shall have to untrain you."

Jamello reflexively began to brag of his notoriety, then thought better of this tact and merely sputtered. The paladin continued, "I sense in you great stamina and quickness of mind and foot. These will not be enough." Xephard shouted, "To your guard, man!" He splashed from the water to retrieve his blade.

Jamello dropped into a classic swordsman's pose, his center of weight equally balanced over his legs, knees bent with the right cocked forward. His jeweled smallsword's slender tip spun lazy circles in the paladin's face. Jamello smirked. Xephard's broadsword, even wielded by that cabled wrist, could be no match for the blindingly quick fencing strikes he could launch against the unarmored knight.

Xephard made a slight advance. Confidently not bothering to parry the slower blade, Jamello sprang into a low forward lunge to score a quick touché against Xephard's front, meaning to tickle the paladin's scarred hide.

In a deceptively fast swipe with his empty left hand, Xephard slapped aside the narrow blade and contrived to clap his meaty hand over Jamello's right, crushing it over the smallsword's golden hilt. Though little taller than Jamello, Xephard extended his arm to simply lift the lighter man to dangle helplessly. Jamello made lurching attempts to draw his long poniard with his left. Xephard shook him like a dog with a rat until Jamello relented, dropping his sword to hang limply.

"So you see," said Xephard nonchalantly as he replaced the thief gently upon the turf, "we have much to accomplish."

Jamello harrumphed, retrieving his blade and smoothing his garments before affecting a dignified stroll back to the camp.

In the morning, Apieron made an offering to the little stream with a drop of wine from a skin and a prayer for guidance. The travelers elected to follow its course. Two days of dawn to dusk effort from Apieron's cache took them deep into the fastness that was the Wyrnde. Blisters within hot boots formed, ruptured, and formed again. The mounts became scratched and surly. Even for experienced outdoorsmen, the terrain was oft treacherous, and great care had to be taken of the horses that they not take a bone-wrenching misstep. Tussocks of rush grass disguised deep holes in the muck and, on occasion, a steed needed to be pulled free with ropes while sucking mud weighted each footstep. Despite his heavy load, Henlee's sturdy burro proved to be the least encumbered.

Wild boar could be heard thrashing in the denser bracken, passable only to their own kind, and none were ever seen. Brisk rain showers would spring up although the sky was bright, causing the companions to pause under broad-leafed sycamores while fat drops rattled the canopy overhead. The rain would clear as quick as it came, and the company would press on while the ground steamed in the sunlight. At times their watercourse would dive into the shadows of centuries-old trees indiscernible in type, so strangled were they with lichen and vine, and where the horses' hooves and the voices of the men were muffled as if stricken by the ever-gloom that lurked under darksome boles. Then the trees would open up, and the rickle would divide into multitudinous rivulets that branched crooked fingers across flat stands of waving grasses and horsetail. Occasionally tracts of this were beaten and trampled into muddy puddles by the rootings of the destructive tuskers. Always, however, their little stream gathered itself to continue determinedly on south and east, and so they followed.

On the sixth day, there was no path, for a great bog rose steadily around them. Afternoon's sun cast long shadows over the marshy woodlands. This day's toils had been the hottest of all, and the companions were oft forced to backtrack when their course always seemed to lead to a deepening pool. The day grew short, and they pushed hard, having no desire to halt for the night in green, standing water. Sweat lathered the horses while swarming flies bit anything that moved. Even Giliad's light-stepping mount had stockings of caked mud and eyed her master reproachfully.

Jamello pulled his leg free from a mucky hole and regarded his soiled boot with dismay. Henlee's dark face beamed from his perch atop Bump, the only animal capable of carrying a rider in the morass.

"I think I spy a doubloon in the water, Master Dwarf. Don't you wish to come down and help retrieve it?"

Henlee laughed and clucked to Bump, who promptly shook his mud-splattered hide like a soggy dog, further soiling the thief. Jamello cursed under his breath, silently vowing revenge on the ugly burro. As for his master … Jamello turned to the others in exacerbation.

"Why could we not have taken a path of less discomfort?"

"Know you any better?" growled Turpin, slapping at a particularly vicious deer fly behind his neck.

"Actually, I think Apieron drug us hither that he might spend one last night at Windhover," teased Xephard.

"And would *you* begrudge him that right, thief?" challenged Henlee of Jamello.

"Nay, not at all. I only wish he had made his home somewhere more pleasant!"

With that, Jamello slipped again, miring to the groin his already sodden breeches. A laugh was shared, Apieron more so than the others. "Well said, friend."

Jamello persisted, "Did not our learned mage hint at several of these Hel gates? Why not one in a nice dry city?"

"This is the path revealed to me by the Sybil."

"It is the correct path," added Turpin. He wiped sweat from his face. "In fact, young Jamello, others besides houseless peasants and ignorant beasts dwelt here. Long ago."

Jamello speared a bluebottle fly on a quirt. He flicked the creature away in disgust. "In this beastly swamp?"

Turpin nodded. "They were a mighty people before they faded. Have you heard of the Nessur?"

Giliad joined the discussion for the first time. "That was an evil race."

"They fell into dark worship," admitted Turpin. "Nonetheless, their works were many and their power far-reaching. Even now we tread the outliers of their great city."

"I sense no lingering evil here," said Xephard. He sounded disappointed.

"Well enough," said Apieron. "We have other worries. See? Our gay, little stream flows not at all. Something has dammed it ahead."

"I will be sad if that is true," said Giliad. "It has been a faithful guide."

"What of these Nessur, Lord Turpin?" asked Jamello. "Did they hoard much gold?"

The cleric shrugged. "Doubtless most is buried under a wasteland of ooze and muck. Of the temples and strange crypts they constructed, it is possible not all were destroyed. 'Twould be a matter of a simple spell or two to answer your question."

Giliad's gaze was hard to bear. "If the Wyrnde has taken that city, there let it remain until the world turns."

"Hear that, my lad?" said Henlee to Bump. "'Tis no treasure and more of this mere for the likes of you and me." The six companions pushed through a tangle of fronded oat grass, parting tall blades to behold what obstructed their freshet. A lake confronted them. Appearing no more than a foot or two deep, it was nonetheless broad and merged into flanking walls of impenetrable vegetation.

Across the water, broken and rotted trees stood drowned in the stagnant pool, their skeletal limbs thrust sadly against a brassy sky. Even the light of the sun seemed sluggish, as if it also waded with effort through the clinging mists that rose from the mere. Ahead and due east they beheld irregular berms of felled and stacked trees that stretched into the distance where nightfall gathered. Waterfowl thrummed overhead before crashing noisily into the water. Feeding fish made circling ripples in the lowering light. Otherwise all seemed quiescent. The thin hopes of a dreary day ebbed.

"I for one," groused Jamello, "cannot sleep while I float."

"Damned beaver," muttered Henlee.

Jamello's hands were on his hips. He kicked the water. "I am a liar. The *prince* of liars, but does *anyone* expect me to believe a beaver did this?"

Apieron's disheveled face had sprouted a dark beard, darker yet with dirt. He smiled. "Say not one beaver, but a clan of beavers, stretching back many generations to the first one that wandered into these parts."

"Damned beavers," amended Henlee.

Xephard secured a rope to Axylus's saddle horn and tossed it back to Apieron, who did the same and so on until a continuous line connected the horses. Giliad, who brought up the rear, held the loose end in his hand, for the blue-eyed elf steed would accept no such tether.

"Axylus shall lead us," declared Xephard. With a tug on the mighty charger's bridle, the procession advanced into the lake. They tried to keep to the larger hummocks of water grasses and cattails that dotted its surface, but even that was no guarantee of firm footing for heavy men and heavier steeds. Worse were the startling bursts of nesting birds or the thrashing of disturbed serpents that lay hid within denser growths. Yet the companions made steady progress, for the mighty thews of Axylus did not falter, nor did the steady hand that guided him. Slimed to the waist, the paladin pushed ahead with powerful, slashing strides.

At last the travelers came to soft-barked cypress, short and thick, with rings of protruding roots like ebony knuckles thrust into the morass. These cast deformed shadows before the party as the sun dropped westward. Hoary willows clustered atop drier patches, their branches falling to cover the loam around them with blankets of pale leaves. The travelers had nearly reached the largest grove of these, where they hoped for a dry camp on the easternmost rim of the lake, when Jamello spied a manlike shape, hunched in shadows below the willows. The thief gave a startled yell and the others gathered around and peered ahead, trying to pierce the gathering darkness.

After a time, the dwarf spoke. "I see nothing."

Giliad held up his hand for silence. He relaxed and motioned all clear.

"What was it that you saw?" asked Apieron.

"I don't know." Jamello searched his thoughts beyond humidity and flies and fatigue. "It was larger than a man but stooped. Its arms dragged the ground. It had a long, pale face and fled when it saw I marked it."

Apieron shared a look with Xephard, who said nothing. Wary was their advance to the copse where they sought for sign of the beast. They found nothing. Jamello continued to squint into darkling mists while the others saw to the mounts, wiping them dry before securing some and putting grain into nosebags. Henlee drew saddle and tack from Bump and tossed it to the ground.

"Like as not, it was some sort of woodland creature," grumbled the dwarf. "City boys don't know a muskrat from a mermaid."

Jamello answered crossly, "What are *you*, Henlee the swamp dwarf?"

"Sweat stings the eyes, and this cursed heat fogs my brain," huffed Turpin, who plopped down heavily to lean against a stump.

"But I saw its eyes. It seemed to … to flash a toothsome grin before it fled."

"Bah. Swamp demons and bogeymen! Our little popinjay saw a granddaddy possum or some such," persisted Henlee.

"Whatever it was," replied Apieron, "we must be more cautious. We are making enough noise to hold a parade." He winked at Jamello.

Camp was set for the night. Despite the appearance of Jamello's mysterious man-beast, all were glad to be at last on dry ground, for the sun did not linger and twilight overtook the willow grove. Gear was cleaned and the horses watered. Axylus and Ingold and the ill-tempered Bump were left untethered as was their norm.

Apieron and Xephard gathered drinking skins and left to search out clean water beyond the beaver dikes and to scout the easiest path beyond the tangled embankment of fallen wood. Henlee busied himself with collecting material for a fire and disappeared into the shadows, grumbling all the while about the lack of dry tinder to be had. Turpin heaved himself up and drew off Giliad to discuss various arcane preparations for the Hel Gate.

Jamello was left alone to watch over the baggage and mounts. After a time, he gave up his attempts to scan the darkness, removing his pack to lounge against a wide, smooth-barked willow. He stretched out his long legs and sighed, sadly making futile swipes at his clothing. It was then that disaster struck.

Jamello sat up to gawk at the hurtling shape that sprang

into the clearing. It paused, swiveling its long neck to regard the lone man and the horses, vulnerable in their hobbles. Jamello shouted and leapt to his feet, drawing his blades. But the creature was quicker yet and lunged toward the frantic steeds, talons outstretched to rend Apieron's mare, who was screaming in the horrible way that only a terrified equine can. Jamello saw vast shapes moving at great speed as Xephard's warhorse, followed closely by Ingold and Bump, plunged forward in wrathful tumult. Axylus intercepted the humanoid before it touched the mare and delivered a vicious two-kick to the attacker's torso.

Although larger than any two men combined, the water troll (for that is what it was) could not withstand the mighty stallion and was hurtled backward to land atop the pile of discarded packs. It grasped one at random and made to spring up just as Jamello sank his smallsword deep into the creature's flank. It bellowed and twisted away to swipe at the thief. Its flailing claw, larger than a wide-brimmed hat, was launched in a roundhouse blow at the thief's face. It met instead the point of Jamello's dirk and was impaled to the hilt.

The troll gave vent to a hideous yell, leapt over the baggage pile, and bounded off erratically into the swamp. The quick-reflexed thief drew and flung two long quirts into its backside as it fled. Each blow was punctuated by a yelp, but there was no sign that the monster was in any way impeded in its splashing progress. Henlee ran into the campsite, shouting and brandishing Maul, quickly followed by Giliad and Turpin. The animals were calmed by word and touch as the howling passage of the retreating troll faded into the nighted swamp.

Apieron and Xephard arrived breathless. They had run far in the darkness at the first signs of alarm. They found Jamello looking aghast at his one remaining dart. They noted his empty scabbards, and his thoughts were not hard to read. His stabbing sword and the accompanying dirk had jeweled crosspieces and grips of twisted gold. Their watered steel blades were crafted by the most acclaimed family of sword smiths in Bestrand, and had cost nearly a thousand golden plates. The matching blades were known by many who had encountered them as simply "the twins." Now they dangled impotently from the hide of a nameless beast.

Jamello wheeled and flourished his lone quirt to his comrades. Apieron repressed a relief-filled grin. He slapped Henlee hard on the back so that the dwarf's guffaw came out as a garumph.

"Anybody need a letter opener?" choked he.

Xephard laid a reassuring hand upon the quivering thief. "This is a good thing, very good. Now we'll outfit you properly, and with new weapons come new skills that I shall be honored to teach."

Turpin was not amused. "Where would he obtain new weapons? Our task brooks no delay."

"From the hoard of the Nessur."

Turpin looked thoughtfully at the paladin. Giliad spoke. "Such is not our mission. I did not leave glorious Amor and travel half the length of the northland to despoil the ruins of decrepit and vanquished human kings."

"Not vanquished by any foe among men, dwarves, or elves," responded Turpin. "Their civilization was lost to the trackless Wyrnde, sunk in the mire of their many sins." He quickly performed a warding in the air before him.

"My sword," moaned Jamello.

"Be that as it may," said Xephard, "our good cleric shall guide us to this lost city, so we may properly gird our boon companion from the many treasures that are said to reside there."

"My dirk!" groaned Jamello.

"I chafe at the delay," said Apieron, "but it *is* true that we cannot expect Jamello to proceed unarmed into the perilous zones we intend. We can expect no outpost whence we can buy or trade betwixt here and the Matog." At last Giliad bowed his concession, and they gathered to discuss their assault on the sunken city of the Nessur.

ILYCRIUM

An inland breeze bore a faint sea tang to Adestes Malgrim as he studied the settlement. Although only a backcountry thorp in comparison to the bustling capital he had quitted, the village of Templemore nonetheless boasted some three thousand souls and an importance to the realm far greater than the number of its occupants. For it was here that the skill resided to mass-produce fine chain links used to manufacture the steel cloth that was the armament for the army of western Ilycrium. The carefully guarded art was passed from father to son, master to journeyman to apprentice, such that the entire town labored in some way towards the drawing forth of gray metal wire to be coiled, clipped, and interlinked with countless others to assemble sheets of life-saving mesh.

Templemore's artisans placed broken pieces of soft iron into crucibles and added an exact proportion of moistened chips of the Pid tree. The mixture, topped with a covering of green leaves, was sealed over with clay and allowed to dry in the sun. When this process was complete, the ceramic vessels were placed in a furnace fueled by clinkers of hardwood and stoked to incandescent heat by the raising and lowering of bull's hide bellows. After some hours, the clay was broken and eggs of the improved metal were retrieved and pounded into bars at a lower temperature until their weight did not change with each reheating. Only then was it drawn into the steel wire that was the basic ingredient of the ingenious mesh. Such was the artistry of its production, that mail of this type was known throughout the lands as simply the gray cloth of Templemore.

Nightfall was nearly upon the thorpe, yet Adestes could see that much labor continued. No doubt enormous orders for product had been placed by those who knew war was inevitable, and the town's burghers no doubt already anticipated great profit. *That would change tonight!* But first, let the little people scurry a bit more.

Adestes retreated to the interior of a densely tangled hedgerow to make his preparations. The surrounding countryside was interlaced with the yards-thick dikes that were nearly impenetrable amalgams of living brush springing from packed detritus accumulated over countless generations of growth. A wind sighed in outer branches but could not penetrate the plant walls. Adestes' boot kicked free a clod of moss-covered loam.

"A fecund place, this bleeding earth."

Adestes settled to prepare his spell place, yet of more importance to him were the mental exercises required for a casting of this power. He recalled mighty dreams that had come when he was ensconced in the Pleven, and various fell beings had oft appeared to him thus.

Adestes Malgrim knelt in his shadowed bay and propelled himself into an inward trance, evoking those distant memories whilst aligning his physical energies until his entire will became an arrow of summoning. There could be no mistake, lest his spirit-self be shattered by the casting. Nor would there be a second chance should he otherwise fail, for it mayhap he never attempt such a spell again. Certainly every drop of blood he had spilt in the crimson weeks spent in this soft land would be offered—all except the exploding coin he had proffered that crippled beggar in Sway. Malesh smirked. That one he would keep for himself.

The soft winging of a low-flying owl rushed overhead. It

stalled, thrashing away from the unsettling magics of the little dell. Berating himself, Adestes reacquired his focus, seeing the bloodstained star in his vision though his eyes remained closed. It was heavy, sinister with portent, and tugged at something. He felt a yearning to explore the strange realms from whence it came. His spirit searched thither. The wind died and a raven croaked in the distance. A name came whispering to his lips.

"Ulfelion, servitor of Darkness. Come hither!"

Adestes gritted his teeth against the pain. A small part of him left. With a shout, energies geysered from him in tremendous surge, yet he remained connected to the magic. Mighty it was! And ever growing. He beheld a rupture in the night and sensed the presence beyond. He saw an unholy angel that traversed a lightless void, trailing nimbi of evil phosphorescence. Adestes stood in alarm but did not draw blade. A summoning this strong could not be of his doing alone, a dark deity pushed this Gorgon to him, magnified by Her will.

It came to him like a thunderbolt, streaming in reverse glory halos of visible hate, bent on its mission of destruction. Malesh narrowed his eyes, ever suspicious, and braced himself. With a soughing clap, the air before him was riven. It was there! A silent, vaguely manlike form hovering black against the lesser dark of the night. Wisps of unlight streamed behind it like mighty pinions, for even the starlight that illuminated the clearing could not reveal its features and was thrown back in twisted radiances of green and yellow. Adestes felt the pull of its vampiric nature.

He boldly fronted the spirit of unlife. "I know you," he gritted. Time dimmed as recollections of a shadow-veiled infancy stirred in him. The figure nodded its affirmation.

Adestes Malgrim, Kör's Malesh, pointed towards Templemore and stepped aside. The Gorgon flowed through the hedgerow, leaving a blackened hole where the organic substance was instantly withered. Adestes followed to behold Ulfelion's remorseless descent onto the village as it poured into each small dwelling, and all sound of life and laughter therein ceased.

As the unbeing made its passage, so did the quiet like a knife of silence. The lesser sounds of bird and insect, dog and fowl, were not spared—likewise absorbed by the null without call or yelp to mark their passing. Even the glow of fires set for cooking or the comforts of warmth and light were doused into the still darkness of death.

Adestes was riveted by the tableau. In a mere span of minutes, the once thriving town was plunged into the stasis of a charnel house. He knew he might live for many years hereafter and never again witness the purity of such absolute destruction. When he slew, he partook in the intensity of the life riven. These villagers each held but little personal power to shield them, and yet the smotheringly swift passage of such numbers as this into unlife was astounding.

Adestes regarded the vampire, now risen into the upper airs … a thing of bloated menace, and knew his business with this dread spirit was only begun.

Adestes summoned his stallion. His mission to outworn Ilycrium was complete, but he could not savor the moment. He felt robbed. The mighty spirit was gone, hidden against the nighted vault. Where it hied he cared not.

Adestes paced his horse before the town that lay motionless in streaming moonlight. Not bothering to loot or burn, he focused on the greater task ahead. He spurred the stallion into the night, south and east to Duskbridge!

Chapter 17

Nessur

Hard scratches and sodden clothing were the reward for breasting the last of the beaver dikes. Apieron and Xephard attached a pull harness of twisted hemp, three fingers thick, to Axlyus's breast strap. With much advice from Henlee, they selected the correct logs to tug free and thereby return the stream into its natural bed.

The six travelers and their mounts turned rightward and paused to gaze out on the vastness that was the southern Wyrnde. The spread of marsh before them was brown and cheerless. Swamp trees and sullen meres dotted the peat, as well as odd-shaped hummocks that were covered by thorny vines and strange, twisted trees that sank mighty roots into the bog like hungry eels. The party slogged southward. Passing close by one of the mounds, they discovered it to be a rotted dome, tumulus of some structure buried in bygone ages by the encroaching marsh. Birds cried forlornly and the sun was thin behind low clouds.

"This place is dreary, Sir Cleric," said Henlee. "I think our elf friend must have been right, and this sky is like milk. Eh, Bump?" A day passed, then another. Xephard's packhorse was bitten by a viper. From its frothing convulsions, surcease was granted by a merciful stroke. Axylus stomped the serpent into bloody ruin.

"If I had not lost the twins," Jamello apologized weakly, half-poisoned himself by the plethora of insect bites that dotted his slender frame.

"Once we set our lucky stream free of the wood dam," said Apieron, "I felt in my heart that we should follow its guidance the easterly route. Instead we are here. Where in all this ruin (for surely these gray mounds are forgotten towers and temples) shall we search for a weapon that has not been corroded by the marsh air?"

"The Nessur were a warlike people, and worshipers of many demons from times beyond myth," answered Turpin. "'Tis said by historians they entombed their royal dead with many artifacts to last until they be summoned from the long sleep to serve again dark masters."

"Like Apieron said, how do we know these weapons have not been ruined?" said Henlee.

Turpin shrugged. "Doubtless some have, but long was Nessur's lore in the arts of preserving themselves and their houses 'gainst the decays of time."

"I like not disturbing the resting places of the dead," growled the dwarf. "Lead on anyhow, holy man. I've had a bellyful of the thief's whining about his lost toys."

"While you debated," sighed Giliad, "I cast a spell of seeking, and there is entry to an atriolum such as you describe under yonder crest. It drew my spell powerfully as a lodestone. Beyond that, I cannot say what lies within."

"Leave that to me," answered Turpin excitedly. "It is as I thought, this land is rife with treasures."

"Like your ring, Master?" inquired Jamello.

"Your eyes are quick, my son," said the cleric. He pondered his answer. "Nay, Nessur did not forge it."

Giliad waved his impatience. The companions gazed at the area he indicated. Crawling vapors and hazes of sweet-rot made distances difficult to gauge. The ground appeared to rise somewhat to a ridgeline, deep green with trees against the drab sky. Apieron eyed the tableau carefully. "We have come far in little time. If we do as well tomorrow, we can arrive at Giliad's escarpment by noon. Let us camp here for the evening."

"Name not any feature of this unclean land after me!" said the elf.

During the night, the wind switched from the south. It brought faint smells of the distant sea. Even so, the mists did not clear and the humid air was, if anything, more close the next day. Apieron's predictions proved accurate, and an hour before midday found them before a tree-studded upslope that appeared to end a mile distant in an overgrown edge. One could faintly hear the deep murmur of a river running.

Apieron spoke. "I believe beyond that tree line we will find a cliff that shields the channel of a river known as the Arda. I have never heard tell of any who have traveled its course to see whence it comes and where it goes. Just as I have never heard of anyone come to this place."

"That river is properly known as Ardus Nessur," said Turpin. "And in its day was the water highway hereabouts. It is said it overflowed its banks and thus drowned the city."

"It's back in them now," said Henlee, "and I am grateful for that."

"Like as not it took its origin from an ancient swamp," said Apieron, "although not as large as this one. My guess is that eventually it finds its way to mighty Ess far to the south."

"Rivers don't climb up hills," said Henlee. "That channel must have been constructed."

"There will be no river journey today," said Giliad. "The entrance to yon lichgate is somewhere nigh the foot of the slope."

They spread out to search for an entry, soon finding that what they had perceived to be a builded wall atop the ridge was in fact a fallen ziggurat, its great height strewn into the waste like the bones of a stricken titan. Their work was not easy, for the ruins were covered in dense bracken. There were many thorns, some grown into mighty trees that wielded six-inch spikes. Eventually Jamello gave a call. He pointed excitedly to a hole below the fallen tower. Hand axes and Maul chopped a gap. Bump pulled aside a thick curtain of thorn brush and Jamello was lowered with a lantern. He shouted for the others to follow. Giliad placed spells of warding upon the steeds and whispered a few quiet words to Ingold.

The party anchored a second rope. One by one, they scaled down to join the thief in what appeared to be a gateless and broad entryway that once formed a base for the fallen tower. It was flanked by low columns that must have looked out over the city from its slight prominence. In places there was standing water, and every surface was swathed in molds and slime. Apieron lowered himself last, being most agile after the thief. Once he joined the others, Jamello again took up the lead, tapping lightly with a thin stave he had whittled, occasionally stopping to listen or press gloved hands against wall or floor. Next in line came Apieron and Xephard, who were followed by the spell-casters. Henlee stumped alone in the rear. The way below the tower and into the hill was straight but long. Soon the companions bore torches that crackled in the moist darkness. Jamello sounded a low exclamation, and the others gathered round to view a portion of the wall that he scraped clean of shaggy fungus, revealing a flowing script carved into the stone with no little artistry.

"I cannot cipher these characters," said Xephard. Henlee chortled softly. The paladin continued on, unperturbed, "Surely evil things are written here."

"This is no speech of elves or that of sad mankind that is spoken today," replied Giliad.

Turpin's eyes gleamed as he mouthed strange words under his breath, excitedly following the meaning within. "Would we could see more of this! What little I have read tells me that we have come upon a great funerary and a mighty temple of their faith. Only the greatest of kings would be here entombed."

Turpin brandished his ringed hand. "I could cleanse it with fire, but I fear the message would be lost."

"I don't feel like spending my afternoon scraping mold," said Henlee.

"Nor I," echoed Jamello.

Giliad held forth his white hands and beckoned to the ground. He made a pushing motion while speaking a short command. A thick mist arose to fill the passage. It blew ahead to disappear beyond their lights. Eyes watered and skin prickled, and they beheld its wake left the walls gleaming.

Henlee whistled, "I'm not sure I'm glad you cleaned the walls, Master Elf."

Xephard's voice was thick. "It is as I thought. One does not need to be a paladin of the Lampus to sense the depravity that once resided in this place."

Xephard drew Leitus but did not lift shield from his back. Jamello resumed his place ahead and now bore his last quirt in his ready right hand, the walking stick in his left. Henlee held Maul before him. Apieron pulled forth a throwing javelin from a sling, and even Turpin grasped his long mace yet held it loose as he eagerly read the rune signs revealed as they walked. Only Giliad left his longsword in its silver sheath, although his face was stern as he gazed about him with flinty eyes.

There appeared to be a graying of the blackness ahead, and they discovered that the tunnel debouched into an enormous vaulted chamber. Here the roots of one of the swamp giants they had seen above penetrated the structure, sinking its questing, man-thick feelers through the very stone, thereby allowing a smattering of light to penetrate the last passage. One by one the companions doused their brands as Jamello knelt at the entry and signaled back that he detected no trap or creature.

The wall glyphing ceased at the chamber entrance, yet its final depiction was the greatest. On wall, ceiling, and floor was carved a mighty demon who stood before a throned dais whereon sat a king of the Nessur, a bared and gold-hilted sword across his lap. The companions trod with itching feet over a portion of the image and into the room beyond. Passing a receding wall, they stepped down onto a square platform of cool, black stone.

The ceiling was vaulted with massive buttresses cut from the living rock, and the companions saw that they stood in an underground amphitheater with stone benches and canopies stretching around to dark recesses. To the left and ahead were steps to rows of seats beyond a low barrier. There was also a hallway that continued opposite the entry, although it appeared to be smaller. To the right lurked an open space, its low ceiling set with squat pillars blackened with soot. How deep this second chamber lurked they could not discern. A feeling of uneasiness filled Apieron and the others as they stared. Here the elf's spell had not penetrated, and vapors clung to the begrimed floors.

"A temple of the elder gods," breathed Turpin.

"Yes," said Giliad. "Worshipers of the Lost Ones gathered here to enact their grisly cabal."

"What sort of ritual?" asked Apieron slowly, swallowing a slow foreboding.

"Behold," cried Giliad. "See as does an elf lord of Amor."

The eyes of human and dwarf were unveiled. A seething multitude of wraithlike forms crowded in audience from the seats, and the platform around the companions teemed with flitting images of man and beast rended and slain over the course of generations in a vast and bloody orgy of torture and spectacle. Individual torments were interspersed with gladiatorial combats and wholesale slaughter, yet in the end it was always death that earned the adulations of the ghost crowd. Often the victims would be dismembered and consumed in macabre rites of mass cannibalism. Afterward, portions of their bodies would be preserved for totems. Apieron now noted that the floor was not of black stone, but stained so by blood.

They stood silent for a moment. Xephard gave vent to a roar and leapt amongst the stands, slashing wildly. The images parted before his shining sword and reformed without hurt. Apieron and Henlee rushed to his side but did not strike out.

"Put up your weapon, Son of Light," said Turpin. "What you behold are but impotent ghosts of another age. Here they are doomed to reenact endlessly the dramas of the dark gods they worshipped."

"The snake-writing resumes on the farther passage," called Jamello.

"I will cast another incantation to cleanse and decipher it," said Giliad wearily.

"No need," answered Turpin, who strode forward. "There is enough here to understand plainly." He waved his arm to the right. "Away yonder is a temple. I sense no power resides there any longer. Ahead lies the crypt of a great king. The writings speak of a curse to befall any who come to violate its secrets."

Giliad dispersed his enchantment. The wraiths faded from view, but Apieron felt he could yet perceive their faint whisperings. The companions passed cautiously into the farther passage and found that it continued in the original direction of its opposite. Torches were relit, and the explorers crept on for what Apieron reckoned to be a half mile until the way was blocked. A round portal was closed against them. It was of crumbling stone, coated with a rind of white lime. The walls of the passage were streaked with the same.

Henlee tapped softly against it with Maul and listened. A broad smile lit the dwarf's features. He drew back and blasted his heavy weapon through the water-weakened rock, jerking it back with a spray of dust and pebbles. Beyond the hole they beheld a tree-shrouded terrace, and the weak light that streamed within seemed bright as a seashore day. Henlee punched through the remainder of the door with his gauntleted fist and kicked out the lower margins with his iron-shod boots.

They stepped outside, breathing deep, each glad to be gone from the noisome airs of the temple. They stood on a broad shelf. Above them on both sides, a ravine rose in sheer walls to tree-lined heights above. There was a fallen portico of sorts that once led to a landing. Of its bridge there remained only a few feet. The far cliff face was thick with hanging vines, and they could discern no entry beyond a narrow ledge.

Below lay the Arda, churning slowly in its canyon. Several of the great, smooth-barked trees had grown far out over the chasm in search of light. Twisted roots anchored them into the seamed rock. There were also many holes in the face of the ravine, more so in the depths nigh the water, but several only feet below.

"Poor construction," complained the dwarf, "else we could simply stroll across this creek to Giliad's crypt." The mage shot him a dark look.

Apieron gazed at the narrow strip of sky above. The feeling of elation at leaving the temple departed. They stood outside, yet the towering rock face and its cloak of trees made him feel as if they were still within an enclosed structure.

"We spent more time in that hole than I hoped."

"Bump will be getting angry with me for leaving him so long," said Henlee. "How are the steeds doing, elf?"

Giliad made an exaggerated gesture of placing a well-manicured hand to a cocked ear. "Ingold assures me all is well. She and her brothers are happy that it is we who must crawl about in this foul drink like worms, and not they. However I am sad to inform you, she also says Bump is still the ugliest burro in seven realms."

"I wonder what lives in those holes?" asked Jamello.

"Climb down and find out," suggested Henlee. "I'll hold the rope."

"Maybe Giliad can fly across and attach a line," said Jamello. "It appears no more than fifty feet."

"I think not," replied the elf archly.

Apieron smiled at Xephard. "How fast do you think we can fell one of these leaning trees?"

"Best idea you've had all day," said Henlee.

He tossed his throwing axe to Apieron and grasped Maul in both hands. The wood was green and the work hard with such tools, however the three fighters soon chopped through the base of a medium-sized tree. It fell with a groaning crunch such that its shaggy top was wedged against the entangled far wall at an acceptable angle. A rope was tied to Jamello. He tested the new bridge and found it sound. After a time and many objections from the dwarf (who insisted that he was no spider to dangle thus), they gathered on the smaller outcrop of the far side.

A profusion of hanging vines, some as thick as a man's wrist, obscured the rocks' faces. These were hacked asunder to reveal a second stone portal. They broached it easily and came into a downsloping passage that apparently had been flooded many times in the past and was filled with a cloying, unwholesome air. Torches were blown to life again, and the companions pushed into the darkness. Here there were no painted pictorials, but horrific writings again scrolled the walls, bolder than before and dizzying to focus on. None needed spells of seeing to discern the intent written thereon. Spells of warding and death.

How far they pressed under the escarpment, only the dwarf perhaps could guess. Side chambers and small rooms were bypassed as these appeared to be only work areas used in the construction of the great barrow and of little importance. It was an hour of cautious advance until they reached the central funerium, where their torches betrayed a large crypt.

Jamello halted and stared behind the light beam of his small shutter-lantern. When he did not signal the party for "safe" or "danger," they advanced to his side to view what so perplexed the experienced thief.

On the ceiling of the entry was inscribed in jet and gold leaf, a dozen feet high, the likeness of the tyrant who had ruled the city and its far-flung empire for seven decades. Jamello looked to Giliad, who nodded and waved weakly to the others that no traps lingered. When they stepped forward, an enchantment of the chamber propelled them into a waking dream, in which they witnessed the history of its occupants and objects therein, and the black deeds that were done were many.

A foot of standing water filled the chamber, obscuring many things fallen into decay. Countless niches had been cut into the walls and the very ceiling. Chained therein were moldered bones of slaves, wives, children, and animals set to serve in death their god-prince as in life.

"Gawks, there must be ten thousand!" exclaimed Jamello. In ordered rows, wound around the perimeter, stood great terracotta figures—each bearing the individual likeness of a fierce warrior. Henlee kicked one over. It burst to reveal the remains of an armored soldier, garbed as if for battle.

"Bleghh," said the dwarf, coughing on the dust that rose from the corpse within. Artifacts of the buried king had been placed in profusion around the room. Chests of stone and rusted iron and tall, porcelain amphoras contained goods and wealth of every kind. There were even intact chariots with mummified horses slain in their tracings, but it was the central dais that captured their attention.

"By the mother of the potbellied god," breathed Jamello, "what is it?"

On the platform there was a rectangular slab of a clear crystalline substance, open from above. It contained a pink gelatinous bath in which reposed a man of sorts. A mighty figure he would have been if standing upright. He was bereft of all clothing and ornament, and of bodily hair. His skin was translucent, and faint pulsations could be seen along greenish veins and wet muscle beneath.

Turpin spoke. "I believe, sirs, that this is what is left (or is yet to be) of the principal of this tomb."

"He looks like a yolk-chick whose egg cracked too soon," muttered Henlee.

"This is no funerary vault, but a womb of evil," said Giliad. "Kill it."

Apieron looked up. "To strike an unarmed foe?"

Xephard drew Leitus. "If you will not, brother—"

"Wait!"

Jamello sprang to the dais and plunged both hands into the sarcophagus to retrieve that which he noticed at the man-creature's feet. It was a large, leathern bundle, oiled and tightly bound against the moisture. The thief strained as he lifted it from the bath.

"Look at him," intoned Turpin. "Nessur's evil king, he dreams the long sleep of the waiting dead."

Xephard plunged his sword into the figure's breast. The broth reddened as the buried king died his second death.

Gathering into sacks what they could quickly salvage from the chamber, the explorers departed the crypt as fast as they might. At length Jamello sat on the near outcrop and opened the bundle. Once he was satisfied that it posed no danger, he slowly unpeeled his find.

"Good boy!" congratulated Turpin, peering over his shoulder.

Jamello smiled as he withdrew two blades to flash in the light. The larger of the two was a longsword of the same length as his own, but that is where the similarity ended. Its cutting surface glistened below a thick sweep of proud steel with enough curve to strike from horseback, yet not enough to encumber a straight thrust. That gave onto a heavy golden grip with a thick bolster and a wide guard, all inlaid with small, red and yellow stones.

"Ah, at last a weapon that will stand up in the fray!" said Xephard. "I fancy even your troll would not have so easily escaped had you cleaved him with that."

Jamello examined the curiously wrought companion weapon. It was a double curved jambiya, fifteen inches of the same construction as the other. The undulant weave of watered steel along its blade shifted hypnotically with each turn of the wrist such that it never appeared to be exactly the same. Apieron patted him on the back. "The weapons of a king, my friend."

"Overlong have we stayed here," said Giliad. "The sun has abandoned this crack, and I do not wish to be trapped betwixt crypt and temple when she seeks her west-bower."

"Very true," said Apieron. "This place is foul enough whilst he shines."

"Lead us on and out, Sir Thief," said Xephard. The paladin shouldered a large sack, bulging with clinking metal. "I have brought a sampling of more practical gear, but it will have to wait until the dark temple lies behind us."

"And I saw a vase filled with golden ingots," said Henlee. "I left it there, for it was too heavy to carry." No one knew the dwarf to shirk from carrying such a treasure of any weight, yet none questioned his decision, for the taint they felt lay on the barrow, and the desire each felt to bear from it only what they must. The party prepared to recross their tree bridge when Jamello's shout echoed in the narrow canyon.

"There's that fucking troll!" Below and from an aperture in the cliff peered a malformed face. "I'm going down there to get the twins."

"That is unwise!" called Giliad and Turpin simultaneously. They glanced in brief consternation at the other before focusing their respective glares on the busy thief.

Brooking no argument, Jamello secured a rope to his waist with a second loop under his foot so that he could be lowered ready to fight. He passed the loose end to Xephard. The paladin grinned and quickly lowered Jamello twenty feet to hang before the tunnel mouth. Jamello peered into the dark burrow. "He's brave enough, at least where his wealth is concerned," commented Henlee. The dwarf shook his head although not without a small note of respect in his voice.

Giliad gave a cry of warning, and Apieron ran to grab Xephard's arm. An angry stirring came to them as many trolls poured from the myriad holes in the lower cliff. Some milled on the riverbank while others swarmed up the rock face, their gibbon-like limbs and long hands finding holds without difficulty. Xephard and Apieron gave Jamello's rope a mighty heave. Henlee leaned to lower an arm to the ascending thief. White-faced panic was writ on Jamello's face as he was hoisted up in mere seconds, yet before he could grasp Henlee's proffered hand, several things happened all at once.

A weighty impact struck Jamello's leg, and to his horror, he saw that the troll had leapt from its cave to catch his dangling foot in its filthy grasp while its other claw flailed about his chest and neck in an attempt to pierce his leather jerkin. The rope over Xephard's knee, sodden and abused in the swamp passage, snapped with a muffled *pop*. The thief began to plummet.

Henlee's hand shot out and grabbed Jamello's forearm. For a moment, dwarf, man, and troll paused, wondering what would happen next. Henlee grunted and with straining effort began to heave both thief and the snarling troll.

Apieron drew his bow and ran to the edge. He saw two dozen of the swamp trolls climbing rapidly toward the landing while half a hundred more began to set up a tremendous din. He swung the great arc about and snapped an arrow at close range, directly into the ugly face of the monster grasping Jamello. The cloth yard shaft, with its razor-barbed tip, embedded itself with either end protruding from the beast's head.

Xephard stood poised on the brink with Leitus raised to cleave the troll once it cleared the rim. It was a wasted gesture, as with a shriek it flung its limbs wide and fell free of Jamello to crash onto the rocky shore three hundred feet below. Without the extra weight, Henlee easily jerked Jamello to safety.

"Guess it was a different troll," breathed Jamello. The dwarf looked at him, a broad smile on his dark face.

"We have to leave—now!" shouted Apieron. "Quick! Onto the tree and into the tunnel."

Xephard took up post at the entrance while the others dashed inside, not bothering to relight torches. All fled except Giliad, who at the first sign of trouble had cast a quick incantation and flew to meet the attackers. Xephard laughed in appreciation as he saw the enraged elf right himself before the frothing beasts that uselessly flailed at the hovering mage.

Giliad raised his arms and shouted powerfully. The cliff face collapsed, hurling clinging trolls with tons of shattered rock into a free fall that crushed a score more when the frantic amalgam struck bottom. White plumes of the river were thrown up as if in anger.

Giliad rejoined the paladin and caught up the others who halted just beyond the first walkway. They raced across the open temple and proceeded with speed through the noisome airs and stagnant puddles of the last passage. Scrambling out of the hole beyond the temple's portal, they found the steeds, nervous but unmolested.

All six breathed deep, taking mouthfuls of water to cleanse themselves of the taste of the mausoleum. In doing so, they did not stop to rest but saw to the horses and swift preparations for departure in what little was left of the day.

Turpin spoke as he heaved up onto his stallion. "A mighty ruin, but grown foul for all that."

Apieron stood frowning as he stared out over the marsh. It was dotted with the overgrown hillocks that marked what remained of the once proud Nessur. "This is how Ilycrium shall appear in future years should we fail. A necropolis."

"Aye, a haunt fit only for ghosts and ghouls," growled Henlee.

Turpin spoke again. "Master Elf, let us scorch this place with cleansing fire."

Jamello interjected, "Fire will take in this bog?"

Turpin ignored him, a strange glint in his eyes. "You and I, mage. Let us summon holy flames to destroy this blasphemy." Giliad appeared withdrawn and did not reply.

"Why not use a *power* to—?"

"That is not the way of elves," replied Giliad softly. "This rotting pile was here ere you and I were born into this world, and shall remain after we are gone to dust. I will light no fire here." The elf pulled his hood close over his head. Turpin opened his mouth to protest but snapped it shut when Giliad turned Ingold's head onto the path of their exit journey.

The cleric stared a moment at the others, then smirked. He breathed onto the ring of heavy gold and sparkling rubies that he bore on his left hand, and pointed at the tunnel entry. The ring's gold turned red as arching flames shot forth in rhythmic waves until a conflagration engulfed the entire upslope. An inky smoke streamed from the entry until, with a rumbling crash, the embankment crumbled upon itself.

Turpin turned to go, a triumphant look upon his face. The dwarf eyed him thoughtfully. He wagged his beard and turned Bump to follow as rear guard. They made steady progress into the long shadows of the east while a great smudge was cast into the sky. Burnings set in the dense peat would smolder for many days. The companions pushed hard before halting for the night. Apieron reckoned that the detour south had ended their travel in that direction for the present, lest they pass below the realm of the Starfall. In the morn, they would walk to the rising sun.

Camp that night was fireless and glum as each was filled with unsettling thoughts after the trials of the necropolis. Xephard drew Jamello aside to reveal his plunder. A variety of armaments were spread out on the ground. With Xephard's guidance, Jamello chose a hunting sword as a secondary blade. It had a wide, cleaving tip that men call falchion. He also chose cuirass and heavy helm, but the thief did not display this last to the others.

The men ate sparingly of the provisions from Windhover and Apieron's cache. There appeared to be a great deal more swamp ahead, and doubtless wilder as ever more distant from settled lands they strayed. Henlee mused as he champed on a piece of biltong, "Sir Elf, why do you not again summon the enchanted feast of the night you joined us?"

"That would not be wise. We are not in dire straits, and to

flippantly make magic in unknown lands might invite attentions we do not desire."

Apieron, who knew Giliad as well as any, felt he detected otherwise in the elf's explanation. Rather an emotional reluctance, perhaps explained by the elf's erstwhile mysterious female companion.

Jamello fiddled with a pair of newly acquired daggers, testing their draw and attacking with a filing strap any hint of blemish. He addressed the elf. "It is said that your master, Galor, is a student of the Lords of Time who can peer into the past and who also ken much of the future. I have heard they visit the past and future to witness the trials of mortal kind as it pleases them."

"Elves take no master," corrected Apieron.

"I'd say your brain was addled, and that it is *time* to practice your shield work, or you'll have no future," added Henlee.

"The imagination of a dwarf is like a sapling planted in a cave where it cannot grow, closed in darkness and cold stone."

"Nay, for once the wastrel is correct," said Giliad. "At least in part." A loud harrumph issued from Henlee's bearded lips. Giliad continued, "My Lord Galor's vision is indeed far reaching, an' yet the gods suffer none of living blood to physically enter the past."

"Of the past I care nothing," answered Jamello. "It is the future that concerns me, our future … to be specific, *my* future."

The dweomorcaster paused a moment. "The future is a mansion with many, many corridors. Explore one and you may not find another. Which path he will walk, no mortal can know, for that itself is contingent on one's actions. Besides, I have not the power to attempt it." A variety of assorted shiftings and another harrumph sounded from Henlee's vicinity.

Giliad paused to favor the dwarf with a glance that one might find on the face of a feaster who discovers a hair in his soup. "I might add this, however. I know of no other mage who can do so, and if there were such a one, I doubt if he (or she) would cast such an enchantment."

"I'll drink to that," quoth Henlee, tipping a cup from his small cask of ale. He measured out a share for each to cheer their dreary encampment.

"What think you of these things, Your Grace?" asked Jamello. "Are you not Patriarch of Sway? An equal to Cynthia herself. Gods bless her for sending me on this quest!" He shot a quick glance to Xephard, who listened intently for the cleric's reply.

"Equal?" snorted an irritated Turpin. "To begin, the clarity of vision given one whose eyes are opened by heaven's knowledge exceeds that of mere practitioners of magical arts, as much as their's surmounts that of the common man." If Giliad took umbrage at this, he did not reveal it.

"For another," Turpin took a second cup from the little barrel and nodded to Henlee, "the ways of the races are estranged." His finger wagged. "But perhaps there is an underlying truth. Surely the dwarven folk are sons of the Crippled God, so much do they enjoy the fiery crafting of metal."

Giliad flicked something invisible from his garb. "Or perhaps this god was patterned by men after the dwarves, and that is why he resembles *them*."

"Dwarves have our own gods," mumbled Henlee. "We care not for those of short-lived men."

"Outrageous," said Turpin.

Giliad spoke again. "Men seek to label that which they see, no matter if they have little understanding, for it comforts them to name all things, even if these exist far beyond their ken."

Xephard, who had been silent, now spoke. "Some say elves are of the golden race, held close by Sky and Sea until the times and turmoils of making were at an end."

Giliad's eyes were remote when he answered. "Elves also have our gods. They speak to us in the remote voice of the blessed heavens, and of secrets whispered in the wind. Like dwarves, we heed not the myths of unhappy men."

"Then what say you of the third race, the race of bronze?" asked Xephard. "Perpetua taught me that they fell into the earth, there to dwell in anger, waiting for a time of war. Perhaps *they* are the guardians of the Helfast we seek."

"Greeaat," said Jamello softly.

Turpin turned to Xephard. "What you say may be so, my son. No one truly knows what awaits beyond the Matog. The gods themselves cannot spy the doings of Tartarus. After their hard-fought victory, they were fortunate to isolate the evil behind walls of imperishable bronze. Earth holds them, but she also holds many secrets. Perhaps the Thunderer's enchanted walls have weakened. Demons roam the lands again where none have been in living memory." Turpin wagged his jewel-heavy finger. "What think you of the ancient prince you slew in the crypt? Perhaps this occurs in preparation for a day when the eldar gods themselves can issue forth."

The circle became silent. At length Xephard's baritone rumbled, "That would be a black day."

"How can mortals face titans … these fathers of gods?" stammered Jamello.

Henlee glared at the thief.

"A fair question," Apieron put in quickly, "and one I asked the Oracle. She told me not to search every room in Hel's vastness … to seek one hall only."

Jamello was not assuaged. "Oh, what a relief! Only one titan."

The companions saw to their bedding. Henlee leered at Jamello as he downed the lees of his cup. "You should be more worried about Hel trolls."

"You jest." Rudolph Mellor rubbed his hands nervously on his breeches.

"Thick as flies, 'tis said, and heftier than those scrawny things you stirred up yonder." Henlee jerked his bearded chin back west.

"Miserable, cowardly creatures I deem them," waxed Xephard, his voice disembodied from his bedroll, invisible in the darkness.

"Not the trolls of Hel, I tell you," persisted Henlee. "They breathe fire and swarm like angry bees."

Apieron laughed. "I hope we never get to see one. Today I've had enough of that accursed race to last till the end of my days."

"Hel trolls?" asked Jamello.

"Thick as flies, I tell you—" Henlee drew his blanket over him.

As usual, being youngest, Jamello had first watch. They had no fire, yet he could discern slow, swirling fogs illuminated by light of the first stars, in which were shifting shapes not unlike hideous, grinning faces and malformed torsos that sprouted knotted limbs.

"Hel trolls," he murmured glumly.

Chapter 18

The Wyrnde

The pallid light that came before sunrise lifted fingers of mist from the Wyrnde. Shining droplets of moisture hung in hair and beaded on clothes, and spider webs in marsh grass glistened like nets of woven pearls. Xephard stood from his guard position to waken Jamello. The others were roused by the thief's vigorous protests in finding himself facing the holy warrior for an early lesson in the weaponry of a knight. Henlee hunkered down to observe as Apicron and the spellcasters prepared for the day's travel. Xephard addressed Jamello, who wore a sour expression.

"Assume, Sir Cutpurse, that your foil play is ineffective against a larger and impeccably armored opponent."

"Not a hard assumption to make," guffawed Henlee from the sideline. Jamello directed his surly stare at both.

"Further," stated Xephard, "assume that your daggers, coils of rope, caltrops, jumping jacks, bits of string, and hard candy are likewise useless."

Henlee hooted, flapping his arms whilst Jamello prepared a cutting reference to overgrown men suffering a lack in the romantic arenas, but thought better of it with the renowned paladin addressing him from three feet with drawn blade. Instead he fidgeted the toe of his boot, elevating a fascinating plug of moss.

"Then, Sir Thief, your choices are but three. One, learn to hold position with shield and heavy blade. Two, die. Or three, run." Jamello looked up hopefully. "Of course if you run, you will also die, for without cohesion, defending units are quickly cut apart. Now, strap this on." Xephard lightly tossed Jamello a shield plundered from the mausoleum. It was wrought of etched steel that sported panels depicting scenes of the hunt and was rimmed in gold. Xephard apparently had attached leather straps to the frogs on its concave interior. Jamello caught it up with a grunt. It seemed to weigh more than the rest of his burdens together. The thief hefted it and attempted to appear fierce.

Henlee hooted again, his mouth full of something. A minute smile played at the corner of Xephard's mouth. "Defend!" he shouted and leapt at Jamello, who quickly raised the shield and braced for a mighty blow. Xephard simply stopped and punched the shield with his heavy gauntlet to send the thief flying. Off to the side, Henlee sounded as if he was choking, and so it went for the next hour until the party leisurely assembled, ready to travel again.

"Ah-h, Henlee," called Apieron. "What is that Bump is eating?" The broad-backed burro was calmly chewing white-flowered fronds. Sap from crushed stems ran down the donkey's chin.

"I dunno."

Eyes narrowed, the dwarf approached his steed and inspected the clump of greenage rapidly disappearing into Bump's champing mouth. "Looks like carrot tops." The dwarf began to search about for more. "Where did you get those, Bump my lad? Carrots would go well in tonight's stew."

"Stop him!" urged Apieron. "It's poison."

Henlee wheeled and swatted the remnants from Bump's mouth. The donkey bit his hand. Not taking his eyes off the treacherous equine, Henlee tossed back over his shoulder, "What kind of poison?"

"It is known as *horse poison*."

"Oh." Henlee scanned the area for more of the deadly flower. Finding none, he nonchalantly began adjusting saddle and tack.

Jamello was incredulous. "Aren't you going to do something?"

Apieron fingered the scattered remnants of the plant. "There is no preventative anyways."

"No worries. Bump will be all right."

"What?" called Apieron and Jamello in unison.

Henlee stood and regarded the twain, exacerbated at having to state the obvious. "He's not a horse."

Apieron glanced at Turpin, who shrugged. "I cannot heal an ass. Besides, if the steed has acquired anything of his master, he should be fine."

Henlee stepped over to Jamello's mare. He eyed a large bulge in the thief's saddlebag and wrapped his knuckle upon it. The contents emitted a hollow, metallic ring. "That the helmet you've got, boy?"

Jamello clapped hands to forehead. "Egads, the mental prowess of this dwarf is awe inspiring."

Unimpressed by the display, Henlee stood, hands on hips, in front of Jamello's horse. "Well, you gonna let me have a look at it?"

"You'll see it when I need don it, not before."

"And when will you know you need it? When your head is all stove in? 'Tis not doing you any good in your bag."

Jamello tapped his temple with a finger. "The power of the mind, good dwarf. Why stiffen my neck without cause?"

"When the fighting starts, don't stand next to me."

The clearing fog found the wayfarers pushing eastward as fast as safely possible to enter the heart of the Wyrnde. Drifting seedlings in ages past had become thirsty trees that anchored themselves into the bog, yielding groves on small islands as the slow accumulation of debris in the mire piled against delving roots added to by generations of leaf and twig-fall from the trees themselves. Thus the party found many bridges of passable land on which to guide their mounts, although wildlife and flora alike became alien to the knowledge of the travelers from the West.

Herds of rust-colored, shaggy deer watched them with wide eyes before scampering off. Once, a velvet-antlered stag stood and bugled his challenge echoingly across the marsh. Butterflies by the thousands crowded small pools where gaudily plumed kingfishers darted after fish and bald-pated storks stood sentinel. Swamp roosters and their dun mates clucked under canopies of leatherleaf and a dozen varieties of ivy, creepers, and sedge that Apieron could not name. There was also a short bamboo grass that cut like knives if carelessly brushed against, and the wounds burned for days.

Apieron's encouragements and Xephard's boisterous nature did little to assuage the fastidious thief or the dwarf who groused and grumbled about soggy clothes, clinging mud and bloodthirsty flies that no salve of ranger or cleric could dissuade. Despite the nature of the terrain, clear water ponds and rills were rare, and without cart or wagon, no more than a day's supply could be carried. It took the combined skills of priest, woodsman, and mage to locate and purify enough to meet the needs of thirsty steeds and Turpin, who sweated much in the clinging heat. Red-faced with effort, the priest made to push aside a stand of waist-high, fleshy-stemmed flowers to set himself down for a rest. Apieron laid a restraining hand on him.

Turpin returned an impatient look but followed Apieron's gaze to the yellow-orange blossoms. He started in alarm, noting that the flowers had begun to align in his direction. They stumbled

236

back at quick pace as the flower tops followed on their pale, tumescent stalks. A sweet scent filled the air, albeit it was faintly reminiscent of rotting meat.

"Toscaris plant."

"And?" huffed Turpin, regaining a measure of his dignity.

"I have never seen it but heard tell from woodsmen that it shoots a cloud of spoors like darts that germinate within the animal host, later to burst forth. Where the victim dies, a new stand of Toscaris is found."

"A foul growth," said Henlee. "Surely we approach the land of the hellions."

Apieron shrugged. "I'll grant we stand in the midst of a strange land, but we are far from the rim of the Starfall."

During their brief sojourn, Xephard again summoned Jamello to swordplay, and so it would go whenever a halt was called. No amount of protestation, feigned illness, or bribery would dissuade the temple peer from his self-appointed task. The young thief proved to be a remarkable study, though it pained him greatly to suffer any discipline not his own. Likewise other members of the company took minutes here and there to perfect silent signals of body language by day and subtle noises by night. Order of march for various situations was discussed at length. All were accomplished fighters, and they tried to imagine and prepare for the otherworldly conditions that would exist within the darkness of the Hel pits. Nonetheless, circumstance found them poorly prepared for their strangest encounter yet …

The party had made steady progress for three days after their departure from the ruined city by following a series of elevated switchbacks that interlaced the Wyrnde. Dry land grew more plentiful, and moss-draped cypress gave way to stately evergreens of a sort unknown to the elf mage and ranger. Swathed in reddish, soft bark with deep vertical grooves, these towered to unknown reaches and were easily the mightiest growths of height and girth that the adventurers had ever seen. Many birds called from their upper reaches. Apieron signaled halt in a dry clearing with an aromatic carpet of tiny needles where they were surrounded on all sides by the forest giants. He made to scout forward whilst the others prepared to take a midday rest.

Turpin looked up from his saddlebags. "I sense a presence."

Apieron leapt for the cleric. Already he was too late. An arrow streaked across the clearing towards Turpin's throat. It sprang back from Xephard's shoulder armor as the paladin angled his back to the tree line and grasped the cleric in a shielding embrace.

Henlee vented a war cry and hurled Maul two-handed over head. With a snapping crunch, it split through the low brush from which the singing shaft had come. There ensued a brief silence during which many strange warriors, wielding either bows or twisted spears, materialized from shadows beneath the red boles. Jamello, yelling an alarm, pointed as more warriors darted overhead on beating wings. Turpin mumbled arcane words, and the air above his ring began to shimmer.

Several of the ambushers were revealed in the light of the dale, and to the companions' surprise, they appeared to be of elvin kind, although with long, coarse-braided hair and bronzed skin. And wings! A dozen of their rough-hewn spears and sleek arrows were leveled at Henlee, who whirled about like a cornered mastiff, growling and brandishing an axe and his dwarven shield.

Apieron's hand rested on the haft of one of his javelins, still in its back sling. He guessed he might draw and cast one of his darts before being transfixed by a half-dozen arrows from the slender bows. Though much slighter than Apieron's bow of yew, he was certain that elvin marksmen seldom missed, and his own was of little use, unstrung and encased in leather.

Seeing the disaster about to befall, Giliad gave a magically enhanced shout. It rocked man and elf alike. Any that heard perceived a commanding "Halt!" in his native tongue and gave no thought to disobey. To all, Giliad revealed himself as an elf lord of great power, and his golden hair flashed like sunrise on water. The winged foresters appeared as astonished as his companions, and weapons fell unheeded to their sides. "Hold, I say, elves of twilight! This I, Giliad of House Galdarion, do command."

Chapter 19

Fogleaf

Three winged elves emerged from the shadows bearing the large but broken body of an archer slain by Henlee's cast. A warrior of roughly the same height as Jamello fronted Henlee, unmindful of the dwarf's threatening belt axe. He was clad in leathers and dun clothing as were the others, and his chest was bare. Many small totems of carved wood and bone and feathers secured with cleverly twisted wire adorned his person. His wings appeared to be of the same material as his coarse flowing hair.

To the wonderment of the party, he addressed them in the common speech of the West, albeit haltingly. "One of the bearded folk! Truly strange times have befallen the Liflyne."

He turned to the three who hefted the corpse of their slain companion. "Bear Draliks back to Tree Home. Prepare his body for the long rest."

The apparent leader of the forest elves moved to Giliad and bowed low. "I am Sarc of the people of Fogleaf. We welcome a high lord of the North, yet such a slaying demands judgment by the *People*. Will you follow my company without resistance?"

"We have a choice?" Jamello muttered.

Turpin fretted. "We have tarried in this bog overlong."

"Indeed you have," rejoined the winged elf. "Stumbling about our lands for two days! Scouts marked your passage into the forbidden city. Some of the Liflyne deem you grave robbers, or worse, worshippers of the *Darkness*, come again to serve your dead masters."

Jamello glanced at Xephard, and breathed a sigh of relief when he beheld the temple warrior had not unsheathed Leitus, and merely regarded the swamp elves with silent study. The thief discerned at least a score of the creatures amongst the trees.

Apieron turned to Xephard and Turpin. He arched an eyebrow. Xephard nodded in return as Turpin let fall his ring with a snort of disgust. Another winged elf emerged from the bracken, his bronze face dark with infused blood as he carried Maul in both hands. A second warrior moved to assist him. Together they ascended with heavy wing beats to disappear into the upper reaches of the shadowed forest.

"I shall have Maul back," growled Henlee to the elvin leader.

"I am now commander of this squadron," said Sarc. "Draliks is no more. If you wish to see your bloodthirsty weapon again, bearded one, you shall follow us to hear the words of Bragen and the Council of the People."

"And I am Henlee of the clan of Daindran. One way or t'other, I'll have my stick back."

"You shall indeed," returned Sarc, but the edges of his speech were hard.

With a strong escort of swamp elves, the companions struck a smooth footpath suitable for the mounts and proceeded rapidly into a primordial forest composed almost entirely of the rust-barked giants. As they went, elvin sentries flashed hand signals to those who flitted through tree heights and called in melodious voices to others unseen ahead and behind. Apieron pondered the voices of birds he had heard for days.

Two hours' march found them in a glade cut by a rustling brook where good fodder was spread before their grateful mounts. The elves dispersed, leaving the six travelers to freshen in the clean water or recline on a sward of soft grass next to the rill. Winged elves randomly walked or flew by yet seemed indifferent to the presence of such a polyglot troop, seemingly more intent on their own goings on. The company glimpsed dwellings, storehouses, and concourses at all levels in and around the towering redwoods, and some on the ground. Apieron guessed that more than a thousand of the bronze elves dwelled here, and perhaps many times that.

"At least the beasts are well fed," sighed Henlee. He tossed a hard biscuit back into his satchel without bothering to rewrap it.

Turpin faced Xephard. To the surprise of all, he gave a formal bow. "I thank you, warrior. That shaft was aimed with no good intent."

Xephard nodded in deference. "You are our spiritual guide. More so, we who escort Apieron on this venture are companions of a divine trust." Xephard turned in a complete circuit, carefully eyeing the elves going about their daily habits. "I sense no evil here."

"I'm agreed," said Apieron. "This deep forest dwelling, though wondrous strange, feels no different to me than any common gathering of goodly folk."

"Be not so trusting," admonished Turpin. "Your hearts are kind and valiant, and you would have all men so. The doom we pursue is too grave a matter to entrust to such uncouth, wild woods folk. Who can know what dark gods of these troll-haunted fens they serve?"

Giliad's eyes flashed. "You may be held wise amongst your own people, Messire Turpin, but in this you speak ignorance. Elves of any sort serve no darkness."

"So they say," muttered Henlee.

At this, a winged elf approached the edge of the clearing. "You are summoned to Wood Hall," he said. "There will be funeral and feast in honor of Draliks."

Henlee regarded his donkey. "If I don't come back, Bump my boy, you shall have a good life here with these swamp elves. They don't look like they would ever need to ride." The ever-hungry burro ignored him and plucked another mouthful of sweet grass.

They followed the solemn young elf, or so he seemed, along a winding path that debouched into a dell surrounded by trees of diminishing height such that they resembled the amphitheaters of Ilycrium, albeit of living wood rather than stone. Its center was a grassy swale that held a still mere from which rose a twisting green-yellow blaze fed unceasingly by gasses rising through the water.

Evening's wings overtook the tree basin, and the yellow light of the water torch reflected the sheen of many bronze limbs and faces clustered around the clearing in irregular ranks. The party was led to the grass. They heard a light rain pattering in the upper trees, although no drop reached the clearing where there rose and fell the subtle singsong of the elves conversing in their own tongue. A low drum throbbed in echo, and many of the winged ones joined in a thrumming hymn that made a sad and beautiful music. At times a female would add her high, lilting tones at once eerie and wondrous—though forlorn, for she sang of the passing of Draliks the Strong.

The party was greeted by a stoutly built swamp elf whose many years of deeds were written in the pattern of intricate beads of wood and amber strung along belt and plaited hair. "Welcome to Fogleaf, strangers of the North. I am Bragen, priest of the Liflyne and spokesman for this tree moot."

Before the companions could respond, he nodded to several waiting elves who brought forth food and drink on wooden platters with cups and utensils of horn. The elf cleric retreated to converse with others as the party sat on soft pillows of woven grass. Henlee smelled the food with suspicion.

Apieron and the others ate with gusto. The drink was thin and yellow but of surpassing excellence, and they found it greatly lightened their mood. Apieron had long known that elves of all types were suited to their homes, blending with their habitats in looks and custom, and in turn giving back to the land grace and renewal. These creatures were much more so than he would have imagined, seeming to be the embodied spirit of this sequestered and primitive place.

"Lawks, I wish I had a bushel of these carved bowls for sale in Bestrand," exclaimed Jamello as he admired the intricate craftsmanship against the greenish light of the flare. "I wonder if they're magic?"

Tortured by the others' obvious enjoyment of the provender, Henlee took a small sip of his wine. Jamello laughed at the dwarf's dilemma. "Why so shy, Master? Would they bother to poison us when they have us surrounded?" The thief took a mighty pull on a tall drinking horn to further discomfit the dwarf.

"I've been in worse pinches," admitted Henlee, relenting a bit to tentatively join the others.

"Elves of any kind use no poison," said Giliad. "Unless it be the effect strong liquor has on lackwits who drink and speak overmuch."

The stoutly built shaman returned to greet them. His face was grave. "It is time for words. You have taken food and rest and thus are entitled to guest rights. Nonetheless, the matter of a slaying must be decided."

Henlee rose rapidly, discarding his meal onto the turf. "I'll not be judged." The others stood as well.

"Call it what you will. The death of a war chief of the Liflyne demands a hearing."

"Relax," whispered Jamello to Henlee. "I've some experience in these matters. Contrary to popular belief, they never feed you before killing you."

Henlee scowled at the thief. "Been killed a few times, have you?"

"Who will speak for Draliks?" intoned Bragen. He faced the gallery.

"Draliks hunted for me when I lay invalid from a poorly healed fracture," said a slow-speaking elf. Apieron could not mark the speaker in the shadows behind the flare.

"Draliks trained my sons in the way of war," added a female voice so high it seemed to the humans more like that of a bird. Several of the winged elves spoke in quick succession, relaying various deeds done by Draliks for the benefits of the tribe. When they ceased, a heavy silence filled the glen, broken only by the night sounds of bird and insect and the fluttering mere-light. A basso throbbing filled the airs above like the passage of a mighty avian creature, yet unlike any bird the companions had ever heard.

Henlee mouthed to Apieron, "Bat?"

Apieron shrugged helplessly in his ignorance. The noise faded, and their attention was returned to the Bragen, who again addressed the assembled swamp elves. "Who will stand witness for the outlanders?"

After a pause, Giliad strode forward. His voice lifted like the clear tones of a bell in the clearing, authoritative and harmonious. "Our hearts are saddened by the death of Draliks, and each of us partakes in the blame of it. Yet I ask, why did a war leader of the Liflyne attack without warning?"

There was a muttering among the elvin assembly. "You came to our secret place, unbidden," countered a voice from above. "You entered the dead city and lived!" Other voices were raised in angry assent.

Giliad replied, "Are the ways of my distant kin grown so fierce that travelers are greeted with violence before kindness?"

Bragen inclined his shaggy head. "Alas that you come to us during days grown dark."

"But that is *why* we are come," interjected Jamello. "We are quested—"

"Stay your tongue!" boomed Turpin.

"Come to slay the Fogleaf people?" called a strident female voice.

"Peace to you, Iifir!" commanded Bragen.

Apieron stepped forward. He stared at his feet a long moment before raising his head to search the tiers. In the flickering light, the lines of his face were revealed in sharp angles of light and shadow. His gray eyes were steady. "I am Apieron, son of Xistus Farsinger, lord of Windhover, and your closest neighbor in the lands held by the king of Ilycrium."

There was a chorus of banter at this, but none gainsaid him. Apieron spoke with earnest passion. He detailed the reasons for their arduous journey, itself merely a prelude of their hopes to strike at the inner heart of the evil that threatened to well up from its hellish prison to befoul all the land.

When Turpin heard such forthright speech, he started forward. "It is not your place to speak thus!" The Patriarch of Sway snapped his mouth closed when he felt Xephard's heavy hand on his arm. Turpin eyed the paladin long and hard, though he said no more.

"A noble sentiment," countered a loud, sarcastic voice from the trees when Apieron finished.

"Who speaks?" said a flustered Bragen. "Show yourself."

"Enough!" boomed a powerful voice from behind the shaman.

A tall, winged elf warrior entered the circle to confront the newcomers. They saw that it was Sarc, the same scout leader who gathered them earlier. They had not marked him where he had sat in the shadows, quietly observing. "I claim the right of challenge, for Draliks was my kin by my father's sister. None here may deny me."

Henlee rushed forward to study Sarc. "What be your challenge then, winged elf?" The dwarf's words sounded as a growl. "Let us get it over with. My ears are starting to ache." An angry chorus erupted at the dwarf's words.

"Only this, bearded one. For weregild of my cousin, you shall ..." Henlee's beard bristled, "—take me with you."

The noise grew clamorous as each turned to his neighbor to shout and debate. "Impossible!" boomed Turpin.

"I like him," countered Xephard quietly.

Apieron shared a look with Giliad, who smiled and spread his hands in acceptance. "It appears we have no choice, Your Grace."

"And who appointed you leader of this venture, young Apieron? This is a religious matter."

Henlee turned to Jamello. "You can put up your gambling dice, thief. There'll be no fight tonight."

"Whist, whist," said Bragen, pushing out toward the crowd with his hands, "we may argue until the trees are dust; Sarc will not change his mind. In this he is like his cousin!"

"You would send our ablest warrior off with these outlanders?" accused a voice from the trees directly above.

Bragen addressed the assembled elves and the party where Sarc also stood. "In this I believe his feelings are sooth. Who can deny we Liflyne feel dire tremors in the depthless roots of sacred trees? Who would desire the dark future whereof the ranger lord spoke? I (for one) would that the People partake in these bright deeds before we retreat into our swamp vastness, and are sundered entirely from the world."

"You would have to flee farther than your wilderness, brother," said Giliad. "Did not Apieron state the Hel Gate lies not fifty leagues hence?"

"We know that place," said Bragen. "Dry and barren it is since the great light struck thirty summers ago. Fell peoples live there. We go not that way."

"Until now," corrected Sarc.

Bragen nodded. "Tonight our friends may rest while we make funeral for Draliks. Forest daughters will see to the needs of the outlanders and add what provisions they might. Tomorrow will see you on hidden paths only Liflyne have trod." Loud in the still night there came the braying of Henlee's restless burro.

"I'll not be leaving Bump," said Henlee flatly.

"Nay. I urge you take your beasts. We have not much of the food they require."

"We thank you," said Giliad. "You have the friendship of the peoples of Amor, and aid should you have need."

Bragen bowed deeply. "Who knows where our paths lead? Even to your northern home where the trees are strange and waters grow still in winter. I will tell you this, your company seems odd to us, and none more so than yon dwarf. Even so, the name of Apieron Farsinger was not unknown to us ere now. Although we are not noticed, the people of fen and fallow range wide and hear much."

"And to you, my brother," Bragen addressed himself to Turpin, "I say that we who are leaders of our peoples do our best to train and guide but must leave the remaking of the world to these young warriors."

His composure regained, Turpin gave a polite nod before seeking his way from the tree hall behind Giliad and Xephard. Despite the obvious racial differences between the two clerics, it seemed to Apieron that they were much alike in size and temperament, at least it held true for the Turpin he knew a fortnight ago.

"I imagine we all look the worse for wear," he muttered, seeing Jamello abuse his priceless new kindjal by flicking bits of dried mud from his long-suffering boots.

"Now to more important matters," said Henlee, addressing himself to Sarc.

"Where's Maul?"

The Liflyne warrior strode to the shadows and turned, bearing the strange, heavy glaive to Henlee. The dwarf studied it closely for a moment, then slung it from a back strap. "You had it ready! Now tell me this, winged elf. Had things been decided otherwise, would you have relinquished it as promised?"

Sarc laughed in his sonorous voice. "Most assuredly, stunted one. It is the judgment custom of the Liflyne to slay one who kills with the weapon and method by which he killed."

Henlee was flabbergasted. Jamello slapped his knees in mirth.

The companions repaired to a close grove of the mighty trees and were aided into the middle reaches by means of a stair that wrapped around a massive trunk. They stood on living buttresses where organic debris and seedlings had accumulated over the centuries such that it resembled a grassed and hedged forest dell rather than a floor two hundred feet above the ground. There, funeral was held for Draliks.

One by one, members of the tribe passed by his body, cleansed and radiant on a soft bough, to say a soft word or simply touch him fondly. The elves' voices were lifted in praise of his life's journey. Orisons were spoken for swift transport to the spirit realm, to be ever young amongst immortal groves of blossoming trees. Apieron noted that the warrior's body was enclosed in a light, fibrous winding whose stray ends floated loose above him in the nigh imperceptible breeze. How long they stood thus he could not say, but it seemed that soon the heavens opened to reveal a pure white light of clustered stars against its depthless vault.

They felt the deep fluttering before they heard it, and a gigantic shadow obscured the sky. Jamello and Turpin gasped as it lowered. With a whooshing flap of its wings, the filaments about Draliks rose and the body was jerked and borne away into the night.

When the ceremony was done and funeral feast begun, Henlee turned to Apieron.

"Moth?"

Bragen nodded. "That is a better guess than most. But no, the creature is one of which we call Aerald. The people of Fogleaf grow them. In turn, they serve us."

"*Grow* them? You make them sound like they are a crop of beans."

"It is true that they are neither plant nor beast. Maybe some of each. The natal grove is not far from here, but difficult passage for those that must go on two legs or four."

"I long to see the birthplace of the Aerald more than anything in recent memory," said Apieron, "except my home. And yet we tarry here overlong. I fret at the slight delay that has already transpired."

Bragen spoke. "You are wrong, friend of the Liflyne. You have gained three things—"

The others perked up their ears.

"Firstly, you have won the friendship of the winged people, and that is a rarity in this wild corner of the world. Second, you have acquired a stout companion, for Sarc was second only to Draliks in the dance of battle. And third, you are gifted a measure of time, more precious than food and laughter for short-lived humans. Tomorrow's light shall see you gone by swift trails known only to the Liflyne. On occasion, even we have need of such. No more blundering in beaver ponds for you!"

Apieron wondered again about the voices of many birds heard

and not seen. The companions breathed deep the night's clean air, scented crisp by the trees. They found again their bivouac, and despite the odd happenings of the long day and evening, each found his sleep to be of the dreamless and satisfying sort. No guards were posted, and Giliad refused to set even minor wards, saying that such would be offensive to hosts more honorable than many princes and potentates he had met in various realms. When leaf-dappled light of morning filtered down to illuminate the little clearing by the brook, Bragen and Sarc came to greet them. They were followed by several Liflyne who set breakfast before the companions and returned several garments that had been given over for mending.

"Greetings, my friends. It is time to up and away," said Bragen, his smiling, bronze face glowing in the eastern light. Jamello whistled when he beheld his riding boots handed to him with a luster more rich than the day he purchased them.

Sarc left the clearing and returned leading a muscular, short-legged steed of tan coloring. It had vertical brown stripes and a bristled mane that continued from crest to tail. The elf was clad as the day before, with bow slung at his back, but he now bore a curiously twisted stabbing spear, and a bolo was at his belt. The spear was covered in bark, and there were small sprigs along its length that bore green leaves.

"What is the twig for, elf?" asked Henlee. "Is it for your, er, horse to eat if he gets hungry?"

"Beg is no horse. His kind wandered into Fogleaf long ago from the great grasslands past the lands of dawn. Wild herds of Tarpan, as we call them, roam the swamplands. They serve the Liflyne people when we have need. I cannot fly all the way to the Starfall! As for my spear, you may judge its usefulness when you have seen me wield it."

"Okay," said the dwarf, shrugging.

"Of your courage, we have no doubt," said Xephard. "My apologies, but I fear that 'gainst the dark beings we must soon embattle, your weapons prove too frail."

Giliad responded, "There is a dweomer upon Sarc's war tools that is not the same as held by weapons of crafted steel but is equally mighty. It is rather like the place magic I sense here."

"The vision of an eldar lord sees truth," said Bragen. "The Liflyne do not dig in the earth for minerals or seek to remake one element into another. Our arts but enhance nature's givings. Should you come this way again, we will have opportunity to share more with you.

Regrettably, the end of this day must find you far from Tree Home. When the light of yestereve's moon faltered, I beheld the demon star entering the house of Fogleaf. Dire events unfold! You must haste to meet them." He turned to Henlee. "I am glad to have met one of the dwarven people of which my father spoke and to have met valiant men besides." Henlee bowed.

The companions gathered their mounts to trail after Sarc's oddly striped beast. As they filed past a small crowd of elves that gathered, Bragen called out to them one last time, "We will not forget the coming of our neighbor: Apieron Farsinger, master of Windhover."

Apieron could think of nothing to say and only nodded. Henlee confided to Sarc, "And you can tell your chieftain later that me and yonder paladin are never late for a feast, whether at table or the feast of swords."

"I believe you," replied Sarc solemnly. "You can tell him yourself when we return."

While the others were thus occupied, Turpin pulled Jamello aside to whisper, "What think you, thief, of the motives of the winged one?"

"Oh, I don't know. Mayhap he takes himself a bit seriously—not unlike certain of our warriors."

"Keep your eyes peeled, my boy. Could he not simply disappear after leading us hopelessly astray into some dark fen?"

Jamello stroked his moustaches thoughtfully. "What do you ask of me, Eminence?"

"I fear Lord Apieron and others are enamored with the charms of this new race and so forget the dangers to our mission." Turpin paused to ascertain that they still spoke in private. "I ask you to keep a ready blade for any sign of treachery."

Jamello stared deeply into Turpin's pale, quick eyes. He patted the daggers at his waist. "My blades are always ready, lord." Seemingly satisfied, Turpin kicked his mount forward to hear what had passed between Apieron and the cleric of the swamp elves.

A few hours' time found the travelers on deep forest trails invisible to all eyes except those of Apieron and Sarc. The others were soon bewildered by the many switchbacks and direction changes chosen to ease the course for the horses and confuse any who might seek to track them. Jamello expressed his amazement at the path-finding ability of human ranger and elf of the fens.

"I am also a stranger to these lands," replied Apieron, "so I keep close to good Sarc to learn what I may."

The winged elf was silent a moment, putting his thoughts into speech. "I have heard of the great cities of men. They seem strange to me." He swept his arm out to indicate the forest. "Just as you are no doubt intimately familiar with such a place, the Fogleaf is to us. Each tree is different and speaks to the people its own voice."

"I wager living here for three or four centuries doesn't hurt either," added Henlee.

The first day from Tree Home became three as the companions encountered terrain more unusual than any seen thus far. Hanging, wide-leafed plants, with enormous crimson blossoms, hosted black bats that pressed greedy faces into the flowers to feed. Other bats with orange bellies and four-foot wingspans flew in daylight, swooping overhead to gorge on fruits that hung from oddly sinuous trees, and there were colonies of monkeys, with faces like wizened old men, who set up a clamor whensoever the little column passed under their leafy homes, although Sarc was able to shush them with words that sounded much like a parent addressing unruly children. The horses started in alarm when a herd of smooth-flanked bison crashed through the long grass of a nearby pond, snorting and bellowing as they swam to the bank farthest from the party to disappear into its thick undergrowth.

"Ware your step!" called Sarc, too late.

Apieron wheeled to find Jamello stopped, one foot within the drooping fronds of a large honeysuckle. From twenty paces, Apieron could smell its syrupy pollen. The thief stood poised, motionless as a street performer Apieron had once seen in Sway, except that person had not worn a fearful sweat as angry hornets hovered inches from her face.

Their plate-like eyes and throbbing hum were fraught with menace. Fast as Jamello was with dagger or quirt, Apieron knew that no such action would save him from a vicious attack. Worse, these were dagger wasps, large as one's thumb and known to have predilection for the eyes. A dozen of the creatures circled their quarry whilst thirty more stared at Jamello's face with their merciless yellow orbs.

"Easy, Jamello. Make no sudden move."

"No shit!" squeaked Jamello without moving his lips.

"Whew!" said Henlee. "Those bees have knives larger than yours. It's a standoff … you'd best stay here whilst we find a place to sleep. We'll come back for you in the morning."

Curiosity turned all as Sarc emitted a staccato vibration. Apieron could not discern if it came from deep in his throat or along his pinions. The wasps seemed to hesitate as if listening, then flew as one to alight above the thief to regard him from a branch.

"Come to us around the bush," urged Apieron.

"Yes," said Sarc. "Do not fear. I told them you intend no harm to their home. Of course they choose to watch anyway."

"He talks to bugs," Henlee said to Apieron.

"Of course he does. As can I. Can you not?"

Henlee harrumphed and tugged on Bump's lead rope. The burro tossed his head in annoyance and cast a look of regret at the sweet vine.

Despite Turpin's misgivings, the paths chosen by Sarc were dry and easier to walk than any since entering the Wyrnde. Many turnings and loops notwithstanding, their passage eastward proceeded swiftly. The only obstacle occurred on the evening of the third day when their course debouched onto a nameless river whose only ford was encumbered by a sandbar upon which rested a dozen cruel-looking crocodiles. The largest of these was a giant over twenty feet in length, and it eyed them malevolently under horny brows.

Chapter 20

The Wyrnde

"Too bad the winged ones fixed your boots so well," quipped Henlee to Jamello. "You could've had some nice new ones from these big lizards."

"I see no way around the beasts without a detour of several miles," said Apieron as he reached to help the thief and Turpin steady their nervous horses.

"Who can say but that the next crossing will not be similarly occupied?" Xephard's cloud-blue eyes regarded the river up and down its length. "Like as not, they infest any stretch of bank shallow enough to invite game to cross."

"What does our guide say?" asked Turpin.

"I do not know of another ford," responded Sarc. "Some of the croc people are filled with hate, and the death they offer their victims is a hard one. Yet we need not fight. Follow me, quietly."

The winged elf led his mount, with one hand in his mane, across the shallows into the midst of the waiting reptiles. All the while he piped a singsong melody. At first the reptiles tensed as if to spring upon the foolish trespasser, but soon cocked their toothy heads at the song and lowered long snouts onto the warm sand as if all will had been drained from their hearts. To Apieron they appeared so many well-fed hounds in repose before their master's fire.

In single file, the companions led their reluctant steeds within paces of the stricken beasts. Only an ancient giant tracked them with its baleful eye, yet even his evil wisdom was insufficient to overcome the spell of the swamp elf. When the little column gained the opposite bank, they heard him roar in frustrated rage and splash heavily into the water.

"That was a nice trick, elf," said Henlee. "You could join a circus." Sarc bowed, teeth white in his bronze face.

"Do all the Liflyne possess such abilities?" asked Apieron. Turpin perked up at the question.

"Some more than others," replied Sarc. "Of course the druids among us have greater powers nearest the glades of our home."

Turpin huffed at the reserved answer and retrieved the lashings of his mount from Apieron. The thief came forward to congratulate Sarc, who cocked his head in the cleric's direction and raised one sandy eyebrow.

"Oh him," said Jamello. "Pay no heed. He's famously dull."

Apieron nodded in agreement and, joining Sarc, turned to lead them. Once beyond the unnamed river, the ground rose incrementally and grew more firm. There was now little water not confined within a banked course and Xephard did not neglect his purpose to teach Jamello the complexities of heavy sword and shield. The scrape and shuffle of shifting feet, metallic blows, and shouts echoed in the opening forest whenever a halt was called. Midday of the fourth from the enclave of the winged elves found the paladin admonishing Jamello once again against his reflexive tendencies to reach for a throwing dagger when range was opened betwixt opponents.

"The white lady is the noblest and most deadly of weapons. Why think you we traversed the gods' cursed shrine of the Nessur but to find one as fine as that you now bear?"

The fighters stood on a wide stone that rose above the forest floor. Bristly pine saplings had taken root in weathered cracks across its surface, and yellow lichens swathed it flanks. "Besides, to strike thus with a missile would be deemed cowardly."

Henlee could not help but to inject, "Yeah, who would toss away a perfectly good knife anyways?"

Jamello rounded on the dwarf. "You have obviously never fought a giant or brought down a fleeing horseman." Henlee was dumbfounded. He walked off slowly to dig into his pack for aught left to eat.

Apieron said, "Henlee *Gerakundoom*," at which Xephard guffawed and all the party chuckled, except Jamello and Sarc.

"What?" At this, the laughter grew louder.

Giliad finally met his eyes. "Gerakundoom means 'giant slayer.' The dwarf has many such accolades."

Henlee was smacking loudly on a long, thin loaf supplied by the winged elves. He mournfully shook out the last dregs of his beer cask. "I never thought to grow tired of seeing Jamello getting knocked on his ass, but aren't we nigh on the star crater? Besides, elf food is running thin."

"You are correct, mighty dwarf," said Turpin. "Last eve I cast an astral calculation, and we are less than two days' walk from the crater rim."

"I also agree," added Sarc. "Trees tell me that we will soon pass beyond the land where their fathers and children live and grow. Already we have left the lands of the Liflyne."

"Then what say our leaders to an early supper?" asked Henlee. "This rock is as good a campsite as any, and the last of my beer would taste sweeter if I knew a roast pig were to follow." An odd glean caught the dwarf's eye. "What do you think, Apieron? Can you outshoot a winged elf with that fancy bow of yours?"

"A golden plate says he can't," said Jamello.

"And *I* shall back my friend," answered Xephard enthusiastically. "With what?"

"With this silver dagger," proclaimed Xephard, smugly patting the hilt of a splendidly adorned poniard at his waist. "We did not name Apieron 'The Archer' for naught when he served with Royal Pathfinders, the only bow in seven realms that can outshoot Tensel is that of an elvin ranger, our friend Tallux, hundreds of leagues westward, and no doubt its owner is drinking ale with the King's scoutsmen."

Jamello bowed, a subtle smiled playing on his lips. "This I shall enjoy more than many a fortune I've won at the gaming tables."

"I think not," rejoined Xephard. "To lose your ill-gotten gold will do you good. A warrior must have humility. How else to recognize his weaknesses before an enemy does so first?"

"Then we are decided," said Giliad. "Henlee and Jamello shall prepare a cooking fire whilst Sarc and young Apieron hunt for our provender."

"Why include me with him?" asked Henlee.

"It should be obvious," stated Giliad imperiously. "Those of little skill must serve as they may."

"We shall not have to hunt to eat well," said Sarc. He plucked up several thick, fan-shaped fungi that sprouted from a rotting log and piled them upon a smooth stone so that they looked like a stack of griddlecakes.

Henlee sniffed in his beard. "An' that is no food for man or dwarf. Eating that 'twould be like nibbling plaster, a bit seamy for even an elf."

"Observe," said Sarc. He pried several green filaments from the back of the pale fungi and twisted them together. "Prepare the others thus and dip them in boiling water. You may be surprised."

As he spoke, Apieron drew Tensel from its scabbard and

strung it with a fluid motion, one end braced against his foot. "Care to retract your wager, thief?" grinned Xephard. "Have you ever gazed on a more fearsome bow?"

Jamello did not need to answer. Apieron's great bow was indeed mighty. Before strung, it stood six feet of polished yew, engraved with many subtle runes of power and accuracy. Apieron pulled on bracers and a finger guard and readied several cloth-yard shafts with hunting tips, although he carried his armor-piercing arrows with him. With a nod to Sarc, the two hunters disappeared into the forest.

Giliad and Jamello, Turpin and Henlee, fell to readying a comfortable camp for what would be their last night under the protective eaves of the easternmost arm of the Wyrnde. The next stage of the journey would take them into craggy uplands whose dangerous repute would disallow cooking fires and the sounds of merriment.

The cheer of day's ending was shared by the steeds who were happy to be free of swampy trails. Giliad attended to their hooves with a small pick and a cantrip that allowed him to heal bruises and cracks. A merry blaze was soon nestled in a crook of rock, and Henlee was amazed to find yellow-green fruit like a skinless grape dangling on the twisted ends he held while the fungus melted into the boiling water. He popped it whole into his mouth, and his rehearsed grimace turned to pleasure as he crunched the sweet nectar, smacking his lips.

"Tastes like peaches or ... anyway, 'twould make a better brandy," he added mournfully.

Giliad smiled at the dwarf. "The moulds of the Wyrnde are not for the inexperienced. Prepare a clean pot of water. I shall find us something better!"

The elvin mage furrowed his brow in concentration and sniffed, then signaled Jamello to follow with a spade to the base of a spreading oak where the loam appeared barren of all plant life, and small multicolored flies circled. Henlee whistled when they returned a brief time later bearing a clothful of truffles. These were cleaned and added to a pot with salt and a handful of water onions and the leaves of a blue-flowered parsley that Apieron had taught them to harvest. A pleasant aroma filled the campsite as the horses of the sun rode westward, drawing long shadows from the surrounding foliage.

Henlee sat cross-legged atop the weathered stone and drew a soot-black file across the cutting edges of his maul with a grating rasp. He would finger the edge and repeat the motion. All the while, he hummed a ditty in his native tongue, and a small smile lifted the brown beard in his seamed-back face.

"Why sharpen that hand glaive?" asked Jamello. "Apieron once told me there's few weapons in this world as enchanted as Maul."

"'Tis true," said the dwarf, stroking his beard, "but then, so's the file."

Jamello favored him with a sardonic smile, yet his gaze remained fixed on the dwarf in admiration of the many gems and clever loops of electrum, gold, and platinum that set them in his beard.

"What are you thinking, thief?"

Jamello made an off-handed gesture at Giliad, hoping to dissuade the dwarf's ever-suspicious mind. "'Tis said that the wealth of that one's liege is beyond counting."

Henlee coughed. "Surely even your addled brain does not conceive thoughts of thievery from Amor, a land that none may enter without alerting the six immortals who keep it. *The Ring.* And Galor Galdarion, that one's master, you have met." Henlee chucked darkly at the memory.

"Nonetheless," persisted Jamello, "I should like to see the splendor of the tower by the sea, and ships of white timber with silver rigging."

"You would be made most welcome in Amor, Jamello," called

Giliad from the opposite side of the wide stone. "And, you may come away with more than you desire. That is, should we survive our current quest."

Xephard looked up from oiling Leitus with a rag. "That is unimportant. Each moment we live and breathe is a gift from the Goddess in which to rejoice, to live fully."

"You are a testament to your order, my son," said Turpin from where he reclined. "I deem you to be remembrance of a more gallant age, an age of heroes."

Giliad idly drew, then erased various sigils with a white stick. "I agree with our esteemed priest."

"Is it true that elves can commune with their ancestors?" asked Jamello. "I have oft desired to speak with my father."

"Spilled beer and dancing devils, boy," exclaimed Henlee. "Know you how long one of those elves lives? They don't have to commune, they just turn and ask him something."

Xephard looked up. "Our hunters return."

"Quick, lad!" said Henlee to Jamello. "Your eyes are sharp, do our friends bring fresh game? or is it more elf biscuit for us?" Jamello scrambled over the stone face.

"Aye," called Xephard, "an' tell us who was the huntsman. I would know if my sword brother hast finally met his match."

Jamello shielded his eyes. He beheld two figures, small in the distance, leaving deeper forest shades to wend their way up the tree-studded slope of the little crest whereupon their friends waited. "The twain are yet two stades distant, and their raiment masks them well, yet it seems my lord Apieron carries a burden over his right shoulder, on his left is the great bow."

"Aha," shouted Xephard. Giliad sprang up to join Jamello. The figures were more clearly seen, picking their way carefully but swiftly amongst rock and bole. "The man-child does indeed bear the greater prize. Perhaps a hind."

"But the winged one is not empty handed," said Jamello. "I see a string of woodcock around his waist."

"More the better," chuckled Henlee, fueling his fire while fashioning a spit for the roe and a stone oven for the hens.

Jamello and Xephard descended the outcrop as the hunters crossed the final hundred steps into the camp. Xephard poked Jamello in the ribs rather painfully. "Well, gambling man, it appears your bet was poorly placed. Surely that spike buck outscores a brace of fowl. Rest assured, I shall donate your golden lucky to a just cause."

Jamello grew agitated at the thought of his precious coins so disrespected. "I do not doubt, noble Xephard, that all your thoughts and deeds are painfully noble. An' yet I prefer to keep my wealth until I see the arrow wounds, perhaps the poor animal was simply tired and begged our kindly ranger for a ride." Apieron and Sarc crested the outcrop and moved to lower their burdens.

"What ho, elf?" boomed Henlee. "Two hundred years of practice and you can't outshoot a whelp?"

"Apieron of Windhover is lacking in no hunter's skill that I can discern."

"I always hate to see an elf begging excuses," chuckled Henlee.

"Judge me how you will," continued Sarc. With that, he lay out five plump, long-beaked woodcock in a row. Each displayed a single wound centered on the upper portion of the neck. Henlee emitted a low whistle and bowed. Jamello began to smile.

"Come now, Apieron," protested Xephard. "Show us your hunter's prize."

Apieron stretched out a yearling buck. It also displayed a single punctate mark placed cleanly and high on the neck. "That's a fine piece of shooting, brother!" Xephard clapped Apieron on the back. "Let us see your gold, thief. I wish to test the weight of your coin before we feast."

Apieron smiled ruefully. "Actually, the foliage was a bit dense to wield Tensel, so I stood guard whilst Sarc did the shooting."

Xephard stared incredulously at Apieron's face. Henlee roared with laughter and slapped his mailed thighs. Giliad and even Turpin joined in.

"You loosed no shot?"

Apieron only shrugged. "Whomever said it was wise to wager against a famous cutpurse or compete in bowry with a winged archer? Where is water for cleaning? We hunters shall take our ease whilst you camp lizards prepare the game."

Xephard composed himself, then withdrew the silver dagger from his belt scabbard and presented it, hilt first, to Jamello. "Well, sir, have you naught to say?"

The thief gathered it up and flipped it a few times before returning it to Xephard. "I'll take it *after* we return. You may save my life with that! Also, they sing in town that any man who is rich in pride is inevitably poor in substance."

"They also say," said Turpin, "that fools ever put money before wisdom." Xephard and Jamello shared a look; apparently neither could guess at whom the remark was aimed.

A small freshet where Henlee filled pots was put to use, and willing hands soon had the wood fowl cleaned and the venison dressed and spitted. Choice morsels were added to the stew such that a pleasant variety of roast hen, deer-shank, and truffle was poured over the remaining bread provided by the winged elves. Apieron did not protest the light of a goodly fire, and so they built the popping blaze high as night drew on. The airs above the cairn were cooled by a clean breeze that lifted over the elevated campsite. The place possessed a wholesome feel, and the cheer of food and rest after much toil was welcomed by the travelers.

"What are you drinking, elf?" asked Henlee of Giliad.

"A draught as cool and refreshing as virgin snow," said Giliad. He handed his gem-studded cup to the dwarf.

"You conjured it?" asked Henlee suspiciously.

"I moved it from another place to here," replied Giliad archly.

"You stole it," pronounced Henlee. He swirled the wine, staring into its dark red depths as if trying to discover some secret that lay hidden at the bottom of the chalice.

"How come I can't smell it?"

"My good dwarf," explained Giliad, "a subtle vintage such as this delights the tongue and cools the throat. It does not offend. One might be reminded of coastal berries and rarified fruits, not the breath of a stupefied orc."

Henlee quickly lifted the chalice and imbibed a mighty swig before wiping his lips with the back of one hairy hand. He handed the cup back to the elf noble.

"How did you find it?"

"Delightful."

Henlee rose and strode to the far side of the camp to sit by Apieron and Jamello. "Tree piss," he said with lowered voice.

"Here boys, try a real drink." He reached into his jerkin to produce a flask that appeared of iron. "I keep this little secret for times such as these." He took a swallow and proffered it to Apieron, who tilted it sparingly and handed it over to Jamello.

"How much harm can it do?" said Jamello to the flask. "After all, we are going to have to share a great many things on this journey."

"That'll put hair on your chest, and back," laughed Henlee, relieving Jamello of the flask to imbibe another gulp before tucking his treasure away. Jamello sat motionless, staring as if transfixed.

"How did you find the special liquor of my people?" asked Henlee. "*Redhand's Repast* we call it."

"I am indeed fortunate." He rose and walked stiff-legged to Giliad, who smiled up at him in the darkness.

"And how was the distillation of mountain dwarfs, whose making is held secret?"

"Dragon piss."

"May the knowledge of its making remain secret," laughed the elf. He handed Jamello more of his wine, then rose to share it out to all. As Giliad dispensed his cordials, Apieron noted that the gemmed flagon was no less full when he was done than when he began.

Snatches of song and explosive laughter echoed down the crag. Even Henlee relented to partake again of the elvin vintage, although he often looked with the longing of a lost lover at the empty keg he had strapped to Bump's kit. Apieron studied his friends and companions. A dire task faced them, and yet the faces he beheld were relaxed and happy. Xephard sat guard upon the stone, constantly fingering his platinum wedding circlet as he sipped a bit of wine. Apieron realized the sacrifice the temple captain made without complaint. How he must desire to lead his company of knighted peers on gallant steeds to the battle gathering of the West!

As always, when Apieron beheld something remarkable, he thought of Melónie, wishing she could see what he could see, to share the joy that was within his heart. "By the gods, I truly miss her," he said in a low voice. Xephard's eyes fell upon him, and the paladin smiled.

To the surprise of all, Sarc produced a long, intricate pipe of white bone and gathered a coal from the fire. Shortly, sweet-smelling smoke emanated from his direction. Henlee was impressed. "There's something I'd never thought to see. A smoking elf!"

"Neither I," added Giliad without the same enthusiasm.

Ignoring the mage's remark, Henlee continued, "And that pipe weed smells sweeter than a cherry-wood fire."

"Then join me."

"Gladly I would, but I fear I'm near the end of my stash, and what's left is none too good for the wet and wear, I'll wager."

"Don't do that!" chuckled Xephard.

Henlee dug into his pack, and his eyes widened when he felt the weight of his tobacco skin. He opened it and peered within, his expression turning to one of delight when he sniffed the contents and found them to match the sweet-smelling smoke that emanated from Sarc's slender pipe. He stood and bowed low to the winged elf, whose stern, bronze face broke into a wide grin.

"Did I tell you people what an excellent idea of mine it was to have this fine fellow join our little expedition?" The others shared a laugh.

Apieron took some of the dwarf's provender and pulled a bit of flame from a twig into his own pipe bowl. "Do the elves of the Wyrnde cultivate much pipe weed? This is the best I've ever tasted."

"The soil of the Fogleaf is rich beyond belief of the drylanders, should they know of it. I have heard of human husbandmen who speak of topsoil that must be guarded in the uplands lest it blow away. In Fogleaf, the topsoil is a thousand feet deep. Tobacco and many other fine crops are raised there, though we grow only enough to provide for ourselves and do not destroy one of the forests' children to make room for another, save for those born of evil."

"I think that is wise," added Apieron. "Should the cities of East and West know of such things, you would have a highway of trade caravans to your very doors!"

"Then I am doubly glad of our solitude," laughed Sarc, "for I would rather fight noisome trolls than bicker with greedy humans."

"You may soon get your wish," said Turpin. The cleric raised himself to address the entire party. In the flickering light, his fleshy face cast ruddy highlights, and the remainder of his form was near invisible, wrapped in his voluminous mantle. The priest's sonorous voice filled the clearing, giving the impression of a disembodied oracle speaking momentous words to each of the journeyers.

"Tomorrow we begin ascent of the outer rim into the valley of the Starfall. Once in that haunted vale, who knows what we shall encounter? There is none who traveled thither and returned. Once therein, the elf lord and I shall ascertain the location of the Hel Gate, and thence to the climax of our quest. Each of you must search his heart, for what awaits is greatest peril."

The adventurers were silent as each pondered the cleric's words. "What mean you, Your Eminence?" asked Xephard. "We are all here pledged to the end."

"Are we?" asked Turpin. "Of your prowess and true faith, none may question, my son. But there are others here who must weigh my words on the scale of their own devotion." With that, he turned a keen look upon the winged elf and Jamello. It was on Apieron, however, that his gaze lingered. Apieron felt as though his soul was caressed by probing fingers.

After a space, Turpin continued, "Have you ever encountered a being of such purity in its evil that your very life is an affront to it? They are legion."

"You have met such a creature?" asked Henlee softly.

"Fearsome," said the cleric. Seemingly satisfied with the effect he had on the others, Turpin reseated himself and tilted his cup in a long gulp of elfin wine before refilling it and repeating the gesture. Jamello fidgeted.

"Ahem, boy—" said Henlee, indicating the thief. The dwarf proceeded to mumble something while crunching noisily on a piece of hot fowl, bones and all.

"You were saying, noble Henlee?" Jamello asked with exaggerated politeness.

"I said," reiterated Henlee, clearing his throat after a mighty pull from his cup and wiping his lips on his sleeve, "the problem with demons is they don't fight fair. You can't hardly sneak up on one, and they can smell a durned elf a mile off."

The dwarf waved a dripping fowl leg in the general direction of Giliad. "That one, probably *two miles*." Giliad smiled and gave a seated bow. "And when you do get close, they just up and fly off, laughing as much as they please, and there isn't much you can do about it. An' they are strong, strong as dwarves, but bigger." If possible, Jamello looked even more glum. "That's saying nothing for quickness either, boy. As quick, or quicker than you." Henlee emphasized his point with several jabs of the drumstick. "Rip your throat out faster than you can say *boo*."

Apieron added, "We are in for a quick strike, not a pitched battle."

Henlee continued unperturbed, "And you can bet your precious cockels that these demons will have something especially nasty in store for us, or I'm a furred rabbit."

"Say no more, O Master," said Jamello. "I'll take first watch as sleep is furthest from my thoughts."

"I wasn't trying to scare 'im," said Henlee to Apieron's reproving look. "Just give him a bit of encouragement, a sense of challenge and adventure. The boy never would want to go on if there was no excitement in it."

"Ah, but you neglected an important point," said Xephard. "*I* will be with you." The paladin displayed his long blade. "See, thief? Demons hate Leitus, she is not kind to them."

"If that's true," said Henlee brightly, winking at Jamello. "They'll all probably leap on that big, shiny fool. We can just sneak up and bash them from behind. Besides, that pretty little wand is so bright, maybe it will hurt their eyes." Xephard laughed, and launched the sword into the air where it hung, turning in the light of the fire before falling with a single tumble back to his easy grasp.

"It *is* a pretty pig-sticker," admitted Henlee. "An' he do know how to use it."

With those words, conversation ebbed, as Turpin's speech and the dwarf's jest had given each much to ponder. Despite Jamello's offer, Sarc stood to assume first watch, ascending the outcrop with a spring and graceful flap of broad wings. In the lands they departed, summer was in full bloom and the Wyrnde behind them sweltered, yet here a brisk draught of air slid from the eastern enescarpment to find their camp. Jamello leaned upon one elbow, swirling his last portion of Giliad's wine. "A fine meal is finer yet with drink, Sir Mage, even if the latter *was* conjured." He raised a toast.

"Perhaps," said Apieron, "you might have pursued the magical arts had you known of such rewards, eh, Messire Rudolfo?"

"Indeed, ranger. Unlike you, I've no taste for endless meals of hardtack, dried venison, and spring water. No wonder you've such a dour disposition, your bowels don't function properly." Apieron's face grew crimson in the firelight, although he smiled in acknowledgment of the thief's barb.

"But you are mistaken," corrected Giliad. "Not about Apieron, of course, but of the wine."

"Thank you very much," said Apieron.

"Not at all," beamed Giliad. "A good vintage must not be maligned, and this one is quite real, crafted by master druids in blessed Amor."

At that, Henlee tilted the dregs of his cup and banked their fire to burn down while they slept. "Master Dwarf," protested Jamello, "did you sense my toes were becoming cozy?"

"We have enemies," Henlee muttered, and proceeded to prepare the camp for a speedy departure should it become necessary.

"Fear not," called Sarc from his watch position. "Tonight there will be a bright display of starshine to warm your spirit and light your dreams."

"Come hither, and bring your cup!" Jamello mounted the rock ledge to stand nigh the winged elf. They beheld a blanket of glistening stars across the indigo firmament.

"Hand your wine to me." Staring down into the liquid, dark within the shell of the cup, Sarc intoned softly—first into the wine and then to the stars above. He flung up his arms, hurling the wine into a shower of amber that separated into shining droplets, hanging against the sky like a mantle of diamonds. The ensorcelled wine brought into relief several large constellations. Jamello gasped, and Sarc laughed aloud. The others came forward to stand at the foot of the outcrop.

"Truly a wondrous enchantment," exclaimed Apieron. Turpin and Xephard stared silently while Henlee stroked his beard and muttered to himself, naming the formations he beheld. Giliad beamed and gave a silent bow to Sarc, who returned it deeply.

"Now, Jamello," said the winged elf, "even a city-dweller can see our Lady of Evensong, whom we of the forest name Bradamante." Jamello followed Sarc's pointing hand and marked the outline of a shining woman with hair that fell in an arching cascade to join graceful wings longer than her body. "Bragen says dwarves call this *The Forger*; her arms and breasts a great hammer, her head the anvil, and hair—the leaping sparks." Henlee nodded in confirmation.

Jamello answered, "I see how this could be true, but I prefer the winged maiden with the flowing hair." Sarc proceeded to instruct him on the nature and meanings of the star signs as known by his people of the Wyrnde. With the aid of his spell, never-seen bodies and patterns became beautifully apparent as they wheeled slowly overhead.

Xephard found Apieron's distant look and placed a hand on the taller man's shoulder. "You think of home?"

"Yes," answered the tall knight without turning to his friend. "At times like this, I do so very much."

"Soon, my friend. Soon we will breach the Hel Gate and solve this fateful riddle. Then you can go home, this time with lasting peace."

Apieron briefly patted Xephard's scarred hand. "You are my true friend. I know I do not have to ask that, should I fall in the fire, you succor Melónie and the children. For you know as well as I that not all my enemies are before me."

"Do not fear for them. I have already so pledged."

Apieron sought his rest, but his thoughts were troubled by a star the elf did not name. It was fully risen in the east. X'fel the Accursed.

WINDHOVER

A busy spring's eve drew to a close at Windhover. Apieron's fortifications were complete, and Duner and Telnus devoted their time to drilling the garrison in contingencies for defense of their strong place. The community was blessed with a bountiful growing season and neared the time of harvest. The troubles of cities and rumors of blight in the provinces had seemingly neglected this outlying corner of the kingdom. Freemen's crofts rippled with ripening grain, and fat flocks bleated whilst children sang happy songs and made pretend war in barns and behind hedgerows.

Duner was uneasy. The news of the King's passing was momentous. The son was able, no doubt, but would he get a chance? Of similar blood to that of his lord, the Candors retained the soul of a warrior people in unbroken tradition. Would it be enough? A boy of eighteen!

Duner shook his head and sighed. Weighty matters were not for such as he, who but longed for his lord Apieron's return. Then all would be made well. By thunder! he had a mind to board up this lonely pile and march off to the aid of his lord, devils and royal courtiers be damned! He heard the sound of Melónie singing from her high room. Doubtless she was at the loom, finishing the mantle she made for Apieron. Allowing none to aid her, she spent hour after hour at her spindle, weaving and singing songs of love and protection. *Nay, he would not leave. Windhover would be held, come what may.*

"What're you looking at, Skels? Dress that weapon, eyes front! If I was a goblin archer, I'da shot you through your worthless brainpan. Probably woulda improved your thinkin." Duner tramped off, muttering about the quality of recruits in this modern age. The sentry gulped and tightened his grip on his halbard. The seneschal was old, some said as much as fifty. Nevertheless, he was fierce as an old boar, and getting worser the longer his his lord was away.

Melónie smiled when she heard. Duner's gravelly voice and gruff demeanor comforted her. How far away were her father and brothers! Tonight more than usual, Melónie felt the absence of her man. She betook herself beyond the tower and bailey into the garden where her slipping stream chuckled merrily. She walked to the bank of its small pond that collected in an elbow where the stream made a turn before angling down the green slope. Its still waters exactly mirrored the star-strewn vault, and frosty starlight limned the drooping limbs of her willow and set gems on the water. She wondered if Apieron gazed on a night such as this. Did he see the same stars as she? Was her name on *his* lips?

Melónie wept silent tears that struck the water, making tiny rings. She raised her face to the blessed heavens. White starfire blurred in her eyes to become one shining light. "Hear me, gods of justice. Succor my husband, and keep safe his gentle spirit."

A cool wind nipped at her bare ankles. *How odd this country is!* She wondered if the immortals heard her prayer. The silent stars winkled on, unperturbed and impassive to the woes of one, small woman. Melónie stifled her weeping and drew close her veil to wend a lonely way back to her bridal bed.

Book II

There was a battle to be fought,
With fine, whetted swords.
Rings of honor did we win,
When we smashed Hel's brazen door.

Chapter 21

Broken Country

Tallux stood his horse in a high place. A vast landscape unfolded before him. Uncounted miles of broken hills blanketed with foliage lay behind, and to his front reared cragged hilltops rimming northern passes to the Haunted Vale.

A mighty journey of more than two hundred leagues had led him from the salt tang and wet cobbles of Sway to this remote wilderness. Ignoring conventional wisdom, he chanced a diagonal course to the Gorganj, knowing he could never hope to make his rendezvous by the southerly route. Instinct told the half-elvin ranger that the forest between the knoll he had breasted and the high southern valley secreted many hidden meadows and pocket glades of wild grass, but these would grow scarce as the land inclined. The yellow light of the westering sun marked areas of darker green that denoted the path of a winding stream or river. He knew that ancient watercourses would have carved tunnels and caves in the soft rock of such defiles, rendering the footing for mounted animals perilous except in daylight. He pondered if it were best to set Windstrong free, for on foot with Sut he could match a horse's pace for days without tiring.

In the distance, a mist blended the forest against brown slopes that sheltered the wide vale beyond. Somewhere in the wild walked his quarry. In his mind's eye, Tallux pictured Apieron of Windhover—tall with brown hair falling upon broad shoulders, and whose long, purposeful strides no doubt led a group of stalwarts such as Tallux could well imagine. Tallux swung off his horse and set before Windstrong the last of the enriched grain he had carried from the fertile eastern marches of Ilycrium. While the beast happily champed, Tallux squatted and fingered the rich loam at his feet to begin his reverie. Short blades of young grass, green as emeralds, revealed their spidery roots when he lifted them free of their chestnut bed. Sut sniffed once, and recognizing his master's behavior, the war dog set out in a wide patrolling circle to safeguard the area against intrusion.

Tallux felt magic flow through the earth into him and back again. Although only a half-elf and a warrior, he possessed a measure of the powers wielded by the elvin woodmasters of Greenwolde. Their art was fed by natural enchantments of the living world and amplified within them. Where decades' attunement with nature's harmony left off and the mystic began, none could say—for these were one and same to the peoples who lived and walked leafstrewn byways amongst first-growth forest but three days' ride from the capital of Ilycrium, though few there knew aught of the woodland kingdom save by myth and the stories of children.

Tallux summoned a spell view of Apieron, remembrances of their long association aiding him in the task. He saw Apieron's face and felt this slanted sun warm upon his neck whilst a strange, chill wind blew from the fore. There was a glimpse of barren cliff tops close behind. Tallux smiled and replaced the turve. Those he sought were not far. Neither were they easily reached. Moreover, he sensed a shadow of danger lurking where his friends trod. He watered the gelding at a nearby rill and spoke words of keeping and blessing to the animal after removing what light pack it carried. The beast touched its soft mouth to his neck and snorted, then departed swiftly whence they had come, setting the sun on its left shoulder.

Sut returned and regarded his master with yellow eyes. "We go, dog. My lord Apieron has need of the messages we bear, and perhaps more besides!"

The elvin scout fingered his mighty bow as he spoke. Then he shouldered the famous weapon. He checked longsword and dirk at his belt before lifting his pack. "Let us run through the cool darkness. With luck, before sun seeks her rest tomorrow, we shall join those we seek." Sut swung into a loping gait at his master's side. The two warriors disappeared, silent and swift into shadows of solemn pines that carpeted the hills north of the Haunted Vale.

Tallux's chest moved deeply and rhythmically after his night's exertion. He had run without pause, covering twenty miles in the darkness onto the last spur of the Gorganj that lifted to become a northeastern bastion of the Haunted Vale.

Last night was the third of the full moon. Moon man had been a late riser, at midnight only halfway from his eastern breakfast to overhead. Daybreak found him high above his bed, pale white yet distinct against the western sky. Today would be a day of portent. The flat rays of morning's sun invigorated Tallux, and the wind was brisk. He gazed down at tireless Sut who stood like a statue, no visible sign of their efforts revealed on his smooth, gray flanks.

"Today we shall find Apieron."

Tallux looked back whence they came in the night. Low weathered hills, whose pale brows were covered with gorse, lifted undulant shoulders clothed in pearl-green sage. Black pine filled the defiles. He wheeled, his eye capturing the image of a man like shape housed in shadows near the base of the slope they had ascended. Tallux was garbed in drab green and dun and knew he should be invisible to any save an eagle. Depsite this, he had no doubt that the tall figure was regarding him.

They stood thus for a space. The wind blew very chill. Tallux contemplated yelling or walking to confront the apparition, but it turned and disappeared into the gloom-shrouded ravine. He shrugged and clucked to Sut, who stared intently into the defile where night lingered. An encounter in such a remote place could mean many things. Whatever the figure's presence portended, it was unlikely to involve him directly. Nonetheless, the man-creature made him uneasy.

Tallux cut east once he breasted the last ridge and set an intercepting course for those he sought, near to the Starfall. In the meantime, he would keep to deep cover available on the tumbledown slopes of the circling rim. With his camouflaged garb and woodcraft beyond that of mortal men, even canny squirrels and jays would not mark his passage.

Tallux was veteran of unnumbered forays. A half-elf raised among wood elves, he had earned acceptance by ever seeking out the most difficult missions. Similarly, his rise amongst the ranks of the hardened frontiersman of Ilycrium's border scouts came of respect paid by coin of toil and hardship. Tallux knew that when he felt a prickle behind his neck, to heed his instincts, and after this encounter, his long hair fairly stood on end!

He set his face into a grim smile and lengthened his stride. Expert woodsman always chastened pupils to never run in the wild for fear of misstep or exhaustion and exposure, but they were not Tallux of Greenwolde. Already he moved faster than a normal man could run. He glanced to Sut, tireless and steady.

"Come, dog! Let us shed this night dweller. We have appointments to keep." He sped up, elf and beast flitting through the dawn-dappled woodlands like sifting zephyrs.

THE HAUNTED VALE

Under his breath, Apieron cursed their delay. A full day's effort had been required to surmount the bony ridge that shielded the Haunted Vale. The companions hastened to descend somewhat before setting camp such that they might catch warm drafts rising from the valley floor, for the night prior had grown crisp. While vegetation cloaked the outer rim, within was altogether different. What flora existed struggled amongst sunbaked rocks, dramatic temperature swings, and barren earth. Tough cedars and stunted pines clung to small pockets of soil trapped in clefts along cliff faces. Many birds roosted here, but to Apieron, their raucous calls were unfriendly.

The campsite was all together different tonight. No fire was lit, and the travelers nibbled cold venison and woodcock. They drank sparingly, for they had not spied any rivulet on the valley side of the rim. Watches were doubled as the first portion of their journey neared completion. Night slowly gave over to a cold and cheerless dawn. Armor previously stowed on mounts was checked and rechecked for rapid use should urgent need arise.

After a meager breakfast, Jamello finally produced the helm procured for him by Xephard. Apieron whistled as Jamello set it on his head for sizing. It was a boat-shaped morion of black-and-white enamel over steel, with a sail of white metal and exquisitely detailed florals upon gold bolt-heads along the adjoining base.

Xephard at least seemed very proud, slapping the slighter man upon the back. "Now a lordly warrior you shall appear, and strike fear into the heart of the foeman!" Apieron laughed for the changes wrought upon the life-sworn thief.

"With that boar's head, foemen will take you for our king," said Henlee. "Like as not they will try to kill you first, so stay away from me."

"I think it an excellent choice," objected Xephard. "'Twere best to fit it now before we reach the valley floor."

"What exactly lives there?" asked Jamello.

"My people know of the cursed bowl," said Sarc. "Many speak of its evil, yet none ever journeyed hither. Wise peoples do not leave the Everspring for a dead and haunted vale."

Turpin spoke. "It is likely the area of the Starfall already hosted a Hel portal … perhaps that is why the comet struck here. Such things draw evil unto themselves. In such wise, it has no doubt drawn more fell creatures and peoples since the cataclysm three decades ago. I have tried to scry this place many times. Always I am thwarted by some power, mayhap the Gate itself! And yet the *arts* might aid us now that we are within the vale's circumference."

Giliad stepped to a flat boulder and brushed it clean. The stone's surface lost solidity, assuming the identity of the valley. Jamello whistled while Henlee clucked in admiration. Giliad smiled, and they could see the defile through which they had traversed the west rim, the terminus of which they now stood. Of interest, the northeastern edge was open where a great, fan-shaped rent grooved a splaying track into the farther plain. There the stone of Giliad's spell bubbled and hissed in miniature vortex. The golden elf bore a solemn expression.

"*That* is pretty obvious," muttered Henlee. Apieron wanted to offset the foreboding the others must feel at the apparition revealed by Gilead's casting, and where they now hastened, but his throat had gone dry, and the moment passed.

The party swung atop their mounts, intending to traverse a path oblique to the valley floor, but soon their defile ended in dry gullies that branched and intertwined like writhing snakes. They picked their way forward in whichever of these provided the truest course while Sarc at times soared briefly overhead to survey the terrain. Despite his efforts, the ravines were oft choked with tangled brush and tumbledown. By midday, they reached a last shelf above the valley floor. Here Sarc located a small, spring-fed pond. Both elves cast spells of purification, and man and horse moved quickly to the water, for the going had been dusty, and none knew when they would next cross a stream. Jamello laughed at Henlee's wet beard.

"I thought I once knew a dwarf who claimed that water was healthy only if imbibed in the form of beer."

Henlee scowled at him by way of reply and kneeled to fill his flasks. Their rest was short. It was Apieron who spotted the footpath leaving the waterhole—it wended its way north along the ledge and parallel to the valley floor. Sarc leapt to the low height of the nearest tree. Hand above eyes, he scanned the distance briefly before sailing ahead. He reported back within minutes. "Not far from here, this goat trail becomes a well-worn track that keeps to the slope and loses itself away beyond boulder and tree. Two-footers have trod there within a day. Orc signs, I should say."

"That should not have been hard to discern," snorted Henlee.

Sarc shook his flowing mane. "Normally I would agree, but these did not defile the area greatly with their passing and left little spoor."

"This place needs a little defilement to add to its charm," said Jamello.

"They went in haste," said Giliad in half question, half statement.

"Yes," answered Apieron. Sarc nodded his assent as well.

"As should we," said Turpin. "Let us take this track as far as it suits our route, then leave it to its mysteries among the hills. It may save us much time."

"I like this not," growled Henlee. "Our rangers say this is a dark place, though they know not why. Now we march to unknown perils whilst letting all the orcs of the hills at our backs."

"Did you not listen earlier?" asked Turpin. "When the holy powers of the high cleric of Sway cannot pierce the sorcerous veil guarding this place, is that not enough?" Apieron stirred slightly but said nothing.

"Be that as it may," replied the stubborn dwarf, "Your Wisdom is standing here with the rest of us wasting what little light this day holds. I for one do not fancy battling goblins after dark, and who is to say the trail does not curve back down to the valley floor and the very doorway of your unnamed evil?"

"Or into a blind sack where we might be set upon in ambuscade? Or that the menace of the valley actually resides in these hills?" Henlee kicked a dry stone off the slope with his heavy boot. As if to emphasize his master's point, Bump hunched back, pulling on the reins, his ears laid back as he bared his long, yellow teeth.

"That is a possibility I have considered," conceded Apieron.

Jamello heard a small movement from where Xephard was standing. He spun around and said alarmingly, "You're not going to blow that thing, are you?"

Xephard had retrieved his war horn, a mighty shell of ox horn bound with silver scrolling, fingering it in preparation to set forth a mighty blast. He fixed Jamello with a glare. "Of course, knave. This banter of hidden paths and waiting ambushes slays my patience." The paladin straightened, swelling his chest. "Let us challenge the Valley of Shadow and press straight through to our greater purpose."

"Well, Bump," addressed Henlee to the burro, who perked up his long ears, "a stand-up fight it is!" He unslung Maul from atop the donkey's kit.

"Of course he will not," snapped Giliad. "Let us please be serious and consider our best course."

"Waste not thy breath on lonesome rocks and broken stumps, my son," consoled Turpin.

Henlee touched his nose. "These stones and roots have ears."

"Very well," said Xephard, shrugging as he replaced the oliphant at his belt.

"I have a proposal," said Apieron as he scanned their unhappy faces. More than they, he was beset by the feelings of a weary anxiety after a great journey, now faced with greater dangers.

"Sarc and I shall rove ahead, on and off the trail, while the rest advance after one-half hour. We will scout the orc path and return when a direction change needs be made. Hopefully we can skirt the heart of the vale and leave it behind our right shoulders as we approach the Gate."

"This seems sooth to me," added Giliad. "We shall follow after a time but advance no more than we can swiftly reach you should the need arise."

"Aye, Apieron," said Henlee. "Signal us with your hunting horn or a rattle arrow." At this, Apieron and Sarc left packs and mounts and moved off swiftly past dust-gray trunks and sandy rocks.

The valley was indeed inhabited by such folk as the Archbishop of Sway guessed. A dozen miles in diameter, a variety of peoples and monsters dwelled therein. Some were allied, and others held themselves apart, but all paid heed to the repute of the powerful shaman that dwelt at the vale's center. He was a renegade cleric of more than a little orcish blood, with the hand of an assassin and the heart of the blackest foes of light.

A shrine of sorts he had there, and from its subterranean halls none that went thither as captive had ever returned. The smoke of sacrificial burnings cast a reek that covered the valley's floor with a gray pall. Many slaves had he, and more useful yet were spies and murderers, both free and embonded. Bizaz bestirred himself, the game was afoot!

Chapter 22

The Haunted Vale

Ongush, son of Chip Fang, eyed the tall human who picked his way carefully up the path. At twenty years old, Ongush was a goblin warrior nearing middle age and in the prime of his strength and fighting experience. For this and his proven bravery, chieftains chose him to lead his party of three on this difficult, daylight mission to waylay the rim trail. The valley's strange shaman (curse his black soul!) had sensed a presence. So now he, Ongush the Bold, was stuffed in a miserable crack, watching this huntsman navigate the goblin's secret road with no more noise than a night cat.

Although his hiding place was under a rocky bank cut over the trail, the light of day stung his eyes and rendered the man nearly invisible, rot his balls! Even so, Ongush could see well enough to note the great bow the man held ready and the steely javelins on his back and the four-foot sword girt at his waist.

With a barely audible grunt, Ongush signaled his companions in their holes across and down the trail. Maggots eat their eyes if they were asleep or cut and ran when the big warrior came to the ambush point. The attack had better be perfect, for if that bastard human was alone, he—Ongush the Cruel—was a halfling bitch.

Of course maggots would not get the chance if Gul and Half Ear botched this, because Orc King would first scoop their eyes out with a sharp rock. Ongush hissed silently at the pleasurable thought, although his expression turned to a grimace when he realized such an eventuality meant he would have to face the human scout alone.

Ongush's fist tightened excitingly on his scimitar. His eyes widened in surprised pleasure when the hunter paused at exactly the right spot to cock his head as if listening. This one was dumber than most! Gul and Half Ear came boiling out behind the man, yelling like banshees.

The warrior wheeled with appalling quickness, drawing and releasing the bow in one smooth motion. A three-foot shaft took Half Ear exactly in the middle of his low-slung head, somersaulting the goblin completely over to fall flat on his face and snapping the shaft beneath him. Gul paused and stared at his dead companion, then whooped and ran at the man with a wickedly edged axe raised over his long arms. The man calmly dropped the bow with his left, cross-drawing his sword with his right.

Ongush saw the scene played before him as if in slow motion. Worms of perdition! But that blade was a pretty trophy, if a bit large. He put on a burst of speed to close with the warrior from behind. No time for anything fancy here, he'd simply hook his scimitar through the man's right kidney.

Gul didn't last long. The axe had barely begun its overhand descent toward the human's chest when a precise fencer's thrust took him in the diaphragm. Arms and axe fell limp as the goblin soldier sank to his knees, eyes closing forever. Ongush didn't care, all he saw was the man's broad back filling his vision as he took a final step and lunged forward, scimitar tip leading.

Apieron felt the danger and prepared to duck and roll forward. He had deliberately avoided encumbering blows with the pair of goblins so that he could react to any peripheral threat, yet strategy and quickness could not save him from taking some wound with the scimitar's killing point scarce feet from his flank.

Ongush's chain shirt was as well wrought as any borne by goblin or man in the Starfall Valley. This was so because the mail links had been forged for goblin masters by a hamstrung dwarven slave, long since dead. The shirt of supple metal and its countless rings riveted with consummate skill availed him little. Sarc's twisted lance took him square in the back, parting the links like rotten paper. The lance head burst through his barrel-chested body where it tented the mesh over his chest from within.

Ongush died silently, although his eyes bulged weirdly at the strange apparition from his chest. Black blood gushed from his lips as the winged elf's momentum jerked the goblin clear of the ground over Apieron, who ducked and cursed, getting a wayward kick from an orc boot atop his coifed head. Sarc laughed grimly and shook his burden free before alighting next to the ranger.

"Tough little buggers, and well armed!" said Apieron. "No doubt these were forewarned of our little expedition." Sarc only grunted. Drawing his odd-shaped knife, he bent over the corpses.

"Come, my friend," said Apieron. "Leave the carrion for the kites. Our companions must be told we are spied out. I figure the master of these wretches will send swarms once darkness falls."

It was already dusk in the shadows. A spidery wisp of a questing touched the half-elf. Prone behind a crumbling red boulder amidst one of the many rock-strewn ravines fanning north and eastward of the Haunted Vale, Tallux cursed.

Silent as the imprecation, he fitted a shaft to the bow named Strumfyr by the elves of the Malave, and had been given into his hand by King Dryas himself. No other could bend it. The men of Ilycrium's border scouts simply called it *Farstriker*. With the mighty weapon, Tallux could place a cloth-yard shaft into a palm-sized targe at two hundred yards whilst winging three others into flight before the first struck home. Tallux had augmented his camouflage with small sheaves of parched grass that bristled about his person, and daubs of clay to obscure the forestland colors of his garb that would have betrayed him amongst the wind-parched gullies. His concentration fell inward, weaving a subtle enchantment of concealment. A lone raven croaked in the still.

Tallux's eyes hardened. The cold fingers of a powerful searching spell probed the evening gloom like a grasping hand. Sut growled deep in his throat. "I feel it as well," Tallux whispered. "An unholy will guides this violating magic."

He shared a look with the yellow-eyed hound. "As we have done many times before … you shall seek and flush our foe. Then I shall slay." The massive hound nudged him and crept forth amongst the rubble. His pale form flashed briefly in the darkness. Tallux smiled grimly, fingering a taper-headed arrow whose enchanted steel tip would pierce any armor cast by man or elf. There was no doubt that his pursuer had (incredibly) managed not only to track the powerful hunting twain but to keep pace and now drive him to cover. Tallux ground his teeth. No more. The hunt ended here—in blood, as it always did.

"Halloo the camp," called Apieron softly.

"We were resting, not camping," said Jamello.

"Come on in!" returned Henlee. "Glad to see you back so soon." Presently the forms of the tall woodsman and longhaired elf detached themselves from a shadowed ledge. "Some lookout you are, thief!" said Henlee as he poked Jamello. "They were nearly on us, and you, standing there like a barnyard sheep."

Jamello shook his head in disgust, more so at himself than any words of the dwarf. There was some magic of concealment about them, he was sure. Even when the two strode into the mist of the party, the keen-eyed thief barely marked them until Apieron smiled and lifted an upturned hand in greeting. He had seen Apieron do this before, and he suspected that the winged elf was even more skilled at it. *Damn forest druid types, man or elf!*

"I felt them," said Turpin.

"At least one of us is a worthy sentry," said Xephard. Turpin inclined his head.

"What have you there, elf?" asked Henlee. Sarc let fall the heads of three goblins he had bound by their lanky hair. The winged elf looked at his hands and whispered a minor spell of cleansing.

"Well, well," said Henlee, eyeing the swamp elf whose bare chest was flushed with the exertions of the hunt. His wild, long locks and barbaric dress added to the measure of respect in the dwarf's estimation. "I never did see an elf like to you, winged one."

"Three scouts," said Apieron, "set in ambush against us. We are being tracked." Apieron looked up at the waning sun, already hours past its peak.

Giliad spoke. "Then let us haste while the light of day persists. With one strong march, we should hope to turn the north corner of the vale and put your orc tribe behind."

"Would I had been there," exclaimed Xephard mournfully.

"We will have to march hard if we are to outrun goblins in their homelands," said Henlee.

"Agreed," said Apieron. "We will do so and pause not for darkness as long as the trail holds." Within two minutes, the travelers were moving at a goodly pace. Sarc's trophies were left in a grim, little pile on the dusty rocks, their dead eyes staring at nothing.

Goblins did indeed come forth. Once the slanting rays of the sun failed to burnish the tops of the vale's peaks, night descended on swift wings. Well-armed mountain orcs boiled forth in their hundreds from their gates like black soldier ants. Their fortress was called Thousand Eyed—a strong place that commanded the northwest corner of the valley and was set in a cliff face opposite the ledge trail. Parties of goblin soldiers were detailed away eastward along the path, as well as straight out onto the valley floor to fan out on a deadly night hunt of the sort at which the dark-loving goblins excelled. By far the largest force was directed away south by Orc King, for it was in that direction whence had gone a trusted scouting party of which there was no word. The loping strides of his soldiers were matched in the opposite direction by the companions. They collided scarce two hours after nightfall.

Sarc wheeled. His eyes and teeth flashed in the low light. "Many orcs on the trail. They come rapidly!"

The companions looked around. The full moon was low in the east and cast a cold light over their surroundings. This portion of the trail offered little in the way of concealment, especially to the sharp night eyes of goblin-kind. Here the path hugged the escarpment that overlooked the vale floor, now an inky well to the right. On the left, tall shoulders of the border slopes crowded the track.

"There is nothing for it," growled Henlee. "We shall have to defend this miserable goat path."

Sarc began a rapid incantation, briefly touching his feet and ears, then those of each of the travelers. "I have cast a cantrip so that we shall hear them well before they us."

Apieron nodded in appreciation of the winged elf's druidic mastery, for with a simple spell, he had removed a great advantage the goblins held. The magic was no sooner cast than the jingle of weapon and harness and the scrape of rushing feet gave evidence to a well-armed company approaching with haste.

Apieron clambered atop the ledge rocks to find field of fire for his heavy bow. He set arrows with armor-piercing tips before him. The conical points were of lead encased in steel and designed to punch through any but the most enchanted armors. He planted his throwing javelins in the ground, ready to hand.

Henlee gave into Jamello's hands the reigns of the mounts to lead back to what shelter he might find. Giliad called softly to the thief, "Do not secure Ingold or Bump. If the goblin people find you, those two can fend for themselves. Defend instead the others." Jamello nodded and silently thanked Xephard for the gift of shield training. It would appear that, for the first time in his life, he would be obligated to defend a set position.

The black dwarf unslung Maul from his back harness and set himself in the middle of the path on widespread legs before Turpin and Giliad. Beard bristling, his eyes smoldered with dark fires, for his people hated mountain orcs perhaps more than any others.

In the meantime, Xephard completed donning his heavy armor and secured barding to Axylus with the help of Giliad and Sarc. The paladin had worn most of his over-gear since striking the orc trail and grinned as he set a high-plumed helm upon his head. He could not restrain a laugh when the elvin mage withdrew a foot-long, miniature lance and commanded it to grow. Within moments, he handed to the paladin a twelve-foot war spear, its long tip sheathed in bronze. Xephard inclined his head and raised the proud weapon to his lowered visor in salute.

When all was ready, Sarc sprang into the air. The clamor of running goblins arose. Xephard turned the great stallion's head and set in the spurs. Axylus neighed his war challenge and leapt into a thunderous gallop up the trail. Sarc's druidic spell allowed all to hear the cries of alarm and dismay when over a ton of man and horse hurtled into goblin ranks.

In this narrow place, the enemy formation was three abreast and twenty deep. At the paladin's onslaught, the first five ranks were blasted apart. The remainder recoiled in shock. Sarc plied his unerring missiles against any that approached Xephard's flank. The winged elf's light arrows struck exposed necks and forearms, or pinned leather-shod feet to the trail, his rapid shots echoed at half pace by the deeper thrum of Apieron's great bow. The human ranger could not match the elf's eagle-sharp sight, but it did not matter. He aimed at the closely packed rear ranks, where goblin soldiers found their armor shredded by the weighted arrows that punched through metal and bone. The entire rear was thrown into milling havoc.

Giliad produced a small wand. He angled it over the fray and set off a volley of starbursts that arched over orcin ranks, illuminating the battlescene as bright as day. Some goblins cowered against the painful glare. More screamed their rage and pressed the attack all the more fiercely for their desperation. Next to the elfin mage, Turpin stood frowning, mace in hand. Arms crossed over his chest, he surveryed the scene like a master gamesman, his quick eyes more upon his allies than the goblin host, as if weighing the performance of each of his colleagues.

After his initial charge, Xephard flung down his bloodied lance, useless in tight quarters, and produced a heavy morning-star that he swung with terrific force to crush helmeted skulls and upflung shield arms as he wheeled Axylus in a rampaging circle of steel death. Many of his foes threw down their weapons and fled back against their advancing column, further worsening the press and often struck down from behind as the paladin charged time after time into their ranks. A party of orcs slipped forward past Xephard, dazed for a moment and glad to escape the maelstrom when they spied the dwarf and the two spellcasters behind him. They yelled in fury and charged these seemingly weaker opponents, only to rebound in shock and dismay.

Henlee's magically forged armor and thick legs repelled their feeble blows while every two-handed swing of Maul slew a goblin outright and drove back the rest. If the paladin's blows were fierce, those of the dwarf were terrible to behold. Maul's killing edge caved in chests and splintered shields like rotten tin. Man-sized, battle-hardened orc captains were hurled aside like broken dolls.

Of the dozen or so goblins that fled behind the paladin, none escaped the dwarf's fury. Soon even the broken sounds of those maimed were stilled as Henlee methodically ran down first those able to limp away, then slaughtered those that could only crawl. Their hate-filled curses were silenced forever by Maul's crunching blows and Henlee's metal-shod boots.

In short minutes, it was over. Only one orc sergeant had marked Apieron's location and crawled up the ledge at him, only to be cast down with a javelin throw to the teeth. Axylus slowed to a walk, flanks sweating and twitching as Xephard turned his plumed head in search of more opponents. Many of his foes had fought bravely, and his legs and arms were bruised and abraded.

Apieron surveyed the carnage in the failing light of Giliad's illumination. "I do not think more than a handful escaped us."

"Exactly four," replied Sarc, who alighted nearby, "and two of those will not live out the hour."

"Is everyone hale?" shouted Apieron.

"We are fine!" huffed Henlee, doffing his helm and swiping his brow with a hairy hand.

"Whew," whistled Jamello as he brought up the steeds, "that didn't take long."

"Long enough to draw the remainder to us," said Giliad.

"Just so," agreed Apieron. "The others will hasten to this position, as we should make shrift to not be here when they arrive."

"They would be smarter if they took their time," said Henlee. "But then, no one ever said goblins were overly smart."

"They are clever and will change tactics," countered Giliad.

"Let us begone!" said Apieron.

Xephard recovered his lance and trotted at the head of their procession. Whether the companions outpaced the pursuit or the goblin companies were of the same mind as the dwarf, none could say. Thus the party was unencumbered by any resistance until they drew abreast the stony windows of Thousand Eyed. They gazed westward. Here the trail widened onto a rocky flat dotted with scrub trees and mounded colonies of round-eared cactus. The moon was peaking, and the orc stronghold was readily viewable, in which black holes appeared at random intervals in the cliff face that rose a full two hundred arm lengths from the level. A road of sorts debouched from a yawning gate and bisected their trail. Off to the right, the valley was a dark lake in the dim light. The companions saw they had completed their northern course and could bear with the trail nearly due east.

There was a yell and a brief clash of arms as three sentries sprang out. Xephard impaled the first with a lance thrust. He executed a perfect turn to wheel and take the second cleanly betwixt the shoulder blades. The remaining goblin shrieked louder and rolled out of the path of the thundering stallion only to be silenced as a slim arrow from Sarc's unusual bow sprouted suddenly in its throat.

"There appears to be nobody home," said Henlee. "At least not now," he chuckled darkly.

They walked the horses forward until they stood halfway from the trail to the entrance. "I suppose we should purge this robber's den," said Xephard.

"Is that wise?" asked Jamello. He looked apprehensively over his shoulder. "Surely the goblins we met on the trail lived not alone in there. Like as not others will return, and we'll have to defend from that nasty hole." Henlee wrinkled his face in distaste.

"You are both correct," stated Turpin, waking from the reflections that had occupied him since the battle. He stepped up boldly, flipping back his mantle such that it streamed from his shoulders and uplifted the hand that bore his ring of heavy gold. In the uncertain light of moon and star, it appeared vaguely serpentine. He called forth in an arcane tone. Giliad frowned at this, but none heeded him as they beheld the spectacle of the high priest's casting.

Undulant streamers leapt from Turpin's hand and snaked rapidly towards the orchold. A goblin head bobbed briefly in an upper window, and an arrow was lofted toward the party. Turpin ignored it as the power of his spell grew. Filmy tentacles were flowing into every hole and crevice in and around the fortress, some exiting to loop between portals until the entire complex was bound as if with winding thread.

Turpin's eyes gleamed as he again raised his hand with a pulling motion. A woven band of the spell substance was drawn through the central doors of the fastness into the golden ring. The misty loops stretched tight, and with a stone-splitting heave, the force of the constricting weave simply imploded the fortress, which collapsed in on itself with an enormous roar and a geyser of thrown chips and billowing dust.

The steeds reared and snorted. Tiny bits of stone rebounded from mail and helm whilst all but Turpin coughed and sputtered in the dust. Henlee growled at the rapturous cleric. "Next time, holy man, tell us what you intend. I shall find a place to hide."

"Magnificent," said Xephard. "Although a bit too easy for honest work."

Apieron and Jamello were dumbfounded. It appeared to them a faint glow remained about the heavy ring on Turpin's hand. Giliad eyed the cleric closely and was ignored in turn. Sarc remained stern-featured as always. Henlee spoke. "I suppose we could camp in this lovely place or continue on the elf's heading."

"Raiding parties may soon return," reminded Apieron. "How many battles must we fight this night?"

Before the mushroom of dust fully settled, the companions already set a strong pace. The rising sun found them clearing the northeastern rim of the vale into a broken desert blasted into rows of serried rises and deep channels parallel to their present course. In all, the formation was like to a spread fan. Of the remaining orc companies, there was no sign.

By noon, men and horses were stumbling weary. The adrenaline surge of their victories had long since dwindled, and the bleak terrain offered little cheer. "This place is worse by daylight," muttered Jamello. "Where are you taking us?"

Apieron and the spellcasters did not reply. The diffuse orange sunlight revealed a panorama much worse than the one they had departed. In this desolate place, little life stirred, aside from a few strangled conifers that strained to maintain a root's hold amongst the crags to push twig and leaf against chilled eastern gusts. Apieron gazed at the sun's orb and marvelled aloud, "Barely is it midday, and this red sun is at its ending." The wan rays seemed spent and dull, and a cold wind was in their faces.

"The very stones are broken and hold no voice. I like not these wastes," growled Henlee. He kicked up a shower of loose rubble for emphasis. The black dwarf's speculations sank into grumblings in his native tongue.

Sarc shook his head slowly, his mane swaying to and fro.

"That Sun Goddess should have so little power is the worst thing." He stretched forth a long hand to stroke the gray bark of a bent and sallow creosote. "These trees have never seen pure light or change of season," he said sadly. "From seedling to deadwood they have known only this pall." He withdrew his hand, dusted with crumbling bark. "Its life force is weak."

"Let us begone," stated Giliad. "We must search for a grotto in which to secure the steeds before we attempt the neighborhood of the Gates."

"Secure *me*, I'm dead!" groused Jamello in weariness. He was ignored.

Henlee pulled up. "Not so fast, Sir Elf."

"With this here sun setting early, those goblins will hotfoot it down our trail."

"In these gullies, you can hide a dozen regiments of orcs and never see them," said Xephard.

"And one small party of men, elves, and a dwarf," added Apieron.

"When we find a suitable place, I shall reconnoiter," Sarc assured Henlee. "No goblin can stir that I will not mark, the wind and trees will spy him out for me. I can spot a darting swallow a mile distant."

Henlee harumphed. "I hope so, winged elf. Bump would not like to share his sleeping place with filthy goblins."

"Oh, he has told me a great many things that annoy him."

Henlee shot Bump a wounded look. "He didn't!" The deep-chested burro snorted. Apieron and Giliad shared a helpless look. They started forth, leading their mounts toward the rocky defiles. The ranger's high boots set a brisk pace that the companions tried to match despite their fatigue. Slow settling clouds of dust billowed onto the rumps of the horses as the little file slipped amongst the stone channels, each face grim with its own private foreboding of what lay ahead.

A soft chuckle emanated from the rider's lips. He regarded the downcast travelers who trudged mere furlongs below. "If thou liketh not the Starfall, thou shalt find little comfort in what lies beyond."

Swathed in a voluminous sable mantle, the figure sat as a shadow upon a black horse yet greater in stature than any beast tamed by man, and perfectly still. Drannôk knew well the rift and oft patrolled the region. He also knew its rightful name, for it was here that he had first burst forth in fury and flame to claim his share of this fecund plane.

Acutely attuned to magic and the life-force emanations of all creatures that crawled, slithered, walked, or flew, Drannôk sensed the strength of the travelers moving below. In particular, he was troubled by the erect paladin as well as the poorly cloaked power of the golden elf. His scowl deepened when he beheld the tall human forester who walked at the fore. Regardless of his unnatural abilities and Hel-forged lance, he did not desire meleé with such as these. "Nay, let them break themselves on the Matog."

And *if* they should pass through, they would hardly find the regions beyond hospitable. Then there was Malesh!

Short weeks had passed since Drannôk served as guide and herald for that evil champion. Though standing nearly seven feet tall and of thirty stones' weight, the ever-confident Drannôk had humbled his demeanor before the most deadly human he ever beheld.

By now, Adestes Malgrim would be thoroughly entangled in the webs of intrigue at the seat of the Dragon Queen. Drannôk shrugged his mighty shoulders. Such was the human's destiny, and welcome to it! *That one would not have shrunk from the elf-wizard's cast*, Drannôk chuckled, *but would rather thank the dark gods of yore for the chance to strike down the holy warrior and his miserable companions.* Should these travelers be turned back from the Matog and return hence, they would doubtless be harried and worn. Perhaps then he might convert profit from their fool's passage. A single day's ride into the vale lay a hidden place wherein dwelled a half-orc shaman of bestial deities, and it was *he* who engendered the valley's dark repute.

Drannôk regarded the diminutive figures retreating slowly eastward. The orcin cleric would pay well to learn of their passage. No doubt he would seek to waylay any stragglers flung back from the Everfire.

"Yes, foul Bizaz shall pay with two hands to learn of these things." A basso laugh rumbled from the rider. His dark horse wheeled and sprang down the stone shelf. Even so, the rippling rows of close-set barding and the steed's mighty hooves made not the slightest sound.

As the dark rider spurred forward, a slighter being was jerked to his face and drug a space. With a remarkable feat of dexterity, the tethered creature managed to avoid being rendered unconscious amongst the stones, somehow gaining his feet to manage a stumbling run behind the cantering stallion. Although battered, and gagged with painfully twisted leather, and coffled at neck and wrists, Tallux's green eyes burned with promised vengeance at the broad back of his captor.

Chapter 23

Arid Country

Giliad halted. "I believe we have found what I desired." The others drew up and followed the golden elf's gaze. Of all the party members, he alone did not appear weary or even footsore from over two days' continuous fighting and running. The companions had spared the horses as much as possible, yet chests and forelocks were flecked with foam. Even proud Axlyus's mane hung limp and dusted. The sun westered behind the rim mountains, and its slanted rays turned gully ridges to burnished copper. Set in a narrow rut before them was a dry streambed of sand and fine gravel. Giliad stepped to the outer curve of a sweep in the aged watercourse and motioned to Henlee.

"A hole, please. Four feet across and two deep."

"What do I look like, a badger?"

"You should be so fortunate," said Jamello. Too tired to exact any physical retribution on the thief, Henlee merely gave an unblinking glare.

"Come, friends," chuckled Apieron through his weariness, "I think I know what our esteemed colleague has in mind." He extracted three spades from the packs and tossed one to Jamello. "For your penance, you must dig."

Discerning Giliad's intent, Sarc flew some hundred paces distant to a stand of desert sage that here grew as small trees whose pale leaves hid delicate purple blossoms. In short order, the hole was dug and lined cleanly with stone. Already a dark hint of moisture spread into the filled rock bottom. "You see, the stream only sleeps," said Sarc, who returned bearing a bag of fragrant greenage. "She awaits only her lover, the rain, to renew her song."

"You gonna do a rain dance?" asked Henlee.

Sarc ignored him and began a minimally audible chant to the spirit of the stream, a plea for her blessing. Giliad poured a single drop of water from his crystal flask into the pit, speaking softly in archaic elvin. Sarc tossed in a frond of sharp-odored sage. There came a welling of unpolluted water to fill the dig and spill over its rim onto the thirsty sand.

"The spirit of the stream is well pleased to aid us," said Sarc. "I thanked her for her boon."

"As will I," added Apieron.

Two by two, the companions partook of the sage-perfumed spring and laved away as best as possible the grime of the trail. The horses were allowed to drink until their bellies swelled. Giliad addressed the party.

"I did not bring us here to merely refresh ourselves, though we need it sore! A short ways down this channel is a grotto where we may set the horses, for they would not survive the Hel fire." The companions followed his brisk steps until they spied a dark opening in the rocky embankment that overlooked the watercourse.

Sarc laid a bronze hand upon the stone. "It is uninhabited."

The climb was short but steep and the mounts reluctant, yet once within, they relaxed, snorting and stamping for food. The cave was roomy and aerated by many small fissures at the top. The final contents of grain bags were emptied onto the floor. Giliad produced a small vial and poured it over the provender. To the others, it looked and smelled like molasses. The horses fed greedily as the men prepared sage-bough pallets for themselves. To the astonishment of Jamello and Henlee, the steeds soon appeared well sated, and the small piles of grain were not diminished in the slightest.

Giliad chuckled at their stares. "'Twould not do to let such loyal beasts grow thin ere we return."

"And if, Sir Elf," asked Henlee as he eyed Bump happily masticating the fortified grain, "we do not return?"

Giliad nodded respectfully. "The provender is ensorceled to last six months for these few steeds, minus one—I intend to send Ingold back when we depart tomorrow. She will bear word to my people. After that time, we shall have either returned to reclaim the horses or the portals will fail and they may seek their freedom."

"What of the watercourse?" queried Jamello. "Should the stream rise, won't this hole fill with water and drown them?" Giliad stared at the thief as if he were an idiot student, too dense to rebuke.

Sarc laughed. "The stream will not let that happen."

"How do you know this?" persisted the thief.

"She told me," said Sarc.

"*She told him*," mouthed Jamello to Henlee.

"Be not so glum, Uncle," said Apieron cheerily. "Of course it would be my fondest hope that when we return it will be to find a merry stream here. And return soon we might, for we seek only the surface of Hel, not the deepest abyss." Henlee gathered a handful of the grain and rubbed it between his palms and sniffed absentmindedly, his mind elsewhere.

Apieron looked around. The others already sought their repose. Giliad was at the entrance of the cavern where perhaps he contemplated the wards he would place in the morning. A gentle breeze stirred there, and the chamber was soon filled with the sound of horses and men in slumber. Apieron stretched sore legs, placing his heels on a pack, wondering if he were too tired to remove his boots. He could not remember feeling so exhausted. A sound turned him to regard Xephard.

In the faint glow of the few coals Henlee had kindled, the paladin's cloak and armament gleamed. He was strapping Leitus against a polishing leather in long, even strokes. The brilliant sword caught and held the light of the coals in a mesmerizing sheen. As he fell down the long paths to sleep, Apieron's last vision was of steel, and fire.

THE RAT'S LAIR

A smoking candle on a plank revealed three figures who sat at table in a dank, soot-darkened vault beneath the Haunted Vale, whose master was Bizaz. A chill wind gusted down a slime-encrusted stairwell to buffet the flame of the taper. When it righted, a looming shadow waited at the bottom step.

"Greetings, reaver," said the half-orc, though he licked his lips with trepidation.

"A gift to you, conjurer," said Drannôk, dragging Tallux forward by a choke leash, completely occluding the half-elf's windpipe. "I found this one lurking about the east rim, undoubtedly scouting for the strikers who are even now on the Starfall Stair." The massive knight handed the half-breed shaman a blazon torn from Tallux's jerkin.

"Why bother, spawn?" said a rangy man clad in the leathers of a bounty hunter. A sneer of contempt was stamped on his cruel features. "This creature would have stumbled into our snares soon enough. As for your powerful posse of elf lovers, the cleric here has divined they are already to the ravines and make straight for Duskbridge." He snapped his fingers before Drannôk's face. "This is how useful your spying has been!"

Drannôk gazed briefly at Bizaz, who nodded in affirmation of the bounty hunter's words, then squared before the human male who called himself Slysbeth. Neither drew weapon, yet a palpable tension filled the room. The handle of Tallux's leash dropped to the floor, and the strangled half-elf began to gasp mouthfuls of air.

"And if *he* had slipped through?" asked Drannôk. He motioned angrily at the prone figure who was struggling to breathe. "That is no regular army scout, idiot. Canst thou not smell the elvish blood in him? He hast resisted my inquiries, not a word dost he speak. Mayhap the priest of rodents can do something with him."

"Has the mighty Drannôk lost his touch?" asked Slysbeth. "But then you were never one for subtlety. *Off with their heads!*"

"Fool!" boomed Drannôk. "Even thou remembrest the injunction. This entire vale is to be closed to all traffic but that direct to Matog."

"Maybe he *was* for the Gate," quipped a voice from above. Drannôk peered up and scowled. A mongrel dwarf with bleary eyes and a scraggly beard sat perched amongst smoke-stained beams, safe beyond arm's reach. He drank noisily from a leathern jack.

"Bah," growled Drannôk, "thy brain is besotted."

"Aye, the eldritch has the right of it," said Bizaz, moving forward to stand beside the dark knight. He threw a neat kick to Tallux's stomach, doubling him over with his iron-shod boot. "This one is too weak for the Gate."

"And the others?" sneered Slysbeth. "Did you find the courage to stop them and inquire as to their business?"

"I have said it. Thou art a fool."

"And you are not the leader here!" shouted Slysbeth.

Drannôk took a menacing step but hesitated as the bounty

hunter, with well-practiced reflex, snapped up a small blued-metal crossbow. Its short, thick quarrel was of blackened steel and etched with tiny devices that glowed faintly to Drannôk's magically attuned vision.

"This is *my* burrow!" screamed Bizaz. He gesticulated wildly, bloodshot eyes bulging. Spittle flew from his mouth. "All blood spilt here is done so by me!"

He gestured to the captive, and four malformed servants emerged from the shadows. Gathering up the half-elf, they dragged him to a black passage. The perched dwarf poured a measure of beer down the back of one of the shambling slaves. No response ensued. Deuce shrugged and returned his attention happily to the spectacle below. Any death or maiming of the two principal warriors would only increase his own standing.

Slysbeth tried to peer around the half-orc's broad back to line up a shot on Drannôk. The black knight stood immobile such that he appeared an image cast in iron. The taper's light flitted redly on his midnight armor. It seemed the slightest event or motion would plunge the room into screaming chaos. Then a rotting odor filled the arched chamber. It was a musk, overpowering and dank, like the underbelly of some unkempt beast. They perceived its harsh respirations, and a thudding heartbeat was faintly discerned.

Deuce crawled higher into the rafters. Slysbeth leapt back against the stones, his crossbow alternating wildly between Drannôk and the unseen presence. Drannôk ignored him, drawing blade to face the dark recess from whence came the stench. The dwarf's neglected drinking jack fell wetly to the flags.

Bizaz smiled. "So, you sense *He Who Feeds?*" The half-orc fixed them with his rolling eyes. "Cease this prattle, lest a sacrifice become necessary." Bizaz eyed the badge torn from the captive's coat. It was a stallion in chief, regardant a field vert. "King's scout," he spat in disgust, tossing it to the flags.

He turned to the others. "The woodling will be questioned by me, in time. You knaves may leave. Or stay, I care not." With a threatening gersture and flanked by two hulking slaves, he departed the room to ascend the flight of worn steps.

Drannôk slowly sheathed his sword as the monstrous presence receded. "Cowards. It seemeth to be gone."

"It is luck for you that the beast was summoned," smirked Slysbeth. "Else you had tasted my sting." He petted his diminutive bow and tucked it into the folds of his huntsman's cloak. Drannôk's eyes glowed ferally as his stare bored hard into the evil human. Without further words, he spun to depart as another party entered the subterranean vault—a tall, gangly figure with a prominent forehead and the robes of a spellcaster. His gaze shifted from side to side with innate paranoia. His fingers twitched.

Deuce snickered and dropped from the rafters. He and Slysbeth gathered to the spellbinder, who spread forth a map of the vale and surrounding environ. The previous excitement was put aside at the savory prospect of an ambush of the captive's friends once they were driven from the Gates.

DUSKBRIDGE

"Apieron needs help with the flasks. I volunteered you."

Jamello wrenched himself upright. He had thrown himself onto the hard floor of Giliad's grotto the preceding night without bothering to prepare a pallet. It seemed comfortable enough until morning, when it became apparent that several stones had made it their purpose to bore holes into his backside.

"I'm only twenty-three," he voiced aloud. "This is ridiculous."

The others paid him no heed, and soon all were assembled by the springlet. Those provisions not needed for the next phase of their journey were separated and carefully stored in a nook within the shelter. A small pile was made of those designated for the Hel trek. Jamello dubiously eyed rope and spades and other bulky items that he had taken for granted whilst on the backs of the steeds. Of note were three large prochooi of red glazed ceramic that Turpin and Apieron handled carefully. Each had two sturdy handles. Turpin nodded meaningfully to Jamello whilst Apieron prepared a harness for each to be borne by a walker. With the cleric and Apieron, apparently it was he who would have the honor. Henlee snickered.

After the men performed their morning ablutions, their steeds were watered and walked for a space by Sarc, who guided them a final time into the grotto. Ingold remained without. Laying a hand on the elf-steed's proud head, Giliad spoke to the beast in the same ancient elvin tongue that the companions heard him utter at times before. Ingold's blue eyes regarded the warrior-mage until he was finished. She shook her flowing mane, bowing to touch forelock to nose before sending forth a neighing call, then broke into an easy gallop northward.

"A magnificent animal," said Apieron.

"A good friend," said Giliad. The companions could hear the remaining mounts neigh impatiently within the grotto. The gusty voice of Xephard's stallion rose above all.

"The elf-steed rouses their blood," laughed Xephard. "Axylus wishes to follow." The paladin climbed to the grotto entrance to speak soothing words to his warhorse.

Giliad spoke. "Where Ingold goes, none may follow. In three days' time, the morning sun will usher her into the sanctorum of Amor, where she shall present herself before the lady Dorclai with news of our quest."

"And how will she accomplish such a feat?" asked Turpin. "It is nigh one hundred leagues to Ilycrium, and more than thrice to your native forest between mountain and sea."

"Look," called Sarc.

In the distance, they saw the white mare leap onto a low ridge, and her figure altered, graceful wings unfolding from the horse's back. She surged into the airs and accelerated like a shot bolt. Apieron laughed aloud, giving a bow to the elfin mage.

"Now that was something," said Henlee. "Why could you not have summoned flying steeds for us all, Master?"

"Or whisked us here on some spell carpet or something?" added Jamello.

"Speak for yourself," said Henlee.

"I did not summon Ingold," said Giliad. "She is my friend. As for the other, you have heard it said before, it is unwise to circumvent the path fate has laid at your feet. The *athelas*, the hidden way, is discovered only through knowledge gained on the quest itself."

"It is done, mage," called Xephard from the grotto entrance where he had placed a barrier of large rocks such as were not easily moved by man or beast. Giliad ascended to stand by him, and one by one, he touched each horse's nose to cast enchantments of soothing rest. Turpin's stallion and Apieron's racer, and also proud Axylus with Jamello's pony, and finally Sarc's bristle-maned Beg, and Bump.

Henlee covered over the well whilst Sarc retraced their footsteps and those of the horses, removing all signs of their passage by his efforts and druidic art. Henlee scampered up the short incline to the horse cave. Giliad noted the dwarf's concerned demeanor. "The air and fodder will remain clean and fresh. Bump will eat better here than he has for a month."

"I thank you, elf. But, er," stammered Henlee, "I could use a moment alone with my boy."

"Of course." Giliad inclined his head and retreated.

"If'n this here elf enchantment don't last, Bump my lad, kick your way out o' here and follow that funny-lookin' striped horse back to the winged folk. I'll find ye there." Bump laid his long ears forward and chewed on Henlee's beard. "Stop that, overstuffed rabbit!" cursed Henlee affectionately. "Take care o' the others, and mind your manners."

Henlee stomped back to rejoin the party and busied himself with his overlarge pack. He wiped his sleeve across his eyes, "Damned mountain ass will probably gnaw the tails off the others by the time we return."

Burdens were distributed and hoisted upon aching backs, and the companions pressed eastward, leaving the Haunted Vale behind and over their right shoulders. They followed furrowed ravines sheared as though with a knife to reveal colored strata in the exposed rock. Once again each wondered at the cataclysmic force that had apparently cut miles of solid rock in such fashion. Vegetation grew more strangled and twisted than ever. They saw pines with many trunks like the mangroves of the Wyrnde, but prickly with yard-long needles like green javelins. A heavy rustling from under a shadowed creosote brought heads around as an enormous hedgehog emerged and scampered forward to regard them, beady eyes squinting against the light, nose quivering to gain their scent.

"Boy-buggers!" said Jamello. "Do they normally get that big?"

The beast was six feet in length and four across. Each sharp quillion was eighteen inches from base to tip, the mass of which rolled over its twitching skin like trees waving in wind. "It is an aberration," said Giliad, "as with all we see so near the Duskbridge."

"Maybe it's related to Apieron's granddaddy beaver in the swamp?" speculated Xephard jokingly.

"Perhaps," answered Giliad dryly.

"In any case," said Jamello, "we had best skirt this beast before Henlee falls in love."

"If you weren't carrying that amphora, I'd knock you down, sissy boy."

They shared a frugal lunch and pushed on east by south as the furrows angled slightly. A cold breeze got up directly in their faces, nipping at exposed skin despite the orange sun. There was no game path or watercourse, and their heavy packs made for leg-jarring jolts with each step on the uneven terrain. The chill in the air grew, and within short hours, the beleaguered foliage ceased altogether, painting the vista a bleak desert of tortured rock.

"This is truly a land fit only for robbers and trolls if there ever was," quoth Xephard.

Sarc's bronze face gazed up without blinking. "Even the life orb is beset. See how heavy She hangs … weary from Her travels."

Henlee looked up and muttered, "Like melting gold."

"Nay. Sun god is wrathful," said Apieron as he strode up to join the odd twain. The finely knit elf next to the blocky dwarf, framed against the setting sky. "His anger waxes large. The pure gold you see are the bit and harness of his stamping horses, and wheels of his chariot. His anger is for our enemies, whose schemes he sees from his fiery perch."

"Angry or not," answered the dwarf, "like as not it shall be up to us mortals to do all the work." The gloomy dwarf looked hard at Apieron. "And *you* sound like your father." He moved off, still muttering.

Sarc turned smiling to Apieron. "Surely you are amiss, the sun kisses the world, giving life, that is why you should say *She*, not *He*."

"How can a people so long lived be so uninformed?" answered Xephard. "Sun is wrapped in fiery splendor like a peacock, not the hen. If you wish to see a *she*, wait for mysterious moon."

"Again you are confused," stated Giliad, not unkindly. "All

wise creatures know the moon is a *he*, for does he not sit waiting the night through, drinking from his silver cup?"

"Elf's right for once," called the dwarf.

"Heathens all!" rejoined Turpin. Once again, none could tell if his abrupt remark was token of a foul mood or merely a manifestation of his dry wit.

"Do you know what else is strange about yon sky?" said Apieron. "No birds. We have seen neither lark nor desert swallow since leaving the grotto."

"We are very close to the Gate," replied Turpin. "I can feel it in my breast, I can see it in my mind."

"Let us haste," said Giliad. "We will make one final camp when this pallid sun departs, for I do not wish to test the powers of the portals in darkness."

"Think you, Lord Mage, that your gates have spawned this cold wind?" asked Apieron.

"I know not," answered Giliad.

A last brisk march soon negated the chill effects of the wind, manifested by sweaty brows and aching limbs. "Look! A tree, and on it, a bird," cried Sarc. He pointed to the crest of a small rise, a mile or so before them.

"We shall encamp there," declared Giliad.

They trudged the distance while the dying sun cast haggard shadows. As they neared the tree, it was revealed to be an ordinary scrub cedar standing alone on a headland before a vast depression cloaked by encroaching darkness. The incessant east wind had bent the tree from earliest growth such that its faded green stood stiffly behind it like a girl's long hair, and its bark on the lee side was shabby as the heavy beard of a shut-in. On the windward side, it was polished smooth.

An angry cawing disrupted the travelers' observations. At their approach, a mighty black crow took flight from recesses in the cedar. It passed low overhead, calling to them in strident tones. "Two heads?" asked Apieron, unsure if his wind-stung eyes deceived him in the failing light.

"Oh, is that all?" said Jamello. "I'm glad it wasn't four."

"Not as alarming as what he uttered," added Sarc, shaking his head unhappily.

"What was that?" asked Henlee.

"Look before you, gentlemen," interrupted Turpin, motioning to the bowl below them, "We have come to the land of the Starfall. Behold the Duskbridge." Gathering to the weatherworn edge, the companions gazed out onto a crater. Its rim and rocky floor was a mystery painted in shadows.

Camp was quickly set. A brief debate over whether to set a campfire or no ensued. It was Turpin who decided the issue, hinting that fire would prove useful for what he intended. Henlee produced a pile of hardwood cones from his pack. Bracken shed by the tree soon fueled his flint spark to a robust blaze. A warm meal in the comfort of the campfire was welcomed, for the wind was bitter and blew ceaselessly. Sarc stood beside the windswept cedar. "I am glad we have found this little one." He lightly stroked its gnarled and twisted trunk. "The spirit of this tree is alive, but consumed in its struggle to survive, it has no voice for us."

Xephard stood close, and with tenderness he touched a tufted branch. "I find it quite brave. It stands alone, undaunted before a wasteland of enemies. I will remember this little valiant later, as an inspiration. As should you all."

"And I shall plant a grove of hitherto lowly cedar amongst the forest denizens of Amor," said Giliad. "They shall be in remembrance of this young and old one who stands betwixt realms, half-living and half-dead, like struggling mortals."

His voice sank to a whisper. "They who have one foot in the grave, and the other in the heavens ... and so muchly neglect the world about them." The golden elf stood and moved past Sarc to the leeward sweep of the cedar's branches and returned to open his hand before them. And lo! Three small, gray-horned kernels, such that is the seed of that type of tree, were seated on his palm. Giliad smiled and secured them on his person.

Jamello and even Henlee raised their cups to him and the tree in salute, albeit their toast was only water. Of the companions, only Turpin and Apieron made no gesture or speech at the tree. Apieron was overcome with many thoughts. He felt more acutely than any a familiarity with the stunted tree, and when they had first spied it, he knew he was meant to come here. This ordinary scrub cedar that struggled alone made him ponder his place in the world more poignantly than anything else could, his heritage ever a burden for himself, alone.

King's man, Apieron mouthed silently.

He gazed again at the tree, its dusty scent clean on the cold wind. Silently strong, it now reminded him of the wife he left behind. Melónie never questioned his course—had done her best to hide her grief. Now she too owned his terrible birthright, purchased by the coin of her love for him. Apieron bowed his head, eyes moist with unspoken feelings of doubt and angst.

For a time, Turpin seemed to note neither Apieron nor the others, and his glinting eyes obviously fixed on vistas far beyond their camp, onto the nighted pit below. Apieron looked up. Xephard was calling his name as the priest bade others gather round and unseal the ceramic prochooi. Rinds of wax were peeled away and the tops broached to reveal a creamy unguent that resembled reduced fat in texture and density.

"Remove your garments."

Turpin's tone brooked no objections. Soon they stood thus before him while he uttered sonorous prayers in his basso voice, anointing foreheads and breasts. They took the jars and proceeded to apply a sheen of the material over every surface of their bodies.

Henlee's chuckle was wry, "Now we're all basted in batter like fat fryers."

"If so," added Xephard, "the meat cutter tricked the goodwife by adding bony Jamello to the batch."

"What about the elf?" protested Rudolph Mellor.

"Elves are supposed to be skinny, boy," said Henlee. Sarc ruffled his wings much like a bird that has gotten doused. His strange, sinewed muscularity rippled beneath bronze skin and tawny hairs.

Jamello shook his head in wonderment. He sniffed at the amber emollient. It bore no discernible odor and absorbed evenly into the skin. "How do we know this stuff will work?"

"Because a high priest of Sky gave it to you," returned Xephard.

"A high priestess of Wisdom sent me on this mission, and look at me now … standing like a fool, naked and cold on the very edge of the world! How chill the wind is." He shivered, clasping arms across chest and flexing his knees.

"In the cerstae of my youthful years, we ran naked each morn through snow to draw water," laughed Xephard. "If any were to spill, it froze on your backside. We did not spill water often."

"A fine story," said Turpin, "but the thief's question is valid. Who will first test the unguent?" Henlee and Xephard made to step forward.

"Nay, not the dwarf who is inured to flame and already muchly burnt. Neither Xephard, who can deny any pain. Let it be the one who is most doubtful, nor possesses any mystic ability."

Eyes turned to Jamello, who was surprisingly nonchalant. "I knew it would come to this, and there *is* a bright side. If this does not work, I go no further." The thief moved to the fringe of Henlee's campfire and paused before the dancing flames. A bemused expression crossed his face, and he walked directly over the fire. To the delight of all, the flames were immediately reduced to mere embers, which rekindled when he stepped free.

Sarc leapt onto the renewed blaze, his long hair and wings trailing down onto the tongues of flame as though they might be suddenly kindled and consumed. He vented a roisterous laugh and shook his mane to and fro before gliding free. "The one thing my people fear above all is *fire!*"

One by one, each of the companions tried the flame test. "Congratulations, cleric," said Henlee when he donned his garments. Turpin bowed slightly. It seemed his old energies had returned.

"But I too have a question," Henlee continued.

"Ask away, noble dwarf."

Henlee addressed the entire party, his gravely voice cutting the wind. "We know we are protected from fire, if this holy grease of yours holds up. Yet what if this here cold wind comes from yon Hel gate, and it is colder inside?"

"Oh, great," moaned Jamello. Apieron popped a grin, Xephard's and Sarc's faces were unreadable. Giliad moved to answer. "I, at least, can assure you this is not so. From whither this wind hales, I know not. It is high summer in most of the realms south of proud Ilycrium. Perhaps here is ever-winter."

"*Assure?*" echoed Henlee and Jamello together.

"Within the Hel Gate, it is not cold," stated Turpin heavily. "It may be soon that you pray for a breeze such as this. The blessed unguent will shield one from Hel fires, but not all the discomforts thereof." With that, the companions occupied whatever nervous energies they had for the morrow in the manner that best suited each. Packs were reorganized, and excess items were hid by the dwarf in a cleverly concealed cairn he made, marked by Giliad with a rune symbol for hidden things, visible only to them. The golden elf bade them rest the night through. He and Sarc would stand guard, their bodies not requiring the sleep of oblivion as with mortals.

Henlee's fire spent itself, ashes falling onto coals in gray mantle. The dwarf mumbled and fretted over every joint of his armor and meticulously attacked minute burrs on his weapons with the file he always carried. Xephard sat cross-legged across the fire pit from him, the dying embers reflecting at times from his casque and Leitus that he rhythmically stroked with an oilcloth.

Jamello fidgeted. He rearranged his kit a half-dozen ways before cursing some omission and beginning anew. His fingers flew between the various weapons about his person. His new sword was finally seated on his left hip, the hunting falchion slung on his back, daggers and quirts on girdle or in boots. A small bag of blackened coltrops depended from his belt whilst he coiled a wire garrot into his left sleeve. Two unusually heavy balls of metal that he was wont to fondle were rechecked and pocketed.

Turpin wandered a short distance into the darkness on the crater side of the knoll. They could hear his footsteps on the broken shale cease after a few careful minutes of picking his way down the slope. Similarly, Apieron sought a measure of solitude and knelt facing the windswept cedar. He fingered the padded jupon that Melónie had given him, feeling a silken warmth and inhaling her scent, which seemed to emanate from the garment whenever he touched it. *How like her*, he smiled, to bind and enhance a small thing with her feminine arts such that it became, in time, a powerful reminder of her love.

Apieron's eyes squinted as his thoughts raced back to Windhover. Melónie was surrounded by retainers whose loyalty he could never doubt. And yet the Sybil's hint at the death of the old King, corruption in the capital, jealous courtiers who resented the tales of Xistus Farsinger, and Candor's friendship with Apieron himself, all weighed in the pit of his stomach like a burning iron. He pictured gentle Melónie, unused to the customs of the West, vulnerable in that great pile of Windhover on the edge of lawless lands that knew no king.

A sense of urgency filled Apieron to speak now his prayer, *for who knew if gods could hear once one traversed the Hel Gate?* He unfolded a small piece of waxed leather and rolled out a single coal he took from Henlee's fire. He leaned forward, blowing it to new life, then gently lay upon it some of the cedar's husk-like bark. A small smoke arose, gray and fragrant in the blackness.

Apieron was well pleased at the omen. He evoked the brave spirit of the tree to speed his prayers, naming also the small gods of his household and homeland. He thought of Cryse, Melónie's gentle goddess who delighted in jests, a mistress of color and scent, laughter and perfumes … and the gentle kiss of lovers. Apieron spoke aloud, his voice low and fervent, his hands tightly bound about the jupon she had woven him:

"Merciful Cryse, though I know you not, I ask a boon, not for myself, but for thy faithful servant, Melónie dark-eyed, my wife. She is wise as ever a woman could be, knowing all the virtues of patience and compassion."

Apieron felt a white heat rise in him, and he flung his arms wide, staring at the twinkling vault above.

"Far have I brought her from her father's home to a land besieged by evil. Gracious Goddess, grant her, my love in life, thy sweet succor."

All went black before Apieron's eyes, and when his vision cleared, he found himself kneeling, hands on knees and head bowed low. The little coal was exhausted, the cedar bark reduced to a white dust blowing free in the wind. He rose and returned to sit near his friends. Soon Turpin returned, although sleep did not come readily for any. The moon had got up, a cloudy smear in the east. Stars hung low in this place, but the red star eclipsed all, directly overhead and menacingly bright. By such light, the companions were bulky shapes. The tree's bristly boughs rasped in the wind.

Jamello's voice cut the darkness. "I have a question for our learned mage, though I suppose if anyone else has aught to say, I would fain hear it now." When no answer was forthcoming, he continued, "What will we face on the morrow?"

Giliad's gold hair was illuminated briefly as he shook his head free of his hood. "We know there is a door hereabouts. Tomorrow we shall find it, and with luck enter within."

"And I am no sage," persisted Jamello, "yet I have never seen a gate of worth that did not have a guardian." Henlee grunted in agreement.

"Remember," replied Giliad, "the place we seek to enter is its own guardian, and its very nature would soon subdue us were it not for the protections of our learned cleric."

"Jamello's words reflect, I'm sure, the foreboding each of us shares. I too feel as if there is some sentry," said Apieron.

Giliad answered, "No doubt there are powerful beings aplenty, any one of which could be named as such. There is also and always She who we will not name so close to the Duskbridge … She who waits below. I must needs spend most of my energies attempting to spell-cloak us from all of them."

Henlee's words came out as a growl. "But the Gate itself?"

"Your words depress me because I fear all you say speaks true. The portal itelf may be of amazing complexity or itself alive. Of these things, there are none among the forces of good that can teach us, even my lord and spellmaster, Galor Galdarion."

Apieron mused, "We know the gods imprisoned those they condemned behind mighty walls of bronze. Mighten the Gates themselves be valves of that same metal?"

"Perhaps," said Giliad quietly. "I know not."

"And I have heard it said that if one dies in that dark place, your soul is lost forever," said Jamello, a slight tremor in his voice.

"Blasphemous nonsense!" said Xephard. "The immutable spirit of the warrior is his weapon, not the steel he bears." He brandished Leitus, silky white in the dim illumination. "Defeatist words devour the iron of one's will worse than rust will eat his blade."

"My friend," said Apieron softly to Jamello, "it were best to speak not of such things. Why worry over what we cannot control?"

Jamello regarded Xephard, again absentmindedly burnishing the famed sword with a scrap of cloth. "And you, Xephard, paladin, are you not afraid of what we shall meet on the morrow?"

Apieron answered for him. "All of us are afraid, Jamello. This is not some quick battle for unschooled levies whose bloodlust be roused with fighting words. I even know a minor casting or two to evoke such, though it would have little effect on this gathering."

Xephard spoke. "Each moment is a gift to rejoice in fully. Enjoy yourself."

Turpin finally stirred. "Our holy knight is a throwback to a more gallant era, a time of mighty heroes. Heed me now! What we *will* face is a journey of uncertain length into certain peril. Where the end will be, none can say. Prepare yourselves."

Henlee interjected vehemently, "It is a quick end we seek." He punched a fist into his hand with a solid slap. "We hit 'em fast and furious, I say, with never a look back." The dwarf stood, and the others could see gems in his long beard winkling, the links of his shirt rustling. "Remember well the paladin's lessons! Other folks here use what talents they may." He nodded at Giliad and Sarc. "Those of us who cannot fight in the air must take heed to not be overwhelmed."

Apieron stood and moved next to his friend and mentor. "I

agree heartily. Hopefully we shall be into the enemy's lair before they are aware."

"That being so," added the dwarf, "if we are leaguered, it will be a stand-up fight." He laughed and turned back to his pallet. "It always is."

Jamello regarded Sarc, who picked his way some distance apart to stand vigil over the benighted knoll, soon joined by Apieron for a low, inaudible conversation. He saw Giliad, who was in silent repose, sipping thoughtfully from his chalice. Turpin was again withdrawn, laying on his back and staring upward. Only Xephard remained sitting as was he.

"Xephard the Fearless. How does one accomplish this?"

The paladin's deep voice was slow and serene. "I have thought on your question. It is one I have answered before, yet never well. I will make amends now.

"Simply this … it is easier to be brave than not. The ugly part of fear is that it immobilizes one to action." The paladin paused, gathering his thoughts.

"The rabbit runs, not because he is afraid, but because that is his nature. If fear covers him, he freezes in the face of danger and is taken. The secret of courage is then to do a positive action despite one's fear."

"And you?" asked Jamello softly.

"I have no mantle of courage to slip on, having no need of such virtue. From my northern fathers, I know that the thread length of my life was wound by the Norns at the time of my birth. When it plays out, I will die. This knowledge is a mighty gift."

"Is that all?"

Xephard smiled warmly. "No. Long ago, I gave our goddess of wisdom and war, the soldier's friend, every breath and shout and fiber of my being. I have no hidden self to fear or hurt. I have been shriven."

"Nothing left to lose?" said Jamello wryly.

"Exactly!" beamed Xephard. He lapsed into silence. Jamello thought him done, until the temple peer lifted his head once more.

"The holy mistress of Lampus says that *how* one lives out his days are what is important. If one's deeds in this life are found worthy, Spear Goddess will gather you to Her circle of champions to live again as a chosen of her court, to be a hero most excellent. Do *you* this thing, Rudolph Mellor." The paladin's cloud-blue eyes gleamed in the dark as he spoke.

That said, Xephard lay back and fell apparently into untroubled sleep. Jamello groaned inwardly. He always knew that Cynthia would lure him into an inescapable fix. At last he reclined, troubled by shivering nightmares and dire, waking images such that he was surprised to find Henlee's booted toe nudging him awake after the others had apparently risen with the dawn, such as it was in this bleak and blasted place. He sat up and blinked.

A limpid sun climbed the eastern horizon, and the wind blew chill as ever. There was no obscuring cloud, and yet the sun's light was thin and the sky cast with a yellow-gray film. Stars remained visible, and although the companions did not speak its name, X'fel shimmered directly overhead.

Apieron and the elves touched the windswept cedar, speaking words of thanks and farewell to the last tree. The travelers hid all traces of the campsite and filed down the face of the knoll, finding that the rise they had vacated was indeed a portion of an encircling rim, eroded in places by wind and stonefall. The broken shale of the declivity was a crumbling, sharp, and dangerous schist that gave onto a hard stone floor, seared and cracked in places. Its topsoil and loose rock were blasted away. Henlee cursed in his native tongue. The wind's mutter grew to a howl, and soon all realized it indeed flowed from the center of the scooped depression.

"Look yonder," shouted Sarc above the wind's yowling. They followed his pointing finger to the right. Horsed figures regarded them from the height of the ridge, some half-mile distant, the riders' cloaks whipping in the wind as did the manes of their mounts. Otherwise they sat motionless.

"Thirteen horseman on mountain ponies," said Sarc. "*Crimson* mountain ponies."

"Garbed as human nomads. Armed with scimitar and recurves" added Apieron. Instinctively the party turned and spread before this new threat.

"I like this not," growled Henlee. "It stinks of a trap."

"We were not followed yesterday, I swear it," said Sarc.

Giliad spoke. "These warriors look to be a long-reaching horse patrol. No doubt they spied us when we entered this naked bowl."

"I agree," said Apieron. "And I wonder whence they came. Armed horsemen do not exist in isolation, there must be a base camp or village for the mounts and refit."

None of the companions guessed the magnitude of truth behind Apieron's words. Osum gazed down at the seven infidels who dared approach the Matog, and his eyes blazed with wrath at these transgressors. How he longed to hurl his reavers down the slope in a whirlwind of sharp-edged death, whilst calling forth dire powers from beyond the Portals to trap and crush the trespassers betwixt!

Osum bit his lip and chewed his beard for a moment of indecision. He touched a dull metal circuit fixed to his brown robe.

"Depart!" he commanded, wheeling his scarlet horse to spur off the height, his riders streaming after their captain to find southern trails.

"They're gone!" cried Jamello.

Henlee did not lower Maul. "A flanking maneuver?"

"I think not," answered Apieron.

Xephard nodded. "They would gain little by such in this open place." Sarc alighted and reslung his crooked bow.

"Riders. Nomads," mused Jamello aloud. "They seemed to my eyes to be garbed as monks I once saw in foreign lands. Whence came they, I wonder?"

"With luck, we shall never know," said Sarc. "So many things are strange. My people know that mighty Wyrnde once covered this place and may still reign beyond these defiles. Three times ten years ago as men reckon, a light from the heavens fell here to wither all green things.

"After that, a mighty reek covered the east for nigh a year. Our divinations are scattered and confused whenever they search hither. Now I know the reason wherefore, this has become a twisted place of *unnature*. Fell beings, and now fell peoples are arisen here."

Jamello blew through his teeth. "I still do not know how I landed in this mess."

"Whatever their presence portended, it is done," said Giliad. "Haste. Haste! The crater's center is but a league before us." Turpin grunted his agreement, and they turned into the rising wind.

Within two hours, Osum hailed sentries at the mud-daubed walls of his hillside redoubt. Harsh commands were shouted. In mere minutes, fast couriers were racing down hard, packed trails that gave onto the wain roads of Mogush, slave city of Panj.

An oligarchy ruled by warrior priests, its tendrils of influence spread to a dozen cities of men who lived and toiled in broad lands undreamt of by men of the West, save for worldly adventurers and enlightened sages. The ruling caste of Mogush revered the awakened power behind the Hel Gate nigh to their walls. That will became manifest at times, as it was now ...

The companions were only lightly encumbered, yet the opposing wind stretched the three-mile march to the Gate into several hours. By reckoning of the time since they set out with dawn, the sun should have been halfway to its zenith. Now the limpid orb hung already in westward descent.

Brighter than ever, X'fel cast an angry light. What lay before them was a furrow of glazed slag, like dirty glass, two hundred steps in width and sharply concave on its opposing rims to form a low, open arch. Beyond this was a slow vortex of darkness. The wind screamed in the half tunnel, and ice glazed its sides.

The dwarf clapped Apieron on the shoulder. "Well, that is about as uninviting a door as I've ever seen."

Chapter 24

Tiamat's Palace

Malesh stalked the ghaddur. The catacombs, vast beyond comprehension, throbbed through the heels of his boots, the walls, the air itself! Below the threshold of hearing, nonetheless it bespoke something alive. Adestes knew It was aware of his deeds, and in an evolving way, kenned the sights he beheld. Adestes Malgrim glided to the lee of a column. Its living bronze twisted, seven serpents entwined, that slid and blinked brassy eyes but hindered him not. He paused, pondering the Presence. He recked it had witnessed countless internecine conflicts—survival of the strong.

Malesh resumed his stalk and pictured Bolechim, Chamberlain of Hel. The fiend had mocked him before many and cast a veil of fire on him. Feigning injury, Adestes had fled whilst taunting words stung his ears. *"Think you to be a spy of Kör? Weak of flesh and small of mind! Bide here, slave, until I summon thy soul to torment never ending."*

The ghaddur's back was turned. It appeared to hold silent converse with three pale, bulbous creatures. Their saucer eyes gleamed like polished jet, reflecting the horrific visage of the Chamberlain of Hel. Bolechim turned, its piggish eyes alight with mirth and hate.

"So. Where is thy trumpet, Herald?" The ram's head jerked, indicating the four-pillared altar that loomed beyond. "Think you the Dark She will save thee? She favors only the worthy."

Adestes hoisted an unadorned shield of steel from his back, nigh as long and heavy as himself. He pulled a thick visor over his face. With supple mail of gray mesh, this completed his armament.

"Exactly fatty, bring it!"

The ghaddur charged, roaring with each thudding step. At the last instant, Adestes flung his body aside, his right arm extended. A small dart shot into Bolechim's open maw. Adestes dived into a crevice. With mace and claw, the ghaddur ripped free chunks of stone. It punched and tore the shield, finally flinging it like a discus, and a firestorm engulfed the crouching man. Malesh only laughed.

Bolechim stooped to grasp up the impudent human and dash his brains against the rock. A brand of lodestone threatened, but such a thing could never daunt such a mighty fiend as Bolechim. A strange look slid beneath the ghaddur's features. After a pause, the ghaddur lunged at the man, but instead died in a heap atop him.

Malesh hacked his way free. "You are doughty, Lord of Swine, for I used enough poison to slay a whale!" After a time, he gazed up, pleased with his work, and whistled softly. "Disgusting dietary habits."

"And one thing more." He grasped Bolechim's fire mace. When its faceted ruby surface shrank to proper size, he hefted it one-handed. An iron statue stood there. It towered, a fusion of fish and devil, perhaps an evil merman. The mace flared vermillion. A single blow and the casting shattered like a riven bell. Adestes regarded the scintillant surface of the mace, and it gleamed its delight.

"Very well. I will bear thee." Movement caught the periphery of his vision. Adestes wheeled and beheld that the three diminutive, grub-like slaves remained. They bobbed their obeisance. "Ever kill snails with a stick? I suppose not." Malesh hefted the mace.

"Come, I'll show you."

Stars were falling in the sanctum of the Dragon Queen.

Oily droplets hung pendant from every surface. In each winked a light, a trembling star whose brethren fell like a galaxy of rain. Slaves and regents, soldiers and principals stood to behold the crucified body of Bolechim. His four mighty limbs were suspended from the spiral pillars of the very altar. The archfiend hung head down, his face frozen into a ghastly leer. A gut pile steamed below, and on it, small kindlings lit and smoldered foully whensoever a droplet struck.

Countless murders had the shifting corridors witnessed, but none so reckless. A babble of speech, both audible and telepathic, swelled and ebbed. Outside, Aurgelmir's iron-plate features deepened their scowl. A terrible sight. The Warden of the Wall shook out pinioned wings, and resumed his ponderous tread atop the battlements of his queen.

SWAYMEET

The many hued tents and bustle and multitudes of onlookers resembled more a summer's fair than an assembly of war. Such was the atmosphere on the parade grounds before Swaymeet, keep of the Candor kings, capital of Ilycrium, mightiest realm of the West.

The sun bore down on the muster where each contingent of men at arms, attached to their respective lords, vied for prime space near a branch of the meandering Swaywynde. Longhaired northmen fingered the hilts of straight swords and stared suspiciously at sun-browned coastal levies, whilst inland companies, clad in leather jerkins, cast down bill and fork to claim a bit of shade. Depending on the wealth and inclination of each district leader or noble overlord, the quality of dress and gear varied greatly.

Scribes with lists in hand pushed through formations to tally men and equipment while the camp itself became a tumultuous circus of braying mules, barking dogs, and stamping horses of types from farmers' steadfast hackney to proud destrier, bred to war. Men called and shouted greetings of laughter or dispute over space and provisions. The majority, however, strayed little from fellow countrymen and spoke in serious tones of the death of a king, and tidings of unrest.

Trakhner, general of the armies, gladly gave over his cursing attempts to impose any semblance of military order on the gaggle when a page summoned him. Within a small dell, ringed by guardsmen bearing polearms, Gault and the Council of Ilycrium gathered at roughhewn benches set on a greensward before a tributary stream.

The creek gurgled lazily under afternoon's sun. Flies were brushed from victuals scarcely touched by those present. Prince Candor stood, clad in a warrior's tunic with an open lambskin surcoat, blazoned on either panel with the argent horse of the royal house. His belt was conspicuously barren of scabbard or blade. No little rumor followed the discovery that the old King's corpse and chambers were bereft of Ilus, heirloom of his house and traditional weapon of the king.

Councilors not present for the funeral rites moved to greet the stolid prince and offer condolences. Some voiced private words of support for his ascension to the throne, yet fully half held their remarks to a politeness for the passage of his adopted father. Gault stood with his hair unbound as befitted one in mourning, the dark circles of sleepless nights framing his eyes, although his bearing was upright.

"What a pretty gathering you have assembled, Dexius," said Exeter.

"Bah," spat Trakhner. His forehead was seamed with lines of worry under close-cropped, gray-blond hair. "More like a refugee camp."

Gault searched the faces of those gathered. More than one were new to him, such as the handsomely dark youth of his own age next to Tertullion and clad as a mage, who no doubt was his understudy. Rumor marked the young gallant with a repute for fast women and flamboyant friends, many of whom were those who loudly proclaimed a hawkish throne to blame for the problems that beset the land.

Of more concern to Gault were those notably absent. One of those was Buthard, son of Wulfstane, March Warden of Ilycrium south and east. Whatever the reason, Gault breathed a silent prayer of thanks for Buthard's departure from the capital. Yet there were those he hoped to find and did not. Tallux had not returned, nor Apieron of Windhover, nor Xephard, captain at Lampus and mightiest knight of the realm. Belagund was dead. Gault had hoped for welcome news from a trusted face. Now to him the bright day grew dark.

"If I may, Prince?" asked Trakhner. "Gentlemen, word has come from Bestrand of a raid. Yesterday morn, that harbor was razed by a trio of fire ships which exploded in the very butt of the shipyards. A third of their fleet is burned, and much of their dock stores and wharves are lost. For the nonce, Bestrand is closed." The flat delivery of this news from the blunt warrior gave each man pause. Trakhner was not known for exaggeration or verbosity of speech, or even to string more than two sentences together unless the need was dire.

"An invasion?" asked Lysander.

"Nay, a raid without sign of troop ships or a supporting force by land."

"And anonymous," added Tertullion. "All evidence no doubt destroyed with the fire ships. Clever."

Trakhner ran thick fingers through the stubble on his head. "A sore loss," growled he. "I had counted on the strength of Bestrand's fleet for resupply and to safeguard our coastal flank."

"And this, with no word from Farseps?" demanded Exeter, turning to fix fat Lysander with his eagle-like glare.

"None at all," moaned the obese merchant. His normally infused complexion had become pallid over the preceding weeks, and he merely pushed his food about without sampling. One sleeve of turquoise silk dragged across a greasy roast, although the normally fastidious burgher failed to notice. "It is as if my brethren of that isle have sunk into the sea."

Candor spoke forth. "Our naval officers have taken counsel with such of the independent captains as remain in Sway. Half of what vessels we have will be dispersed along the Ess north and south. The remainder are commanded to remain at port, for they are now too few of number to risk encounter on the open sea."

"Lord, what news of Kör?" called D'Istre, an upland lord who came far in haste at the news of the King's death with a company of fifty horse soldiers. He was understandably concerned. The mountain fortress of Uxellodoum could be seen from the walls of his keep. Fifteen leagues beyond the dwarven city crouched Alkeim, and the Vigfil Stair to the southern passes of Kör.

Trakhner replied. "The White Throat is quiet. Of Kör our scouts report little, though most remain here, on my orders attached to the army until I can find better use for them."

"I see none of their officers," observed Exeter.

"Aye, where is the elfin bow wielder?" demanded Wulfstane. "Is he not one of their captains? And where is Apieron of Windhover? Did he not achieve a goodly measure of fame and reward from his service with that company?" The castellan touched his nose with a sly gesture that Gault found repugnant. "My son sends word by carrier bird that Apieron's household remains stationary. They see to their own fortifications, and the old keep is made strong."

Candor was secretly glad Apieron had at least done so and feared his friend would have need of such defenses ere long. Trakhner slapped his thigh in disgust. "Apieron of Windhover would not be the only rural lord who looks first to his own walls. I know others of higher rank than he who came not hither."

"Witness the troth of elves, dwarves, and those of foreign descent 'gainst that of true men," declared Exeter. His brown cloak fluttered over a creamy doublet. "By ancient custom such as he forfeit land and title. An assembly of war has been called, and they do not answer. Mayhap they will not think their walls strong when they see the hosts of Ilycrium encamped without."

Gault's face betrayed nothing of his thoughts when he spoke. "We will gather these lords to us on the march as we may," he raised a hand to placate Exeter, "and if they enjoin not to us, you shall enforce your office, Seneschal. Mark me! I do not intend to divert this army against our own, whilst the true enemy gathers in force."

"It would melt away if we did so," murmured Trakhner.

"Do you then truly intend to march this—this army of yours, my prince?" asked Dexius.

"Here, here!" called a rough-looking knight, one of the few present in armor, the metal of which was dulled and scarred but well kept and clearly serviceable. "A sooth question, milord," he continued. "Is this then to be a true campaign? Or sneaking ambush and brigand work?"

Gault said nothing to the knight, who he had seen before but could not place a name. Instead he bent to retrieve from the sward a bulky object covered with cloth. When he rose, he held aloft a mighty axe, twin bladed with a handle of iron-girded hardwood and a worn leathern grip. He brandished the weapon one-handed. "This belonged to my grandfather, the Old Marshal.

"Some of you will recognize it from the wall display in the room of the throne. When I requested it of a page this morn, a question of discretion was asked of me. *Me*, whose father lay smitten in that very chamber a fortnight gone! Are we grown so refined that a weapon is kept from the hand of one who rightly owns it? Gods help us against a less-cultured and more-practical foe." Gault lowered the axe to the ground. He leaned with both hands upon the haft. In that moment, the young prince with his broad shoulders, tawny hair, and flashing eyes looked more akin to his warlike grandsires, both by blood and by name, than to those of his own generation.

"Understand, gentlemen," voiced Tertullion, his wintry beard tugged by the lazy breeze, "that we face no ordinary foe! The slaves of Kör practice every savagery, sparing not their own children from grisly banquets at times. We must not allow this rabid beast into the heartland of our country."

"Fear not, Wighelm," added Trakhner grimly as he addressed the burly knight and nodded to Dexius and Exeter. "When croft holders and tradesmen see their lands razed, wives and children sold off like cattle, they will flock to us." The old soldier growled into his throat. "The time for skulking in our cities is past. This army is a shield, we move to receive our enemy's blow rather than stand idly until we are bled dry."

Trakhner's meaty fist smacked his palm. "See our strong prince? With him we shall take the passes of White Throat and Alkeim. If dwarves and mountain tribes be not steadfast or seek a separate peace, we will take their high places to hold against Kör. Let him rave behind these all he wants! Or rot until another demonling seizes his throne for all that I care." Trakhner's clean-shaven, weathered face was lined with determination. A true professional soldier who had risen in the ranks without political affiliation, he cut an inspiring image of competence to those present. He was of medium height and barrel-chested. His thick hands and forearms rested confidently on the pommels of plain-hilted broadsword and fighting knife.

Dexius fidgeted. "What if you are wrong about from whence the blow shall fall?" The ivory pointer twitched. "What of the religious orders? Should we not await what strength of arms they will spare us and the wisdom of their counsel?"

"I also wonder wherefore the Lampus sends no strength of arms to our assembly?" asked D'Istre.

"They will not come without direct order from the Throne." Tertullion shook his locks sadly. "They await their most puissant knight, Xephard Bright Helm, who walks with young Apieron on a dark quest."

D'Istre's tones were rueful. "I had hoped to swing a blade beside him. Now I shall hope no more."

"To lose such a one to foolish errantry galls me sore," nodded Trakhner. "Had it been mine to command, my word would have been nay. Only the gods know the mind of the old King … may they gather him to their eternal feast."

"Amen," whispered Gault.

Tertullion stood, arranging his beard upon his front. "As to your first question, noble Dexius, he that holds wisdom sees many disparate events as evidence of the spreading disease of Kör, so that without a war of cleansing, the two lands become as one in time. Kör is a hegemony and would welcome another corrupted sister without a battle having been fought. That her prince has allies from realms we cannot touch is beyond doubt. Such were the warnings of the religious, but *our* task is here and now."

"'Tis a poor party indeed when the invitation of a prince is ignored," countered Dexius.

"We must put aside all complaints and hindrances." Tertullion stepped forward, waving his hands and wagging his bearded chin as if to banish a bad taste. "By the grace of God, we have an opportunity to seize the initiative from our adversary. The legions of Kör will march soon enough, yet her tyrant is wise and so first probes our resolve. No one here must doubt that the attack on Bestrand was conceived nigh seven hundreds leagues distant … on the living throne in Tyrfang." His piece said, Tertullion plopped down unceremoniously. With affected gallantry, his dark-skinned understudy held his chair. Gault noted the exquisite robes of the youth and how he reseated himself with many a flourish.

"And this noble city of Sway?" asked Dexius. "Are we to leave the very capital of the realm undefended?"

Trakhner made to reply, deferring to Gault, who looked up from the helve of the axe planted before him. "Not undefended. A governor general will be appointed in our absence. Perhaps old Hardel, and you shall be his viceroy if you will. Levies from city districts who have not assembled, or for which there is yet no equipment, will augment the ranks of the city guard, whom I will leave intact under Brockhorst." Dexius bowed, his face inscrutable.

"But the merchants must have protection!" protested Lysander.

"And Sway cannot be held in forfeit of the remainder of the kingdom!" shot back Exeter.

"I doubt that she could anyway," added Trakhner. "She is broad and cut by too many waterways to be well defended. Her walls are old and scavenged for their bricks. Even if rebuilt, they could not hold back such a force as Kör would bring should he gain intact the resources of the eastern kingdom."

Tertullion shook his head sadly. "Would that war had been

averted, that these hard choices not been before us. Maybe our course was set long ago in a place and time veiled to us. Perhaps beyond this very earth."

"The security—" began Lysander.

"We are a nation rich in history and wealthy in the diversity of our peoples," interjected Gault in low but earnest tones, "but we are newly united. How do we honor the fealty of folk left to the whimsy of Kör whilst we huddle in the lighted streets of Sway?"

Gault shook free his unruly locks. "Nay, my father had little patience with intrigue, a sword leaving its scabbard sang sweeter to his ears. He knew that the glue of this nation was the willing valor of its knights to sacrifice all for the meanest croft." The Prince dropped his head as if in reverie. Others began to hold converse, but he again raised his gaze, and the noise was stilled when they beheld a fierce light in his eyes.

"The Old Marshal paid skaalds mouthfuls of gold when they sang of brave men and worthy foes. My birth father was such a one. How easily our people forget the ravages of a land torn asunder by war. Now to be left naked to the demons that lurk without?" A sweat sheened Gault's brow. His breath began to heave, and his arms were knotted with the strain of his grip upon the planted axe.

"Some name them Children of Darkness, but I say they live under the light of day. They draw air and hold converse just as we, and declare us mortal enemies. Such a one as this left my father gutted like a suckling pig on his very chair." With a strangled roar, Gault hefted the mighty axe. Whirling it overhead, he brought it down with a thunk that split a stump placed there for a stool.

The silence of the dell was filled only by the soft-throated gurgle of the stream. Trakhner and D'Istre grinned broadly. Wighelm stood. Gault spoke again. "Now, gentlemen. You have none of these heroes of old, only a boy prince without crown or sword. Even thus, by the blood of Gor du Roc, my birth father, that he shed to birth this kingdom, and that of the Candor kings, I swear that we shall take this army, such as it is, to reck bitter vengeance 'gainst the black prince of Kör."

The soldiers encamped nearby were roused from cooking fires by the chorus of eager yells that erupted from the greensward. Gault rocked his axe from the stump and slung it over his shoulder. "At last it is decided," he said thickly. "Tomorrow we march."

THE MATOG: STARFALL GATE

Sarc and Jamello stared, dismayed at the forbidding aspect before them. Apieron led them to a side channel outside the wind's blast where they might gather and converse. Apieron took Sarc to scout an encircling route around the structure and was not surprised to find a normal vista just beyond, a low line of broken hills tossed up as the remnants of the land scooped forth from the mighty furrows they had traversed. They rejoined the others.

Jamello mumbled about a bad dream as, mechanically, the companions set about making final preparations. Few words were said. The thief jumped, startled as Xephard's heavy hand was placed on his shoulder. He looked into the paladin's steady blue eyes and easy smile.

"Come, Jamello, the wise among us wish to admonish us one last time."

Giliad searched the faces of each in turn. "My friends, we are come to the edge of darkness. The athelas is revealed at last. I salute you!

"Finer companions on a hard road I could not ask. Even thus, the trials we have faced are nithering against what we front now. Think not the land beyond yon portal as the plane of existence where our adversary happens to dwell. Nay, Her very essence is bound to it, and Her will gives it shape. In return it adds to Her strength."

Giliad's keen glance found them again before continuing, "At its core will be a nexus where She is most strong—Her place of power. That is where we must go. Know you, to seek Her there will be quick death if our first blows be not lethal. Hark well the lessons of teamwork! When in doubt, look to Turpin and myself, who can see things hidden to the eyes of elf, dwarf, or man." Sarc shuffled uneasily. Henlee muttered.

"Listen to me!" said the gold elf. "Our foe does not dwell alone in Her creation. In countless ages, other powers gathered to Her. Some serve Her directly, others have reigns apart, thinking only to serve their own malice, but all further Her will in some fashion, else She would not suffer their presence. We must quickly slay, or better avoid those who would oppose us before our final destination. We must not tarry in endless battles with armies of Hel kind." Giliad fixed Xephard with a searching look.

"Ah, mighty mage," queried Jamello, "what would you, er, suppose would happen to certain individuals in that place if She were to be, um, banished or greatly wounded?"

Giliad's clear eyes fixed on the thief's, yet none of his usual hauteur was evident. "For once you have asked a worthy question. I have no ready answer."

"Why, we fight our way free, of course," stated Xephard.

Turpin addressed Jamello and the rest, his tones ominous, "Whomever is not ready to meet his death must now turn away. If through these gates you pass again, you will have left the life you knew behind." As his words trailed off, the tunnel's wailing rose to a wild cacophony.

"Enough banter," growled Henlee. "Unless our wise men think endless talk will silence yon yowling tube, let us make an end to this."

"Heed a final warning!" said Giliad. "The powers I exert will be used chiefly to cloak our forms from the denizens of this place, an' yet some of us bear artifacts of the powers of light." Xephard grasped the hilt of his sword reflexively. Giliad continued, "Our very natures are foreign to this place. All beings therein and some things not truly alive can sense us. Some from great distances."

"Then what hope have we?" objected Jamello. "If—"

"Gods of Sky and Wisdom have called you," said Turpin. "That should be enough."

Jamello continued to fidget. "I am wont to place my faith in hard facts and harder men."

Giliad gazed into the vortex. "Who knows how even the brave will face his fear?" With that, the golden elf strode forward, raising his hand in invocation. His final words were blown on the gale.

"I bless you all by the powers of Light!"

Belts were cinched and outer clothes fastened tight. One by one, the companions walked the gate path and were smitten by the freezing blast such that they were forced to lean forward. Xephard led the file after Giliad, followed by Apieron. Jamello kept close to Sarc, who kept his wings tightly folded such that he appeared to be simply a woods elf of some barbaric tribe. Jamello's teeth chattered, and he alternatively prayed and cursed every god that he knew. Turpin followed. Apieron glanced back, noting that the cleric's ring of heavy gold held rubies within its coiled mass that flared within the Duskbridge. Henlee came last. The companions pressed forward, and then surprisingly, they were through.

Chapter 25

Limbo: The Guardian Of Hel

There stretched a gray and featureless plain beneath a void of deepest black, pierced only by X'fel, which burned with a fierce light, seeming very close in the gloom. Initially pleased to be out of the howling ravine, each looked to his nearest companion. Here was no sound save their own muted exclamations and small shifting noises of kit and harness. They felt neither warm nor cold; all senses seemed dulled. Behind and to the sides, the flat gray extended into infinite limbo. It was only to the fore that there was change where a reddish smudge lined the base of the horizon, end to end.

"I believe that to be east," said Apieron, "if such things have meaning here."

In that direction they walked, speaking little. After an interval of unknown minutes or perhaps hours, they beheld the Guardian. All noted it at once. The horizon was clearly demarcated by a roiling burning, although somewhat removed, like a lamp seen behind a cloth. In its midst was a motionless, solitary figure of manlike shape, and as they approached, the flaming grew bright, and its true dimensions became apparent.

"Whew, the cutpurse was right," exclaimed Henlee. "That *is* a whopping big doorman." Forty feet from crown to heel stood the Guardian of Hel. Encased in shining bronze was he and armed with a triple morning star of black iron.

"This is no living being," said Sarc.

"Mayhap he merely stands to block escape rather than prevent entry?" said Apieron without much conviction.

"Perhaps," answered Giliad. "I prefer to not find out."

After a look to Turpin, who was lost in thought, the gold elf waved the others to follow, and for a space they sought a circumventing path around the figure. They pressed on, a line of somber, ashen walkers in a shapeless land but, after another indeterminate time of march, the glowing horizon stripe grew no closer and the sentinel was now tiny over their right shoulders. Without signal, they came to the same conclusion. "It is as I feared," sighed Giliad.

"I think we are all of a mind, but there was nothing gained without trying," said Apieron.

"And now?" asked Henlee.

"Now, oh dwarf, we try something new!" snapped Giliad. "I do not grow weary by mere foot travel, yet I deem we might walk here a hundred years and never touch yon conflagration. Surely that is our destination."

Jamello groaned. "A hundred years? My beauties at Perla's Parade will be crones when I return."

"Heck, thief," said Henlee, "their daughter's granddaughters will be of age by then." Jamello looked hopeful.

"Enough nonsense," said Turpin. "Try your casting, mage, though I doubt not the result."

"A teleportation?" asked Henlee dubiously.

Giliad nodded. "Of the strongest variety."

"By Obdug's gravel eyes, I hate these," groused the dwarf. "But I'll let you fly me through the nether realms this time, only because I am in one anyway."

"Then join hands around me. Quickly!" cried Giliad. When they had done so, he spoke softly and withdrew a luminous pendant near his breast. It blazed with a brief flash, and they tumbled into a spinning free fall. Muffled, as if by great distance, they heard Giliad's urgent calls, and they were back in the circle on hands and knees, the least movement leaving them vertiginous and helpless.

Jamello was flat on his face. "Yegh, this gray dirt tastes awful."

Apieron helped him rise as Henlee glowered at Giliad, who explained, "When we touched the barrier, it cast us into the void. I had to reverse the spell before we were lost."

"We must face the Guardian," stated Apieron.

After a moment to clear dazed heads and a sip of water, the journeyers walked until the figure loomed. They halted some three hundred paces from it.

"What now?" asked Henlee. Xephard grew impatient, testing the draw of Leitus.

"Wait! We must try my idea," said Apieron. "I am the fastest runner. Let us see if he reacts when I threaten to pass."

"The thief is the quickest to duck and dodge," countered Henlee. Jamello shot him a withering look.

"Nay, you are both wrong," laughed Sarc.

His voice, like theirs, sounded flat in the gloom, yet his humble merriment cheered them nonetheless. With a flap, mighty pinions thrust behind him. Muscular thighs tensed, and he bounded into the air to circle once before heading directly for the silent sentinel. When he crossed some unseen threshold, it sprang to life.

Moving with surprising alacrity, it swung its weapon into a whirling arc while turning to track the winged elf. Sarc flew higher, appearing to strain against an invisible force that prevented further ascent. The construct stepped forward, launching a roundhouse blow at the stalled elf. Sarc folded his wings and fell beneath the strike, although the passage of the iron balls, each nearly as tall as he, buffeted him mightily. Mere yards above the ground, he recovered his balance and shot back to the companions. A wicked foot stomp by the golem followed him, churning up a cloud of dust in his wake. The party felt the ground shake.

Xephard and Apieron ran forward and were the first to greet Sarc, supporting his arms as he sank heavily between them. He gasped as he was led away. "I could not overtop him." The swamp elf recovered his breath. "He moves like a striking snake, and his face is very cruel."

"We must assault him," declared Xephard, never taking his eyes off the Guardian, which had resumed its motionless station. "When he is drawn to the attack, I will harry him whilst you others enter the Helplane." Henlee passed into Xephard's hands his war hammer, retaining Maul in hand and a throwing axe on his back.

"Peace! We can do better than that," said Giliad.

"Turpin and I shall batter him with spells while the rest of you rush beyond." A brief discussion ensued in which all partook except Jamello. A battle plan was agreed upon, and the seven adventurers spread out for the attack. Sarc again took to the air, this time with bow ready while Giliad and Turpin strode to the fore. The golem turned its front to them.

With a shout, Giliad hurled a blinding spray of light that struck the monster full on the brow. Once more Turpin summoned the vaporous essence of his ring. This time it appeared with greater size and speed than before, and shot from the heavy ring to entangle the mighty thews and lower torso of the beast. The golem reared back its head and roared like a hundred brazen trumpets, then surged toward the spellcasters like a juggernaut, morning star whirling overhead.

The servant of the ring was broken into fragments of

dissolving mist, and the lights of Giliad's spell blinked out. Sarc's arrows struck the monstrous face and head in a rapid tattoo of ringing metal but had no discernible effect. Seeing the peril of the charging beast, Giliad quickly summoned a dangerous magic of unbeing. He clapped his hands.

Dark wings of nothingness closed on the upper portions of the beast. A second volley of Sarc's arrows was caught therein and winked into nonexistence. As the darkness folded like a shutting door, the gray horizon of flames beyond disappeared into an empty, black vista. The sentinel gave vent to a second roar, greater than the first, and a concussion shook the area, tossing up fountains of gray dust and swirling smoke. Then it was among them.

Xephard and Henlee shouted and charged to intercept. Apieron led Jamello behind one of its great legs, hoping to find a joint of weakness. Henlee and Xephard struck mighty blows with all the power in their massive frames. There followed a clang and a flash that left Xephard staring stupidly at the sundered half of Henlee's war hammer. Maul did little better. While it did not break, it nonetheless rebounded from the Guardian's adamantine skin with such force that the dwarf spun completely around and tumbled to his knees, where he was promptly kicked by the construct thirty yards to land in a crumpled heap.

Apieron hurled his steel-tipped Javelin into the fossa behind the knee of the creature's planted foot. Jamello shrugged, then slashed behind the ankle with the broad-bladed hunting sword of the Wyrnde tomb, forged for such chopping blows. Both weapons shattered instantly. With a horrid ripping of the air, they saw the morning star flash. Xephard shouted a warning to Giliad, who remained in the center of combat before Turpin. He flew aside, heaving the cleric in tow with him. Xephard had half-drawn Leitus but snapped it back, seeing that his companions were clear, and bounded up just as the iron balls hammered home in rapid succession. Where cleric, mage, and paladin had stood, deep craters were torn into the ground. They scrambled back to a safe distance.

Apieron supported Henlee, who was dragging his shield, dazed but amazingly unhurt otherwise, cased within his dwarven armor. Apieron gave him a drink from a skin. Henlee wiped bloody spittle from his lips and grinned at Xephard, jerking his head in the direction of the now quiescent sentinel.

"I've softened him up for you, boy. Now go in and finish him off."

Jamello hurled down the useless hilts of his broken blade. "I never liked that one anyway. Too heavy." He grasped the hilt of the king blade, testing its draw in scabbard.

"This Guardian is indestructible," said Sarc. "My small magics would certainly be uselessly spent against such as this, for I have witnessed the mighty spells of the lord Giliad and holy Turpin cast in vain. Is there no other way?"

"There is no other way," Turpin answered. His gaze never strayed from the fires visible between the golem's legs.

"Perhaps this creature is protecting us from nightmares 'twere best not to face?" said Jamello hopefully.

Giliad ignored the thief. "I agree with Sarc. To assail this sentinel further is nonsensical."

"To leave a foeman unscathed seems unright to me," countered Xephard.

"This is no living intelligence that has chosen the path of evil," replied Sarc.

"Yet it serves evil," said Xephard.

Apieron's aquiline features were dust coated and streaked with sweat, yet his voice was strong with passion. "I did not forsake my king and household and gather dear friends onto a perilous journey to be thwarted by a mere door warden.

"If we must slay this thing to enter, we will find a means. Now that we are come hither, I feel more than ever that our cause is just. There is a dark will here that casts its hate on us. I know it is the same that moves with fell intent upon our homelands. Now that we stand nigh the source, we must not falter." Ever before, Apieron's power of leadership had been the voice of moderation and patience for careful consideration. For the first time, certain of the party glimpsed the upheaval that filled his soul.

Xephard beamed at Apieron's words. "Well said!"

Henlee pursed his lips. "Someone must have made that shiny turnkey. I guess then someone else can unmake it." He scratched his beard. "An' I never swung Maul so hard to no effect."

Turpin exhaled heavily and focused his attention as if reluctantly on them. "The priests of my order must oft journey by trance into the twilight of the inner mind. There each discovers his own guardian that separates his life in the waking world from the mysterious deep that lies within. Unless the initiate can wield a strength of mind and spirit, he cannot pass into the realm of the hidden self. He must first defeat his guardian."

"Do you mean the guardian comes to him as some monster to be slain?" asked Jamello.

Turpin's golden ring flashed heavily in the gloom. They saw now clearly that its substance was coils, as if of serpents intertwined, with eyes of glowing ruby. "Nay. It is only a shadowy device called into being to shield one's mind from the unlogic that lives within us all.

"It can be person or monster, oft simply a puzzling barrier. Whatever the form, it may be broken or slain, but most oft a way is found by appeasement or trick. This is sooth, for in this way compromise is gained so that the barrier remains as an obstacle to return visits, and the dream traveler risks not his immediate destruction in direct struggle with his guardian."

"But—" interrupted Jamello.

"Moreover, such a guardian is easier to defeat the second, third, or tenth time. Erstwhile it remains to not only shield the hidden realm from the light of reason, it also protects the waking world of man from the dangers of insanity and possession. Only the most wise can exist in both realms without such sentinels."

Giliad's eyes searched the cleric's face. "Yonder barrier, learned priest, will not protect us from the arms of Hel that will surely assault us should we tarry here overlong."

"I do not think we've weakened him, though he has nearly killed us," added Henlee.

Giliad ignored him much as Turpin had Jamello. "Yet perhaps your words hold the key, Patriarch. Valiant Apieron, you mistook my remarks if you deem I intend to retreat. There are none of us here who feel not the urgency of this quest." The gold elf gestured broadly back the way they had come.

"Back there, a war will soon rage, our skills will be sorely missed. It is for our very love of kith and kin that we leave them when their need is greatest, that we dare the very heart of evil." The elf mage's eyes were cerulean, and his golden hair glinted as if they were the only objects of color in the drab twilight.

Apieron bowed. "As always, the words of a lord of Amor hold wisdom."

"Now that we are thinking more clearly, I believe we can try the Gate again," said Giliad. "Jamello is nimblest. He shall engage the construct, tempting another strike. At that moment, we shall rush past to our destination."

Jamello sputtered, "Engage it?"

"Good plan," said Henlee, "except that thing is too quick. One or more of us is like to get stomped or kicked."

Giliad smiled. "Not when I have imbued you with the speed of our friend Sarc. With your permission?"

Sarc nodded, offering one wing. Giliad drew a gemmed poniard and deftly severed six hairlike feathers from the understructure of a greater pinion. He passed one to each of the others, retaining one himself. "With this casting, you will be as light of foot as a winged elf of Fogleaf, at least for a short while. Take heed not to leap into the air or you will be a floating mark for the golem!"

"Probably won't work on dwarves," muttered Henlee.

Turpin spoke. "The elf mage saved me from the Guardian's stroke but moments ago. I will trust him now."

Henlee squinted at Giliad's hand and shifted his feet uncomfortably but otherwise submitted to the brief spell. When it was over, the tiny quillions they held vanished. Jamello gave a little hop, then raced a circle before coming to a gliding stop before them. "Would I had use of your magic when I cat burgled half the merchants of Bestrand," he laughed. "I would be retired! Since we are not leaving, I will lead you. Come quickly when it commits. I do not wish to dodge a second strike."

"We will come," said Apieron.

"The blessing of Spear Goddess be upon you," pronounced Xephard.

"I'd rather have one of Lady Wingfoot," said Jamello.

"The enchantment will not last forever," reminded Giliad. Jamello sped away, his form growing dim against the gray.

"Ware his kick!" called Henlee to the receding thief.

In mere moments, they saw the creature react. The morning star began to whirl. This time the golem's movements did not seem so quick next to the evasive leaps and bounds of the tiny figure at its feet. The party trotted forward. The weapon began its descent.

"Now!" shouted Giliad.

They put on a burst of speed, Sarc maintaining a position a dozen feet above the ground and to the rear. Henlee was utterly amazed to find himself keeping pace with the longer-limbed humans and the graceful golden elf.

The triple-weighted morning star flailed into the ground with another thunderous impact. They heard Jamello laugh as he ran between the creature's legs. A monstrous bellow cut the vapid airs as the construct raised a leg to stomp them, the enormous foot trailing a streamer of dust.

As one, they flashed underneath and its impact behind them was like a detonation, bouncing them briefly into the air. Flames roared directly in front. They saw Jamello look back, but Giliad waved him forward, his cries lost in the tumult before and behind. The thief disappeared into the burning, and they trailed him, pursued by the Guardian's wrathful bellows.

"That's Jamello!" Apieron leapt forward. The companions heard a wailing as they dashed through the maelstrom. After a distance, the swirling fires cleared, and they found the thief hunched over a crimson bush. Its leafless branches were of elongated and segmented gems, like a living garnet. Jamello's right hand grasped the branch nearest him. He put back his face and screamed.

Apieron's second javelin passed with a harmless rattle through the bush. Xephard dropped to the ground at Henlee's warning. Maul tumbled overhead, the heavy black sledge striking the main trunk of the gem tree, which fell into shattered fragments. Jamello sat down, his face ashen, then vomited. Apieron placed a hand on his trembling back.

"It was sucking the life out of me," stammered the thief.

Henlee bent to retrieve Maul from atop piles of powdered garnet that already drifted into the wind. "You should know which jewels are for looking and which are for taking, thief."

"Foolish," added Turpin.

Apieron helped Jamello to his feet. The thief examined the leathern gauntlet of his right hand. It was fused and useless. He cursed and tossed it away in disgust. It burst into flame and windblown ash before it struck ground. Xephard approached and laid a heavy hand on Jamello's shoulder. "I believe, Jamello, that you are a true warrior. It was your courage that led us through Duskbridge."

"Oh, right," said Jamello. "More wisdom for those of us who lack it most."

Xephard laughed and moved to join the cleric and elves. Henlee shook his head and followed. "You don't understand," said Apieron. "He was serious."

Jamello looked at Xephard's broad back, glinting silver in the Hel glow. "Oh."

With the immediate peril of the Gate passage behind them, the nature of their surroundings imposed itself upon the travelers. Side by side, they gazed in wonderment and dismay. It was a land of vivid chaos, an ugly barren of blackened rocks and soil stretched before them, its surface broken by jagged rents where lurked yellow fumes. Occasional jets of venting steam shot forth in mighty plumes that were immediately sundered by howling winds. The air was heavy to breathe, foul and oppressive, and overhead, the horizon was a vertical clash of jarring colors like the palatte of a mad artist. The overall effect was as if the firmament upon which they stood was falling up into the sky.

"I feel nauseated again," said Jamello.

"As do we all," shouted Apieron into the wind. "Your spells are wondrous, wise Turpin and noble Giliad. Without them we would already be burned alive." He indicated several tongues of flame, many yards across, that billowed from the ground or fell from the roiling sky or originated in the wind itself. Swirling gales jerked these to and fro across the landscape, and slung sharp grains of obsidian or caused clapping pressure changes that slapped the travelers' ears like a giant's hand.

"Confound it!" complained Henlee. "No matter which way I turn, this durned wind is in my face." The dwarf's jewel-plaited beard flew about as he urgently sought to retuck it into his weapons belt.

Apieron examined his recovered casting lance. Its once bright head was pitted with rust. It crumbled in his hand. He swept the wooden haft, already burning, around in a slow circle. "Is there nothing living here?"

"There is," intoned Turpin somberly.

"There!" shouted Sarc. Their gazes followed the line of his outstretched hand to behold a cluster of black specks far in the upper airs. Hard to mark against the disjointed horizon, they appeared to wheel and turn like some nighted flock.

"Birds?" asked Apieron.

"Bats!" growled Henlee.

"Neither," said Sarc. "I know not what they be."

"Now we must decide what is to be our direction," said Giliad. "I have cast a scrying magic. It was destroyed before leaving my hand. The will of this place thwarts us well."

"There is no need," said Turpin. He glanced back to the Guardian as a wayfarer might imprint the location of a landmark. The sentinel was indistinct and small behind its veil of fire and smoke. With his boot, Turpin traced a line in the charcoal soil north by east from Apieron's prior estimate of that direction.

"The Goddess be praised that you are here," said Xephard. Turpin nodded, his mantle of crimson and ermine alive in the gale.

"Let us be about it," spat Henlee. "This isn't my choice spot for a picnic."

"Agreed," said Apieron. "Now that good Turpin has said it, I feel he is correct." Without further words, they set off on the cleric's line, taking great care where they placed their feet amongst the many hazards. After a hundred paces, the heat, even protected as they were, drained their energy as if each had already come to the end of a long day's toil. When the wind was still, the air shimmered in undulant waves as they trudged onward into the swirling miasma.

Once and again, Apieron beheld a shadowy form, glimpsed only in the corner of his vision, yet each time he turned, it faded into the swirling darkness of the Hel plane. Apieron did not call out or seek aid of cleric or mage. He knew it walked only with him.

Chapter 26

Helheim

Jamello lay back and closed his eyes. He folded his once fine cloak around his head to keep the stinging grit, borne on the Hel wind, from his face. Giliad had called a halt once Henlee discovered a meager windbreak nestled low amongst an outcrop of gleaming obsidian, its faces worn shear by the incessant grist of the storm. Giliad had asked Apieron and Turpin if they felt any different from before. They had both shrugged a no. Jamello knew how *he* felt. Miserable, and likely to be more so in the near future.

The elf mage had mumbled something about the need to strengthen his shielding magics. Exactly what that entailed, Jamello was not certain. He recollected Turpin stating that once beyond the Gates, nearly every entity would detect their foreign natures and seek them out. Therefore, whatsoever the nature of the elf mage's casting suited Jamello well.

Thus far, they had been "attacked" only once, and he was unsure if one could call it that. A smallish, gray-skinned creature of spindly limbs and a bullet head had materialized before Henlee and clambered onto his front. To Jamello, it appeared some cross between a monkey and a lizard. Oddly enough, when Henlee throttled it, the creature's gaze never left the gems and precious metals woven into the dwarf's beard. Eyes glowering, Henlee had kicked its limp form to ensure its demise.

"Damn thievin' Hel womprat."

Jamello unfolded a tiny corner of his cloak and raised a flask to his lips, carefully wiping both flask cap and its mouth before letting a small amount trickle down his throat. Although warm and flat, he let the sensation take his mind away to wander into a cool, aquatic fantasy. He looked from side to side. Henlee and Sarc also sipped at water skins. The dwarf shook his head with distaste, no doubt suffering the trauma of actually having to consume water rather than a more lively spirit.

Jamello toasted him, "More precious than gold," chuckling when Henlee grunted his disdain.

Jamello cherished another sip. "When I think of the times I have nearly drowned in this stuff, I'm smitten with the irony. Now I'll likely die from lack of it. Ah, Henlee, 'twere better to have drowned back in Bestrand than desiccate here like a worm on a pavestone, stranded and stretched out to shrivel after some summer shower has lifted him from his cool burrow."

"Bah, thief!" exclaimed Henlee. "If it makes you worry less, I say you are more likely to have your head ripped off by a Hel troll long before you die of thirst."

"Oh, thank you."

"I like the story about the worm," said Sarc.

Jamello was searching for a pithy retort when Xephard's steel-cased hand touched his shoulder. "It is time to wake and walk the paths of honor, friend. Our guides say we must go."

Jamello stepped out of the shelter with the others, checking the draw of his blade. "Oh!" he exclaimed. A patina of scintillant dust immediately coated the weapon. He saw Henlee swipe at a similar effect on Maul whilst Apieron carefully cleaned his bow.

He glanced to Turpin's hand where he bore his heavy ring, but saw only the unaffected gleam of its serpentine gold.

"Powdered diamond, or I am no cousin of Dangmar the wealthy," said Henlee.

"Not on our cleric's ring, nor on Leitus," proclaimed Xephard, holding its gleaming surface aloft.

"Nor on me," echoed Sarc, who conspicuously wore virtually no metal. Jamello smirked, and Henlee guffawed when they beheld Giliad. The aloof and debonaire sword-mage swatted clouds of the stuff that swarmed onto every aspect of his person. His once silvered mail resembled a powdered pastry. At last with an angry gesture, he mouthed something that sounded more like an imprecation than a spell, at which the dust promptly fell into obedient piles. When his haughty gaze lit upon them, Henlee snickered.

"Now that all have rested, we must do better before we stop again," said Apieron. "I feel we are far from our destination." Apieron turned his head as if tracking something in the corner of his vision. His gaze returned to the line of their march, his face set in grim determination.

"We are far indeed," intoned Turpin, his heavy ring flashing redly.

"That is a mighty talisman you wieldeth, Priest," spoke Giliad. "How well suited to the dark powers of this Helpit it seemeth."

"That was a rest?" asked Jamello. No one answered.

They moved off. Jamello regarded their course, slowly swiveling his head. He had abandoned his customary habit of quick darting glances at any new surrounding, followed by a more thorough eye scan. For the last time he had tried, he spent the next several minutes helpless and dizzy.

After a time, the ground upon which they walked became red, like crushed iron ore that Jamello had once seen piled nigh a furnace. That stuff, he recalled, did not have wisps of orange flame or plumes of jaundice-brown smoke pouring from its surface. Vermillion dust, sparkling with mica, powered the legs of the party. The sky roiled, and oily black clouds scuttled across its surface while cords of blue lightning fanned across the bottom of the wrack in lacing webs that lit the whole with a sickly purple glow. Jamello hated this place. He knew it hated him back. Jamello hated Apieron for bringing him to this hateful place.

"I hate you, Apieron." A foul gust swept his words away. Giving no sign whether he heard the thief's words or no, their leader bowed his head into the storm and trudged on. They marched, always into the wind. The gusts grew progressively more violent.

Jamello's eyes wept as he alternated between sneezing, coughing, and gagging. His legs were leaden, and he fancied that he felt the added weight of each grain of metallic dust that clung to his leggings. The wind rose to a howl, driving pieces of sharpened jet against their faces and bodies, and soon the air was entirely peppered with flying debris. Jamello ducked a spinning shard as large as his fist only to catch a particularly vicious chip through a seam in his cowl. He slapped at the wound and looked to curse Apieron when he saw a trickle of blood, dark on Apieron's coif below the neck. In unspoken agreement, the party came to a halt.

"Your casting, my lords," shouted Sarc to Giliad and Turpin, "is wondrous against the Helfire, yet will do no good if our flesh is shredded before we reach Apieron's demoness."

"Aye," said Henlee. "I, for one, cannot stare into a storm of glass chips, and I durst not wrap my eyes lest I step into a pit." The dwarf's thick eyebrows and beard were filled with red dust. Jamello would have laughed had he not felt so miserable. Besides, he imagined he looked equally ridiculous—perhaps like a skinny, orange mummy.

The wind took on a deeper note as it gathered more velocity. Jamello was buffeted into Xephard, who steadied him. Sarc appeared to suffer the worst, his wings tightly tucked as he leaned forward into the blast, every muscle straining. Giliad regarded them. He stood without discomfort, only his billowing cloak and streaming hair gave testimony to the gale, and no grit came nigh his person. Turpin at times waved his ring hand before him, thus protecting his face, although his torso and legs were as affected as the others.

"That isn't fair!" shouted Jamello.

Giliad reached into his jeweled belt and pulled forth six pairs of oval, yellowish membranes, each looped by an encircling twine. "Strap these to your head. Sarc shall have mine." He handed them to Apieron, who quickly distributed them, helping each to center the discs over their eyes.

"These will tint your vision slightly," apologized the elf, "but I daresay in this light you shall hardly notice."

The mage spoke a singsong cant while touching his hand to his lips. He touched their ears in turn, his voice carrying easily through the shrieking gale. When he was done, Jamello found he could hear without straining or reading lips. "What did he do?" asked the thief, but Giliad had already turned to converse with Apieron and Turpin.

"He repeated 'listen' many times," said Sarc. "In ancient elvish."

Jamello looked at his companions, faces clad with the bulging goggles. He donned his own. "Perhaps if we are spotted by some hostile scout, he will think us merely a troop of giant Hel insects and leave us be."

"I hope so," said Sarc.

"Surely this storm will confuse prying eyes," said Apieron, returning to them.

"If we don't get lost ourselves," grunted Henlee.

"Perhaps," said Giliad.

"This membrane, Master Giliad?" Henlee stroked one of the lenses on his face. "Of what substance is it made? It is transparent, flexible yet resilient."

"It is taken from the processed membrane of the afterbirth of a western sea cow."

"I thought so," replied Henlee seriously. He stepped forward to resume the march.

"What is that groaning?" asked Jamello.

"More like the blowing of horns," said Apieron.

Xephard stroked Leitus. "A hunt?" The paladin said no more while each of the others imagined what might be the object of the huntsman of Hel.

"Methinks," added Sarc, "it is a natural music that rises and falls on the wind."

"Music lovers or game drivers, either way I have got a greeting for them." Henlee slapped Maul with his gauntleted palm. The travelers marched as they spoke, and soon the source of the noise became apparent. The gritty soil upon which they trod gave way to rock, slate black and increasingly pockmarked with holes, small as one's wrist or several feet across. The wind across its surface produced an undulant sound like a gargantuan wind instrument blown by some mad god.

"This outcrop is too wide to skirt," said Apieron. "Ware your footfalls."

Henlee bent to peer into one of the dark openings that emitted a particularly loud piping. He turned to wink at Jamello. "Hi there, thief, you are skinny enough to slip right in." He spat into the hole. "Why don't you drop a line and tell us how deep it goes?"

"I do not trust this music," murmured Sarc. "Something lives in the black wind." Despite the swamp elf's misgivings, their journey across the rocky expanse was uneventful, if slow, for many minutes as they picked their way between twisted rises and furrows in the honeycombed stone.

"Dwarf!" shouted Sarc. Behind Henlee rose an eel-like creature from an aperture he had overleapt. Its fleshy body was more than a yard in thickness, its length as tall as a mast and terminating in a snapping maw like that of a turtle, with a blood-red interior and a black, leathery tongue. It was eyeless, but a ring of searching stalks twisted to and fro at the base of its head.

It lunged down at the dwarf, although found no purchase on his helm and skillfully presented shield. Henlee scrambled to bring Maul to bear one-handed while pushing against the man-sized beak. Failing its attempt to bite through the dwarf's defenses, the creature reared back and gave vent to a high-pitched shriek. The call was joined as a host of the creatures erupted from fenestrations in the stone.

With a shout, Apieron hurled this third and last javelin. It passed through the creature's body beneath the head and flew off to be lost amongst the waving throng. Three of Sarc's arrows embedded themselves in rapid cadence below the head, followed by a string of Giliad's blue radiances that lassoed around it before exploding. The creature ignored these attacks. Pausing, it arched twenty feet above Henlee, then whipped down, maw extended wide enough to engulf its target whole.

The canny mountain dwarf was prepared, his bushy brows furrowing in concentration as he tracked the strike. At the last moment, he sidestepped and shield slammed the head to the ground. He released his buckler and brought Maul down two-handed in an overhand blow. With a resounding crunch, his heavy sledge crumpled the creature's mantle and splattered plate-sized pieces of chitin and ichor onto the rock. The beast descended into a frenzied dance of death, whipping its mangled head about on its thick neck to thud repeatedly against the stone. Shattered portions of the outcrop fell amongst the party, and they dodged and sidestepped its passage, all the while taking care not to traverse into the radius of the beast's howling neighbors. Eventually it passed too near one of these and was promptly snapped in half and swallowed. The proximal end lay limp and oozing at its hole.

"Looks like intestines," said Jamello, disgusted.

"A mighty blow!" enthused Xephard.

Henlee beamed. "Like stepping on an egg."

"The Forest of Hel," said Sarc. In all directions was a wide expanse of the creatures. They gave forth a clamorous moaning to blow in the wind. Occasionally one would sway near another that would whipsaw its boneless body in attempt to snare its comrade. A savage struggle would then ensue.

Giliad beckoned. "This is no place to linger!"

Huddled together, the party wended through the surreal forest for hours. Sarc repeatedly wielded his twisted lance to fend off snapping attacks. Xephard ran several through with Leitus while Apieron spent most of his remaining arrows but did not think any of their actions caused any serious hurt. Giliad attempted no less than a dozen castings that either fizzled in the air or had no effect. During one such attempt, he opened a small bag to obtain a pinch of black dust for an explosive incantation. He instead dropped the sack as each grain had become a scurrying black beetle, three-inch pincers waving wildly.

Of habit Henlee would have scoffed, instead he shook his head. The futility of their actions and the tedious, winding trek across the honeycombed labyrinth began to tell on even his iron endurance. Oft the wind gusted in cadence, and the creatures would emerge from the stone to extend their full length like waving water plants fifty feet above the blackened terrain. Each would then moan its own timbre such that they joined in weird chorus.

Whether this was a means of communication or merely a behavioral anomaly, none could guess. "Maybe they're all but portions of one enormous jellyfish?" speculated Jamello.

"By the snaky locks of the god beneath the waves, I hope not!" said Apieron.

"Me neither," said Henlee.

"It does not matter," said Giliad. "We are near the end of this cursed rock."

They crested the last bastion of the shelf to look out over a new landscape. It was a zone of blackened rubble, scarred into pits and furrows. Great reeks of acidic gas gathered in low places as the ever-present orange glare lit the horizon in all directions. Without a word, they filed down onto its surface. The skyroof was lower and composed of the same dirty plumes that crept the burning ground. Minutes stretched into hours with pause only for sips of water, and not even the dwarf had a stomach for food as they trudged their weary, winding way around the worst of the reeks. Apieron fell into his warrior's stride, setting the pace brisk to maintain momentum, albeit not enough to cause the inevitable cramp of muscles.

"My legs feel like they have been beat by a dozen of Procrius's torturers," moaned Jamello. Little clouds of dust trailed behind each of his dragging steps.

"Normally I would fly a bit ahead to mark the terrain," said Sarc, "but I durst not." He indicated several shifting shapes in the cloud deck above.

"How much farther must we walk?" asked Jamello of Apieron, who merely shrugged. The thief turned to Turpin. "Why can't you use your holy powers to detect the distance to our goal, Your Worship?"

"Only a fool looks direct into the light of a lantern to see who is carrying it. The wise man shields its light to see whose face lies in shadow. Were I to open the eye of my soul here to evil, I would be awash with such in every direction."

"More good news …"

"Besides, I have tried squinting the eye of my spell such that the sea of hate would be less. The result is meaningless. Sometimes I glean a focus of evil intent that cuts the air like a knife, bearing down on us with malice from the sky roof, or welling from a spot on the ground. Such redes tell me naught."

"There are creatures in the sky, we have heard their braying," said Apieron.

"A mage's searching mind might hunt the distant airs like a falcon," joined Giliad.

"And the ground," said Henlee. "Remember you the eels of song?"

"I know not," said Giliad with a glance to Turpin. "The next time you sense such a thing, tell me, and we shall see."

Xephard came back from point, having heard some of the conversation. "Delay not, sage. There is a Well of Hate twenty paces from where we stand. Leitus tells me so."

Henlee scrutinized the area indicated by Xephard with a scowl. "I see nothing but the same voiceless stones we have been tramping over for a day and more."

Giliad raised his hand. "Patience, good dwarf. A knight pure of heart may be our greatest ally in this foul place. We would do well to explore all that impacts his senses (if we can). While my skill lies most in warcraft, I have learned something of sagery from my studies and the tutelage of my lord Galor."

"Lead on then," gestured Henlee broadly. "This is as good a place as any to call a rest while you witchmen spoon out one drop in Turpin's soup of hate."

Giliad smiled. "Of course take a mouthful of blessed water,

but do not rest! For this task we shall need your strong back and skill with a pick." They moved to the area Xephard indicated. Gilead's booted toe drew a mark in the dust.

"Dig here."

Turpin's eyebrows arched with curiosity. A curt smile played across his face. "Of course here, Xephard and my lord Apieron, ply to while myself and good Jamello keep watch."

With the expert aid of the dwarf and the great, looping blows of Apieron and Xephard, it was discovered that the stony crust was only inches deep, and overlay a passage of sorts. Skillfully hewn steps were revealed that led down to a cavern mouth. Henlee took the fore, his energy returning at the sight of the hidden stair and the prospect of undiscovered treasure. Jamello and the spellcasters came behind the paladin and Apieron. They quickly descended from view of Sarc, who stood guard at the surface. Rather than darkness, the companions found the walls to be of translucent crystal wherein weapons of many sorts, both strange and familiar, as well as trophies of war were somehow embedded. They halted at a door of iron, speckled with rust but obviously very strong.

"Stand back, boys," said Henlee. "Put away those skinny toothpicks. This be a task for a real weapon." He raised the hammer surface of Maul aloft and two-stepped forward to deliver a charging blow. At that instant, a white light blazed from Giliad. The dwarf stood as before, but instead of the dull gleam of metal, there was a smoky glass, warped and bubbled. Henlee jerked to a halt.

"Stealing my glory?" He restrapped Maul, and before any could object, he gathered his short legs beneath him to leap forward, shield and helm leading through the barrier with a crash and spray of splintered crystal. Apieron rushed past the others but halted and teetered on the edge of a chasm over which the dwarf had plummeted, arms flailing wildly.

Giliad shook his head in exacerbation. With a disdainful wave of his hand, the tableau shimmered and changed. Rather than a yawning pit, they beheld a chamber of sparkling black granite. Its flagstones were littered with glasslike fragments of the broken door. A prone dwarf lay before them, arms and legs pumping rapidly. "Never before have I seen a swimmer on dry land," said the elf mage dryly. "Truly this is a marvel."

"And I have never known a dwarf so apt at the sport," laughed Apieron. "He could be an otter."

The dwarf leapt up sputtering. Fragments of the door speckled his beard and eyebrows, and his eyes were wild. "Thought I was falling. Damn Hel illusion!" His palms slapped his steel cap to clear his head. "Next time, young Apieron, *you* go first."

They regarded the room. A square-cut block of the glowing quartz dominated the floor. In it and suspended within a gelatinous bath lay a man of sorts. A mighty figure would he be if standing upright, yet he appeared incomplete. Translucent skin and faintly pulsing veins made him appear vaguely embryonic. The man was partially clad with gleaming plate armor. Henlee reached into the fluid and slipped free a tall, visored helm that lay next to the head. He placed it on the floor and struck it one-handed with Maul, then bent to examine it closely.

"Not a scratch," he breathed. "*Wodensteel.*"

Apieron frowned and prodded the man's half-armored chest with the butt of his bow. "Is this one of your dark droplets, Turpin?" The cleric nodded slowly, his pale eyes studying Apieron. The ranger shook his head unhappily. "I like not that we have discovered his ilk before. The decrepit temple of the swamp was too much like this cairn, albeit lesser in power."

"And this one better equipped for battle, though the t'other be a prince," stated Henlee.

"How many more lie about, waiting to emerge?" asked Jamello, fingering his goatee nervously.

"A cocoon," said Apieron. "And alike, how many hide in the world above, not distant from the lands of men—an army of evil kings awaiting some fell summons."

Xephard nodded gravely, his horsehair plume suspended white in the glittering darkness. Leitus flashed silver in his hand. "One is too many."

"Up the steps, quickly," commanded Giliad. At the urgings of the golden elf, they fled the chamber to gather Sarc and stand back. At a small sign by Giliad, a gout of incandescent flame burst from the stone in the excavation, the structure collapsing in on itself before settling into a slow whirlpool of molten glass that bubbled thickly.

Henlee whistled. "Well, that's that."

"Another push, then we shall set wards and take a well-deserved rest," said Giliad. "We have destroyed the howe, nonetheless, I care not to linger."

As they left the ruined cairn far behind and marched deep into the Helscape, Xephard would often frown and indicate with sword drawn various points on the charcoaled ground. Turpin and Giliad returned curt, negative nods. The companions were surprised to find signs of eroded ramparts and roads, and bridges of iron cast over crevices. Now and anon, they bypassed areas of lingering magic that Giliad would point out, yet appeared no different to the others. At these times, his eyes seemed unfocused.

"Battles," he muttered, "terrible battles once raged here."

Henlee gave an excited shout, pulling a protesting Apieron aside. "I see nothing but windblown flame under a rock. There are many such here!"

The dwarf clucked his disappointment and heaved aside a boulder to reveal an unworked defile, ten paces across, where a vent of flaming gas burned with blue heat under a natural dome. The rock was fenestrated, and the whipping wind fanned the torch to a great heat that caused Apieron to flinch despite Turpin's magical balm. Henlee pointed to flecks and slivers of bright steel shining from a bed of black carbon that crusted the upper dome. He pried one free with a work hammer and fingered its slick, gray surface.

"Wodensteel," he said thoughtfully, regarding the Hel kiln with furrowed brows.

"What did you see?" asked Jamello of Apieron when they rejoined the others.

"The forge of gods."

"Oh."

The terrain grew more difficult. Strange spires and swirling drifts of stone forced them into many circuitous detours, although Turpin never lost his bearing, always starting back to a course that to ranger and mage seemed an unerring line from the moment they left the Gates. Nightfall did not come to ease the ever-present heat, and the only thin shadows flitted from fingers of drifting gas. At times the ground itself seemed transparent and lit with an eerie light. When this occurred, Henlee would stand and mutter, then swallow it back and shrug forward when he saw the others' unheedful expressions.

As with the dwarf, each traveler experienced his own particular variant of malaise. Whether up or down, the path seemed always a jarring incline to protesting muscles and straining joints. Sudden rigors or bouts of vertigo would leave them shaken and weak. Apieron could see Jamello grow increasingly more agitated, jumping and starting at random sights or movements, drawing and resheathing every weapon he carried, his face a mask of twitching paranoia.

Apieron could only imagine the suffering of the swamp elf, whose visage was set in a grimace of pain until he at last hid it under a cowl and cast his eyes downward. Worse than heat or pain for Apieron was the return of the riding shadow at the periphery of his vision. It had grown in strength and now possessed a sibilant voice. "Begone, Whisper of Despair," he muttered, too low for the others to hear.

"A Hel troll!" called Jamello. He loosed his last quirt into a fiery curtain that billowed briefly ahead.

"You're hallucinating," growled Turpin when they rushed to the spot only to find Jamello's weapon, broken but unbloodied. Jamello glared, kicked the broken dart and trudged forward, his previously nimble feet dragging along the rock to leave furrows in multicolored soils. That was when Henlee began his song.

First he hummed in time to their footfalls, soon he interwove a chant in the dwarven tongue that cut the blowing wind. Apieron took up the rhythm where he could, shaking his head to cleanse all shadows from his vision. The companions followed the marching song until their feet seemed trotting automatons, ignorant of pain or thought. In this manner, a great distance was covered.

"See yonder hill?" pointed Giliad. "We shall camp at its summit and take counsel for our next journey."

"I feel that we have come far," said Apieron. "We are close."

"We are close, indeed," echoed Turpin.

Struggling to the top of the rise, the companions cast themselves into a crack while Giliad pronounced a cloak of warding over them. "I will stand first watch," stated Turpin. None argued, and despite their many discomforts, the travelers fell down the paths of sleep.

Henlee threw down his flask with a curse. When the companions stirred from their rest, unsure of the time that had passed, they sought jars of unbroached water, carried with no small effort from clear springs of the topside world. Upon hastily stripping the wax rim from a random flask, a swarm of tiny blood leeches materialized therein, swirling from its depths. Other vessels were quickly opened and inspected, and of the two dozen remaining, only half were unpolluted. Six of these were hastily consumed. Similarly, foodstuffs were found to be infested with red maggots and were tossed down a crack.

"Bump would be mighty mad if he knew he carried these all the way from the Wyrnde for this."

Apieron observed from where he had cast himself down. The dreams that assailed him had been the worst thus far. Beyond the nightmare images described in terse tones by the others, his sleeping mind had been battered time and again, and, as long as he had lain, his subconscious had struggled against the intrusion of an irresistible power. It was an entity, alien and immortal. One who knew and hated him from birth.

Apieron felt blanched. He sat shaking, his soul caressed by an unclean hand, and as if by a careful eater, his memory had been picked clean: the turmoil of a life consumed by self-doubt and unattainable goals; a land sliding inevitably into war's embrace; an old king and boyish prince, both long friends; shy, dark Melónie, the youngest child of his body nursing at her breast ... all was now clear. No longer would he harbor any small hopeful doubts of *Her* existence or intent. He knew now Her form and name.

"*Tiamat*," he breathed. Apieron blinked, and his vision cleared, and the resolute defiance of his warrior fathers rose within him. "Tiamat!" Apieron stood.

Turpin looked on. He made a gesture of warding.

"Tiamat, I'm coming for you!" The others started at the sudden noise. Xephard strode to his friend, proffering an armored arm to Apieron. The paladin smiled in the strange light.

Henlee's brows were furrowed, his expression perplexed. "I'm upset about the loss of the grub as much as anyone, but—"

Turpin fronted Apieron. "Do not utter or even *think* such words, it is more than dangerous."

"She knows we are here," replied Apieron. "Her assaults shall worsen regardless what words we speak."

Giliad pointed. "Look where we hied in yesterday's gloom."

They followed his gaze south and west to the pitiless crags over which they came the day before. To the north, immense pillars of flame intercoiled with inky smokes dotted a barren flat whereon the smallest burning was greater than the largest tree of the surface world. Random geysers of flaming oil and reeking brimstone added lurid glares of strange, luminescent gold and crimson against the black distance.

"The Hel troll!" cried Jamello. Indeed, the companions saw a smallish figure that shuffled betwixt naptha fountains. It was caught in a flaming gout and dissolved.

Face ashen, Jamello looked to Giliad, who shook his head. "Nay, fortunately for us, our way lies not through the Devil's Cauldron."

Their gazes fell eastward, where there was a rise slightly higher than the one upon which they stood. Sarc squinted under his hand. "It appears no more than two miles distant, though my reckoning is faulty since we came into this *unplace*."

Apieron looked at his travel mates. Soot covered Jamello, who shook and cringed. Sarc's hairlike feathers drooped dull and desiccated—many were scorched or broken. Apieron wondered if the winged elf could even manage to take flight should he desire. Xephard and Henlee would endure any hardship until life left them, yet their expressions were haggard.

Henlee caught his glance. "No food, little water. We're a sorry lot, and you're no better!"

Only Turpin appeared animated, his face as red as his vermillion wrap. Apieron guessed him cognizant of spiritual perceptions indiscernible by the others. "What next then, Master? What course would please the gods of light?"

"Let us ascend yon eastern scarp. From there we might spy out our best course."

Giliad nodded to Apieron. "I do not disagree."

Apieron tested the draw of bow and sword. "Whatever path we choose, we must tarry no longer. Our purpose is grim."

Ulfelion regarded the seven struggling figures midway between the farther ridge and the hill on which he stood. To undead eyes, they appeared frail shadows, each clutching a wavering taper of soul-light within their breasts, save perhaps the golden elf. In him, spirit and body seemed more tightly twined. "Pathetic," he voiced to the figure beside him.

That figure spoke, his new gem-encrusted plate mail glinting in the flickering light, a gifting from the She. "What say you, litch?"

The vampire's faceless cowl turned. Adestes Malgrim did not flinch. "Your kind, mortal, are but thinking cattle. See how they hurry to our feast."

"I find no comfort in your chill presence, wight, though I stand amidst the fires of Hel." An amused susurration escaped from Ulfelion's low-slung cowl. "One thing intrigues me," continued Malesh, his tones light, "when I once opened the gate of summons in unhappy Ilycrium, you appeared more fell than the present form in which you stand."

The vampire was silent for a pause. If he was concerned with Adestes' thinly veiled insult, his response bore no clue. "When a naming is cast, I feed on the very essence of the deity. I thirst for such a time again! Yet such as those worms below will suffice for now. Defend the crossroads of Hel, that is your assigned task!"

Malesh bridled at the dismissive tones. He would bear it, for now. "They come anon," he answered. "We will await them from the walls of Llund."

Adestes was not sure if a vampire could smirk or scoff. The angle of this one's head certainly made it appear so. "Observe and learn wisdom," intoned the spirit.

The black-swathed figure stooped and gathered a handful of red iron grains. Ulfelion brought them up and lowered his cowl. To Adestes, it seemed he made as if to breathe a low incantation, although he knew no breath had ever passed betwixt those unseen lips. Ulfelion pinched a few of the grains with invisible fingers and let them fall. Where each struck, a small burst of flame pinwheeled downhill like a fiery tumbleweed.

"That's a neat trick, conjurer. Now I must go prepare a suitable welcome for these trespassers."

Ulfelion said nothing but hurled the entire handful of enchanted mineral in the direction of the walkers. A great flash lit the cliff face as a thousand ignitions raced down the broken slope in a churning ocean of flame. Where it passed, the black slag was fused and split.

"Harken!" said Apieron as a billowing roar drew his eyes to the distant plateau. He shouted an alarm, "A great light approaches!"

"It is a wave of springing flames," cried Sarc. "Already it reaches the narrows!"

"Back up the slope," shouted Giliad. "Our protections cannot withstand that!" Moments ahead of the tumbling inferno, they dove into a crevice to curl up behind shields, cloaks, and packs. A rush of too-brilliant incandescence struck their hideout with a great clap that sucked air from lungs and collapsed the stone rim over them.

A blackened pike-head burst through a layer of pulverized stone, and a small egress was thereby created by a cursing dwarf, who stood a moment gasping, with hands on hips. He stooped to pull six dust-blowing figures free of the cave in. Garments and packs were charred. Soot overlaced skin that was scorched red or merely hung in waxen tatters, as the companions gazed at one another, each shocked at the sorry state of his neighbor.

Giliad cursed long and low in elvish, shaking his long hair in disgust. Even his golden aura was diminished. "Priceless spell components, food and blessed water, so much lost."

"And I cannot cast spells of healing in this place," added Turpin.

While the others bandaged their wounds as best they could, Xephard banged soot free from his heroic silver shield. "Fit or frail, it must suffice. We must move ere the firewave returns."

"I don't wish to seem paranoid," Jamello choked and coughed up something, "but is it not obvious the river of fire was aimed at us?"

"We are vulnerable to another until we crest the slope whence it came," said Apieron. "Let us haste."

"Who says it can't run uphill?" growled Henlee.

The travelers quickly discarded damaged gear and consumed the last of the potables. No further onslaught hindered them in the hour spent crossing the narrow valley to ascend the crest of the rise from whence the firestorm originated. Once the hillock was breasted, they beheld revetments of stacked basalt enclosing a maze of walls and passages. All was ruinous and open to an unquiet sky.

Chapter 27

Lampus at Hyllae

Isolde bent over the font. Her summer-lightened hair hung damp and lank. Up and out in the cool dark, she had run her exercise around the Sacred Vale bearing a spear. Now it was day's end, and on the water she saw the mirror glint of the wedding circuit she now wore as necklace.

"He walks in darkness," said the Matron.

Isolde straightened. She regarded Cynthia's bright eyes and upright manner, her wrinkles lending more of dignity than frailty. "Your words, Donna, cast shadows on my soul."

Cynthia touched the dwarven twine that bore Xephard's hair. "Can you see the Brighthelm, child?"

Isolde swept back her water-heavy hair. Her smile was forced. "I was never much the seeress. Now that a man has touched me … I disappoint you."

Cynthia's laughter surprised Isolde. "I once knew a man, Skinfaxi."

Cynthia gestured. "He built these defending walls and oft manned them himself in sentry, although I think his eyes strayed more to that which lay within than to dangers outside." The Matron chuckled again. "That was a long time ago."

Isolde gawked. "You seduced the Fulcher of Gladheim?"

"Indeed. He was a powerful man, and brutish, but generous and forthright. His embrace was akin to that of a bear."

"But, Mother! You are a priestess of the Virgin Goddess."

Cynthia's smile was creased with kindness. "And that I remain. I did not say Skinfaxi was the *stronger*. Better so, his yearning builded for us a better wall by frustration than it could have in fullfilment."

Isolde joined her laughter. "Besides," continued the Donna, "in the end, I believe he left with better treasure than the maidenhood of one overly thin priestess, the vessel of his mind was filled with a measure of wisdom."

The women shared a look. "Regrettably, it was a small vessel." Cynthia held up her forefinger and thumb only inches apart. They shared a cackling laugh.

Cynthia tugged Isolde's sleeve. "Come with me to prayer and forget not your spear. I deem orisons alone be not enough 'gainst the gathering crowmeet."

HELHEIM: FASTNESS OF LLUND

"The dragon sleeps," said Xephard. Before them, on the surface of a gleaming wall, was inscribed a serpent of seven heads. The eyes were closed. It appeared very ancient.

Giliad touched the relief, jerking his hand away quickly. "Heraldry of a *beast*, dormant. We have come to the right place. Ware yourselves! All does not sleep here. A magic simmers, similar to that of the firestorm."

"This is our destination," spake Turpin. "I have *seen* it."

Henlee nudged Jamello. "He's getting weirder and weirder."

Jamello's throat was too parched to reply. They pushed into the hilltop ruin, past blocks of windscarred basalt whose flat

---

planes mirrored distorted images in the garrish light. At length they came to a central chamber fronted by a metal archway, tall and pointed, rimmed onto the surface of the stone. Henlee ran his fingers along its gray surface; it was cool to the touch.

"Wodensteel," he breathed. "In such amounts!"

Beyond was a darkened room where rifts of black sand snaked across the flagged floor. Henlee kicked a pile of discarded pottery and grunted in surprise when one rolled free, obviously intact. He squinted suspiciously at the red sigil emblazoned on the ceramic. He felt its weight, heavy with liquid. The dwarf shrugged, then smashed the bottle's neck against the archway. Smelling its contents, he quickly upended the jar into his mouth. Apieron and Jamello regarded him with horror, wondering if some fell dweomer forced him to finish the contents once tasted.

Henlee finished his long pull, fondly regarding the empty flask before tossing it into the pile. "Fire ale!" he said. He saw this meant nothing to them. "Dwarves have heard of it, yet not even Bardhest Redhand has tasted it. Now I have."

"There is nothing for us within the keep," said Turpin.

"Not anymore!" huffed the dwarf as he toed the broken pile without much hope.

Apieron was not completely convinced that his friend was unaffected. "Are you well?" The dwarf looked up. His dark face sported several pink burns, his brown beard was fire-blackened in places, and several gem-laden pleats were charred free.

"Never better," he beamed, smacking his lips.

They retraced their steps to an outer embrasure, its broken length facing away south and east. The terrain was now gloomcast by an inky darkness that dwelled in the sky, deep as blackest night as streaming fingers of the pall reached toward the abandoned karak. Several were nearly overhead.

Jamello turned to Apieron. "I suppose you mean to tell us that our next destination lies under that storm?"

"It must be I was astray," murmured Apieron, a look of doubt in his eyes.

"I am uneasy," said Giliad. The golden elf raked their surroundings with his crystalline gaze. Bits of black grain drifted amongst the fallen stones at their feet. Winds howled in the ruins they had quitted, partially abated by the cyclopean blocks of flanking walls.

Seeing the apprehension of the elf mage, Xephard swept Leitus from its sheath. It glowed like starlight, illuminating the decrepit courtyard. "What think you, Master Turpin?" asked Henlee. The cleric stood off to the side, regarding them with an inscrutable expression.

"Well, what?" demanded Henlee. The darkness was advancing fast.

"Not a storm," cried Sarc. "It is Nilfering, the flying Evernight!"

"The wall, Apieron," shouted Giliad.

From the height of the basalt palisade leered a dozen demonic figures who made to cast javelins of barbed steel. Almost as one, ranger and swamp elf wheeled, nocked shafts to cheek, and released. Their arrows flashed into twin targets, dropping the demons out of sight. The pounding of heavy feet sounded from the depths of the keep, and brazen yells filled the air as a score of swart-faced devils came hurtling from the interior arch.

Xephard and Henlee ran to meet them but were borne back by the momentum of their weighty opponents. Apieron and Sarc sent shaft after whistling shaft into the charging press behind their companions. An armored demon peeled off to strike Jamello down with a mighty hammer but was frustrated by the dodging thief's nimble parries and slashing counterstrikes. A second made to grasp Giliad with claws extended like iron nails. The golden elf gave a cry of rage and in one motion drew his glowing sword to shear one hand on the upslash, the second on the return to the sheath. The demon stumbled past to howl and roll on the rock. Giliad ignored its dying and cast a fanlike ray of pure light over the embrasure, burning down a half dozen of the yellow-fanged attackers at its height. Ten more took their place, although these shouted less and did not expose themselves to the deadly elf mage, preferring instead to hurl weighted javelins with little thought whether they struck friend or foe.

Xephard and Henlee stood a sea of slashing blades and gnashing tusks. An enormous, steel-clad monster charged to drive Xephard backward onto the waiting flamberge of its confrere. Xephard pivoted swiftly aside and swung, arm outstretched, so that his sword fist came about like a weight on the end of a swirling rope. The blow took the running demon on its peaked helm, knocking it sideways several feet to lie with its head at an unnatural angle. Xephard ducked under a second helion's blow, thrusting Leitus with a whistle ending in a scraping thud as the famous blade sheared clear through the softer flesh onto the stone wall behind.

From the corner of his vision, Henlee beheld a shapeless darkness that fell upon him. "Net!" he shouted. He stamped a heavy boot onto its edge and hooked Maul's back-spike into the steel mesh. Henlee set the razor surface of the spike, thinking to rend the snare in one muscular effort. He heaved mightily. Only one shiny glint of a sprung link revealed itself among the innumerable ringlets of the net.

"Cursed wodensteel!"

He whirled the entire mass to keep at bay a ring of demons who taunted and jabbed with pikes and hooked blades. He scrambled away from the overhang whilst javelins and pieces of stone hurled from above were deflected by the encumbering mesh, his armor catchingt the rest. A silver blade scythed before his eyes as Leitus descended in a slashing stroke that tore a screaming rent in the protesting metal, tiny dots of blood flecking Henlee's neck and arms where riven fragments of the net found openings in his plated armor. "Thanks, I think." Paladin and dwarf turned in tandem to confront a ring of threatening forms. The helborn no longer scoffed with derision, but howled hate-filled curses, their eyes alight with feral rage.

Xephard laughed. Under his harness, the muscles of his chest rippled as he swung his sword in a sweeping arc that took the nearest devil's shield on its upper rim, thus snapping its heavy boss against the monster's chin. The momentum of the heavy blade carried it upward and onto the brim of the helm. Leitus sheared through its crest and knocked the helion senseless to the ground where it was summarily stomped to death by its charging comrades.

Xephard felt a quick rush of footfalls behind him and wheeled to see an imposing demon half again his own height bearing down with an iron voulge. Leitus leapt into his left, and the Shield of the Maiden dropped to the ground as Xephard pulled a backhand, transverse cut at the demon's scaled torso. Perhaps this fiend was more skilled than its companion, or it witnessed the power of the paladin's strikes, for it held up short, thus allowing Leitus to sweep wide a full foot from its chest. It laughed and leapt onto Xephard. The helborn's polearm sought Xephard's unprotected front in an overhead chop that would rend the impudent human neck to crotch.

The looming demon halted, releasing its voulge to sag helplessly onto the jagged rock. Xephard's iron-hard hand twisted an eighteen-inch dagger within the demon's chest until he saw the light of life leave its malevolent eyes. Releasing the knife and snatching up its weighty voulge, Xephard took three steps and flung the ten-foot weapon into the back of the devil that confronted Jamello. The spear point of the polearm took the monster low in the back with a sickening crunch of riven mail and shattered vertebrae. The monster made one staggering step forward before Jamello's crypt blade swept head from shoulders.

Xephard never saw the deathblow. Sure of his throw, he turned to retrieve shield and dagger, then made off to confront the last demons who emerged from the arch. The plumed crest of his helm nodded with deadly menace while his goddess-blessed shield gleamed like an argent moon descended into the deeps to illumine the deeds of Her warlike son. Five demons, each larger than Xephard, gave back before the holy warrior, for as he advanced, it seemed death itself considered them from the shadowed eyes of his pitiless helm.

Henlee regarded the behemoth before him. Once free of the net, he had singled out what had to be the largest fiend in the ambush, and dashed low to topple the nigh six-hundred-pound monster. Even so, the immensely strong dwarf should have been able to trip it up. He was unaware, however, that the demon somehow transferred its center of mass to its lower legs. Henlee strained and pulled, then looked up in disbelief at the leering face of the monster eight feet up. The demon chortled in triumph and began a roundhouse swing with a flamberge that trailed blue flames. Trapped weaponless against the trunklike leg of his opponent, the dwarf could not attempt a parry.

"Oh drats!" The great war tool began its descent.

The demon's sword was four cubits of rippling death, forged by the immortal thrall-smiths of Hel. It arched through the yellow airs, trailing flames of enchantment. The dwarf could not hope to roll away and set a stance before it caught him halfway into the move and severed him. Of course the towering demon meant to cut him in twain if he stayed where he was. Henlee glanced to

Maul, which lay useless two feet away. He let go of the scaly leg and frantically shifted his back-riding shield up and over, using both arms to brace it whilst keeping both legs bent, one knee on the rock.

The mighty flamberge struck the dwarf's shield with an explosion that drove Henlee's compact form flat against the smoking ground. When the acrid fumes of burning iron cleared, the demon stared in disbelief at the hilt of the sword that remained in its hand, a hand span of steel yet attached. It could not have known.

Axebreaker had been forged in the fiery heart of Dwarvenhome. Cast in laminate layers of purest metal, each oval was perfectly formed and fitted, and magically enhanced by high craftsmen whose secrets were cherished for untold generations of long-lived dwarves. Axebreaker was the heirloom of a clan that traced its proud lineage back to the first dwarves to wake in wonderment under jeweled night skies. The demon could not have known that Axebreaker was of sterner stuff than the very throne of dwarven Allfather, who stares out over gulfs between worlds with lowering brows.

Henlee dazedly pushed himself up, hands and knees lacerated from the sharp crystals that formed the rocky floor of this part of the underworld and that somehow had penetrated his armor. Shaking his head to clear cobwebs, he regarded the demon. It held itself perfectly motionless. Bits of molten steel had pierced its hide in a score of places, and thick ichor oozed below a chest wound where a length of its flamberge protruded—a half-yard shard of shrapnel had driven straight into the beast's black heart. It gave a hideous shriek and fell backward to measure its length on the rocks.

Henlee pulled his shield around to gaze at its lustrous ebony surface. Its steel-wrought sigils known only to mountain dwarves bore a single fine scratch from end to end. "A scratch! Bagwart said it could not be harmed." He kicked the corpse. "That *thing* scratched my shield!" Gathering up Maul, Henlee ran to find another demon on which to vent his anger.

Adestes Malgrim studied the party's actions. His first victim called to him like none ever had. Out of a shadowed postern he materialized behind Apieron, who was doing deadly execution with his bow against demon missilers. Whether the blow came from the air or stone itself, Apieron never knew.

A mail-clad arm descended against him. It bore an iron-black blade set with scripted runes that glowed and swam. It struck the hind piece of Apieron's hauberk where neck meets shoulder, and into the arched muscle therein. A gout of blood sprayed the air as Apieron stumbled forward. Six more times the rune-blade hewed his falling form with sweeping, two-handed strokes that cleaved his armor into broken tatters. Apieron rolled away in agony, his sword protruding upright from a stony crack. His mighty bow lay riven on the rock. Tendrils of smoke already crawled its length.

A figure of black-swaled power appeared atop the palisade, and those demons nearest it cringed and slunk away. It held a longsword of pale light that did not illuminate the dark around it. Fear flowed from the invisible face.

"*You*," growled Giliad in recognition. Sarc cried out, and within seconds he sent four arrows streaking toward the fell being, but the shafts incinerated before they struck. "Quick, Jamello!" shouted Giliad. "Aim true if you ever have."

With rapid, well-practiced motions, Jamello began a barrage of strikes against the dark sorcerer. His brace of daggers was emptied, followed by sharp pieces of obsidian and shale, each shot unerringly towards their target. Hearing Apieron's cry of anguish, the gold elf turned from the undead abomination he longed to destroy and released a second volley of radiant light from an upturned palm at Adestes. The gem-faceted cuirass caught up the ray and reflected a cloud of jarring color that obscured him for the nonce. When it cleared, the human knight appeared largely unharmed, although he stood bewildered, lodestone sword forgotten in his hands.

Ulfelion fixed Jamello with an invisible stare, and a wave of despair rippled over him. The thief set himself and continued his barrage. A broken quirt, a loop of chain, a rock ... all were systematically dissolved as they neared the vampiric mage. Nonetheless, the shadowed form waved its arms in frustrated rage and faded.

Giliad flew to alight near Apieron and staunched the ranger's wounds as best he could. Glancing about, the golden elf noted that their foes appeared routed. Apieron and Sarc had slain or neutralized the missilers atop the wall whilst Henlee was destroying the last of those who attacked through the arch or dropped from the rampart. Xephard ran toward Apieron, the silver of his shield, helm, and blade undiminished in the gloom. Giliad turned to Malesh. A rage swelled in him, his luminescent blade appearing in his hand.

"Nay, Master, save Apieron," called Xephard. "Leave that one to me. And hark! A winged threat descends from yon fume."

Giliad looked to see outstreamers of the storm cloud overtop them, strange shapes writhing within. For the second time that day, Giliad turned from combat. Frustration ground his teeth, although he knew he was the only one able to defend his friends from this new danger. With a cry, he sprang into the foul air and speared against the descending demons, his hair and cloak streaming gold behind him to reveal the iridescent sheen of his fish-scale armor.

Xephard placed a restraining hand on Apieron's chest. The ranger lord had regained his feet, his left arm hanging limp at his side, a poniard gripped in his right hand. The temple peer stalked Adestes, and the Hel knight staggered back before the paladin, then set himself with fluid grade to stand akimbo, his sword's tip pointed unwaveringly at Xephard's chest. The script on his blade came alive and writhed serpentine fire.

"Ahh," grinned Xephard, "so much the better." He stepped toward the waiting assassin.

A third white radiance preceded Giliad to strike his foes, and winged demons wailed as portions of their anatomy and the roiling essence of the storm itself melted before the blast. In quick fury he was amongst them, and none could withstand the bitter sword of the immortal warrior-mage who assailed them.

Leitus's steel sparked on Adestes' sword and helm. He leapt back a step and saluted, his teeth white in the dim. Xephard made reply and advanced. A nighted figure materialized at his side. For an instant, Leitus revealed Ulfelion's hate-filled face as a stream of black blood spewed from his mouth into Xephard's eyes. The paladin was blinded, and Malesh's laugh echoed from the pitiless rocks.

Giliad turned in horror to behold the fate of the holy warrior. Incredibly, Xephard drove Ulfelion back, then pressed an attack on Malesh, his movements flawless and his feet sure. Adestes *umphed* in surprise and retreated, knowing time favored him against a sightless opponent, no matter how skilled.

Leitus struck again. Adestes angled his weapon to allow the deadly blade to pass partially through his defenses, thus encumbering Leitus for a fraction of a second. He was rewarded with a shield strike that cracked a rib and drove the breath from his lungs. It was worth it. A trio of low-flying demons had evaded the golden elf's wrath and dove silently on Xephard. In quick succession, three Hel wrought lances were flung into the paladin's back.

Malesh's blade screamed as it clove Xephard's breastplate and into the flesh beneath. Henlee, Sarc, and Jamello rushed to the spot but not sooner than Apieron. He menaced Adestes with his dagger. The dark knight did not engage but rather stooped to gather Xephard's faltering body and melt away. Apieron dropped his weapon and stretched for Xephard. The paladin shared a last look with him and thrust Leitus into Apieron's hand. Then he was gone.

Ulfelion had gladly retreated before Leitus and the deadly arm of the temple knight. He gathered himself and streamed toward Giliad to give battle. The golden elf was nothing loathe. Each hurtled to the other armed with sword and spell—one wrapped in light, the other in deepest shadow.

The sorcerers met amidst the roiling cloud. Quiescent until now, Turpin raised his heavy ring and disgorged a streamer of smoke that caught the golden elf, binding his limbs in midair. Giliad saw Ulfelion's pale blade pass into his flesh, but instead of the piercing agony of impalement, he felt the vitality bleed from his limbs. The demon cloud coalesced. Horned claws seized him up, and he knew no more.

Apieron cast frantically about. He was joined by the others, yet no art of forester, thief, dwarf, or elf could discern any trace of their missing comrades. The demon cloud vanished, and with it

Gilead Galdarion. The corpses of their slain opponents began to smolder, and a tearing panic seized Apieron. The dark knight was fled, bearing the body of Xephard, hero of the Warrior Goddess. There was also no sign of Turpin, Hierephant of Ilycrium.

"They are gone, lad," rasped Henlee.

With swift, sure motions, Sarc rebound Apieron's wounds and fashioned a sling for his left arm, although the ranger seemed not to notice. "Now Hel entire casts her spite at us."

Already there approached a new streamer of the dark cloud, and a welling of basso voices filled the ruins behind them. They felt a rhythmic, low thrumming that vibrated from the ground. "The heart of darkness," said Sarc.

"I am afraid to stay," said Jamello. Bellowing screams filled the airs of the hillock, further polluted by the burning flesh of the demons they had slain. The four companions ran.

"A parting gift for unwelcome guests," quipped Malesh from his perch atop the highest wall of the keep.

He drew back an iron bow until the knock of the arrow caressed his cheek, and the mighty weapon creaked in protest. A winged demon swooped from the wrack onto the party's rear and cast a javelin that shattered on Henlee's shield as some instinct caused the dwarf to wheel under cover of Axebreaker. Adestes' own aim was spoiled, for in the time of the javeliner's attack, the companions entered a declivity in the terrain. Malesh tracked his new target, the bolt passing unerringly through the flying devil. It fell dead with a squawk. Malesh shrugged and tossed the weapon aside to find the place where the holy warrior had fallen in order to search for the temple knight's famous blade. He spied a straight sword, hand and a half, its squared quillions protruding over a cleft where it had stuck.

"You are not the sword of a hero." Adestes made to turn away, then wheeled and kicked out with his heavy boot. Apieron's blade snapped in twain.

"Attend me, dark one," came a voice, deep and commanding.

Malesh walked to a strange tableau. The traitorous patriarch of Sway stood fronting Ulfelion, who was cowled once more, dark and silent. The man's face flushed with excitement, and lines of sweat trickled through the soot that besmirched him. He cast aside his ermine-collared cloak, revealing the fine-patterned leather of a nobleman. His ring glinted, bright and heavy.

"Priest, you have earned glory this day," boomed Malesh. "The infidels have fled with much hurt, and they leave a great prize. I deem their days of misery are just begun."

Turpin nodded impatiently. "Yes. Yes. What you say is true, I'm sure. To business, black knight! Who will serve as channeler to guide my thought to the She?"

Ulfelion's tone spake hollow as if from far away. "Place thy hands on my robe and on he." The invisible head nodded at Adestes. "We, Her servants, will attune thy prayers to Her essence. It is strong here."

When he touched the undead being, Turpin felt a cold that seared up his left arm. He ignored it. As a high priest fully attuned to this newly awakened goddess, he would make these boorish slaves fear his name.

As instructed, Turpin also offered his right hand to Adestes, who grasped his wrist to seat the cleric's open hand on his shoulder. Turpin's fingers felt the slick, sticky gore on Adestes' shoulder plate and smelled the heavy sweet smell of blood—*my companions' blood*. Pushing aside such whimsies, he prepared his mind for the link.

"Order your thoughts, priest," hissed Ulfelion softly.

"I know my craft," snapped Turpin.

"Then ... behold!"

A swirling, nighted mass filled Turpin's vision. From its center, a pinpoint opened and grew. From this nexus lanced rays of darkness to dance about him, pure and perfect as black diamond. Beyond these, he felt the Presence. Old, and fixed in Her malevolence, eternally evil. A shape behind the vortex began to emerge. For a moment, Turpin's heart leapt with the utter beauty revealed therein.

A muffled cry echoed from the interior of the pile behind them. It was a voice weighted in chains of anguish, yet for that deep and powerful. "Turpin! Priest of Almighty Sky. I name you faithless. Accursed!"

Malesh laughed down in Turpin's face. His taunt rang mockingly and harsh in the flat air, "Now be you twice damned." His dagger plunged low into Turpin's belly, ripping its way to his chest by the brute strength of the arm behind it. The enraptured cleric never looked down, but stared in horror into the climax of the vision. There a ravening beast of many heads devoured his mind.

"Treacherous sack of shit," said Malesh, spurning the mutilated carcass away. "Think you the Black Goddess would harbor one so flawed?"

"Leave, Adestes Malgrim," moaned Ulfelion. "I will feed now. It has been long since I tasted the blood of a high cleric of Ilycrium. Victory hast proved sweet."

Malesh gave the vampire a hard stare, considering whether possession of the cleric's vital energy would give the evil spirit an edge of power over him. "And what would happen, mighty lich, if the blood on which you feed were tainted by a deadly poison?"

Ulfelion's head raised itself from the corpse. "It would do no hurt to me." In the low light, Adestes normally could not discern the vampire's features, yet smeared with a mask of blood, its face was brought into macabre relief. "My essence is immortal and cannot be harmed by disease or corporal maladies."

Ulfelion turned back to Turpin but paused before plunging into the cleric's open body. "Yet I would discover such a taint and seek out he who attempted the folly. Then I would feed again."

Adestes made no word or gesture by way of reply. As he had leaned down to fix Ulfelion's mind, he slipped free the ring of serpentine gold. Frozen in death, the cleric's face stared into invisible gulfs, an expression of horrified revelation stamped on his features. Adestes wended his way back to the ruin. He must safeguard what little life remained in the prisoner. The aureate ring grew heavy on his palm, and he slipped it onto his finger. *At last you come to me.* Well versed were the monks of Pleven Deep in the lore of the ancient ring of the serpent. Its location had been unknown for an age … until now! Its pattern slid into its true form, that of a seven headed dragon. Its ruby eyes blazed in triumph.

"Ah, Fafnir," chuckled Adestes, "at last you find a proper hand to wield you."

GLORIOUS AMOR

In Amor, between mountain and sea, autumn's golden hand rippled across treetops. A beech stirred in the arbor, as if a wind shook its uppermost boughs, while those around it were still.

Chapter 28

Tiamat's Palace

A spirit of great malice was he. Outwardly clothed in semblance of human form, his scaled bulk was such that the helm of the tallest of men would reach only the middle of his torso. Broad-pinioned wings were attached there, and his flat, impassive visage could have been hewed from black granite. Never had his brain considered mirth or pity. His swart eyes were red, the mouth fanged white and dripping venom.

In a forgotten age, Aurgelmir gathered an army that raged across Hel, striking down all in its path until facing the very goddess in final conflict. There She beguiled him, while his army She withered in a fiery storm and piled blackened bones in a great drymoat before Her gates. Should any again threaten Her walls, it was said the army of Aurgelmir should rise to defend the indomitable fastness they had recked to assault.

"Fair art thou, my daughter," gurgled his voice. So deep was the sound the huge windpipe issued that it was unlike any speech ... rather acid should it boil and split rock. A scaled claw caressed her face.

"Ever useful to me hast thou been, and soon shalt be again. I send thee to the fastness of Pankaspe. There, my mate, shalt thou encumber a man with thy guile. I have seen him in my thoughts, a great doom is before him. "You will bring to me a gift." The rumbling voice faded in the thick air.

Aetterne smiled with wicked delight. "Ever has it been my joy to serve thy every will, who art warden of *She Who Waits*. This man you seek," Aetterne spat the words with hate, "this man of your dreams, I will bring misery to him and shrive his soul of every gladness ere death." The vastness before her inclined its head in acknowledgment, and Aurgelmir turned to merge with the towering shadows of the rampart.

For a spell of time, Aetterne stood silent as her mind turned imaginings of how best to accomplish her father's command. Her form, beautiful and menacing, swirled and contracted, assuming a measure of feminine perfection. Bounteous curves were tempered by a mysterious, smiling face, all carried with the grace of an elvin acrobat. Becoming invisible, Aetterne floated high into the reek, then bent her course to the fort atop the last ridge.

THE WESTFORT, PANKASPE

The party ran. Whether by random chance or the loss of Giliad and his cloaking magics, it seemed the once desolate landscape now teemed with enemies. Some were grossly visible, others half-seen whispering shapes that leered and grasped at tattered cloaks and recoiling limbs. The companions beheld staggering humanoids with leperous skin and gibbonlike limbs, all aflame.

"Hel trolls," gasped Henlee, "and walking about fancy as you please whilst taken with fire."

"I told you," cried Jamello. "They're everywhere!"

These shambling monsters they circumvented as best they may, although Jamello's crypt-found kilij severed a grasping talon and dissolved the wing from a fiend who chanced too close.

Apieron remained fleet of foot despite his terrible wounds. Henlee grumbled with every thudding step, urging on his more agile companions as one encumbered mile passed, then two and eight more until all slowed to a labored walk.

Apieron's shoulder and arm seemed encased in a shell of pain, and each step jounced breath-stealing splinters into his chest. Unable to retrace their way, the four companions kept the firestorms of the devil's cauldron to the right and headed in the general direction they regarded as that of the outward gates. One encounter was unavoidable, a plunging mass of the same airborne creatures the companions had marked from afar on their entry to the Hel plane … many hours and a lifetime before. This time the companions found themselves striking up at flat-bodied animals with plate-lined mouths filled with boiling blood that sprayed forth when they were sundered. Apieron cursed for loss of his famous bow and two good arms to wield it. Nonetheless, he struck looping blows with a shield borne on his right. The beasts' leathery skins were stretched tight over exoskeletons that cracked whenever the edge of his shield smashed down. Soon a pile of broken and thrashing forms snapped mindlessly at his and Henlee's booted feet, but it was Sarc who broke the attack.

After he killed a great many with his treebark bow, the winged elf leapt to close with his crooked lance. This allowed his friends to flail through the greater mass of the monsters without halting completely. "These dastards are like flying, biting rays," shouted Jamello. He skewered a final beast with his crypt blade and whirled it such that the heated blood fountained harmlessly aside.

The party broke through onto a glittering expanse of large, rounded stones like river rock that was flanked by encroaching buttresses of basalt and merged to become a towering escarpment, horizon to horizon some furlongs ahead. They came to a halt behind a tallus of white, powdery stone. Henlee reached out to straighten Apieron, who was bent over at the waist, his face pale. At a nod from the dwarf, Sarc saw again to Apieron's dressings.

Recovering somewhat, Apieron cleared his throat to speak but did not spit, jealous of even the moistened grit that lined his mouth. "I reckon we are at the level of the singing eels," he breathed heavily. "I do not mark them in any direction."

"Fine and fine," said Henlee. "I don't feel like seafood anyways."

"A castle." Jamello pointed excitedly ahead. The middle airs cleared, and a rumbling as of thunder carried to them.

At a low point in the traversing ridge, perhaps a pass of sorts, a line of fashioned stone was dimly visible. Tornados of whirling debris raced across black cliffs to either side of the construction. Its wall, wreathed in smokes, appeared the height of two men and not overly wide. The funnel tops of the twisters reached into a reek of leprous green that swirled slowly in response. Flashes of red and yellow erupted from fiery geysers that were rent by the roaring twisters to suffuse smoky interiors with orange magma spinning up to be hurled aside as boulders of porous stone. The companions realized the wagon sized rock they stood behind was one such cast.

"I do not know how far off course we are," said Apieron. "But there is no going back. We must surmount the cleft between the storms, inhabited or no."

As they trotted, the companions regarded the fastness more closely. It appeared merely two wings of dressed stone backed by a low central keep. Crafted by unknown hands in a forgotten past, it appeared cousin to the Helfort where so much anguish had befallen them. For a moment, a flaming gust ripped aside the veil of smokes from the face of the distant rampart. Tall figures stalked the battlement.

"Yon sentries appear to be alert," said Jamello. "Looking for us?" The thief squinted. "Those are arbelests they bear. Gawds, the size of them!"

"It is said the eyes of demons pierce all murks," muttered Henlee. "Any attack must be launched upslope and fully exposed. I never did mind an uphill march, but ever did I know there was to be a downhill side. This everlasting climb is staler than gnome bread."

"There is no choice," said Apieron. "We durst not loiter, the plane entire wakes against us. Besides," he forced a wry smile onto his pained face, "that run limbered up my shoulder nicely. I do not wish it to stiffen up again."

"Well, why tarry?" growled Henlee. "There be only a dozen or two of those flying vermin. Er, no offense," he added, nodding to the winged elf.

With reluctance, Apieron drew Leitus and held it before him. "I am not he who should wield thee. Forgive me, but one boon I ask. If ever you loved your master as did I, strike now this last time, keen and true!"

"Wait—" began Jamello.

"Think on this," said Sarc. "I shall fly in retreat, then loop as close as I might to the sky-burning to come on our foes unawares whilst you make your advance."

"But those heavy crossbows are steel, and—" continued Jamello.

"Good plan, elf," said Henlee.

He flourished Maul and charged. Apieron sheathed Leitus and sprinted after him. Jamello stood alone, fidgeting and trembling, and alternatively cursed and prayed, promising to sacrifice what gems were left in the dwarf's beard to his god of thieves. He braced his heavy shield and followed, easily catching up the others.

Whoops and calls of jeering laughter drifted from atop the rampart as iron darts whizzed among the attackers. Two of these sprung from Jamello's raised shield with metallic clangor. Wise in the geometry of battle, Apieron took a swift but zigzag path that maximized what meager protections the pitiless landscape provided. Henlee simply lowered his head and pounded for the center of the wall. When the companions were only a hundred paces from the wall gate, two demons hoisted up a long, bronze tube and pointed one end at the charging dwarf. A rather tall, skinny devil balanced the device across the shoulders of his squat comrade. Grinning toothily under a beaklike nose, he placed a burning finger to the rear of the device. The blunderbuss roared, spewing its deadly charge over the dwarf, engulfing him in a puff of black.

Consternation lit the cannoneers' faces when they beheld a yelling dwarf emerge from the near side of the cloud. Dragging one foot, he nonetheless closed with haste on the gate. The mighty dwarf smote it a blow that vibrated the entire wall. Quarrels and hurled pieces of masonry fell harmlessly to his rear as he was under the very parapet upon which his enemy stood.

"Open the doors. *Cowards!*"

Maul thudded against the iron portal, shattering foot-long rivets. "Or not!" *Thunk.* The door sagged. Henlee kicked it over with his wounded foot and cursed away the pain. "You call this engineering? I am coming, cheating dogs!"

Then came Sarc's assault. Yard-long shafts of roughened texture, some sporting bits of bark or an occasional leaf, struck time and again with terrible accuracy. The defenders attempted to counter with their unwieldy arbalests but could not match the rate of fire or swift agility of the swamp elf. Those that soared aloft were slain first. The blunderbuss fired again, its iron shot soaring harmlessly behind the acrobatic elf.

Henlee bellowed and burst from the gate stair to cave in the chest of the first demon to oppose him. Leitus gleamed with delight as it cleaved the astonished expression from the next. Behind ranger and dwarf, Jamello parried and struck with his heavy crypt weapons, standing firm as rear guard to his friends, who swept the battlement within a minute. The last action saw Henlee strangle the tall demon with its own bronze gun after braining its squat companion with the heavy barrel. Sarc lighted nearby, his shafts protruding from the majority of the corpses that littered the walkway.

"By my granddaddy's beard," called Henlee, pulling what remained of his, "doesn't that elvish quiver run dry?"

Sarc produced his arrow case, clad in lustrous bark. Sap congealed in areas where it sought to heal the scorches and nicks of their journey. A full two-dozen arrows bristled from its depths like new grown branches. "Her name is Quq, and she is alive. Alas, like us, she will die if we remain longer in this accursed place."

Henlee plopped down and propped up his foot on a carven stone. From the top of his boot protruded a piece of iron. He laughed grimly. "Don't worry, elf. At this rate, none of us will last much longer. When the mage's shielding fades, none of us is any better than a steak on the grill, eh?"

Jamello looked ashen. Apieron started to reprimand the dwarf, instead he found himself sitting with his eyes closed. Their bits of humor seemed a weak face before the disasters of the day. At length he flexed his arm gingerly, causing the blood caked there to flake free at the slight motion. He mouthed a prayer of gratitude, naming the god that heals, for his wound and entire extremity had gone numb.

Jamello moved off to explore the upper rim, where he managed to find a half-dozen serviceable arbalests. Never comfortable with the longbows of country folk, he nonetheless had excellent proficiency with crossbows of any type, whether traction, crank, or foot drawn. He loved their mechanical perfection, and these were beauties, large and heavy. He primed and loaded each with a deadly bolt and aligned them along the battlement to face outward. Jamello explored further and discovered an iron bridge from the walkway to a cylindrical keep, partially in ruins. Sharp points of obsidian winked like tapered glass in the chasm between. He gasped.

"A written device! Set in the stone of the tower."

Apieron's eyes remained shut, for he did not need to look. From the framework of his thought, he beheld a scaled and sinuous body. Mightiest of all, She wore seven heads on seven serpentine necks, twisted to witness their passage with malevolent eyes of glowing ruby.

"I know what it depicts, Jamello," he called softly. "A *Beast*, couchant."

With a curved dagger, Sarc bivalved the heavy boot from Henlee's foot. "Now I like this place even less," said the dwarf. The elf druid pushed the piercing slag though the foot and bled the wound. The winged elf then produced a bone awl from somewhere and knotted a twisted cord of his long hair through its eye and proceeded to lace up the boot over the bandaged wound. Henlee clucked in appreciation. "Learn something new every day." He stood and stamped. "Good enough to walk on."

Winged elf and mountain dwarf shared a kindred smile. Apieron nodded in appreciation from where he lay against the rock. "Brothers in arms," he whispered. "We must go," he said to the others.

"I'm afraid we may be staying," said Jamello, who had silently returned. The companions crowded to the parapet and looked out over the stone spit. The demon cloud that had claimed Giliad returned, its searching fingers but a short mile distant. A delicate whimper came to them, and as one they turned.

"Quick, Jamello!" urged Apieron, but the thief already raced across the flying bridge and into the squat keep.

"Apieron. I, you—"

Explanations were not necessary as ranger, dwarf, and elf were soon there. A human female they found, dark tressed and full figured. Her arms were bound with cruel chains set into the walls of a side chamber off the descending stair.

"Stand back," warned Henlee. With a heave, he smote one, then the other of the wall links with Maul. The woman sobbed and sagged forward. For a fleet instant, her large, tear-filled eyes met each of theirs before she curled on the stone, hair veiling her face.

"Strike free her wrists, Henlee."

At Aperion's command, Jamello produced a small spike from his salvage and held it to her links while the dwarf struck unerringly twice more. The woman fell to her face before Apieron, her midnight hair cast upon his feet. She clasped his knees in supplication. Gently he raised her.

"No captive are you, lass. Stay close and stray not. We will be hard beset ere we break free of this place." The woman's eyes were twilight meres as she regarded him. Her skin was fair and supple where tears traced streaks on her face and chest. Already the howling bloodlust of their foes echoed into the keep as the demon cloud descended to attack. The companions raced to the wall and set themselves in defense.

Short lived was the surprise on the faces of the front rank of the hoard when they were met with a hail of streaking death from Jamello's arbalests and the long barked arrows from Sarc's mighty bow. Any fiend who penetrated the missile blast was either cleaved by Leitus or smashed to flapping ruin by Maul. The cloud tendril withdrew in dismay. To either side along the ridge, the howling tornadoes and crackling lightning smote the tortured rock, thus rendering impossible any flanking to bring the advantage of numbers.

Apieron stood tall, stricken but stern of mien and steady in his purpose. He met the eyes of Henlee, tasked far beyond the limit of ordinary mortals, steadfast as a beetling cliff, craggy and dark, that stands unflinching before towering waves. They shared a common thought. Haggard and wearied as they were, they could not defend the wall indefinitely, yet to be caught in the open by the bulk of their airborne enemies would mean a quick and brutal death.

The female cowered behind Apieron, trembling with fear. Multitudinous abrasions and welts of lash and claw were evident where scanty rags failed to conceal her flesh. Apieron reasoned that her tormentors must have imbued her with resistances to the heat and poisonous airs. She was clearly overwrought and unable to answer any query. He thought of Melónie in similar circumstance, and his knuckles whitened on Leitus's hilts, the sword of Xephard, first among warriors.

Jamello returned from a second reconnaissance. He wiped a dripping stain from his broad sword. "The cylinder is barren otherwise. There was only a single imp that I found in a side chamber, and he shall never leave! There is also a stepped descent that leads back and down to the flats, beyond the storms … what befalls here?"

"The sky is burning," answered Sarc.

"Oh."

"Jamello," said Apieron, "take Henlee below and contrive such traps as you are able to slow the demon swarm when we've departed. These twisting lightnings aid us. Our foes must spill over the keep."

The thief's haggard smile was broad as he pulled Henlee aside to discuss what misery they might for their enemies. From looted bodies and materials at hand, Jamello quickly strung cutting wires about the battlement, and set his crossbows with the clever trips and pulls known only to a master thief of Bestrand. A frantic pounding interspersed with a dwarf's grim laughter echoed as Henlee rigged a pile of stone to destroy the descending stairwell at the first tread of the enemy.

Sarc and Apieron gazed out to the demon cloud. It twisted in the distance, growing thick and dark as new numbers were added to the milieu. "Bragan, shaman of my people, once said that even a leafless thorn might, in the time of its being, bring forth one pleasing blossom. But here there is no beauty, even deeply hidden."

The winged elf cast back his shaggy head to regard the roiling sky. "Sun has never shone here, nor will she ever."

Apieron nodded, closing his eyes against the sting of the suffocating atmosphere. He felt a bond of kinship to the swamp elf that transcended every difference of race. Sarc's gaze strayed to the human female, and Apieron's followed. Her eyes were dilated with fear, and Apieron saw on their glistening surface tiny reflections of the lurid sky and magma-rent storms, and the advance of the Hel swarm.

"They come again, friend."

"I know." Apieron straightened and beheld a strange, intense look on Sarc's face.

The barbarian elf unslung his bow and rough bark quiver, handing them to the ranger. "Bear these for me. I do not wish them to be lost when I enter the cloud." He brandished his crooked lance and smiled grimly. "Gungnir will serve me well enough."

Apieron bowed stiffly but could speak no words past the constriction that tightened his throat. Leading the girl by the hand, he joined Jamello and Henlee in the cylinder where thief and dwarf applied the finishing touches to Henlee's trap. From within his tattered knapsack, Jamello proudly produced what appeared to be an irregular brick of blackened steel. He tugged free a long pin and the metal block fell into twenty evilly pointed caltrops, which the thief spread on the stairwell and landings.

"Would that the golden elf were here," said Henlee. "He'd rig this entire pile to explode or melt or turn into butterflies as easy as you please."

"Mayhap he lives," said Apieron, a small, tired smile writ on his face.

"Perhaps, an' my hope as well. His kind do not die easily." The dwarf narrowed his gaze at the bow and quiver Apieron bore. "The swamp elf?"

"He will attack on wing, then join us on the farther plain."

From a portal in the western base of the cylinder, the companions and the bewildered girl hurried. Beyond the fastness, the stony isthmus continued and broadened into sweeps of rock, like cresting waves that glittered under firestorms of the escarpment they had quitted. Some of these were razor sharp, and as they hastened as best they might over the terraced rows, there came from out and above a sudden bedlam of guttural voices soon punctuated by screams of alarm and pain, over which rose the war cries of a winged elf.

Sarc stood before the riven gates of the castle of Pankaspe. He gathered a burning chip from the blackened floor. Cupped in his hands, its fierce glow penetrated his flesh, such that together they resembled a porcelain lamp. So brightly did the animate Hel fire flare it seemed the warrior-druid's hands would be incinerated.

"Spirit of fire, obey me." Sarc channeled the intensity of his spirit into an enchantment rendered in his native tongue. Long and low he spoke, then finished with a shout.

"Remember thy true substance!"

The light of the glede faded to a winking coal. Sarc sighed and let fall his hands, and the Hel burning around him now resembled the light of natural flames, tall and fierce, yet deprived of the sinister magic that had animated them. He chanced a glance upward. The bulk of the devil-borne cloud overtopped the battlement behind, and already leathery forms alighted on the walls. Others circled him like predatory birds.

Working quickly, Sarc unstoppered a hollowed gourd he had kept till the end, pouring his very essence into his singing, thus expending his immortal life: *"Purest water, holy balm of Fogleaf, flow free once more. Quench the fires of the underworld."*

His words rang clear as silver clarions in the murk where, with a cry, he flung the contents of the small flask aloft. Amazingly, the water did not instantly evaporate, and instead multiplied in the reek. For a fraction of a second, a deluge from the heart waters of the Wyrnde struck the burning. There was a tremendous thunderclap—and lo! The conflagrations of the Hel floor were doused, leaving only a blackened skeleton of tortured ground. A mighty steam rose in billowing waves that enveloped the fortress and the near part of the stony isthmus. Swarming demons, deprived of a portion of their power, were thrown into confusion and milled blindly. Sarc laughed with the joy of his casting and the sight of his quarry, naked and vulnerable.

He laughed aloud … the first natural sound heard in that place since its time began. Quietly powerful, it smote the polluted airs like a drum; then he was among his foes, gripping his twisted lance in two hands to skewer or to cut. Wheresoever the living spear touched demonic forms, they shrieked and withered and died.

Adestes Malgrim entered the inmost chamber of the Fastness of Llund. It was not barren, as the party had found it, but furnished sumptuously to his tastes. He gazed down at Xephard's upturned breast, bared and vulnerable in the glow of a lamp of priceless ruby. The holy warrior was nearly succumbed to his wounds, lying pale as faltering breaths stirred his frame. The red blood that had flowed so freely from the chest wound had slowed to the barest ooze.

Malesh squatted before Xephard's great shield, the only thing about the paladin he deemed of value. He traced the relief of its rim, admiring the epics of gods and men depicted thereon. "I will bear this, warrior. It shall be the only remembrance of you in heaven or hell." He stood and raised his glyph blade over Xephard's prostrate form as its witch fire grew and filled the chamber.

"Hold, man!" intoned a sepulchral voice.

The dark form that was Ulfelion ghosted forward to lay one translucent hand on Xephard's brow. A moan escaped the paladin's lips, Xephard's eyelids flickering, yet he did not otherwise stir.

"He is not the one." Black knight and undead sorcerer shared a look of unspoken thought.

Adestes passed a hand over tracks of elf, dwarf, and two humans, one of deeper tread than the other. He spoke words taught to him by priests of the Dragon Fells. What were the merest disturbances on the stony soil took on a blazing yellow radiance outlining a line of steps away west from the maze.

"They make for Pankaspe," he mused more to himself than for benefit of Ulfelion, who stood nearby. "What shall we find at the end of this trail, I wonder?"

"Strife and death, and blood ... always blood," groaned Ulfelion. "Let us haste."

"Any sign of him, thief?" called the dwarf.

"None at all." Jamello searched both disjointed sky and fume-shimmering terrain whence they came.

"But who could see aught amidst this ash?"

"Aye, you led us clear of the burning grist and lairs of singing eels, young Apieron, but this here soot makes Redhand's ancient furnace look clean as a winnowing floor before harvest."

The four traveled an ashy plain, often breasting waist-high drifts or circumventing peaked skirls that loomed many feet overhead. Dust filled the airs for leagues, and it coated every inch of skin and garments. Burnings they could see and feel, hot within the gray detritus, although worse by far were treacherous sinks and sliding gullies that would open of a sudden within the ashcake. Twice, flapping devils had flown out of the swirl to be promptly picked off by Jamello's confiscated crossbow. He sported a bandolier of Hel-forged darts across his chest and a dozen more tucked about his person. Shield and blade were slung atop his backriding pack.

"Mayhap the winged one is lost?" coughed Henlee. "I can barely see you three myself." Their entire persons were soot-smeared black and gray such that they were nigh invisible against the ash.

"Sarc has elfin eyes and magics of the druid," answered Jamello. "Surely he will find us." Apieron's lack of response was attributed by the others to pain of wound and the tremendous grind, yet such did not reckon in his mind next to his forebodings for the valiant elf.

Jamello floundered into a soft spot. Arms windmilling, he staggered free, coughing and digging handfuls of powdered charcoal out of his boot rims above the knee. "Of course," he wheezed, "if we suffocate here, *no one* will find us."

"Then keep walking," growled Henlee.

🕴 🕴 🕴

Jamello gritted his eyes shut and followed Apieron's crunching footsteps before him, and the dwarf's foot-dragging shuffle to the rear. It never ended …

He stood listening to the fountain and the water. A woman's bath was his favorite place. Jamello was as yet undiscovered but anticipated that eventuality eagerly, for he knew how dashing a figure he cut. Besides, he wore the perfume women found irresistible—money! So good of the sordid nobleman to encounter the wire slung across the horse road …

Cassandra's whimsical singsong as she splashed and played suited well his mood. Arising well after noon, he spent the day at meal and grooming, and had also arranged a novelty sent to intrigue the highborn wench. Rudolph Mellor smoothed his precise moustache and perfect goatee, touching the golden ring on his ear and the bunched lace at his throat. Deeply he inhaled the scents of Cassandra's boudoir.

"Sirrah!" cried she. "What do you here?"

Stepping from a wide-leafed planting, Jamello doffed felt cap in elaborate flourish, then resumed his jaunty pose, one laced wrist resting on the jeweled pummel of his smallsword, the other touching his chest. A broad smile lit the sharp-featured face, slightly predatory and tanned beyond olive.

"Sink me! Was I spying?"

"Indeed, sir. Your wife—"

"Wife?" Jamello bowed. "You are mistaken. I am too poor for even one."

"Poor?" A moment's perplexity was replaced by a mischievous smile of her own. Cassandra's wrap fell partially aside.

"Today a man, obviously a beggar, sent me a marvelous gift, a jade—"

A rough hand gripped Jamello's pack from behind, jerking him forcibly backward. His eyes flew open. Before him yawned a two-hundred-foot precipice. They had come to the end of the dust sea.

"Sleepwalking will get you dead," stated Henlee.

Rather than his usual reflexive excuse, Jamello wiped a spoonful of dust from his eyelids to examine their surroundings. They stood on the crest of what appeared to be a tidal wave of ash, hardened into stone by some unimaginable blast of heat. Below was a wind-scoured expanse on which were dotted the tiny figures of warriors, stone gray as the powdery rock upon which they stood in frozen poses of sky-beseeching agony. Some held their petrified weapons aloft as if smitten in an instant.

Henlee clucked, teeth white within a face more black than normal. "Don't say it. I am a dwarf of the mountains, and even I have never seen, nor even *heard* of anything like it." The rescued girl dangled her feet from the ledge and stared out over the waste.

"Where's Apieron?" stammered Jamello, realizing of a sudden that he and the dwarf stood otherwise alone.

"Down yonder, scouting our way. He left you this," said Henlee, handing Jamello a charred leather, which had a hopeful swishing sound at its bottom. "She and I already had a sip. Last of the water."

The female's black eyes followed every distant step of the ranger. Both mouthfuls were liquid heaven to the thief. When he was done, he tucked the flask away, although it would have been easier to let it simply fall and immolate. He searched the sky, it was of melting purple.

"And no sign of the winged one," snapped Henlee to the thief's unspoken question.

"He will not come," said Jamello softly.

Apieron's form grew larger though yet slender beside the stony warriors as he picked his way back to the bottom edge of the precipice. Hand in hand, Jamello, Henlee, and the woman skidded down the gentle face of the wave, leaving black furrows in their wake.

"The dust clears beyond the battlefield," said Apieron when they arrived. "The fighting was far flung, it stretches for miles in every direction."

"And beyond?" asked Henlee.

"A last long march. The Gate and out."

Jamello groaned inwardly at Apieron's words. His legs felt like water-soaked strings. Where the Spear Runner found such strength he could not begin to guess; a large man and sorely wounded, Apieron should have faltered ere now. How long had it been since they slept? Three days? And before that, truly rested? His blistered lips counted from their sojourn in the fastness of the swamp elves. Jamello moaned aloud when he remembered that water-drenched place.

"No breaks!" grunted Henlee as he whipped his half-shorn beard around to scowl at the thief. "We'll have a nice picnic once we've cleared the Gates."

Apieron's gray eyes sought the unreal horizon. "Our final flight."

　　　　　　　🕴 🕴 🕴

Silence dwelled before the karak of Pankaspe. A ring of dead or dying demons who flapped feebly lay about a blackened circle some hundred paces across where no fires burned. In its center was a crooked lance. It was singed, but an unmistakably green sprig grew upon its shaft.

"The barbarian elf died hard," muttered Adestes, leaning upon his new shield. He wiped clean his blade of lodestone upon the skin of the nearest corpse. "By this one's actions, he whom we seek is surely out of reach."

Ulfelion did not reply. By the power of his serpentine ring, Adestes clearly beheld the wight as Ulfelion regarded the barren patch for a moment, then waved his hand. The fires of Hel returned, looming larger than before, as if with anger reawakened. The crooked lance began to darken and twist in agony, its sap hissing a nigh indiscernible scream.

"Bring to me some of the yellow stone."

Too piqued with curiosity to disobey, Adestes found a fist-sized lump of powdered sulfur. Ulfelion bent and appeared to inhale, suffusing his translucent form with a jaundiced hue. The necromancer faced westward and exhaled, blowing spumes of vapor that coalesced in the middle airs before roiling forth in the direction of the Matog.

Adestes staggered back, his eyes and dweomered skin stung with the acidity of the cloud. "Impressive, he-witch."

Ulfelion bowed in mock courtesy. "We need not hasten. Let us to the Gate and collect the bodies."

THE MATOG

The scar-gashed terrain that crouched before the Matog provided short-lived relief after the ash basin, and the air grew thick with palpable, vertigo-inspiring waves. The sky was an ever-falling kaleidoscope of muddled colors such that each step taken was out of tilt.

"Curse that false priest!" hacked Henlee. "His unguent is going bad."

Apieron coughed back a bitterness. "My guess is that most of his powers were lost to him when he fell into dark worships. The potions were likely prepared by underlings."

The woman's face held a look of studied concentration at Apieron's words. Whether or not she understood his speech, or rather studied the man himself, was not apparent.

The four gathered themselves, often leaning one on the other as long-suffering feet protested each step over the pitiless rock. They spied lights beneath them, dimly veiled by the interposing stone. "Like a lamplit city, seen from a nighted hillside," said Jamello. What torch could burn so bright, even the dwarf would not speculate, and they hurried past such areas while Henlee muttered in his native tongue.

Once the companions cleared the cloaking dusts, individual fiends began to circle, soon joined by others. Some rushed by in a flapping swirl, others croaked out challenges in hollow voices. One imp, perched atop a finger of glowing tumulus, screeched with glee when Henlee's lame foot betrayed him, causing the dwarf to linger in a burning flare. The torch erupted below him, further scorching his skin and eliciting a stream of vitriolic curses while the demonling's malign laughter lilted in singsong. Maul tumbled from forty paces, blasting its diminutive form into unrecognizable fragments.

"That will learn you proper manners." Henlee hastened to retrieve his weapon. "You'll want to see this, Apieron!"

Jamello and Apieron, trailed by the girl, ran to where Henlee examined the stone upon which the imp had sat. Carved in the manner of the cairn they had unearthed en route to the Helfort, it was lit from within by a spectral light.

"By the besotted gods of Bestrand," exclaimed Jamello.

The others followed his pointing arm, and as far as one could see, hundreds of similar structures dotted the landscape. "The Army of Brass," Jamello breathed. The woman whimpered in fear.

"Come," cried Apieron. "One final push!"

Neither ranger, thief, nor dwarf could well recall their last retreat from the abyss; a running nightmare of tormented muscles, parched and bleeding skin, cough-wracked lungs, and minds numbed by lack of sleep and dehydration. Time after time they beat off attacks by hopping or flying fiends. Apieron cursed again the black-garbed warrior who had smitten him, thus rendering the mighty bow and quiver of Sarc useless. In this place of fire and fiend, he was incredulous that a mere mortal had harmed him so. Leitus flashed, splitting the skull of a three-horned devil who grasped the woman by the hair. In their exhaustion and urgency, the companions durst not stop, countering attacks only when directly beset. If one stumbled, the other three ran to brace him. The girl was strong and played equal part. Jamello mumbled of a time, soon to pass, when all would falter, perhaps not to rise again.

That was when Apieron found the never-ending stride. Cumulative discomforts such as the desiccated tissues of his mouth and windpipe or tortured skin that chaffed against boot or strap had grown to nearly eclipse that of his smitten shoulder and chest.

Apieron bethought himself of the dolichos of his youth, controlling his breaths whilst lengthening his stride. Locking his gaze onto objects to the fore, he willed the fey, sending forth psychic cords that emanated from his torso. Using the litany of his instructors, he tightened these lines of energy until they tugged him forward in his direction of choosing. The muscles of his legs and back unwound like iron springs, becoming supple with the heat of use, thus propelling him over pit and fell. Repeatedly, individual demons or small groups swept down on them. Jamello and Henlee were too exhausted to heed the approach of their enemies until at arm's length, yet Apieron proved himself quicker than any assault, smiting them down with Leitus's ever-keen edge.

"Now I remember," gasped Henlee. "Aperion the Runner." The dwarf's words were staggered with effort, although his scarred face grimaced his approval.

A state of fluid grace washed over Apieron as every occurrence seemed to slow until each slight movement was a continuation of the last, a contribution to the next. Leitus reaped gory harvest on all sides whilst Apieron achieved what his childhood masters had spoken of in awe. *"Warrior Victorious, Champion of Areté."* Even the shadow that ever followed and mocked him grew weak and faltered.

"The Gate," croaked Henlee, and before them, as if rising suddenly from the Hel floor, appeared the erect, motionless sentinel. The wind began to howl, a furnace blast at their backs.

"Not more than five furlongs," called Apieron from the rear.

"Apieron!" cried Jamello in dismay.

The thief's face reflected a yellow cast as he faced the ranger. Behind him loomed a clot of heavy vapors that advanced with speed over the plain they had just quitted. It was jaundiced with poison, and stank on the wind.

"Drop all, save your weapons," commanded Apieron. "Run!"

Before their pounding feet opened the black steps of a cairn. From its depths advanced a mighty figure, a giant of a man cased in shining metal. His face was strong and cruel beneath a high nodding helm. As they leapt over his outstretched hand, Maul descended upon the crested headpiece with an echoing crack. The figure crashed heavily into the depths whence he had come.

"The gas storm gains on us," gasped Apieron. Acid stung their eyes, bleeding throats began to close. "Run, run! We cannot fight this windblown doom."

On rubbery necks they raised their heads for a final sprint. The wall of fire loomed, and the Guardian stood smoking in its mist like an immutable statue, facing west. "What's one more burn?" gasped Henlee. Holding hands—men, dwarf, and woman sped betwixt its legs and through the veil of flame. The sentinel did not react as they staggered into the void of the Gate, whose sole feature was a lowering star.

X'fel glowed in mocking triumph from its sable vault. Hands

clasped, the companions staggered forward on faltering legs, breathing great draughts of the flat air as the wall of burning and the Guardian grew small behind them, until together they collapsed.

Apieron's awareness returned. A sending came to him, and he pictured the wight Ulfelion, cloak and cowl blowing in the gale furnace before the sentinel. At his side, larger than he, loomed the presence of the dark warrior. In Apieron's dream state, Ulfelion's features were revealed. Old and strong, set in liniments of evil wisdom accumulated over untold ages and revelry in perfidy. The lich king spat a curse, carried on the seething wind to find Apieron where he lay.

"Thy lamentations shall be lost on the wind.
Thy tears burn a fiery rain.

"Ashes shall mark thy face and blind thine eyes, then rain
and wind cease. Thou shalt be alone in a forgotten place
until the horn of Aurgelmir sounds its summons."

The dark knight beside Ulfelion bore a rainbow wealth of Hel stones on his muscular cuirass. He threw back his head to laugh.

Apieron placed his good hand on the lifeless soil, pushing himself erect with a painful wrench. The others roused, appearing more dead than alive. "We must not rest overlong," sputtered Henlee. "Who knows what vengeful Hate will come to us from the Hel plane."

Apieron lifted the chin of the girl and gazed deep into her face, her dark gaze meeting his without flinching. She straightened herself and her remaining garments to stand deferentially at his flank. Apieron hoisted Henlee and Jamello to their feet as he regarded their charred and tattered forms.

"We must soon find water."

Jamello wiped his teeth with a rag. "There's water and wine of the swamp elves at the horse cave."

"Three times I will sing wassail for each of the fallen ones," grated Henlee, "but not to he who betrayed us." The four friends plodded onward, and the shadowed landscape opened before them, illimitable on all sides. Were it not for the pain of their bodies, it would seem they had died, their spirits condemned to a gray, wandering purgatory.

After a time, a wind began to stir at their backs. They followed its pushing, sliding course, an invisible path, until its rush filled all the air. They found its nexus was a gale that flowed like a river into a howling blackness before them. Henlee leading, Jamello next with the girl, and Apieron rearward—they surged into the ice-shrouded tunnel of Duskbridge. They raced its length, stung by biting cold, stumbling past the greatest portion of the gullies. The companions inhaled deeply, and the desert air seemed moist and fragrant as virgin rainforest. They raised their eyes. Outlined against a pale, westering sun were two-dozen mounted lancers, the monks of Panj.

Each bore a horseman's bow of recurved wood, sinew and horn, as well as scimitar and javelin. No parley or challenge was spoke as they swung to a well-practiced attack.

Chapter 29

Ilycrium: Upland Country

"Erasmus, why cast your lot with us?" asked Gault. "Are not several of your friends principal among those who believe Kör can be reasoned with?"

"Better yet," gruffed Trakhner, general of the armies, "that we of the West are somehow to blame for the attacks on our homeland?"

At this, the handsomely dark youth performed an eloquent, self-effacing bow that Trakhner found irritating. Gault smiled slightly. The mage-apprentice's tones were silken. "Tertullion says that when mighty deeds are afoot, men who would be great must sacrifice more than others."

"He has been telling me that all my life," commiserated Gault. The auburn-haired prince grasped the slighter man's shoulder with warmth.

"However it is you are here, please be welcome."

"Humph," said Trakhner. "I'll 'ave the men pitch you a tent near to your master. Follow Seamus."

Erasmus looked with distaste upon the lantern-jawed soldier who materialized beside him. The Prince and his general watched as the haughty magician minced off with the expressionless

Seamus while taking great care not to soil his fashionable shoes in the mud and horse dung of the camp's throughways. "Shall I have him watched, milord? He's too clever by half, and I like not his politics." Trakhner's wind-reddened faced was creased with doubt.

Gault sighed. "Heaven knows we cannot look askance at any aid fate sends our way, whatever its form." Gault clasped Trakhner's arm briefly and departed. The old soldier noticed the sleep-deprived eyes and worry lines that etched Gault's face, yet as he disappeared amongst the tents, his back was nonetheless straight and shoulders squared.

Trakhner spared a small grin and murmured, "Black Merlin, he's called. At least the young spell-mummer brought a smile to your lips, my Prince. The first since the passing of old Belagund. Perhaps the fop has his uses after all."

Three weeks' march brought the army north and east of Sway. Trakhner set his line of advance to angle through the kingdom's heart and thence to upland provinces, gathering rural levies and tribesmen of the hills in a push to seal the Vigfil Stair before Kör's inevitable thrust.

Dusk gathered farmlands and villages to her fragrant bosom, silencing the work of harvest. Gault and Tertullion walked their horses through Ilycrium's encampment. Erasmus accompanied them. Uncomfortable on his palfrey, he vented a high-pitched exclamation as his beast shied sideways when they came unexpectedly upon the cooking fire of three armsmen.

"How be the provender, fellows?" called Gault to the dimly seen soldiers. "We didna mean to startle so yer, er, the young gentleman."

"The forage 'as been o' bit lean, milord, but we've a lovely stew brewin'," came a voice.

Gault dismounted. He approached a small kettle suspended over coals by a makeshift tripod. Sniffing over the stew, he was surprised at the hearty odor.

"Care for a wee bit, Sire?"

"With pleasure!"

A grizzled veteran with a short, graying beard and enormous arms handed over an eating tin. He plunked into it a torn portion of coarse black bread, ladling over it a large dollop of the broth. The eyes of the men followed the Prince as he soaked the bread thoroughly and took a large bite, swallowing with gusto. The soldiers beamed their approval and resumed eating as Gault eagerly finished his portion. "You managed spring-buck and marsh onion?"

"Aye, lord. Ye can live forever on the camp marshal's potatoes and thin wine, but who'd want to?"

Gault laughed at the veteran's raspy speech, as did the men. He took the reins of his destrier and mounted. "Gentleman, I owe you the hospitality of my board, yet I doubt it will be better, if as good."

"No need o' that, Sire," answered a second soldier, emboldened. He was a dark-haired farmer, sunburned and slow of speech. "We wouldna wish ta' embarrass the royal chef." Tertullion jogged Erasmus's arm painfully. One of the tasks of the apprentice mage was to serve his master's board, and the camp stew assuredly smelled better than any meal generated in the command tent of late.

"I doubt you not," called Gault, "yet perhaps I can improve on your drink."

He withdrew an embroidered skin from his saddlebag and tossed it to the third trooper … a tall, awkward lad who sported a shock of blond hair. Gault winked and lifted rein, followed by Tertullion and Erasmus.

"What do ye have there, boy?" exclaimed the veteran. The youth shook the heavy bag, which emitted a most promising sloshing.

"Open it!" shouted his companions in unison.

Unable to bear his own teasing any longer, the blond opened the drinking skin, upending it into a long pull. He promptly wheezed, bent at the waist. The veteran grabbed the bag from his incapacitated colleague and imitated the gesture, a trickle of liquor staining his beard, and wiped backhanded as he flung the skin to the other. He blinked water from his eyes.

"Now that, boys, is a king's brew. I would that he took the crown without all this dithering about."

"Maybe then 'e'll get some decent food to e't," seconded the blond youth.

"Calf-lolly!" The black-haired soldier cuffed his youthful companion on the head, then popped the end of the bag into the mouth of the protesting youth. "What he meant to say, Sarge … is *we* too."

The escort of the Prince moved carefully through the loosely ordered camp. "You did well, my lord," said Tertullion.

"By your leave," said Erasmus, "that skin was worth two months' pay for a sergeant, three for a trooper."

"They are good fellows," replied Candor, "and seem a sturdy lot."

"They will need every fiber of strength within them," added Tertullion dourly. "I hope it is enough!"

The riders picked their way through the darkening camp, skirting provision wagons, pens of draft animals, and staked-off sleeping areas where entire brigades of infantry spread rough pallets and lean-tos of cloth or scraped hide over frames. Night had deepened when the riders reached the command pavilion. Trakhner waited within. A messenger had arrived from Bestrand, and the general's face was somber as he handed over the missive. "It is worse than we knew." Candor opened the parchment. It was not sealed.

A wood rot of unheard swiftness struck vessels and warehouses that had survived the attacks of the fire ships. In short, Bestrand's fleet could not sail until new timber could be felled and aged, or purchased, and the labor of replacing the old begun. An ominous addendum was scrawled under the main of the message as if in haste. No careful secretarial script, it was the hand of the Protector himself: By night a terror stalked the streets of the southern port. Mysterious slinking beings slew in darkened alleyways and unlit suburbs. Worse, the horrors found their way into unbarred windows and upper walkways to prey on sleepers or to kidnap maidens and children. Raging fathers and wailing mothers woke to beds and cribs empty, finding rent garments and pillows marked by bloody talons. Families and servants of prominent merchants and notables known to have dealings with Ilycrium were especially beset, and most were now fled. Gault's face was thin-lipped, and his hands shook as he read the last lines:

"Mine own not excepted, I am now a widower. My Beatrice rests with the Goddess, may She pray for us. Yours in strife, Ulrich of Bestrand."

Tertullion perused the note at a glance and returned it to Trakhner. The old soldier tossed it onto a brazier before clearing his throat. "It were best these tidings not be known in camp, many of our coastal levies hie from the neighborhood of Bestrand."

"Will not Sway need those ships for resupply?" asked Erasmus. "The citizens will starve—"

Tertullion hushed him with a glance, turning to address the Prince. "I fear for our campaign, my liege. See how the foe anticipates our every action and thwarts us at all turns. Would he then neglect the southern gateway to his kingdom?"

"Where we haste," added Erasmus in hushed tones.

Gault's features were drawn. "I am torn between despair and hope. Our land takes wounds in ways I never thought possible, yet it seems we have accomplished much. The army grows in strength by the day. Trakhner's idea of dispersing regulars into the levies has worked marvels. We now average fifteen miles in a day's march."

"And we'll do a mile more tomorrow," growled the general.

"They will have to do better than that if we are not to find Kör laughing down at us from the walls of Alkeim," mused Tertullion.

Gault favored them with a wry smile. He drew up one of his boots, revealing a coin-size hole in the sole. "Then it is to be tight belts and sore feet."

"Aye, my lord, it always is," chuckled Trakhner.

"My father once told me a trick of Baemund, the Old Marshal," said Gault. "Have scouts range beyond where we would normally bivouac at sunfall. They will mark a safe course with fires every hundred yards for mounts and wains to follow in a night march until the last hour before midnight."

Trakhner grinned broadly. "It shall be as you say, Highness, though the men will break my ears, no doubt."

"Tell them I ask it and will walk beside each company in turn. At this rate, Tertullion, think you we can make Uxellodoum in time to give battle for the passes of White Throat?"

Tertullion bowed. "We must so hope, lord."

None of them, the experienced commander or Tertullion, holder of many secrets, could know that battle would indeed find them, although sooner and farther south than expected, or as they spoke, deadly strife already raged on the slopes of the Vigfil Stair that men called White Throat, and in the very halls of dwarf lords.

THE VIGFILS

Harold Quickfoot stood watch on the Eagle's Turn, a lookout post situated on a rocky outcrop of Uxellodoum, mountain of dwarves. Harold turned thirty last winter and thereby became eligible for normal soldiering duties, the first of which was traditionally a year of sentry. There were fifty such as he scattered upon various peaks and prominences of dwarf-home. Sharp eyes had earned him the honor of the Turn, as it faced the northern passes amongst which scattered tribes of barbarians made their home, the chief of which was called Alkeim, and thence to the southern marches of Kör itself.

Sentry duty, Harold snorted. "What else with a name like Quickfoot?" The moniker was laughingly bestowed when a fat elder had seen him dance at Springfest ten years gone. *Well*, he smirked, *green-eyed Gunnhild had liked my dancing well enough.*

Harold stamped his feet and flapped his arms to warm them. While summer no doubt lingered in the sun-kissed lands away south, snow already cloaked Uxellodoum, and the north wind blew bitter as ever. Now old Redhand had barked an order to double the number of lookouts on duty, with the direct consequence that Harold Quickfoot found the hours he must spend on this lonely crag exactly multiplied by two.

Those dwarves that did mingle abroad told tales of troubles that beset humans of the low lands. Dwarves had not been untouched in their high places, and elders spoke in hushed tones of strange and foreboding earth signs that grew ever worse. Although their fastness was strong, the dwarves of Uxellodoum were not great in number and were largely sundered from their kin west and east.

Tough as the bones of the mountains that nurtured them, the bearded folk were long inured to the extremes of frigid cold found atop their icy peaks, as well as the fires of their hidden forges. More especially so was that race of dwarves descended from an ancient line of mountain kings; it was said their wiseborn sire had a beard of pure gold and his mighty hand struck diamonds from the stone.

A true scion of that proud line was the present king, Bardhest Redhand. Xenophobic and sullen, he acknowledged no overload of any ilk, and was fond of stating that he held the troth of Candor kings and the wiles of the demon prince of Kör in equal suspicion. Nonetheless, infrequent delegations of humans were hosted that dwarves might secure woven goods and grains from black-soiled lands away southward. In wise like, the men of Ilycrium were ever eager to obtain tools and weapons of dwarven manufacture, of a secret, whole-cast design absent of rivets to shake loose. Even the haughtiest of Ilycrium's ruling elite did not forgo such prizes when available.

Harold chose to believe an amusing rumor that Redhand even grudgingly approved a secret pact with elves of the Malave. Certain woods and greenstuffs were imported (no doubt by night) for utensils and furnishings, as well as a stimulant for the fungus gardens cultivated by the deep mountain dwarfs. Of more importance, however, were cherished amphoras of the fermented pulp of the Limpis Leaf, found only in the airy sanctums of the Greenwolde, for when added to winter ales it rendered a unique and particularly sought-after flavor.

Harold Quickfoot fantasized about the stuff. He would order his next warmed and spiced, and after ten hours on the spur, his bones were nearly as cold as the rock upon which he stood. Although barely midafternoon, nothing stirred in the vales below. Even birds rarely flitted under the leaden sky. What a gloomy day!

Harold's thoughts wandered back to the soldiers' pantry and the warmth of the bright tunnels … *There!* Off in a lower depression, a flash of light as if on metal. In the dim such a gleaming was unmistakable, and Harold knew there was no exposed quartz or feldspar on these slopes to produce such a phenomenon. If there were, he would have noted it during the last eight months. There it was again! He bent keen eyes to a second vale, farther and higher, and next onto trails ascending the White Throat. He squinted under his hands.

"By the bearded gods!" Harold's breath gusted.

Long columns of soldiers marched down the pass like a creeping carpet of armored beetles. No goblins these, but men of some sort—squat, with peaked and fur-lined helms, and wielding small steel bucklers. Their torsos were clad in laced plates of metal and lacquer. Harold took a moment to count and then reached for a brass mallet and stumbled to the signal stone. Embedded low in the lookout wall, his target was merely the endpoint of a vein of acoustically favorable rock that wound its way through the mountain arm and thereby to a listening post deep within the dwarven complex. In mere seconds, his message was received and passed on.

As he waited for a reply, Harold continued to observe the descending columns. He might be young, but he could see this was an organized military division, and no mere migration of tribes unwittingly strayed onto dwarven lands, or a party of raiders intent on bypassing Dwarvenhome. In ten minutes, orders were tapped back along the stone, Harold's knowledgeable fingertips discerning the message from the vibrations as easy as reading a written page. Only eight months a soldier, he was first to witness an invading army in centuries. War had come to Uxellodoum.

Chapter 30

The Mylenscarp Range

"I have set your kit in readiness for the morrow, my lord." Gault fingered his arming doublet draped over a small stand. Of layered linen, it was both a cushioning pad for metal armor and itself a yielding, tough barrier. It was adorned with gold stitchwork on black, and a silken heraldry blazoned on its front. Mountains and sea, and the proud white horses of Ilycrium.

"Conrad, what think you our chances?"

"For the battle when it comes, lord?"

"The battle. The war. The kingship. Take your pick! By Oisin's bones, doubt clutches me like a withered hag. Would that I might glimpse the future."

The serving man made a disapproving, phlegmatic sound in his throat. "Better you than me, that is a game for the young." He touched his fingers, thick with use, although bent and knobby, to his breast. "I am but grateful for each moment when it comes."

Gault chuckled. "Old dog."

"I *am* old, and stiff, and evil." He shot a wrinkled grin under a cocked, aged-festooned brow. Robin's-egg eyes glinted underneath.

Gault laughed briefly and sat with a sigh. "But for a sign!"

"Many times have I envied Apieron Farsinger for the omens I hear tell are placed before him, and not least for the gallant friends who flock to him." He regarded Conrad, whose leather-clad back was hunched over a wooden chest. The campaign steward looked the same as he ever had, save the iron-cropped hair was blanched white, and he shuffled rather than walked. Gault wondered if the old warhorse even heard him, perhaps he chose not to respond.

Conrad turned to face the youthful prince. In his hands be bore a sword, held reverently crossways atop an oilcloth. His legs sounded like broken twigs as he lowered to a knee, proffering the weapon. The sword bore a graceful channel lengthwise in the opposing flats of the blade. It had a simple, squared crossguard of ancient design. In Gault's grandsire's time, swords of its ilk carved out a kingdom.

"Ilus," Gault whispered, "my father's brand."

"And his before," said Conrad solemnly, but his eyes were vibrant with sky-bright intensity.

Gault rose to touch the gold-worked helve and white-gemmed pommel that sparkled in the low light of the tent yet he did not grasp its hilts. "Some said you were lost to thieves—sold in distant southlands. Others that the King's slayer ... my father's *murderer*, took thee prize from his body."

"Say hidden, not stolen," rasped Conrad, "by one who loved your father and his line such that he was set to be servant of the son before your mother breathed her last. May Our Lady bless her soul of kindness." The old squire shook the blade. "Take it."

Tentatively Gault wrapped his hand around the hilts. They felt cool and remote. He could not lift it. "This brand knows me not."

"My Prince, you asked for a sign. I am a simple man of no gilt words, and was a farm lad on my father's croft until I set down scythe and donned sword for your noble sire. Fifty years I soldiered at his side or looked after you. Servant of the Body, and proud of it." Conrad shook the blade again. "Adopted or no, Ilus is yours by right! Let men see and they will follow."

Gault lifted the sword. Under the fitful light cast by a taper, the metal of its blade glistened dully. No tarnish marred the surface despite the nicks incurred in its many forays. It was heavy but not cumbersome. A potent weapon, tried and trustworthy. Conrad rose to his feet, his creaking joints belied by the smile wrought on his seamed face. A voice spoke from the shadows nigh the tent flap. "The man who bears that, is king," proclaimed Tertullion. "Faith! Your sires put more in swords than crowns."

Conrad looked to Tertullion and grumbled past his new smile. "I suppose he'll be needing a drink now that he's here."

Tertullion wagged his wintry beard. "Old rascal, I sensed you were up to something. I was right!"

"But I am no king," protested Gault.

"Without a king, a kingdom withers," quoth Tertullion. "Soon, you must be."

On the twenty-ninth day, the army found itself on the border between cultivated lowlands and mist-clad upcountry slopes. Advance scouts reported tall standing stones set upon a prominent hill that thrust its gorse-covered shoulders above yew and heather. The hillock was called Scaelp by Westerners, Bladenfex by tribes native to these lonely moors. Unknown peoples had carved the granite spires, which sat thereon, and overlay them with symbols of heroes and beasts, whorling flora, and weapons of war that were yet discernible through aged lichens and the flaking wear of wind and water. Tertullion recounted how such folkstones marked places of power where the lords of the land once stood to survey their unfolding realms.

The army encamped on the hillside and below, where there was cover from the wind and freshets for the animals. The sun was setting. Gault stood with Tertullion and Trakhner. He liked this high place, and the standard of his house rippled bravely on the wind.

"What is that menhir, Tertullion, on yonder top? It resembles a finger of stone, shattered. P'raps the ruins of an altar."

"It is called Dromlich. The hill on which it stands is Xambol the Stonefist. Beyond that I know not, these ancient lands hold many secrets unknown to me."

Leagues of fertile farmlands marched before Gault's gaze to a southern horizon. Tree lines and hedgerows, cart paths and stone fences made the flatlands a green-and-russet checkerboard dotted with the occasional cottage or barn, or cut with a random stream marked by a flash of argent through shielding trees that followed the water's winding course. From the lift of the hill, their vision stretched out to a blurred margin where land and sky coupled behind a purpling gauze.

Trakhner cleared his throat. "You wage a new kind of war, Highness. Tradition says one retreats before the overstrong opponent to a high place. Say, the fastness of your birth father. Such could be easily defended, and valor not squandered before the innumerable foe."

"Our country has grown large for such simple stratagems," responded Tertullion. "We know Sway's walls cannot be held against a determined general." He swept his thin arm across the deepening expanse. "Must meadow and bourn be thrown away without a blow struck by us? Only those of the smaller, seaside towns would have hope of escape should we let Kör come unopposed."

"Even so, the duels of war are thusly fought," said Trakhner. "To protect the life, a limb must sometimes need be sacrificed."

There was only the sigh of the wind as the men pondered. Sun's last light slanted from the right, coloring the tableau down country to a hazy gold. At last Gault spoke. "I owe this land and its people more than that."

"I doubt our foe is worthy of your honor," answered Trakhner flatly.

Gault said nothing. Distances were muted into the blues and grays of dusk. The men breathed a breeze freshened from the north. Night unfolded her wings, and dots of firelight that marked a workman's camp or homesteads of simple people arose in the sea of the great vale like friendly stars.

"That does not matter," Gault said softly.

A bonfire of yew was kindled betwixt the standing stones such that throughout the night, clansman might come to pledge arms under the banner of the Candor kings. The smoke was thick and sweet, drifting far on the wind. Captains of the host found themselves drawn nigh the dolman where abode a sense of expectation. Below the indigo vault, stripes of clouds were ordered in serried ranks, their rims lit with silver, and the breeze ceased, accentuating the stamp of cold feet and the rustle of mail. From the downslope came the soft voices of men and the shifting of horses. The moon burst forth, yielding a cold swath of light. It was waning, slung low in its sky cradle.

Renault, a knight champion pledged to Belagund, came forward. His gloved hand touched Candor's arm. "A good omen, milord. The moon is in sickle, a sign for gods who love war."

Gault drew Ilus. He did not know if he followed hidden urges of his own or some prompting of the venerable weapon, but he thrust it into the blaze. When it was withdrawn, men gasped— for the ancient brand held the same radiance of flickering yellow and blue as the fire's heart. As one, peers of the march drew their swords. They paraded past their prince, a circuit of flickering steel, to touch their blades to his until each held aloft a portion of Ilus's radiance.

From somewhere a voice rose in song, then another until at length the airs above the tor resonated with the sonorous joy of warriors singing. The melody was echoed from below as common soldiery found the measure. It was a favorite that bespoke of home and country and the valor of men who go afield. The officers stood thus until moonset while the burning continued, and would till dawn. Pillars of twining smoke were illuminated with glowing sparks.

Gault turned to Seamus, who stood nigh. "You are from this old, old land, are you not?"

"Aye, lord. I was whelped in Fyrfold, but ten leagues distant."

"I have heard it said," added Tertullion, "the men of this country ken the land's spirit because each carries a reflection of the dolmen in his soul."

"I know naught of that, lords," pondered Seamus in his slow, throat-deep timbre. "Though some of my kin can foretell the hunt or find water better than most, I reckon."

Gault's face flickered in the half light. "Tell me, Seamus, what does your upland soul tell you this night?"

The big man shifted his feet uncomfortably although answered in forthright fashion. "That war is come at last to Westlands. Soon it will engulf all 'round." He stretched his thick arm out over the benighted knolls and valleys flowing onto the great plain of the south.

"What then have we wrought?" asked Gault in hushed tones.

"P'raps you shall save this land."

"Are all things so simple in your heart?"

"Yes, milord."

Gault clasped the broad shoulder of the armsman, gladdened by the strength he felt there. At that moment, Renault's voice carried from the tents below. "You have seen the Prince wield the fires of Ilus. You have been called to war with the blessing of the spirit of the Scaelp. Let no man doubt or waiver!"

Men spoke excitedly as they sought their rest. Such omens they had heard tell of in grandsires' tales, but never thought to see with their own eyes. Gault was silent. The melancholy sound of a renewed wind across the dolmen and the rushing of the bonfire played in his ears. He did not fathom the role he played this eve. Tertullion oft bespoke himself of keys that might unlock gates to the future. The venerable mage said such mayhap was the dolmen, or Gault himself. Gault spared himself a wry grin—if only *he* were so enduring.

The wind grew shrill and plucked at their garments with ghostly fingers. Gault shuddered as the weight of past happenings and events forward reseated themselves upon him. *Eighteen years old. It felt like fifty.*

"Do not leave me, Seamus. I truly need thy steadfast spirit."

"Never, lord," spoke the soldier. From within his garments he produced a flask that was small in his great paw.

"A brace, my Prince. Just the thing for a chilly night's work."

Gault gratefully accepted. He imbibed the aromatic liquid, feeling its bite in his head and his stomach. Then came the burning. "What is it?" he stammered.

Seamus shrugged. "Who knows? My uncle makes it. Each time it is different."

Tertullion rejoined them, trailed by his apprentice. He imbibed heartily and passed it on. Erasmus sniffed, wrinkling his nose. "Oh well," he said, lifting it to his lips, "I hope your uncle washed his feet."

The army rested the following day whilst Trakhner and his

officers took the measure of tribesman who came in the night. Tough, dark men they were, unkempt of hair, with armor of skins or boiled leather. Seod they were called, and their wont in battle was to hurl javelins and sling stones, or ply arrows from short bows before mounting slashing attacks from atop rugged mountain ponies. Three thousands presented themselves before the horse standard and with tales of more to follow. Each warrior also bore a bone- or wood-handled scramasax of two hands' length, or a small axe of bronze or pitted iron.

The day passed quickly, and Trakhner was pleased for, although no match for heavy cavalry, the tribals contributed a fast-moving auxiliary, which might deploy first and attack from terrain too rugged for the ponderous destriers of armored cavaliers. There was one, however, who looked upon the exercise and was not pleased.

UXELLODOUM

Finbold Ironshod made his way to the fourth cistern in haste. As a high cleric of Uxellodoum, one of the duties he assumed during his two hundred years' service was to ensure the purity of food and water grown on dwarven lands or imported therein. Finbold's greatest fear had ever been the befouling of his cherished water supply via some clever foe or by accident.

At the third hydrogate, he paused and eyed the portcullis. Of a steel that did not rust, the curtain gleamed softly in the low light. Nothing larger than the smallest fry could pass the barrier, and it emitted a whining noise as rushing water set up a resonance in the steel lattice like some monstrous harp. Finbold dunked his head under the water, the noise intensified until he came up blowing and spouting. *The river was frigid!* He wrung out his long beard. *Thank Goffannon, the gate was intact.* Only the last cistern remained.

Finbold crouched with hands on knees to catch a breath. He thought again of the beautiful, flowing ribbon that was his water tapestry. Others had their schemas and models, but only he had seen it in its naked beauty, revealed in a spell vision. Blue streams of ice-melt collected far to the north under virgin glaciers and seeped through layers of porous rock that purified the otherwise nonpotable water, gathering over long years into underground pools and streams channeled by dwarves into an unending river source for daily use, and even a score of small lakes for fishing and beauty.

Finbold returned to the main corridor, bustling his enormous frame past dwarves who scurried in opposite direction towards the upper assembly areas, no doubt in response to the alarm. More than once he trod on his beard in his haste, each time cursing and simultaneously signing himself for forgiveness. It would have been a comic sight had anyone taken time to notice.

The door to the cistern room was undisturbed, the chamber of the fourth cistern being the final collection point before the water was divided into a myriad channels below. He pushed his way into the broad, cool room. Ghost lights cast from the stirring water threw undulant patterns on smooth stone walls, and the peaceful murmur of its lapping was soothing as ever. Finbold rumbled his nervous relief. What did he expect? To find some adept of Kör or human mageling casting onerous spells of pollution on his precious water?

He gathered up a dipperful and ran his hand over it, mumbling an incantation, sniffing and swirling it before swallowing like a judge at Brewfest. It remained quite pure. Blowing a sigh of relief, Finbold dropped the ladle and squeezed into a service tunnel that led to the water gates above for a final look before he joined the others in conclave.

"By the World Crawling Worm, an attack on Uxellodoum was

foolhardy indeed!" he huffed, not at all pleased with the necessity of his exertions. Eight thousand dwarves could withstand ten times their number. Even if the entire mountain were encircled, the dwarves could endure a siege for years. A swift frontal assault might overrun outlying settlements, yet the outer gates were more than strong. Should they somehow be forced, to pay to take the upper halls against dwarves in their own home would be impossible coin. Each retreat would be to a preset defensive position, rigged with vicious traps and dweomers not to be imagined by surface dwellers.

Hot-faced and puffing like a forge bellows, Finbold made it to the last stretch of tunnel before the inlet chamber. Although smooth and precise, the passage was narrow and long. Ordinarily he would summon a nimble acolyte should need arise. There was no time, for the surprise attack had tripped spell wards that virtually dumped him off his cot during a well-deserved afternoon's repose. There was the door at last!

By Goffannon's brass balls, this was a sorry day. Even the weight of his beard felt heavy. Finbold sighed, only this one last task.

He pressed a hidden catch and swung the stone portal aside on silent hinges to step into the cavern of the water gates … and beheld fifty or so squat beings, busy as beavers. They chipped away at the rock levies, and the outer retaining wall was already sundered while a team industriously attacked the carved river rim itself.

So perfectly constructed was Finbold's tunnel portal, the humanoids failed to note it, and no sentry encumbered him as he stepped forward and stood for a moment of shocked disbelief. These were some new race, or perhaps humans molded by generations of servitude far beneath the light of day. Scabrous white skin hung loosely over their near naked frames. Potbellies and stout legs supported enormous shoulders rolling with muscle, driving pick and mattock against the stoneworks as expertly as any dwarven artisan. Their speech was spare and more like the grunting of beasts to Finbold than the tongues of men.

"Sacrilege!" boomed Finbold Ironshod.

He ran toward the crew undermining the river ledge. The sentry nearest him wheeled to strike at him with an iron maul. Finbold thrust an outstretched hand to touch the creature's torso as he pronounced a word that literally turned the man's heart to stone. The wretch tumbled without a sound. Finbold took no notice as he hurled his mighty bulk into the midst of the invaders like a fat boar into dogs. Two were upheaved into the swift current to pass under the far arch and drown in the nighted, airless tube beyond. The workers at the inner retaining wall never paused in their labors, which must have begun many hours before, and they continued to hack at the rampart like soulless automatons. Finbold never saw the glaive that split his chest and took his life as many hard hands grappled him. The world seemed to explode in a roaring cacophony of pain, followed by the deeper groans of stones splitting under the rushing might of the waters contained above.

His white beard stained scarlet, Finbold was swept away by the deluge with his attackers. The demolition crew had called no word of warning to their embattled brethren when the dike gave way at last. The marauding waters blew aside the chamber's outer doors to pillage down the halls and work areas of Uxellodoum's lower levels. The service tunnel became a roaring tube of liquid destruction. It blew through the mortared walls of the cistern chamber like iron shot through paper, the spewing deluge quickly finding an air vent down onto farm warrens below. Crops were swamped and animals drowned while helpless dwarven farmers could only scramble to safety as the filthy waters settled out to create a broad lake. It had taken less than an hour for a simple act of sabotage to do what no cataclysm of nature or marching foe had accomplished in five hundred years.

Chapter 31

Arid Country

The Khôsh riders advanced at a controlled gallop, steering their desert mounts in a graceful line with thigh and knee, their hands bearing horsemen's bows of laminate wood and horn. In the cold twilight of the Gate, X'fel cast a harsh light. Under its glare, the Khôsh seemed filled with fell grace, as if they drew power from the divinity that guided the red sky-traveler.

Without visible signal, the Gate monks began a broad encirclement of the companions. A metal pot glowing within its smoke appeared on the ground in the line of their maneuver, and as each warrior passed it by, he leaned to dip several arrows that quickly ignited and were set in a brace before him such that their crimson steeds appeared to wear halos of flame.

Henlee turned to the others. "Fire arrows? Do they jest?"

Apieron shook his head, equally perplexed. He regarded the riders who spared not a glance at the four companions but continued their maneuver with the confident ease of born horsemen. The entire tableau unnerved Apieron. He looked at X'fel, and the lowering star winked in mockery. He did not lead his friends from the Everfire to die under that! He swept forth

Leitus, its light frosty blue as the northland sky under which it was forged.

"Think you they mean to make speech? Or seek to charge toll?" called the dwarf. The circle tightened to fifty paces, and the thunder of thirteen cantering steeds grew loud.

"Here's my road tax!" Henlee shook Maul defiantly.

"Watch the girl," called Apieron to Jamello as he and the dwarf separated two dozen paces to either side of the thief and their rescued captive. Wounded and on foot, they could only watch helplessly as the riders ran their circuit.

"Hey!" bawled Henlee.

Before the dwarf could complete his challenge, the riders turned as one in their low saddles and fired a volley of fiery arrows from all directions. The dwarf was struck a half-dozen times. His steel hauberk and girdle repelled the blows. One caught in his mesh skirt and hung there burning. "There's your answer, lad!" he shouted to Apieron, who had flung himself dexterously forward and rolled into a fighter's crouch, unscathed by the missiles.

"I wish I could do that," whistled Henlee, too occupied for further speech as a second volley showered over them, then a third.

Jamello glanced over the rim of his round shield. He knelt behind it with the girl in a small depression. Scant cover, yet enough to channel the horsemen's aim along a single angle. First two, then five arrows careened like fireworks off the shield's sturdy front.

Jamello listened to the sounds of the growing battle. He grew angry. First, devil-worshipping Procrius trafficked in Sadôk such that he, Rudolf Mellor, master thief of Bestrand, was captured, humiliated, beaten, and sold to priests of Sway, only to be turned over to that manipulating witch of the Lampus ... sent on an impossible journey to be robbed by trolls, poached like an egg, and hunted by every freakish monster of the abyss, yet he had, for the first time in his twenty-three years, earned the respect of a man of unblemished honor—a very champion of Ilycrium no less! A man who named him *friend* ... who now lay dead in the darkness, backstabbed and betrayed. Others had died so that he, Jamello, might live, surviving fire and fury. And now these horse humpers wanted to play? He, known as Edshu and Amante the Jongleur, had had enough!

Admonishing the girl to stay put, Jamello drew up the crypt shield and made to set his left forearm in its twin straps. They crumbled and broke. He cursed foully and threw it down with a clang. So soot-besmirched and fire-blackened it was that he could no longer see the fanciful designs embossed upon it. He kicked it, then kicked up a small spray of sand in the direction of the encircling riders, whose initial attack was done. Even so, they kept up a random fire, always swinging by the burning kettle.

"Come get some!" he shouted, brandishing his crypt blade.

Three arrows whistled over his head where he lay face down and spitting dust. "That's the way to draw their fire, boy!" encouraged the dwarf.

Jamello popped up, yet this time his hands bore the arbalest of Hel. With a *clack*, the device was triggered. Its fat quarrel pierced a bronze-bossed cane shield and the rider behind it. The desert monks on their horses paused in surprise of the slaying, Jamello most of all. Except Henlee, who used the interval to close and jerk a raider from his seat.

More agile by far, the Khôsh raider alighted and whipped forth a saber to slash viciously at the dwarf, but Henlee's shield was made to turn the mattocks of giants. The slender blade cracked and fell in twain. The dwarf rotated Axebreaker, pushing wide the man's hand still holding useless hilts. The dwarf lord dealt a crunching blow directly through the Khôsh's lamellar cuirass. The man gave a quick back hop and sank with a groan.

Apieron streaked past to leap onto the crimson mount. Denied by his wound use of bow or shield, he grasped a slender lance and kicked the screaming horse into the circle. Knees and thighs were enough for Apieron to control the plunging steed. Xephard had always laughed when his excellent horsemanship was compared to Apieron's.

"'Tis not fair to judge betwixt us. Apieron is part horse."

Apieron's unexpected attack defeated the smooth, coordinate rhythm of the archers' assault. Two turned backward in their flat saddles to fire. Apieron was the swifter; one he pierced above the hip with an extended jab, the second was bowled from his seat by a throat slap from the flexible spear. Apieron wheeled and trampled him under.

Spittle flecked Osüm's beard. "Kill him!" Arrows flew in volley, then Apieron was amongst them.

Jamello took a backward step. Three dismounted Khôsh pressed him hard. Skillful as he was, his heavy blade and tomb-found jambiya would not be enough, as his defense of the woman negated speed, and soon one would charge him whilst the others entangled his sword. One of the monks, some sort of officer, gave the others a quick nod. Jamello's mind raced. The Khôsh to his right was a tall rogue with a lip split into a permanent sneer by a poorly healed sword slash. It would be the middle Khôsh, the youngster with a lustrous black topknot, who would bowl forward, perhaps even to grapple his legs while more experienced comrades flanked him.

Jamello made as if to set himself to receive their attack but sprang at the leader, raining a quick succession of blows against cuirass, helm, and blocking sword, thus causing the man to grunt and take a back step. The younger one hesitated for a fraction of a second, allowing Jamello's sword to snake out and draw a line across his eyebrows, the young man giving an alarmed yell and falling back as a cascade of blood filled his eyes. The officer turned his head a fraction to order the other to stand fast. Jamello's long blade darted on its wheeling backstroke to the man's throat. Afraid to overextend the blow, Jamello felt his keen blade lightly score the man's sun bronzed neck. It was enough. The external jugular was severed as it crossed the cable-like muscle of the man's thick neck. The experienced fighter clapped a hand over the wound and quickly retreated, knowing that this painless wound would turn fatal if not expertly bound.

Snarling in frustrated rage, the third Khôsh finally cleared his blocking companions and slashed wildly with his horseman's saber at the smaller thief. Supple as a bowstring, Jamello dodged and parried the overeager blows and slid the point of his jambiya into the man's protruding Adam's apple. Jamello stepped aside as the stricken warrior took a dozen ungainly steps while emitting a weird piping wheeze to fall and strangle in the dust.

The younger monk managed to staunch the flow of blood from his face cut and clear his eyes to look for his antagonist, but Jamello was already gone. "Hey, turn around—" said Henlee.

Apieron sat heavily. His shoulder felt like it was being drawn out by the roots, and he coughed up sooty phlegm that tasted like tar, but at least not of blood. "Thank the God that Heals," he breathed.

Henlee upended a leathern bota he ripped from one of the riders' belts, a curse erupting from his cracked lips when only a sparse stream of drops trickled forth. The dwarf cut free three others and tossed them to Apieron, who extricated enough for one swallow past his swollen throat.

"It is the same with the others," complained Jamello from where he looted the last of the bodies, whose robes rippled fitfully in the chill breeze. "To the man they emptied these jacks before the attack."

"To bedevil us?" asked Henlee.

"Water is scarce," answered Apieron. "A disciplined folk, they fought to the last, and their hetman was nearly my undoing!"

"He'll undo nothing this side of Hel," laughed Henlee grimly.

The warlord Osüm had dismounted to do combat after the last of his warriors were fallen. Leitus had cleaved his curved scimitar and carried into the metal cap he wore under his winding cloth, dropping the screaming monk like a slaughtered ox.

"I suppose there's no sign of the horses t'either?" called Henlee to Jamello as he reached down to help Apieron to his feet.

Apieron walked stiffly to join the thief. Shading his eyes, he scanned every direction. The wind was frigid. He dropped his hand and used it to gather his left arm against his body. "The steeds were wise and fled the battle. I heard in their voices desire to leave this foul place far behind and return to their home, wherever that may be."

"Shoulda aimed at the horses and not the men," grumbled Henlee.

"Here," said Jamello. He proffered to the dwarf something scrounged from one of the bodies. "An emblem. They all bore them, the same."

Henlee took the graven oval of dull metal then dropped it instantly. "I'd spit if I could."

"Seven heads?" stammered Jamello. "Ten horns? What means it?"

Apieron bent over in swoon. Henlee bore him up. "Just my shoulder," choked the man, "worse than I deemed."

"I be sore afraid to remain hither," said the girl timorously.

They turned to regard her, so rare of speech had she been. Apieron looked around. The faces of his companions, their voices, their very presence seemed harsh and alien in this surreal place. The riders lay where they died, broken and small. The demon star winked on, soon its unholy light would cover everything.

He gazed again on the men they had slain. The *toll* was death. He stooped to gather Leitus and beckoned the others to follow, then set a path for the crater's rim and the last tree.

The four travelers marched painful miles in the labyrinthian gullies while the wind gnawed at their backs. Apieron set a pace as best he could, knowing they could travel neither far nor fast in their present state, but to linger was to die. Ironic, he mused, that they should be conquered at last by mere thirst and fatigue where the demons of Hel had failed. Bit by bit they progressed at a fraction of the pace they made in the ingress, so long ago. The wan sun appeared, yet seemed already departed for lands more hospitable beyond the Western Rim. Still they walked, afraid to stop lest they fall asleep from pure exhaustion, for none wished to rest within the confines of the Gate.

At last they came to the circling scarp and ascended in darkness, often supporting one another when the way was steep or the footing treacherous, sending a shower of stones to dance down nighted slopes. Although not a high or particularly steep climb, it was nightmarish to the party. Henlee barked each time his lame foot fell awry in the darkness. Apieron often staggered and would have collapsed had there been any level place to do so. Jamello tittered incessantly, at times raising his voice as if pleading with someone not present. Words such as *judge* and *unfair* were oft repeated.

Only the woman seemed little troubled by the shadowed landscape, more than once guiding them around obstacles hidden to their eyes. She searched her surroundings with avid interest as if everything was strange and new. "How long dwelt you in the long dark?" Apieron muttered.

The night was old when they breasted the escarpment with trembling legs and heaving lungs. A glimpse of the last tree or their previous campsite would have brought them comfort, but it was invisible to them. Setting no watch, they cast themselves upon the ground and were overcome by the sleep of the dead.

Sunrise came pale and timorous, its warmthless light a limpid yellow. Apieron's cracked lips parted. "So beautiful ..." He gathered a handful of dried clay at his feet and crumbled it, letting the wind take the dust.

"Thank you," he said in praise to the god who guides the golden chariot from east to west each day.

"Look! We did not stray in the dark," croaked Jamello. "There is our tree."

They walked no more than a hundred paces to find the little cedar. It was broken and lifeless, its drab leaves desiccated by the wind and blown into fragile piles on the rock face. Of the crow, there was no sign, nor did aught stir in the low, milky sky. Henlee's cairn was unearthed, and Jamello fell to his knees when the dust of its pillaged contents sifted from the dwarf's upraised hand. Burned scraps and small shards of pottery were all that remained of the provisions they had secreted there. Jamello sobbed.

With little else to do, they moved on. The need to find water was dire, and the grotto where the horses and extra stores awaited lay betwixt the barren gully-country and the edge of the Haunted Vale.

Leading off again, Apieron wondered if it would be he who first stumbled and did not rise. Conserving his strength, Henlee ceased his grumblings. Even Jamello marched in silence, his face set in pained grimace. At times Apieron would bid them halt and listen in narrow places, hoping to hear a trickle of water. He missed Sarc for the hundredth time, who no doubt would have a druidic spell for finding such—or could possibly simply smell it like a horse. At last in a steep-walled ravine, he found a dry streambed, an arroyo where running water had strewn a carpet of fine debris. He slowly paced its length, boots crunching its dry surface.

Apieron stooped at the outside curve of a bend, where the past runoff had curved to follow the furrowed contour of the land. "Dig here," he motioned to Henlee.

"The man says dig, I'll dig." The black dwarf hobbled forward.

Jamello stood to the side, fingers twitching. "Dig for dust, good dwarf," he squeaked. "Mayhap you'll find a golden nugget."

Apieron spared him a worried glance. "A little more, Uncle?" Henlee grunted and cut farther down into the hard-baked grit.

"I'll be a troll's girlfriend!"

The dwarf's spade turned up a dark clump of moist sand. Two strokes more, and the four companions leaned eagerly forward to see brown water seep sluggishly into the base of the digging. Apieron tore free a scrap of fabric taken from a horse-monk and lined the bottom of the hole. They held their breath, then whooped in croaking laughter when water welled through the cloth. They took turns drinking, lips pressed to the fabric, which they noisily sucked, and paid no mind to its sour taste or the bits of sand consumed.

They stayed by the well pit for the remainder of the day, eventually expanding it and lining the bottom with rock. In this wise they were able to fill drinking skins taken from the horse warriors. Apieron looked at his companions, how woe-begotten they appeared! Although he bore no serious wound, Jamello seemed the worst of all. Burned, bruised, and malnourished, the thief indeed resembled the plucked chicken Xephard had described not far from this very spot. His once lustrous, black hair was thin, his lips scabbed, and his hands would of their own volition burst into wild gesticulations that the others pretended not to notice. Having lost his quirts, throwing daggers, and worry balls, he fiddled and fumbled with pebbles and hand-sized stones.

Apieron's gaze fell on Henlee, whose lamed foot yet resided in its boot, propped up on a pile of scraps like some reclining war lord rather than a battered and sorely wounded mortal as was the truth. He knew the dwarf did not doff the boot for fear he might not get it back on. If ever, the wound would be inevitably slow to mend.

Apieron flexed his left hand and made to roll his shoulder. Crimson pain lanced through the arm. His head swam sickeningly, and he wondered if he would be able to use the arm again. *All for a quest laid at my feet by accident of birth. Had my mother brought me forth a minute sooner, or later, then surely some other infant, red and mewling, would have assumed this burden.*

Apieron thought of his mother. *Astir, the Evoker.* Never accepted by his older siblings, she to them a mere stranger in their house—just as he, her only offspring, held apart. How strange the fate allotted her! Taken by a foreign lord to a cold, cloud-kissed castle to be both greatest and least. Loudly revered when beside Xistus, followed by resentful rumor when alone. How many times had she heard those ugly echoes in the lonely halls of Cloud Home, yet spake never her own words of doubt to her lord, or discouragement to her son?

"Hie now!" The dwarf happily brandished a drinking skin as lustily as he ever did a tankard of ale. "The trouble with thirst, lads and *lady*," he nodded to the woman, "is that once you have it licked, your belly reminds you how hungry you are.

"Still, I am not for taking any of the praise from young Apieron. I trained him myself, you know." Henlee winked at Jamello and the girl. Darkness was falling, and his teeth flashed as he laughed.

Apieron looked over his companions. Better confreres he had never known. He thought of Giliad, so bright and resplendent— arrogant in his unchanging youth, singing the power of creation with his mind and hand. None of it had saved him, his glory swept into the demon wind. He thought of Sarc, slow to speech and strange to look upon, yet also familiar inside, as if one's soul-memory knew that the winged elf belonged in the world as surely as did grass or mountains. He thought of Xephard Bright Helm. Apieron looked to Leitus, gleaming by his side after he had cleaned her as he had seen his friend do countless times. Xephard, captain and peer of the realm, bright star of Hyllae, fallen into darkness.

Apieron bowed his head, tears of grief falling unseen onto his empty hands. Far off he heard the call of a nightingale piping once uncertainly, then twice more and bursting into song. Melónie's favorite, for she said they made the dark hours less lonesome. Instantly Apieron saw her smiling face, lips curled with laughter and sensuality, her eyes sparkling, and on her lap the mantle for him that he had seen her begin. Her tapered hands beckoned. They called him home.

Apieron raised his head to regard his three companions. Their faces were shadowed under the overhang. The moon had not risen, and there were no stars. "Tomorrow," he said, "we find the horses."

"Agreed," echoed Henlee and Jamello simultaneously. The woman only listened. "Never more earnest than I be now to see ol' Bump," added the dwarf.

Before he slept, Apieron prayed:

"Spirit goddess of my home, protect and keep my wife and children. In you I place their care until I return. It shall be soon."

And so the next morning's journey saw the wind grow less and signs of life return to the landscape, albeit it was only wiry flora that clung precariously to the broken slopes, or fingerling birds that fled before their crunching footsteps. Much was their surprise when a large and tawny hare burst out of a thicket before them. Quick as ever, Jamello felled the bounding beast with a flat stone he had taken to carrying. In a trice they had the rabbit skinned and spitted over a small fire, but no sooner had the flames licked up to touch it, the carcass began to writhe horribly on the spit, eventually ripping free to flop grotesquely. Henlee leapt up and grabbed Maul, but by then the dead and skinless hare was skittering away, keening a receding wail that made their hair rise.

"Gods damn it!" The dwarf swung the heavy weapon down onto the fire, pulverizing it into a cloud of dust and sparks. "Fucking haunted vale."

Unnerved, dejected, and hungry, the companions moved on. They were more eager than ever to find their equine friends who awaited inside the hidden redoubt prepared by Giliad and Sarc. Xephard's mighty Axylus and Apieron's sleek mare awaited. With them were Jamello's coltish bay and Turpin's chestnut stallion, as well as the forest beast of the winged elves, and of course, irrepressible Bump.

"Yup. Ol' Bump," Henlee would say as they walked.

He chuckled and shook his head each time he said it, hitching up his belt and quickening his step for a space. Apieron shared Henlee's enthusiasm, for with the horses and extra provisions, the companions might clear the vale without lingering to hunt, and even ride as the terrain allowed.

Cedars and desert pines now augmented the scrub brush and cactus of the lower slopes, and by day's end a warm breeze tossed the yellow heads of dry grasses as the westering sun drove the last vestiges of Duskbridge's chill from weary bones. The party struck a game trail that wound cleverly up the rocky slope they trod, picking its way betwixt boulder and stump until, at last, there was a spur before them that glowed like copper in the slanting light.

"Our grotto," said Apieron.

Jamello leapt ahead, followed slowly by Apieron with Henlee and the female in the rear. The sun glinted off rocks into Apieron's eyes. He felt hot, and wondered if fever had settled into his wound. Each painful step jarred into his spine. "Not now," he muttered, head bobbing with exhaustion.

Drawing a calming breath, he thought of Melónie's garden rill chuckling in its stone borders under willow and greensward, and feeling the shade of her spreading dogwoods. At times she would find him in the afternoon and lead him there in the cool, to speak of little things and enjoy evening's gentle coming … *Billowing sheets of yellow-orange fire descended over his vision, obscuring tree and vine in Hel-wrought fury* … Apieron shook his head and blinked away the tableau.

"By the Archer, no!"

Catching up, Henlee turned a questioning glance to him. Apieron caught the look. "We have failed our task and are late to home. Impatience burns me like fear, Uncle."

"Agreed," nodded Henlee sympathetically. "I did not ever wish to know I could hop about for a week with aught in my belly but water, and none too much of that." He shook a near-empty skin meaningfully.

"The spring at the bottom of that edge is fresh."

Henlee jerked his chin. "Thief's nearly there." He made a trumpet of his hands. "Have ye found it, boy? Watch out for Bump, he don't like surprises."

The woman halted, and her eyes held a strange look. "An Essence. Something foul."

Apieron and Henlee wheeled to her. "Think you it waits before us, lass?" urged Henlee. Not waiting for an answer, the dwarf gathered up his dark shield and unslung Maul to stalk ahead to succor the thief if need be.

"Nay," she said at last to Apieron, "a memory mystic, like a lingering odor." There came an exclamation of dismay on the wind, it was Jamello's voice.

Apieron outpaced Henlee, rounding the last bend and leaping down the slight defile before the cave entrance. The sun burnished the stone but did not reveal its shadowed interior. There he found

Jamello, pale and trembling. The blocking stones had been cast down, and over the lowering threshold, matted hair and bloody hide were smeared over the sigil Giliad had etched. The blood and hide of horses.

Apieron saw that one such scrap was striped, such as that of a tarpan horse of the Wyrnde. Henlee dashed past, shouldering them aside to menace the dark recess of the room. Maul gleamed wickedly. When he turned back to them, the dwarf's features were terrible to behold.

Apieron and Jamello followed. The thief stopped two steps in, then gripped his knees and retched. An old and penetrating reek assailed them. Strewn about the walls and cavern ceiling was the shattered gore of the unfortunate ponies. The rendered carcasses had been tossed to the center. His heart breaking, Apieron began to sift mechanically through the remains.

Jamello stood at the entry, speaking rapidly to himself while his eyes stared at nothing. "Go, Jamello, search the hillock," urged Apieron gently. The thief's hands twitched to the sword at his belt, and he shuffled a step backward but seemed incapable of action.

"Any sign of Bump?" rasped Henlee. The dwarf's voice was flat in the murk. A miasma hung in the air like smoke. It was chokingly foul such that their words were labored.

"I do not know," replied Apieron in half-bitten words. His heart wrenched to see Henlee's wooden expression. The dwarf gathered Jamello by the arm, and the two stumbled forth to ascend the knoll and search for sign of what had befallen their friends.

Apieron remained kneeling. He beckoned, "Come hither, lass." Without fear, she came to stand by the desiccated remains and looked down into his face. "You have some skill of dweomercraft. Sense you aught?"

"Nay, lord. I deem what spirit was here hast departed long ago.

Though the times reckoned by the yellow lamp in the sky are to me passing strange."

Apieron wondered if he was strong as she who had dwelt without hope of sunrise in timeless Hel. He bent to examine the pitiful beasts, then took up a leg bone, holding it up to catch the fleeting light. The coloring of the hide was that of Jamello's palfrey, the leather dried and stuck to bone and sinew, the flesh beneath having since withered. Suddenly he cast it from him.

"Something fed on them!"

The woman and he followed Henlee and Jamello a furlong down the westward slope. Dwarf and thief had discovered the remains of another horse. This time there was no question of the identity. Xephard's warhorse was pinned to a tree, crucified. The body had been savaged as if by a tusked creature that had plowed and chiseled grooves into the destrier's thick bones. Despite the gruesome depredations, the stallion's mighty stature and proud features were unmistakable.

"Axylus," breathed Apieron. "No random monster did this."

"He did not die without a fight," growled Henlee, lifting one front hoof, then the other. These were stained with the flaking, rust-black residue of dried blood. Henlee dropped Maul and shield, unslinging his pack.

"We bury him here."

The deed was not easy, for even in death Axylus was mighty of frame. When they were done, Henlee set there a grave marker. It was a flat stone, shot with quartz, upon which he cut a series of figures. "Here have I made the rune name of Axylus and the symbol for 'warrior'. For that he was, like his master. I also carved the name of Bump, he who was my friend."

They camped a mile west of the horse cave, where the little rock stream vanquished their thirst and refilled waterskins. With Leitus's keen edge, Apieron peeled bark strips from a series of pines. He showed the others how to scrape free the pith between the bark and wood core. The meal was acrid and pasty, but even the dwarf did not complain, and once he realized the stuff was edible, he went through a great quantity of the cuttings, although Apieron did not take more than two or three strips from each tree so as not to wound it overmuch.

They lit no fire so near the Haunted Vale, and few words were said. In the dark, Apieron heard Henlee speaking softly in his native tongue, individual words indiscernible, although they held a chant-like quality. Apieron knew his eldest friend well enough to know that the dwarven champion could only be praying for one thing, a chance to face the defilers of the horse grotto.

All the cold night through the shufflings of small animals and the calls of night birds jarred upon their senses, so unused to the sounds of living creatures they were. At every rustling, the companions woke and grasped weapons in sweaty palms such that there were four sentries rather than one the night entire. Thus they were poorly rested when the ambush came …

Chapter 32

The Rat's Lair

Tallux held Farstriker sideways so that its long silhouette would not mark him against the clay and bracken of the Gorganj. Creeping along a cut in the tumbledown, he would debouch into a dense stand of black pine where his quarry had no doubt been driven by Sut. There was no sign of the mighty hound, nor would there be until their antagonist was cornered and the final battle joined.

Tallux was patient as any hunter in the realms, yet he was eager to bring this episode to quick conclusion, for it only delayed him from bringing succor to his friend, Apieron of Windhover. He crept forward another ten steps, invisible and silent as only an elf ranger could, and readied an arrow whose head was of tapered steel, long and heavy and with a razored point. A killing arrow, the fight would be brief.

Tallux heard a slight motion and wheeled, bringing the famous bow to bear on a charging warrior, black and evil. Without panic, he dropped the bow to turn again to the fore while drawing his sword in one fluid motion. The dark knight in the draw behind him was an illusion. Too close for bow's range, a giant man in forest green was closing with him. A weight of burning ice sank into Tallux's stomach *as he realized his second mistake. He ripped his gaze away from the green hunter to begin a sidestep and parry. Too late he glimpsed a falling form of darkness that crashed onto his head and neck, driving him into oblivion.*

"So that is how you captured the mighty elf, eh?" chuckled Bizaz as he regarded Tallux through the aperture of the cell, feeling the dream slip from the beleaguered form on the slimed stone. The stoic elf had resisted each torture of body and spirit that the half-orc shaman inflicted. Until now.

"How simple, really," said Bizaz to no one.

The boon of sleep snatched in a rare hour of reprieve and a passive incantation of dream-sight had accomplished what days of brutality had not. The information gained had been trivial, but it was a first step. The next would be easier still, as he, Bizaz the Mighty, grew close to his victim's mind, until at last he absorbed all the wood elf had to offer. The broken husk that remained would, of course, be sacrificed.

Bizaz nodded to his apish attendants. Tallux's head jerked up when they charged again into his cell and fell upon his naked form. The elf cursed them through tattered lips but could not curl against their pounding blows and clawing swipes due to the chains that weighted his pain-wracked limbs.

Bizaz fingered again the badge taken from the elf—horse head athwart a green field. A high-pitched cackle startled him, and he turned to regard an unkempt dwarf who eyed the elf's suffering with glee. This one fingered a short knife, pockmarked with corrosions. Bizaz backhanded the leering face.

"Never come upon me in stealth!" he screamed into the dwarf's bulging eyes. The bestial cleric stomped out, not really so furious and glad to have taken the normally wary dwarf by surprise. He would rest and prepare for his next encounter with the elf whilst his acolytes put the subject into the proper frame of mind.

Deuce glared at Bizaz's retreating back, marking well the smug set to head and shoulders. He licked his bloodied lip, vowing revenge, then licked his leaf-bladed knife and slipped into the holding cell that the acolytes had so courteously left open in their haste to savage the prostrate elf. Bizaz would learn the folly of disregard for one such as he. But first, the prisoner would taste his displeasure.

Deuce shouldered two of the temple servants aside and stooped over the wood elf. To Tallux's fading consciousness, the insane light in the dwarf's eyes was more dire than the befouled blade he brandished ...

UXELLODOUM

The dwarves of Uxellodoum lived in a state of readiness for either feud or fight. Nonetheless, the utter lack of forewarning of the attack put them in direst need for a span of time to gather their outdwellers into the security of the mines. Despite the initial frenzy engendered by the arrival of an army on their very doorstep, mountain dwarves were not willing to allow the slaughter of unprotected kinfolk who lived and worked the lower slopes beyond the outflung arms of the mountain fastness. Each knew the invaders from the northern wastes would carry all if they secured entry into the upper halls in the initial assault, yet no voice called for closure of the outer gates' ponderous valves.

When the frantic warnings of various sentries arrived, the force most ready to act was the king's elite bodyguard. Veterans all, each Black Shirt, those who wore the boar's crest of the king's household, was of proven valor. Five score were immediately sent to lead a contingent of ready guards to hold perimeter against the swarming invaders, then to fight a retreat behind fleeing outdwellers.

King Bardhest Redhand dispatched his Black Shirts within ten seconds of the initial signals. He knew that many of these, his cup companions and most loyal servitors, would not survive the day. That the hordes defiling his fair mountain were slaves of Kör, he needed no confirmation. Who else could bring such a force hither?

Redhand's wrath was great, and yet he was not overly worried, for did not the dwarven language hold more words for defense and logistics than those of all other free peoples combined? Everything would proceed according to preset plans, that merely needed proper intelligences to be enacted. Uxellodoum was no sprawling human settlement with a sloppy palisade and a few guard towers thrown up as if in afterthought. Rather, it had been delved over centuries with battle strategy in mind. Redhand snorted, *"These slaves of demons and their pet goblins will break on my walls like water running."*

The King stepped from enthusiastic generals and shouting counselors, betaking himself to a vantage above his gates. He motioned for postern sentries to remain where they were, and pulled a gazing crystal from his belt pouch. The day had begun in gloom, although clouds now lifted from the lower peaks, giving rise to a majestic sunfall.

Redhand could see streaming columns of fast-moving, mounted human steppe-dwellers that the dwarves named Swertings. These bore down on the dwarven field-works as his counter force moved to engage. Farther back he descried battalions of orcs geared for heavy assault. These marched to reinforce the swerting archers. Redhand shouted an imprecation that shocked even the door wardens, for the numbers were staggering and outreached the estimates of the direst of his generals by twice.

"Every miserable goblin that can swing a stick within two hundred leagues must have ran down the White Throat!"

Redhand squinted into his scry-stone to view more-distant perimeter woods, where he beheld loping wolfmen and strange creatures that went more oft on four legs than two, these no doubt released to snap up stragglers and prevent message riders from sending for help. *By the Forger's Tongs, this attack was well executed!* He looked again to his relieving force and the paltry numbers of sentries who rushed from their posts to join the fray. That these would soon be overwhelmed was obvious.

King Bardhest Redhand shouldered Deathhoe, his legendary mattock, and slipped away from distracted sentries. Alone he took himself by a little-known path that skirted the valley of the outdwellers. Twisting along the tumbled stone of the mountain arm, the thin trail carried him beyond the ring of battle. He avoided enemy squirmishers when he could, but encountered one wolf creature that leapt at him from atop a high boulder. The beast seemed a hideous blend of wolf and goblin, with a drooling maw and rabid eyes. As the snapping jaws sought his throat, Redhand crushed its low skull with a single blow of Deathhoe.

Leaving the twitching thing, he ascended a prominence directly above the assembled orcs. Surveying the battle, he smirked in his beard when he thought of how his peers would rant when they learned of this little expedition. Now he could see unaided the roiling masses of invaders.

The dwarven king realized that by virtue of sheer volume and the remarkable unity of the attacking army, the entire North was soon to be engulfed in war. "What a fool Kör hast played me!" Redhand's scowl deepened when he looked again. The Black Shirts were hard pressed. Horses had been brought up, and darting, mounted archers fired at close range into the thin lines of his exposed defenders. Not even dwarven armor could long withstand that steel rain. Where his overextended ranks collapsed, orcish shock troops moved to exploit gaps left by the wheeling cavalry.

Redhand growled as he peered through dust tossed up in the clash, and frowned as he recognized tribal totems amongst squares of ironclad goblins closing in on his beleaguered people. Hitherto only the large, fierce orcs of the summit tribes had the industry and discipline to adopt effective harness and traditional battle tactics. He beheld a dripping eye.

"Tareg," he mouthed aloud.

Many lowlanders thought the fabled under-city of the Tareg merely a myth, not so the King of Uxellodoum. The mighty orcs of the Tareg were the sworn foes of his sires when the mountains were young, and Dwarvenhome was but a precarious colony ringed by enemies. Bardhest Redhand shook his beard in disgust like an old and prideful lion that tosses his grizzled mane in amaze at the effrontery of some lesser beast. The dwarf king vented a mighty shout, and many helmed heads turned to regard him. He flung his arms out wide, revealing Deathhoe to all that could see, his steel hauberk flashing like a rosy beacon in the rays of the westerly sun.

The eyes of orcs burned with fury at the sight thusly revealed. He, their most hated antagonist, had hunted them out of the high places for generations of their kind. To his red hand alone had fallen uncounted numbers of their people, his name cursed by elders and used to frighten goblin pups in their burrows. His head would be the greatest prize of all, thereby assuring a chiefdom and undying fame to any who hung the gray-bearded trophy in his cave.

Two dozen ran forward in rage while many others moved to flank the rocky knoll, and as the wily king intended, the distraction amongst their brethren caused the orcs pressing retreating dwarves to pause their attack. Those troopers charging

Redhand made to scramble up the rock face and come at him in numbers, but the King did not wait. One he brained with a flung stone, three more fell screaming as he severed their clinging hands and kicked them from the rock lip. The rest gained the ledge, yet were winded from the climb and could not match the ferocity of the dwarven king. The valor of his legendary forebears flowed strongly in Redhand's veins as Deathhoe smashed helms and punched through breastplates as if they were cloth, littering the precipice with screaming wounded and gory dead. His own armor was of a spell-burnished steel that defied goblin blows, although his arms streamed with blood from nicks and gashes.

Bardhest Redhand gazed out to see what seemed to be an entire brigade of the monsters moving toward him. "So much the better!" His people made good their retreat, and soon the ponderous gates would be shut. *Then let the lizard-spawn howl.*

He heard a stealthy noise to his rear and spun to see Ivenest, son of his daughter and a Black Shirt. Knowing well his grandsire's mind, the young dwarf had tracked his king to this place. "Ah, Ivenest. I did not wish this to be."

"My King," stammered the other, "I will not be foresworn. Ever the body of a Black Shirt is to be shield for yours as long as you hold kingship, as long as I draw breath."

"Ivenest, son of my daughter," a great sadness filled Redhand's voice, "it was not meant to be thus. You should not have come."

"You would leave us, my liege?"

Redhand shook his head and made to respond, but the frenzied yelling of reinforced orcs as they drew near their prize made speech futile. These found defiles that gave onto the outcrop and scampered in from three directions. The dwarven king tilted his head up to the sky, its steel-blue vault majestically lit with gold-and-vermillion streamers. He called out in a great voice, clear and unnaturally strong.

"Gods of my fathers, I ask only this. Bring glory to my life-end's tale ... and succor to the people of Uxellodoum."

A low rumbling shook the mountain. Trees moaned as if beneath a gusting wind, while their high tops remained still. Charging orcs pulled up mere yards from their quarry and looked about uncertainly. This was the mysterious home of mountain dwarves; there the bearded ones dwelled close to their dour gods longer than the span of memory of goblin tribes, and in the face of their most hated foe, at the very moment of victory, they could not help but quail.

Bardhest Redhand did not hesitate, and with a rolling shout of laughter leapt upon the unsettled orcs, dashing their battle leader to the earth and spilling his brains with one blow of his cruel mattock. He used the partially wedged weapon to swing his body round and plant his keen dirk into the midriff of the goblin's standard bearer.

The advent of the great earth sign and Redhand's ferocious assault took Ivenest completely by surprise, leaving him without an opponent for the nonce. He watched his king move with a dynamism that he seldom witnessed, even in warriors in their prime. He saw Deathhoe split the belly of a third orc, parting its iron link mail to pull free a swinging tendril of black blood. One of the orc chief's bodyguards recovered his scattered wits and thrust a javelin high into the King's back. Ivenest vented a maddened yell and surged forward even as Bardhest Redhand kicked back and whirled Deathhoe to snap the javelin at midshaft.

Ivenest startled as a heavy mailed hand slapped his shoulder. "Ee's dead, boy. Hurry and pull out this wretched stick before the rest regain their courage."

Ivenest's eyes came back into focus. His hand axe dripped gore. At his feet was the javelin wielder. Dropping weapon and buckler to the ground, he gripped the splintered shaft of the javelin, yanking its barbed head free from the venerable dwarf's flank. Redhand grunted but did not stir.

"A bitter wound, my King. Let us move off to bind it."

Redhand's eyes were bright and most alive as he turned to regard Ivenest fully. "Take a message to the clans, boy, as fast as ye can."

"I cannot—"

"You will!" thundered Redhand.

"This I command. Say to them, Henlee of Saemid should be king. Only in unity can the tribes defeat the forces come against us."

King Bardhest Redhand regarded goblins gathering for a second charge, one backed by a thicket of pikes and several of the deadly bowmen from the ranks of the Mgesh. He glanced once more at the blue vault. "Tell them for me … today, I was happy."

"My King, I—" Redhand struck the younger dwarf a mighty buffet on the base of the skull as the other turned to indicate the charging orcs, dropping him to his knees.

When Ivenest gazed up dazedly, he picked out his king downslope amongst the van of swarming monsters. Streaming blood from a dozen wounds, Redhand dealt blows like some god of war. The fell king laughed as he slew, even as his lifeblood flecked his lips and stained the gray of his beard. Foemen lay strewn about Redhand's feet, yet their comrades pressed on relentlessly, maddened to animalistic fury and not to be denied this great prize after such cost.

Ivenest shouted in rage at the betrayal. He leapt to his feet, brandishing his axe, ready to dash down the slide to end his life in the glory of the sword's song. In a flash, he saw again his king's contented eyes as he spake his last command.

Ivenest did not well remember his flight from King Bardhest Redhand's last battle. Tears streamed down his face. He barely heeded three wolf runners that he hewed as he pressed without pause onto the upper concourse, nor was he there to witness the final sword thrust that took Redhand's liver and his life, the mighty dwarf striking out to gut a last opponent as he fell into darkness.

The world was disjointed for Ivenest, and a pall veiled his eyes as he stumbled past shocked sentries at the council chamber. Not bothering with passwords, he burst into the room, quieting its occupants. His body was covered with dust and the spatter of battle. Startled but welcoming expressions greeted him as dwarf lords looked up from their table.

"What word, young Ivenest?" asked Stumfurer Broadbelt, the King's brother and most senior dwarf present. Ivenest read their faces, and could see news of Redhand's death would be little surprise. Many no doubt expected such from their brave leader. Small nods in the group told him the outdwellers had been safely recovered.

"Only this." Ivenest gathered his breath. "Bardhest Redhand is dead. He names Henlee *king*."

Iz'd Yar stood a small ridge before the first gate of Uxellodoum. One step below and to either side were his silent bodyguards, as was befitting a field marshal of Kör, and confidante to he who sat the Living Throne. Iz'd Yar could smell the demon blood in the twins. It was apparent by more than their scaled ears and yellow eyes; they possessed strength and cruelty far greater than that of mere humans. Well they should! For they were his sons. Two of the youngest he had spawned in the long years, they needed his continued benevolence against the fratricidal ambitions of their elder brethren.

Before Iz'd Yar and farther down were clustered his strategists and various commanders of Mgesh and goblin tribes. Their respective kings were sweeping the gate road of the last of the perimeter defenders. That the valves would likely be shut behind some hundreds of dwarven farmers, and a few surviving soldiers, bothered him not at all. Of course the swiftest of his orcs trailed the last fleeing dwarves with rope and spike to attempt the ingress, yet reports were that, not surprisingly, resistance around the gate was desperate.

Iz'd Yar tsked in this throat, producing a horrible sound. The bearded folk placed too much emphasis on the strength of the stone they cowered behind. Was not their very mountain merely the vomitus of the upheaval when the world was born and his deity, the Dragon of Darkness, was cast into ruin? Nay, the dwarves of Uxellodoum would learn that, against the powers of Evernight, stone was not strong.

A great hue and cry came from a company of streaming orcs that paused at his circle of commanders. One came forth. Kneeling before him, it proffered in cradled hands a bloodied head whose gray beard trailed the dirt. "Speak," he commanded.

"King Bardhest Redhand, lord of Uxellodoum," said a greater orc, a war leader of the Tareg, recalled Iz'd Yar, one named Shefang.

"Excellent," said he, extending a claw to seize the trophy. "And of your globin king, Gutr?"

"Slain by the Redhand, lord."

"All hail Shefang, king of the Tareg," said Iz'd Yar dryly. Shefang returned a sharp-toothed smile, then smote his head upon the earth before backing down the way he had come in an obsequious crouch.

Iz'd Yar was well pleased, and could afford a token bit of generosity with the goblin slaves. Were not the closest kin of every commander his *guests* in Körguz? Thus far all proceeded as planned. His movement though the Vigfils had been unsuspected and unopposed. Dwarves had been surprised, deprived of their remote forts, and cut off. No word would reach the low country of their plight until he was in the soft belly of Ilycrium like a ravening wolf amongst fat sheep.

First the dwarves and their fabled treasure! Faquirs assured him that his Drudges had accomplished their first task, and already the secret river of Uxellodoum was loosed. Moreover a message imp arrived from the regiment he had spun off farther up the steep where settlements of northern barbarians were being razed. Soon, the Makis Vodrab and his victorious skirmishers would rejoin him here. When they did, he would break the gates and commence the under-assault.

Iz'd Yar laughed aloud. His sons did not stir, but some of the orc and Mgesh commanders looked over their shoulders in fear. This made him laugh louder, and now there was *this*, he turned the head slowly, inspecting it before retracting the eyelids and gazing into that stern countenance. "What think you, Bardhest Redhand? Will your proud vassals make pretty slaves for Iblis?"

Iz'd Yar scowled, narrowing his slitted eyes and bending his head to sniff. "Ah-h, a pity, your soul hast departed to whatever muddy hell awaits vanquished dwarflings. Foolish runting, you survived not long enough to beg for your miserable life. Despair not, I shall redeem you."

Black talons caressed the dwarf king's craggy features. "Iblis shall be well pleased to receive your offering." Iz'd Yar stepped down to his conclave of counselors, trailed by the expressionless twins as the head of King Bardhest Redhand dangled from his belt, tied by its long, gray hair.

Bardhest Redhand tramped across the mountain ridge, feeling stone tremble with each heavy step. Odd it was, he reflected, how after death it seemed he grew heavier, rather than lighter as his old gam's tales had said. So much for stories! He knew he had recently been amongst the living, fighting a string of battles (mostly victorious) in the general cause of dwarvendom—at least those dwarves with whom he was related or on friendly terms. And he had most certainly died, yet here he was, stomping along very much alive, or so it appeared. His steps seemed to shake the entire range, and from his breath rolled thunderclouds. That was good, he always did like to make a racket.

Below he could faintly discern the swirls and eddies of a raging battle. Tiny figures there were of vaguely familiar dwarves and swarming goblins. Normally this would be of great interest to him, but in his new state, he could see a bright sunset on the distant peaks of his forefathers, and felt an overpowering urge to see them from this new perspective. He turned to trudge in that direction after a final guilty glance at the remote conflict. Oh well, the dwarves would probably appropriately slaughter the orcs, and if they did not, they would gain a worthy new enemy to make strong their sons. Either way, things would work out for the best. Redhand shrugged his shoulders and vented a heartfelt, rolling belly laugh. He slung his great mattock, Deathhoe, and charged off towards the golden horizon.

On the battlefield, thunder echoed in the peaks without clouds in the sky, and the ground trembled. Horses neighed and bucked against their riders while hosts of orcs and Mgesh stumbled on the slope before the gate and wondered what boded. Only bestial wolfings seemed not to notice. The mighty valves closed with a whooshing thump. Thus began the siege of Uxellodoum.

Chapter 33

The Haunted Vale

Bizaz chose his site of ambush well. The travelers below
followed a rainwashed track down an outlier of the Gorganj
lifted from the northern aspect of the vale. *My vale.*

Bizaz the Mighty! was the title given he by himself, half-orcin
priest of an unclean and bestial spirit that he might summon,
when blood was the offing. His veined eyes bulged weirdly as
he watched the haggard figures approach a small ledge where
they must pause before attempting the rough slope. From that
point, every direction open to them lay uphill, with poor foot and
hand holds amongst crumbling soil, sharp rocks, and the thorny
brambles that lined the scarp. Even the rut they now traversed was
treacherous, and they often held hands in the descent.

Bizaz drew his red-hilted scimitar and licked its black
blade. He turned to those with him: Deuce was present, a wiry,
scraggle-bearded dwarf, clad in leather; Dranol Eserhaven, a tall
pock-faced human spellcaster with a beaked nose and chin; and
finally Slysbeth—the bounty hunter had for this fight donned
brigandine, its metal plates encased in forest-dun leather, silent
and nigh invisible. The evil forest-runner also wore a slit-eyed
helm, topped with the horns of a stag.

Bizaz chuckled. "More than a match for those crawling vermin."

"Friends of your wood-elf, no doubt," tittered Dranol. "How he will howl to see their heads roll into his cage."

The orcish shaman pointed his wicked blade directly at the conjurer's chest. "Mankiller will feast this day, win or lose." He favored the others with his jaundiced glare. "Deuce Baseborn, betrayer of kin, murder yon lame dwarf. *You* will aid him, Dranol. And capture the wench, we will sport much with her later." The mageling cackled insanely.

"And I, O mighty general?" sneered Slysbeth, regarding the cleric with an unsavory look.

"Kill the thief," drawled Bizaz. "He is the least stricken and most agile. None of these who destroyed Thousand Eyed and slew my goblin slaves must be allowed to escape."

"As you wish, but 'twill be poor sport." The brawny woodsman flexed bulging biceps for them to see.

"Vain rooster!" scoffed Bizaz. "Ware he does not slice those pretty muscles to ribbons."

"Oh, he might—" added Deuce.

"And ware your filthy mouth, dwarf. Before I split thy greasy skull," boomed Slysbeth's harsh voice from his casque.

"Enough blather, fools!" A file-toothed grin creased the cleric's face. "I have a ranger to bleed."

Tallux huddled in the far corner of his cell, nor was there room to do aught else. The wood elf could have touched each wall with outstretched hands had he still cared about such things. The water-eroded ceiling bulged downward. Its best height was four feet. The first night of his imprisonment, with trembling fingers he broke a piece of its crumbling clay to find only hardened bricks.

His chains were gone, but without a tool, even the cleverest hands could not contrive an exit. His jailers had treble searched his body before throwing him, stripped and helpless, onto the cold flags.

At times he remembered lofty tree heights, the silvan forests of his homeland where open glades were carpeted by grassy swards and studded with wildflowers. Untouched by voice or tread of man, these unspoilt places gleamed like emerald heavens set with colored stars. The Malave's tinkling, crystalline streams sang their soft song by perfumed day and warm, cloaking night. He tried to concentrate, but with no warmth of sun or sound of rain to penetrate the shadowed chill of the dungeon, the reckoning of days escaped him. The cell was fronted by a heavy grate that could be raised like a portcullis only by a locking wheel placed outside arm's reach on the adjoining stone face.

Tallux raised his head. There it was again! A shriek and muffled thunk as if by a heavy blow. Yet no approaching step walked the stone flight down the landing to the pens. An occasional ruckus was not uncommon in the lower temple, but it seemed the place had emptied out, perhaps yesterday. For that he was glad; he had seen no other prisoners, and the sound of booted feet invariably brought his tormentors. Wood elves were a long-lived race. Even so, to resist the cruel ministrations of the half-orc and the demented dwarf, much of his vital energy was depleted.

The only other visitors had been sallow-skinned acolytes and the tall human bounty hunter who delivered savage beatings when his inquiries of Tallux's homeland and of the woodcraft of his people were invariably met with silence. The acolytes came thrice a week to deliver a modicum of half-rotten food and stale water. Tallux's once muscled form was grown thin. Bones had been broken and rebroken, then cruelly manipulated by the leering cleric, yet the forest elf's green eyes burned with the fires of an unvanquished spirit. In the long hours, he watched and waited.

A strangled cry sounded, much closer. A body came hurtling down the steps to land twisted and motionless. Tallux crept forward to see as best he could. An ominous shadow approached the grate, huge and menacing. Before it drew near, Tallux discerned its identity. How many times had he relived the fateful day he fell captive in the lonely wilderness north of the cleric's vale?

The devil-sired man halted outside the cell, drawing himself to his full height—seven feet of towering menace. Helm doffed, the craggy features were a play of darkness within shadow, and the eyes lit by a sinister orange light. The monstrous knight silently regarded Tallux, who took a slow step to the middle of the cell, prudent with expectation of violence yet without fear. Drannôk drew his great sword with a steely rasp and held it before him, expression inscrutable. Tallux held his breath. The sword flashed, and with two heavy blows, the iron crank and winding chain were cloven noisily to the floor.

The creature's impassive gaze returned to the elf. Three items dropped to the floor. Tallux regarded Strumfyr with its quiver and his woodsman's sword. For his own mysterious reasons, Drannôk had obviously kept them from the half-orc who had burned Tallux's other garments and possessions. The man-devil spun and was gone. Silence ruled the prison grotto. Tallux turned to regard the portcullis.

🧍 🧍 🧍

"Let us rest on that ledge," said Henlee. "My foot burns like red-hot pincers."

"Agreed," said Apieron. "We must choose our next descent. The way grows more steep after this, up and out."

Jamello was the last to reach the level from the slope they had quitted, jumping a sandstone boulder to join them. "At least we are atop that cursed vale. I liked it less than Procrius's moldy dungeons."

Henlee sat to undo the binding of his wrapped boot as Jamello and the woman drifted off separately. Apieron gazed out beyond the edge. The slow, picking pace had been rigorous and promised to be more so in the ascent, yet the green of lingering summer touched even such rugged terrain as this. Up and away westward, where lay their destination, he saw the deeper colors of foliage clinging to the Gorganj's distant slopes. A broken country, although clear of the Gate and the Haunted Vale. Soon they would tread hardwood forests where game was more abundant and less wary, then onto the swampy lands of Wyrnde where reposed the serene enclave of the winged ones.

He could almost smell the earthy sweet fragrance of the red, soft-barked giants that grew there. How he wished he was a mage and could whisk his friends on the wings of a spell, thus saving many a hard mile! Once in the elvin grotto, he might cleanse away for good the burning stench of the Hel pit.

Apieron remembered Sarc, and wondered what he would say when he stood again before Bragen in the Dell of Speaking. He closed his eyes, weary beyond any prior imaginings.

"So much death," he muttered. *"Lord of the nighted sea beyond the world's end, how did I ever trespass your dark waters?"* The wind sighed against the cliff, and the sun was warm on his face. He was answered as bloodcurdling yells sundered the still. Attackers were amongst them.

In an instant, the peace of the ledge was shattered by screaming, slashing figures that were immediately into the midst of the party. Apieron leapt for the girl, taking her arm. Within the dilated pupils of her eyes, he caught the glint of a menace behind him and wheeled to see an orc-man, evil faced and leering. An oddly fashioned cloak trailed behind the brutish shaman, and from his upraised hand spun a stream of conjured daggers toward Apieron's torso.

Apieron bore the female to the ground beneath him as the daggers glanced off his covering shield like a pelting hailstorm. Apieron leapt up, leaving the shield where it lay, that he might draw Leitus and charge.

Bizaz completed his second spell, then drew his crimson-hilted scimitar and set himself to receive the ranger's off-balanced onslaught. The air shimmered before him as Apieron closed the final yards, coalescing into a shaggy, hulking form. Apieron drew back in alarm. A familiar smell struck him, the musky odor that lingered in the horse cave!

The conjuring stole away the light around them such that its outline was blurred in shadow, although Apieron could see that it was some sort of quadruped. Vermillion, baleful eyes regarded him from beneath a matted brow, and its shoulder was even in height with his own.

Jamello sought to keep the bellowing charge of the bounty hunter at bay with prodding thrusts of a cane javelin acquired from the Gate riders, but these blows were skillfully deflected by the big man's broadsword and spiked shield. Jamello gave back, herded by the irresistible forest knight, and fell as the ground under his feet became the faux covering of a pit.

As he dropped, Jamello twisted the javelin sideways, grasping it in both hands. Its length fell across the opening, the flexible wood bowing in the middle albeit supporting his weight. The nimble warrior used his momentum and the rebound spring of the horse lance to swing under the shaft, tucking his legs to fly forward and upward to land at Slysbeth's feet as the javelin fell clattering into the trap. With an inarticulate cry, the bounty hunter launched a roundhouse blow meant to cleave the thief in twain.

Jamello ripped out his crypt blade in time to meet Slysbeth's transverse blow with a clang. The ancient brand held, but Jamello was spun completely around. He came back in, sword tip leading, and struck three quick jabs. Two were caught on the shield, the third arrested by the groin guard. This time the great blade came whistling straight down onto the crouching thief. His back to the mantrap, Jamello knew a blocking counter would simply be driven onto his head by the tremendous strength of the bounty hunter.

Slysbeth's sword crashed down, scratching a furrow into the hard soil as the thief rolled to the side to spring back up, his sword arm streaming blood where it had been grazed. Slysbeth freed his great sword with a jerk and bellowed through his helm, "Stand still, trickster! Fight like a man."

Every nerve tense, Apieron took a back step towards his shield, his eyes remaining locked on those of the beast. Its slavering mouth was lined with broken tusks that protruded over black gums, and its breath stank. The woman exclaimed in horror as the monstrosity charged. Apieron ducked to the ground as it struck. Momentum carried it past, trampling the earth-braced shield. The surface was dented, yet the buckler held.

Apieron regained his feet as the monster wheeled, ignoring the rescued girl who was chanting rapidly. It pawed the ground in preparation for a second charge. Apieron regarded Leitus, whose four-foot length seemed woefully inadequate. He fleetingly wished for a great axe of northmen or one of the long phalanx spears of the South, although with only one useful hand, he could wield neither. A mocking laugh drew his gaze to the cleric, whose sword swished idly. Apieron's eyes narrowed when he beheld the tawny, hair-feathered mantle cast over the shaman's shoulders.

A fanning purplish light spun from Dranol's hands. It bathed Henlee's head and torso in its radiance, halting the charging dwarf. Moustaches and beard working in frenzy, Henlee stood otherwise helpless. He let shield and Maul dangle uselessly. Palms down, the magic-user lowered his hands, pushing his spell-glow lower to encompass the dwarf entire.

While Henlee was so encumbered, Deuce's studded club cracked against Henlee's neck and back. Henlee kicked a spray of gravel into Dranol's face and tucked forward to tumble into the mage and managed to punch him under the chin with Maul's haft. Dranol collapsed in a fluttering heap, his eyes staring at nothing. Deuce drew his long knife and charged, yet back pedaled to a skidding stop when Henlee bounded up to face him.

The beleaguered dwarf was a terrible sight to behold as he stood panting, the jagged rents in his armor revealing scars and new cuts that crisscrossed the bulging muscles of his torso. His face, burned and black with rage, was lit with a killing light.

"Get you gone, Lost One," said he in dwarvish. "Lest I bind you and take you before the Seat of Law under pitiless Uxellodoum." Nothing the broad-shouldered mountain dwarf might have said could have produced greater effect. Worse than the fear of death, was the threat of judgment by the grim chieftains of the tribes Deuce had so grievously betrayed. The renegade dwarf took a backward step, feinted with his knife, then spun to scamper up the trail, disappearing noisily into the bramble that lined the path.

The summoned beast stalked Apieron, and he knew it had learned. In its swinish eyes lurked an intelligence that would not again charge blindly over the shield. Instead, it would accept the sting of the sword in order to stamp and mangle the man into red ruin.

A gaily-colored bird passed directly in front of the beast's face, flapping and chirping noisily before its eyes. The creature aimed a biting snap at the bird and turned to reacquire Apieron for its charge. Bizaz scowled at the woman and screamed at Dranol.

"Get up, you idiot!"

Dazed, the gangly mage struggled to his feet and stared stupidly at the strange tableau. The bird came bobbing and screeching back at the beast. Its drooling maw lunged but missed again the agile bird, which ran right under its belly. The abomination bellowed and wheeled to charge after the clamorous bird. The girl clapped her hands delightedly as the bullish monster went crashing onto the slopes after her enchanted hen.

Bizaz nodded to Dranol, who had snuck to within ten feet of the girl and drawn a smoky piece of quartz from his robe. He pointed the item at her back. From it sprung a fuming cloud of fog acid. She leapt into the air and gracefully flew to land in the nearest tree. Bizaz's eyes bulged as the spray headed straight toward him. He dove to the side, yet it caught his trailing legs and feet, burning holes in his leggings.

Dranol ignored Bizaz's curses and stood, apparently pondering how best to attack the woman who was now perched twenty feet above. Occasional bellows and thrashings in the bracken could be heard as the maddened creature pursued her conjured bird.

Bizaz scrambled and rolled and cut away the last of his smoking leg garments. "I'm going to kill you, Dranol. Slowly."

The tall mage shrugged and cast a second acid spray to shower the woman's perch and most of the tree as well. She smiled mockingly and waved her hand with a subtle motion. Dranol frowned at her disrespect then gasped as a twisted cord dropped over his head and drew tight against his neck.

"It's not nice to pick on ladies," growled Apieron in his ear.

Jamello lunged from his fencer's stance and scored several quick hits, yet was unable to find vulnerability in Slysbeth's armor. Slysbeth feinted with his sword and shield-slammed the thief. Jamello rolled with the blow's momentum and came to his feet, then dropped to one knee in the aftershock. His arm and shoulder felt lifeless, and two of the shield's spikes had dug furrows in his shoulder and chest. In a daze, he hoped they weren't poisoned.

Slysbeth laughed triumphantly and waded forward, aiming a bone-breaking kick at the thief's chin. The heavy boot rushed forward … and was slapped aside as if by a great steel hand. Henlee's cleverly thrown shield bounced aside with a clang to vibrate a moment on the dirt.

The shuffling dwarf came on, Maul gripped in both hands. He taunted the tall knight, "An' who would want to fight like a *man*?"

Maul's sharp edge cracked into the nosepiece of Slysbeth's helm, driving the bounty hunter to his knees as blood started from under the cheek guards. The big man's targe angled low in poor position to parry another strike. "Now, treacherous dog," said Henlee. "What say you to the valor of *dwarves*?"

The bounty hunter's left hand twitched within the shield. Shakily his right made as if to raise his notched sword in semblance of defense. It fell open, dropping the hilts to the bloody soil. The broken helm raised itself to regard the dwarf. Slysbeth took a moment to gasp for air. In a voice at first strained yet with gathering strength, he replied, "It seems thou hast broken my teeth, dwarf. I needs must salute thy valor." He stretched both arms out as if in surrender, the shield angled upward. "But of thy wisdom?"

Henlee glimpsed a movement within the buckler's concave surface. A barbed dart arrowed from a cleverly concealed crossbow. It caught the dwarf's thigh as he attempted a dodging hop and instead tripped over a thorny vine. As soon as the device was fired, Slysbeth rolled in the opposite direction to the edge of the outcrop and right over. Tumbling to his feet some distance down, he plunged pell-mell up the close thickets growing there.

Henlee cursed aloud when he saw the quarrel fleshed to its tail right through the chain mesh that covered his thick leg. Glancing about, the dwarf rose painfully and used Maul as a stave to hobble to Jamello who groggily regained his feet.

"I'll wager that shit-head coated the barb with something foul. It burns like seven angry devils."

Dranol's hands pulled futilely at the line, then vainly against Apieron's corded forearm, the spell-user's face turning ashen as he slid into unconsciousness. Bizaz cursed as only an orc could. To see Dranol discomfited did not displease him, but this ambush was getting out of hand! He glared when he beheld the dark she-witch levitate to the ranger, quite unharmed, although her tree was largely denuded and smoking from the acid spray.

The loss of the boar wight had been a sore blow. Now it was time to prepare a final summoning, one to ensure the outcome of this battle and doom the souls of these trespassers. Mumbling under his breath, Bizaz bent quickly to sketch a diagram in the dirt with his sword. It bubbled behind the blade's tip. He increased the strength of his chant as he completed a figure that coiled and twisted like a thing awakened. With gloating triumph, he stood to regard the pathetic humans and their pet dwarf. Only now did they stare in alarm.

The temperature of the glade dropped as an oily mist congealed within the magic circuit. The cleric cocked back his head to laugh; it became a scream as a slender arrow stood suddenly from his eye, thick gobbets of blood welling from the gruesome wound.

Tallux stood at the clearing's edge. He swayed, yet his emerald eyes were clear as he deliberately notched another arrow. Both half-orc and elvin scout knew that the second missile would carry the freight of death. There was nowhere the shaman could hide from the hand and bow that had not missed in a hundred years.

With a strangled cry, Bizaz leapt into his summoning and disappeared. Tallux's arrow sped into its center and also winked away. The runes flared white, then out of existence. A faint breeze dispersed the spell fog to leave the area as if nothing untoward had ever been.

Tallux turned and sped past Henlee and Jamello, down into the ravine and up after Slysbeth. "Hey, elf!" Henlee shouted after him, but he was gone. Dwarf and thief approached Apieron, who was bent over the unconscious mage. They were joined by the girl, who combed bits of twig and leaf from her hair with her fingers.

"My thanks, Lady," said Apieron, bowing low. "But for your device, that foul were-beast would have beset me sore."

"So, an illusionist," harrumphed Jamello as he regarded the female. She ignored him. He made shift to secure the comatose spellweaver. With stray bits of tack and strips cut from the mage's own robes, Jamello bound him as could only a thief of Bestrand, paying special attention to the hands, that they might not weave even the simplest casting. He thoroughly searched the body, and there soon emerged a small pile of items, some arcane, some ordinary, all of little value.

"Mighty wizard!" scoffed Jamello. "More like a thieving mountebank or circus flunkie turned out for his perversions."

Jamello shoved the pile over to Henlee, who promptly ground them into the dirt with his boot. The wizard's ill-favored features stirred slightly at a nudge of Henlee's toe in his ribs. "Donkey killer!" growled the dwarf. He stared for a moment at their unheeding captive, then stalked off. Dranol began to drool.

MYLENSCARP RANGE

Woobora observed the long line of Ilycrium's army as it wound along the overgrown wainroad of the Mylenscarp. Apparently, traitors amongst the Seod guided them hence, and the Sea King's son no doubt meant to swell his ranks with fighters gathered from the tough mountain clans. Should the Westrons follow the ancient caravan track, 'twould be excellent defense from the many prying eyes of Kör. Almost.

Of old and sturdy stock were the folk of Seod. It was they in bygone times who made the road under truce of commerce. Each village, a sparsely settled outpost in an unsettled country, had contributed to the byway within its borders. Woobora recollected the days when chieftains reckoned strength by numbers of tribal sons, for every man fought.

Older still was a sect of priests, keepers of an ancient order— as gods themselves to primitives who needed bright fire and dark spells to ward against fell beasts and monster kind. Unggirat, the Black Druid he had been then, now only Woobora.

He touched the tumbledown altar. Blackened with age and fire and blood, it was slick beneath his fingers, and the coppery taint of more recent sacrifice lingered. Busy lowland farmers scarcely remarked at strange calls in lonely places, or hunters' tales of stolen kills. At times might a youth go missing and searchers abandon hope when tracks of unshod feet intersected their quarry, soon lost in highland wilds.

Air whistled past Woobora's thin and mirthless lips. *Aiee ... standing hither, well he recalled the days of power!* Then had come the northern king with his steel companies and gods of war and science. How the chanting tribes had fallen in red butchery to the iron men of the grandsire of the whelp who now set camp on Bladenfex! New masters had granted their vanquished foes amnesty, and the once proud descendants of the conquered were now grown soft. 'Civilized', just thinking the word hurt Woobora's mind. He paused to listen. Wind and stone spoke of many clansmen marching to serve the steel king in defense of their new country.

Woobora felt the years wash over him like water over stone, and gathered his dusky wraps about him, but not for the cold, his woaded skin had been rescarred many times with the sigils of power. Sun or cold, rain and frost were as nothing to he, last lord of a race more ancient than any hereabouts. Now scarce hundreds numbered his followers.

Woobora laughed. What were numbers to one whose feet walked in daylight yet could not be marked by common men? He watched the settling of the army around the Bladenfex, where camp marshals ordered manned pickets of wood and piled rock as their baggage train was arranged within the defensive enclosure. Fools! Soon their great Westron city would be stricken. Only yester eve had he blown the Horn of Druids. Its gray oak withered in the soundless blast, yet its note reverberated in empty places, and a shadow passed over forgotten battlegrounds and barrow fells.

The sounding of the horn had parched Woobora's mouth, and squatting before a subterranean cataract, he tasted its black water. There had unfolded a mighty vision of its twisting tree-root course far and deep. In the east, men worshipped in a trickling place nigh a lightless cavern. There was prisoned Grazmesnil, eldest son of She Who Dreams. Soon he, Unggirat the ancient, would make mighty sacrifice to that One. Seven times a thousand marched with the grandson of the man who had cast down the temple stones of hill priests and hounded black druids from the Mylenscarps. These would be his gifting to the *She!*

The day waned, and the time of summons grew nigh. Afternoon's sky took on the aspect of molten glass—or the burnings of Hel. Soon the demon prince of Kör would reign over the long vale to the Western Sea, and the echoing hills return to their former state. Then would he lead a purging to quench the thirsty altars of revenge. Those tribal sons of blood comingled with that of Wgend conquerors would not be spared the knife.

Woobora stepped behind a crooked menhir. He waved his hand, muttering words that groaned like a tree's heart that dies in winter, and a low doorway appeared in the stone. Woobora wheezed with pleasure. There and yet not seen, so difficult an idea for these new men, strong only when they understood a thing. He descended deep into the tor.

The frozen air was faintly lit, and serpentine script set in the strata writhed at his intrusion. He ignored the wards. *Had he not placed them with his own hand nigh a century gone?* Before him was a nighted recess in which reposed the mouldered remains of a mountain king. Woobora swept them rudely aside to withdraw from the blackness an unpolished jar. Eagerly he turned it about, pleased that no crack marred its surface. Gathering it up, he wended his way back to the hill's top.

Dusk approached. Woobora regarded Candor's army. Cooking fires were lit in pits, Western captains apparently deeming they were miles from any organized force of their enemies. Thus far they had whetted swords on only a few hapless bands of orcs and the occasional beast maddened by the advent of war.

Woobora glared down with hatred. So much the better the fools bivouacked nearby. He strengthened wards that concealed his own activities and cracked the jar with a stick. A priceless hoard of vermillion Hel stones poured fourth to lie like clotted blood on the greensward. Giving no thought to their material value, Woobora carefully arranged them into a vaguely wing-like shape, and the power imbued in the gems rose in waves like heat on his face.

In the darkness, an eye snapped open. Large as a war shield, its surface glimmered like a prisoned meteor. The summons was heard. From the crags of Pleven Deep rose a wraith of monstrous form. Like a shadow across the moon, it folded benighted pinions to speed westward.

WINDHOVER

Melónie's favorite chair was not the one, tall and formal, required for petitions and high feasts. Hers was rather low to the ground and with a dangling brocade. The hall was warmed by the great hearth and, closer to hand, a small brazier that smelled of cedar and myrrh. Her girls had been busy putting up her garden's yield for the coming winter, and heated sugars or vinegar topped the provender into jars before the sealing of heavy lids with wax. These were placed in cool cellars, and would keep the household in greenstuffs and fruits even though rheumy village elders foretold an unusually harsh winter.

Winter. Such an odd word, as was so much in this land. After her first, Melónie deemed all living things had died forever. She was then amazed by the ferocity of spring's newly born life that raced as if to make up for lost time.

Melónie pushed aside her meal and took up the shawl she had begun for Apieron. A fine base of colored wool and silk was first to take the dweomer she wound into the cloth with chant and finger, spells of comfort, warmth or cooling as needed, with ever-present hints of home and love. The work had taken a life of its own. Countless times she left it, done for the day, and yet returned to pour more of herself into its making. Potent indeed! She touched her belly. When her lord returned, there were many gifts she had for him.

The weave dropped from Melónie's fingers, tonight she could do no more. It had been a long day. The children were supped and abed, and her own duties were done. How her lord's absence multiplied these!

Melónie sought her favorite place. In a room of the tower where she and Apieron had their private rooms, a little altar awaited. Here she was wont to light a votive and say a prayer for his safety and return. Although he was a high lord of a warlike people, she bethought herself of the mundane things that so endeared him to her. She loved the way he danced the native steps of his ancestors, themselves strangers in this strange northern land. She smiled at the way his eyes crinkled at the corners when he laughed. *Old man!* And how those gray eyes became deep wells when he held her, drinking in her every nuance such that she felt he would draw out her very soul.

A wisp of a breeze lifted the embroidered hangings of a window, and she smelled jasmine and honeysuckle from her garden. The flame of her votive bent and swayed, then burned more brightly. She placed upon the altar the wrap she made for him to better invoke his presence, and prayed to her gods and to his ancestors for his safety. It was the custom of her people to name the gods of one's enemies as well, that they show mercy and restraint. Tonight she invoked them not, nor would she ever do so!

"Wherever thou art, Apieron, I send to thee blessings sped by the swift-footed messenger of Wisdom. Look with favor upon my prayer. And, Cryse, whisper words of love and comfort unto my husband, who suffers in a land beyond knowing ..."

Chapter 34

The Haunted Vale

"Warlord," began the woman, "but for you I remain in darkness."

Apieron concentrated, for it seemed spoken words were yet unfamiliar to her mouth. She dropped to one knee and pressed her lips to his hand, her lustrous hair falling over his gauntlets.

"Bow not to me."

He raised her with great gentleness. "You shall return to Windhover as an equal, not a supplicant, where Melónie will speed your recovery. Indeed, we shall all take our leisure. It is the closest redoubt under banner of the Candor kings. There we must hear news and—" Something caught the corner of Apieron's eye. He wheeled.

"Tallux!"

Apieron ran to greet the elvin scout and winced at the pain in his reopened wound. "Blessed be the heavenly gods!"

The elf staggered to them and made to bow but stumbled and fell forward. Jamello proffered a flask of water. Before them rose the grim figure of a wood elf, clad in a tunic hastily fashioned of torn cloth tied at the waist. His hair was long and tangled. Worse were his limbs, which were discolored and swollen in places. They shook.

If Henlee was outraged by the ambush, what he and the others did not vocalize was their horror at the changes wrought on the features of the elf. The dwarf had seen him aforetime, usually in the company of Apieron, who knew him well. Wood elves of the Malave oft served as auxiliary to the King's Scouts, and even Jamello had heard many tales of him. Howsoever they knew him, the wounds put upon Tallux by starvation and torture were overshadowed by the haunted look on his once clear visage. Even thus, as he gazed on them, his verdant eyes sparkled with life returned. The woman stood to the side.

"Why came you hither, Tallux?" said Apieron. "Surely the King or your own people sore miss you in these evil days."

Tallux pulled himself erect and put aside their supporting hands. He locked Apieron's eyes with his emerald gaze. "I came for you, Apieron, son of Farsinger. I bear grave news. The King is dead. Many nobles plot against you."

Apieron swallowed past a painful tightening in his throat. "True friend, you are hurt. We will speak of these things later."

"Nay," said Tallux, "my strength returns. To be under blessed sun heals me more swiftly than thy ministrations." He nodded grimly at the prostrate figure of the fallen mage. "Such as they hurt me less than my fear for you these long months. My mission was failed, and you lost beyond the unholy gate. My heart sings to see you return into the light."

"Months?" husked Jamello.

Tallux eyes strayed over their battered forms, lingering on the bolt that protruded from Henlee's thigh mesh, his lamed foot, and finally Apieron's shoulder that dangled limp and lifeless. "A sorry lot we are," agreed Henlee, reading the elf's thought in a glance.

"Better now," said Apieron.

"Your wounds also will mend, I deem," said Tallux. "I see more pain in thine eyes than in thy limbs. Where is the lord Xephard? We heard tale in the capital he traveled with you. So much for the gossip of Sway!"

"He did," mumbled Henlee.

"Xephard Brighthelm," said Apieron slowly, "fell beyond—" For a space, no one spoke. Deep and mournful, a wind soughed through treetops.

"He bore a great name," said Tallux at last, "and great I know will be the story of his falling. Alas, that I am too weak to hear it in full."

Exhausted by their trials, the companions set camp on the shelf under the midday sun. Jamello discovered a slipping stream nestled in the base of the ravine. The weather was mild, and with clean water they cared for their many hurts as best they might. Without searching far beyond the edges of the clearing, Jamello, with Apieron's guidance, gathered a goodly amount of edible rushes and cabbage into a pouch fashioned from the cloak of their captive mage.

"Lawn clippings," spake Henlee through a clumsy mouthful of the stuff. He shook his burned, half-shorn beard mournfully. "We have come to this."

Tallux fell to with a gusto of the heartiest trencherman among King Bardhest Redhand's house thanes, or so said Henlee. Soon done with his meal and fearing a poison from his embedded dart, the dwarf insisted a fire be made. He beckoned Jamello to cauterize his wound once the offending barb was cut free.

Jamello watched the edges of his kindjal take on a yellow hue in the coals, the best the little fire could do to fine-tempered steel. He was fearful of the dwarf's reaction when he touched the searing metal to the wound. Then a secret anticipation came to him. How the dwarf had belittled and abused him!

Mighty warrior, sniffed he, *we shall see.*

With a nod, Henlee acknowledged Apieron's lame shoulder and Tallux's shaking hands, cutting the quarrel loose himself and squeezing the wound to bleed a moment before beckoning Jamello forward. Jamello pressed the jambiya deep into the gash, eliciting the merest grunt from Henlee. When it no longer smoked, he withdrew the crusted tip and bound Henlee's thigh with greatest care, and in doing so discovered that he felt neither fear nor pleasure, only concern for a comrade, perhaps a friend. Whether the arrow's poison was weak or merely overcome by the dwarf's natural vitality, the wound caused no lasting harm aside from an unusually protracted burning. Similarly, Apieron's chest and arm were attended to by Tallux, although the wood elf oft had to stop and rest during his ministrations.

"That the lung was spared is a blessing of the Healer, Apieron, but the proper care for this grave wound has not happened. I fear in time it will suppurate."

When Apieron's right arm and torso were inspected, they saw many crimson bruises left by the trampling beast, yet no bones were broken. In turn, the lacerations dealt Jamello by Slysbeth were examined, yet these proved superficial and troubled him little. Seeming to have no skill or knowledge of these tasks, the woman merely observed them quietly from the edge of the camp. The fight over, she was again withdrawn and reticent to speak.

"What of me?" whined a voice from near the stricken tree. After a brief interlude of coughing, it continued. "Do any of you barbarian oafs know who I am? It is *I*, Dranol Eserhaven! The mighty—"

"What of thy mouth packing?" interjected Jamello, incredulous.

"I swallowed it," spat Dranol. "Best for you—"

"Silence, dog!" thundered Henlee. "Best for *you* to keep thy lying tongue in your head." Henlee rose and advanced toward their captive. "And no tricks," he boomed, "or I'll cut it out."

The conjurer fell quiescent until the dwarf's broad back was turned, at which point he twisted and struggled against his bonds a long moment before becoming exhausted and merely glaring at the others. Jamello laughed grimly, for had he not secured the mage with clever, undefeatable knots taught only by thief masters in the seafaring city of Bestrand?

Cowed by the fearsome dwarf and the unhappy condition in which he found himself, the sorcerer soon gave up all signs of resistance, cringing in fear when any member of the party made to approach. The woman raised herself and wandered the fringes of the clearing. Henlee returned to front the others.

"Where is this rat's nest?" he demanded of Tallux. "We should hie there and stamp it out. I'll wager Redhand's gold that antlered warrior is skulking there now."

Jamello responded, "Wounded though they were, those villains made ample haste. I doubt *I* could catch them up before they reach their redoubt."

"I feel so as well," said Apieron. "We are in sore need of rest and healing, even if it be only that of a single night."

"You shall rest better when that bug-eyed priest and his slaves are good and killed," growled Henlee.

Tallux spoke quietly. "I have been to his living tomb. Once there, the orcish dwimmerlord can hold out against many times our number." Tallux paused. "I do not believe Bizaz, for that is his name, created that noisome crypt. It is much older than he."

Apieron mustered the energy to speak, "Most like he crept in after the Starfall, to weave his spider's threads in the vale."

"Walk warily when we return you to your own, Apieron." Henlee waved one hairy hand vaguely south by east in the direction of the Duskbridge. "This entire land has grown foul with the taint of yonder gate." Henlee snapped his fingers. "Remember the swamp tomb, where the thief got his blade?"

Tallux gave heed while Jamello recounted their adventures into the Wyrnde and subsequent sojourn in the hidden forest of the winged elves. He told of the sunken city that lay in the bog, and of the ancient spirit of evil they had found there, undiminished down the ages.

Apieron spoke slowly. "We saw others, such as the drowned prince in our escape from the abyss. Godlings, sorcerers, or warrior-kings, who can say? I feel there are many more such as he."

"On *both* sides of the Black Gate," added Henlee in grim tones.

"And think of Procrius, the most powerful man in Bestrand," said Jamello, "who keeps a lair of filthy Sadôk and traffics with demons. I have seen it."

Tallux shook his head sadly. "Events are worse than you know. I came bearing news of the King's death, slain by a flying imp of Hel." Apieron dipped his head in mournful respect, at last acknowledging the tidings Tallux had borne.

"He was a brave warrior and a just king," intoned Henlee. Even Jamello, outlaw and thief, was hard beset by the news. The old king had been a constant in their lives, a symbol of order and justice, and like all, such was never truly appreciated until gone.

Tallux continued, "I came also to tell you that your enemies live not all in darkness. Many walk the lighted streets of Sway, and are counted among the servants and nobles of your kingdom."

"Rivals of your father," stated Henlee. The dwarf smacked fist into palm. "Jealous humans."

"I have dwelt among these men; they are fearful of what is strange to them. Certainly the Farsinger and any such as I." Tallux touched his breast. "But you, Apieron, are a rival for the affections of their prince and thus a threat to their power, which for a baron of Ilycrium is as mighty as that of many a foreign king. Beware."

"I will name them," scowled Henlee. "Wulfstane and his pup Buthard, our friend has mentioned them before."

Tallux nodded. "And others."

Apieron took the elf's hand and grasped it. "For what you have endured, my benisons could never be enough."

Tallux matched the intensity of Apieron's gaze. "That is why, Apieron, it *is* enough. And at least one thing is made clear. My people share many a tale of our brethren, the winged people, but none ever knew where they dwelt, for they left the Northlands when the great forests were young. I am glad our path will take us among them."

"Priorities!" scolded Henlee. "The thought of those churls who bushwhacked us burns me. Such backstabbers will only recover to waylay the next decent folk who pass this way."

"Who passes this way?" said Jamello.

"More like they prey upon their own sort," said Apieron. "Besides, you forget their swinish guardian. He gave me these!" Apieron indicated his livid bruises. "I marked his trampling passage over yonder hillock away south."

That notion settled all arguments, and the cooking fire was stoked high, for dusk was upon them. The woman wandered back into camp and sat at the edge of the flickering light. "Stray not, lady," admonished Apieron. "Whilst it seems we have routed our foes, this is not the king's land. We have traveled this vale before. Who knows what phantom that orcling he-witch might send after us in the night?" Tallux cast a questioning glance toward the woman who sat alert and silent as always, her knees tucked against her chest, arms around her legs.

"Eafora," said Apieron. "At least that is what we have named her until she can remember her own. Henlee calls her Scipflot, for we found her in darkness, captive mayhap, of the fell knight who slew Xephard. She appears merely a lass of twenty, yet I fear she was lost there a great while." Apieron turned to Jamello. "See how the season has passed—though we left Windhover short weeks ago?"

If the woman knew they spoke of her, she gave no sign, darkly beautiful in the twilight as she followed every word of Apieron's mouth with her eyes. He wondered how much of their speech she understood. Certainly her own, rare words had been stilted and archaic. "Despite the hurts we have suffered, I also grieve for her. *Forsaken*," Apieron whispered.

Night covered the barrens. At length Apieron spoke again. "After Windhover, I will take her to Hyllae. Perhaps Perpetua can aid her. There I must go anyway." He lifted Leitus, and the sweep of its blade glittered like liquid silver. As perfect as the sword was, it felt foreign to his hand. Apieron knew there was only one to whom it belonged, and he was no more. "I go to see Isolde, spear maiden, flower of the valley, betrothed of Xephard Brighthelm. I go to take her *this*." He plunged the length of the blade into the earth until only the hilts showed.

After a time, Jamello volunteered for the first watch. "Your cheery talk has quite upset my stomach, and after such a glorious dinner! I'll see if our prisoner enjoys his accommodations." The others composed themselves for rest, but bounded up at Jamello's hoarse cry and ran to where the thief stood over the mage, who lay stretched out under the tree. Across his throat an ugly gash smiled obscenely as if torn by a fantastically sharp claw.

"Ware all," growled the dwarf. "Mayhaps it be a ruse. If some ill has befallen this coward, surely he would have cried out."

"Nay, he is dead," said Apieron quietly. "I have become an expert."

"This is a very evil land," remarked Tallux. "No doubt every tree or bird looks wonderful to those who have journeyed the Everdark, but this place bears a taint, worse so for me. I too will not rest until we are forever gone."

Two days' toil west and a day angling south skirted the remainder of the Haunted Vale. The dry country had grown cool, and on the fourth morning from the ambush, the companions rose and gazed away westward onto falling lands where leagues distant lay the hidden enclave of the winged ones. They heard a baying sound in the broken trees behind, loud and approaching swiftly. Hands strayed to weapons.

A shadow of a smile came to Tallux's face, the first they had seen. He gave a shout and leapt toward the tree line, yet faster than he, a gray shape hurtled to him. It was a short-haired hound, slightly less tall than the shaggy wolfhounds of men, yet broader of shoulder, paw, and head, and more swift than any dog they had seen. Apieron laughed with delight, for he knew the beast well.

"Sut Swifthound!"

"Lo, he comes not alone!" cried Jamello. A dozen paces trailing the war dog, a second beast materialized from the thorny foliage and entered their camp.

"Bump?" choked Henlee. The dwarf hobbled forward and threw his arms around his burro's bristly neck. Bump chewed on his beard, then wheeled and grimaced at Jamello, who had approached and stopped in his tracks, instead turning to join Apieron and Tallux.

Sut and Tallux were face to face, sharing a silent look. The dog's yellow eyes burned like lamps. "Long has been your search," murmured Tallux. "Now you have found me."

"So what be the story of your dog, Master?" asked Henlee. "It seems he and Bump have an understanding betwixt them."

"See?" said Apieron. "The spell weave of that foul orc defeated even Sut, the finest tracker known to elf or man."

"No doubt for the best," said Tallux. "Sut would have harassed the lair until he was slain. See how he hast remained whilst spring turned to fall?"

"An' found ol' Bump," said Henlee. "Is it true you've finally gotten a friend?" He gave the burro's head a playful shake. "Never before has that happened!" Bump shot him a rolling look.

"Watch your attitude! You should have met us east of the vale and saved many a long mile on my lame foot." The dwarf hopped back, narrowly avoiding a kick aimed at the same wounded member.

Apieron laughed. "I think Bump would have been fine without the help of the war dog."

"Sut is a forest hound, a Gelyfin," said Tallux. "My people bred this species so long ago that none remember a time when they dwelled not with us." The companions regarded the hound's mighty stature and the quick, sure economy of his every movement.

Ignoring their attentions, Sut approached Bump, who wheeled at some indiscernible clue, for the dog's tread was entirely silent. Bump bared his long teeth as if to bite, then to the surprise of all, pursed his whiskered lips to briefly touch the dog's muzzle. Seemingly satisfied the burro was in good fettle, Sut moved off a short distance to where he could view the camp entire. He crouched down, lowering his massive head atop crossed forepaws. Under his crinkled brow, his eyes glowed with the golden light of the sun. Tallux continued, "I too am glad Sut has gained such a companion. He is as unique among the Gelyfin, as his kin are apart from other dogs. He was the sole get of his mother, Cinghere, herself a champion.

"Deep in the hidden forest lies a verdant gloaming where is the burial place of Cinghere the Fair, and where the ferns glow emerald and gold. Even our people go rarely thither." Tallux paused a moment, and his eyes held a distant cast. "I think p'raps the energy of her body would have birthed a litter of four or six but was consumed in the creation of one such as Sut. He knows the secret of each plant and animal of the forest. Never again under light of sun or moon shall we be sundered."

There was a space of quietude that followed Tallux's words, broken at last by Henlee. "Aye, elf," he said quietly, "I believe you."

Chapter 35

The Mylenscarp Range

Grazmesnil's dream and those of his two brethren flew low over the hills of Ulard. Coming with the dusk, their approach was unmarked until they burst over the army's palisade with a roaring that a hundred screaming elephants could not match. The blast of their breath simply melted the outer pickets, and those farther in pawed in agony at smoking tatters of rent skin and fused garments as Grazmesnil rolled with glee.

Draft animals surged in madness against their pens, and soldiers behaved in much the same mien. Surprise and the magnitude of destruction overwhelmed the courage of rural levies and tribesman, and when added to the dragon fear, it was simply too much. Whole companies scattered as leaves blown before the tempest.

The three wraith dragons rose from the shattered perimeter to pursue fleeing animals and men to the tree line as great maws and talons materialized to snatch men up, breaking their soft bodies or gulping them whole. Chaos likewise ruled the camp's center, where Trakhner bellowed for information, and his knights made shift to don armor while grooms fought plunging destriers.

In moments, Gault was armed, adjusting a metal cap over his coif as he ran to see Trakhner organize a phalanx of archers at the base of the tor. Conrad ambled past, in his hands was a bow of yew. Renault wheeled his mighty charger to and fro, exhorting the mounted knights to battle, although they milled about without purpose, having no foe to engage.

Gault felt his heart nearly burst in his chest. His fine army, the men who had put faith in him, was dying on the slopes of the Scaelp. Many had fled, and an equal number lay stricken in the broken encampment. The night was not yet full, and scattered fires lit the tableau with garish light. Gault felt a touch on his arm. Seamus was there. The man's thick, pointing finger indicated a remarkable scene. Betwixt the outer perimeter and the forest occurred a strange duel. Spiraling orbs of yellow and white were lifted in succession, apparently from Tertullion's upraised staff toward three dragon wraiths, clots of blackness against the deepening sky. Less frequent volleys of glowing purple leapt up from a stone cairn not far distant from the mage.

"Erasmus also fights," rumbled Seamus.

The wraiths countered. Circling like carrion birds, they bellowed roiling clouds that met mage-spells with barking reports and flashing lights that devastated the surrounding flora and obscured the spell duel from view.

Tertullion and Erasmus had been riding. As evening came, the twain walked their mounts, man and beast alike eager for rest and sup.

"Master?" asked Erasmus. He nodded toward the graying east. They beheld three blurred forms in the air, small but moving with swift purpose. Erasmus's voice held a note of tense apprehension. "Yon fell birds cast shadows in my mind greater than any creature of this world."

At the pause, their horses had stood silent, heads lowered. Neighing wildly, they now began to plunge. "Let them go!" shouted Tertullion, stripping them of bridle and saddle before the frantic ponies bolted for the thin tree line. Tertullion glanced at the sky. "So it is true," he murmured, "the Abomination lingered past the breaking of the earth." Eyes closed, he swayed with a weight of fatigue beyond even his long years.

"Sir?" asked Erasmus. "What shall we do?"

Tertullion turned to Erasmus, hands clenched white on his crooked stave. When they opened, his dark eyes glimmered with scintillant lights. "This young land will *not* wither. Our prince and his hope shall not die. Come, Apprentice. Gird thyself for battle."

The last of the wraith dragons wheeled away in wrath, having wasted effort in confrontation with the magnus rather than harrying helpless prey below. Erasmus rushed to Tertullion, who staggered to one knee, his robes charred along the back, and the smell of burned flesh was on him. The mageling's nut-brown face was wrought with grief.

"Master, I—"

"I command you, wizard's pupil," said Tertullion, "seek those who flee. Gather them in the night, hearten the tribals and peasant soldiers."

"But my spells are nearly spent. You—you need healing." The young man's words faltered.

When Tertullion replied, it was as a kindly father to his son. "You have your rank and your wit. The soldiery will obey you." He looked to the darkling sky where so much ruin had befallen them. "The greatest of the three hies to smite the Prince. There I must go."

"What of your wounds?" pleaded Erasmus.

"Go, now!" thundered Tertullion. Seeing his apprentice stumble into the night, Tertullion gathered himself, moving with a speed he had not in decades, to the apex of the hill where the deep shouts of men and the roaring of the dragon already echoed down the slope.

"My lord," shouted Renault from atop his warhorse. The stallion's eyes rolled with fright, but he obeyed his master, steadfast in his traces. "We have not the weapons to assail this accursed worm whilst he floats 'bove us. If he tires and lights as the lore-masters say, my cavalry will make bold to slay or drive him from the field."

Grazmesnil, greatest of the three, weaved up the Scaelp. Ballistas fired sluggishly, their bolts looping well below the wraith's course. Tribal bowmen shot sporadically with their horse bows while western archers shouted as they loosed clothyard shafts every third second, although with sparse effect against the ephemeral target.

Cursing, Gault snatched up a great bow from the wreckage of his tent. It was an heirloom of his father's. A priest of the Archer God had blessed it, and inscribed on its helve was a sigil of permanency. He knocked a long shaft with a wickedly barbed head and methodically shot the mighty wyvern in its arched neck. The arrow passed cleanly through the blurred margin of the beast, which shuddered slightly in flight although quickly resumed its glide. The great head swiveled and fixed him with a malevolent glare before fading into covering darkness.

"The beast has marked thee, Prince," called Renault. "Let us seek a new position before his circuit brings him round to expend his full wrath on thee."

That was Grazmesnil's exact thought as he wheeled over the camp. The barbarian king's dart stung his pride more than his form. He willed it to greater speed. Time enough for a grand, chasing hunt of the masses once the steel prince was dead and his knights broken. The biting pain of his wound faded to a dull ache within Grazmesnil's outstretched neck. Gathering his corrosive breath, he smiled inwardly at the thought of expending its full blast on the beetle-shelled man whose hand had shot the barb, and doubted even the manling's iron casing would be left. *P'raps he might dissolve the standing stones and the hill's top as well!*

The Seod milled about. Some mumbled prayers for kin before covering their dead where they lay with their shaggy cloaks, others sought scanty cover behind boulders and downed ponies to send ragged volleys at every flying shadow. Many stood their horses and gazed uncertainly at the banner of the Prince that yet surmounted its hill.

"Many will die if we leave the winged devil to his butchery unmolested," said Gault. The knights of his household shifted nervously, gripping swords and long spears.

"There!" shouted a scout. "It returns." All heads turned. In the night, the mighty wraith was as a black crow in the distance.

"Highness," pleaded Renault, "leave swiftly. I will hold with the peers. We will launch a cloud of javelins that, gods willing, might mask thy departure. Seamus, guide him." The stolid armsman ignored the imprecations of Gault's champion and looked only to his prince.

"Your blade, Prince. Show me Ilus!"

They turned to find Tertullion at Gault's side. His body bore grave wounds, yet his face was quickened with a soul animation such that none could refuse him. Gault drew the brand as the magnus explained, "My spells are unwrought by the beast's aura ere they reach their mark, a physical weapon strikes but does no damage."

"Mage," grated Renault, "if you're going to save us and not author a book, make haste." The dragon was now the size of an eagle.

"To fight a dream, so must you be!" shouted Tertullion. He smote the sword with his staff. To those present, it seemed a wave of rippling light passed from the gnarled stave into the ancient brand. Gault swooned, borne gently to the ground by Seamus.

"Shield him," commanded Tertullion. Renault stared incredulously. Seamus unslung his ironbound shield and straddled his prince, thrusting forth his chin truculently and growling like a mother bear athwart her cub.

Grazmesnil swept up the tor like a wave over sand. He roared with enraged glee at sight of the metal-clad witlings who stood the hilltop around their precious banner. *What need of Kör? Victory would be his alone.*

Gault dreamed. He lifted into night airs and beheld many things. On the periphery of the battle, two worms of blackness dipped time after time upon the scattered companies, inflicting more damage than they sustained. He saw Conrad, Servant of the Body, fall pierced by a random arrow from the sky. Ilus glowed like witchfire, unaffected by the mist that seemed to cloak all else, and for the first time felt somehow right in his hand.

The dragon loomed huge and hideous, its eyes alight like some avenging god. Gault saw again his father's kindly face, and heard Conrad's grunt affections, and saw the men below, fearful and dying. Like a gathering tide, the righteous wrath of a king shorn of kingdom filled his breast. He shouted his challenge and shot for the mighty wyrm.

Grazmesnil did not arrest the speed of his advent. Gaping wide his maw, he began to expel his death-promising breath. Ilus's point took the eldar dragon directly in the roof of the mouth. Grazmesnil's eyes boiled weirdly. The head burst asunder in an explosion of roiling gas, its enormous frame simply drifting apart, borne on the wind to leave no trace.

A heavy face, thick jawed and begrimed, loomed over Gault. He had never seen a more beautiful sight. Laughing, he caught up Seamus's arm and was pulled to his feet.

"Your sword, lord," indicated Renault. Gault looked to Ilus. Of its forty-plus inches length, only the hilts survived, and they pitted as with acid.

"Here we shall entomb it with honor. Let the dolmen remember its vengeance for the evil that struck down my father." Gault looked at the faces around him. He saw two knights toiling up the Scaelp. They bore the form of a man who lay strewn on a spear litter. A cloak covered the face. Gault remembered. "Conrad we will also bury on this high place. Where is Tertullion?"

A sob turned them round. They beheld Erasmus sitting against a stone. He pulled his hands from a face lined with exhaustion and heartbreak. "He is gone."

The apprentice rose. "Though sorely wounded, he seeks the summoner of the sky-wingers. See there his stave on the sward. It is empty of power, as am I." Erasmus slumped against the menhir. Beyond him was a nightmare landscape of scattered fires and the broken forms of men and horses. Some meandered dazedly or stared into the black distances beyond the utter destruction of the encampment.

Trakhner cleared his throat. "Of the archers and foresters, most are dead. The cavalry survives. The infantry and tribals are scattered or slain where they stood, scarce a fourth remain."

"What god of evil do we oppose," asked Erasmus, "that his very heralds are eldritch dragons?"

Gault strode to him and proffered his hand. Erasmus clasped it, meeting the hazel orbs with the brown depths of his own. Face to face, Gault thrust Tertullion's staff into the mageling's hand, then crouched before the body of Conrad to snap off the offending arrow. He tossed it into the dark.

"That I do not know, but devil or god, It has much to atone for."

Chapter 36

Hyllae: Valley of Wisdom

Isolde faced the man on the sands of the palaestra. Although she was tall as he, her opponent outweighed her again by half. Clad only in a loin wrap, the muscles under his oiled skin danced and rolled in the sunlight. Isolde smiled inside. Sandos had thrashed her each of the seven times they fought, and once wrenched her ankle so violently that the ligaments burst. After the healing prayers of the Donna, still it remained a sickly purple. This morning she had wrapped it tight, today she would show Sandos a new trick.

He ignored her kicking feint to his crotch and rushed in low to grapple. She bunched, boxed his ears to slow him for the fraction she needed, and leapt up—both hands on the back of his head to cartwheel over and land entirely behind him. He crouched and wheeled to leg-sweep her, but she hopped his leading foot and delivered a stinging slap to his face. Rather than roll away to seek equal footing, Sandos replied to the humiliating blow with hand and feet strikes against her belly and ribs, matching sheer muscle against the leverage of her superior position. For that, he received a leather-clad knee to the face, and another.

The blows were crisp, for Isolde did not wish to allow him a chance to drag her to him where his advantage of size would come into play. His head reeled back as a third knee came crashing in. Near-blinded with sweat and blood, he launched a desperate uppercut at her groin, but the speed had gone out of his arm. She easily sidestepped and returned with a short left kick that placed her calloused foot directly onto his jutting chin. It was over.

When Sandos recovered enough to stand, he grinned through smashed lips and his chronically flattened nose. He embraced her. "Try that bullshit flip on me again and I'll crack your spine for you."

Isolde's clear laugh filled the little arena. "Why, Sandos, how can I ever best you if I use only what you've taught me?"

"I love you, girl," he laughed. "When we're through, you shall have a thing or two to surprise that big lug, soon-to-be husband o' yours."

Well pleased, Isolde bowed and rushed to a meal at the common board, then hastened to her quarters to towel dry and gather the items she would need for this night's adventures. It was all coming together.

Since Xephard departed, she filled her waking hours with a training program of such intensity that the feelings of abandonment and angst and miserable longing had little opportunity to overwhelm her. Physical hardening, mock battles against cleric and mage, weapons practice and meditations left her too exhausted to cry more than a little when she lay alone in her cell each night with nothing but aching muscles to distract her.

Saying nothing, Cynthia had nonetheless signaled her approval by suspending Isolde's routine duties for the long months Xephard had been gone. One by one, masters of the academy pronounced her training complete after nigh two decades' service to the Warrior Goddess of Ilycrium. All but Sandos. Isolde chuckled at the look his face held when he awakened to find her standing triumphantly over him, hand outstretched to help him rise. The grappling champion was a stubborn one, second only to Xephard in free wrestling. Isolde ran her hands over her flat stomach. In the anticipation of the night's events, she scarcely felt where he had struck her, yet knew she would come morning. *But that lay many hours and some miles ahead.* She shouldered her satchel and strode out of the temple grounds and into the deepening evening.

Isolde paused in the middle of a grassy meadow, which lay a half league north and east of the Lampus. The very same where Xephard, with Apieron and Henlee, had recruited the baseborn thief, Rudolph Mellor, that spring afternoon so many days ago …

The night was perfect, and she took a deep breath of the crisp air that stirred her hair. A tang of wood smoke hung in the breeze, and long grasses rustled with each step. Without a hint of haze in the sky, the light of the moon and fainter stars leapt down at her, and she felt that if she stood on tiptoes and stretched upward, she might be able to grasp the fat moon. Isolde laughed softly. While she dawdled, moon woman climbed, and there were miles yet to the Falls of Voices with its ancient temple.

The winding path lay hidden in a narrow defile, invisible to all but those who learned the secret way. Isolde descended through tree arches boughlinked overhead as if to form a leafy tunnel. She trod with stealth, alert for what she might find. Tree roots glistened, and fallen leaves were sodden with dew, for Auroch's misty breath billowed far.

She exited the arbor. The moon was high aloft and now it resembled a shard struck from the argent shield the Goddess bore, *that which none could withstand.*

Isolde counted her descending steps, cut by windborn rain and thirsty root until the path looped sheer right to reveal the echoing falls. So bright was the cascade against the white cliff face that the light of moon and stars became a million flickering luminescences in its watery reef. For a space she listened, although did not hear the enchanted voices such as Apieron once described, and yet the rush of the waterfall seemed almost alive. Nor could she see the darkened receiving pool below that was Xephard's favorite place. He loved its sun-dappled waters by day, its serene flow that became a winding stream to feed Lampus's northern pastures before joining myriad cousins in a journey to the western coast.

Isolde traversed moss-slick stones under the falls, the water billowing from a jutting lip, thus allowing a narrow span behind it, against the abutment, for the trail to continue. A cautious descent for a day traveler, and also by night for Isolde, priestess-monk and high adept of the vale. Her way skirted around the far edge of the pond until she stood before the temple ruins.

Isolde's breath ghosted on moisture-laden air, and the ancient pile seemed to hover above its mist-decked foundation. Half of its grooved columns remained standing, but portico and roof, wall and awning had long since fallen into a rubble-strewn ring. The cliff face of the narrow coomb bore the scars where ancient engineers brought forth its white stone to erect the holy shrine. Cynthia said they were of a race who preceded her own and that of Xephard, whose forbearers had drifted from the North, the wonders of the warming southland bright on their faces, and a song of their adopted gods new on their lips. Here Isolde ever felt at ease, perhaps comforted by their lingering spirits, their watery whispers stirring the dim of her unremembered youth. It was here she first received the white goddess, and ever and anon where she felt most the divine presence. The moon now drifted overhead, and the night sky became so brilliant that even the dog star seemed fitful and wan. Isolde began her preparations.

Shedding her garments and lastly her wedding chain, Isolde stepped into the cool water. She swam and scrubbed with a soapstone. Standing waist high, she combed her tawny hair with a sawtooth cut from the shell of a tortoise. She shook her straightened hair and laughed when it slapped her face, and droplets played in the pale light like falling pearls, she laughing again with the joy of youth and the splendor of her body and hopeful soul filled with love for her beloved, and many hopes for his return … *She thought of the child's name and of the heavy spear of her dreams* … Tonight she would learn if she was to bear the warm weight of an infant, or the cold burden of a warrior's shield.

Isolde clothed herself in a simple shift before gathering certain items from her satchel. All was hush as she entered the nighted temple, its flags frosty in the star glow.

She approached the weathered altar, barren of symbol or carving, and thus to her all the more appropriate. On its worn surface she fashioned a crude bowl from a measure of clay, mixed with small, loose stones of the altar itself. Three strikes of a flint by her dagger sparked the tinder she gathered. This she lay into the bowl and fed with sandalwood steeped in fragrant oils.

Isolde breathed deep, clearing her mind before producing her final items. There was a length of hair she had taken from Xephard the eve of their betrothal. It was twined with an equal portion of her own into a small cord. On this she blew and placed into the bowl. It flared up. She doused the little blaze with water from the mineral-blue pool. The flame extinguished, the colonnade of the temple retreated in darkness, leaving only her and the smoking bowl in the liquid glow of moonlight.

"Blessed Mother, never did I need a man to complete me. Yet the cruel Erinyes have bared my heart to one. Xephard Brighthelm. I obey the dream summons and come before you, child warrior and virgin priestess no longer."

Isolde knelt before the altar and bowed, head to knees. Her hair brushed the flags, and she pressed both hands against her belly. Her world twisted. She clasped arms against her breasts, then flung them out wide, her eyes following the blue-gray smoke into the star-vaulted sky. A rising breeze seemed to lift her to her feet, and silver rags of clouds raced across the vault.

"Maiden Goddess, I offer my life and soul to the spirit messenger of your will."

The soothing voices of women, the thrum and clack of spindle and loom. The mewlings of children all at once happy and fretful like puppies. These came to her … Then the happy sounds were drowned by a cry and clash of arms, a roiling sky shot with crimson that overtopped leering faces and blood-splattered bodies. Flickering steel flashed into men who fell wailing into darkness and were trod over.

Isolde's breasts heaved, her breathing ragged. She held it, and an icy gust extinguished the brazier's last incense and the light of moon all at once, plunging the interior of the temple into frigid gloom.

Isolde cried out with emotional release and fell heavily to her side. Near-blind, she crawled out to her pile of clothes. With trembling hands, she donned her traveling garments and knife belt and took up her satchel. Moon Goddess remained hidden behind a cloud. Stars ventured forth, and she calmed to search her surroundings. The mineral pool and ruined temple, falls and footpaths seemed as they ever had. *Bower or blade?* The Goddess denied her answer. She was unworthy, therefore her path would remain in shadow.

Isolde sighed and gathered up her leathern sack, now lightened of most of its burdens. She eyed the winding trail that would take her from the enclave and squatted to cleanse her hands and gather a palm of water to her lips. It was then that she saw the cave. It was odd that she, who knew this place better than any, had never noticed the hole in the rock face behind the cascade and halfway from the top. Remaining on her heels, Isolde leaned from side to side, and the aperture vanished.

"Odd, but then, not too odd." Isolde retraced her steps with weary feet. Inexplicably, she paused directly under the falling water and looked up to where she knew the cleft lay.

"Foolish!" In the dark, with no equipment, on rain-slicked stone, such a climb was madness. No one would find her until perhaps she washed up days from now and miles west at some bend in the watercourse.

With a heave, Isolde swung her hips over the lip and into the hole. Gathering her breath, she stared into its inky eye and crawled forward. She pushed farther, stirring unseen items that crunched like broken pottery as she moved. Her nostrils flared, and a dusty smell rose as the shards were rimed in a layer that must have settled for years.

Abandoning the cave's perimeter, she sorted through a low pile until her questing hands grasped a heavy handle. She drew forth an object that seemed a weighty amphora near two cubits in height and seemingly intact. She lifted it, and its surface crumbled beneath her grasp. She sighed but brushed away the decayed exterior as unbroken ceramic was revealed beneath. Cursing herself the fool, nonetheless she cradled it painstakingly to the entrance and sat, feet over the edge, to examine it in the wan light. The glaze was etched in patterns too thinned by age to discern any meaning. The lid was fused to the body, not by wax, but as if cast in a single piece.

"Strange." She shook it, something rattled within.

The sound of the shattered ceramic was lost in Auroch's tumult. Pieces arched thirty feet to land on the frothy rocks below. Isolde freed an item rolled in oiled leather. Its desiccated twines broke at her touch. She shook it open and gasped when an object fell to strike between her legs, quivering upright in the stone. Whether this resulted from its incredible sharpness or some chance crack in the rock, she did not know. Isolde grasped it with both hands and drew it forth to raise before her eyes.

The moon blazed behind the water curtain, lighting her face and white arms and the thing she held. It was a mighty spearhead, two feet of untarnished silvered metal, its glow casting the moon into scintillant motes around the coomb that danced and quivered with each tiny motion of her trembling hand. Accompanying it was a butt spike of similar craftsmanship. The Goddess had answered.

A woman's wailing rose in the water's rush, then surpassed it, echoing out beyond overtopping heights and into the nighted airs. Auroch churned on as he ever had.

XAMBOL: THE STONEFIST

"So I have found you, dark child of the hills! What evil dost thou wreck on the land?"

Woobora laughed long and low, the sound pregnant with malice when he spoke, filled with the disdain of the wise who have grown wicked in their long years, finding all else beneath them. "White fool, seek you death thusly? Thou, who might live as slave yet a while beside thy steel prince?" Half light and half dark, the moon gleamed from beneath clouds, revealing the ancient tumulus and the death-haunted altar that crouched like a light-hating beast on the tor.

"Think you earthbound dragons are slain so easily? Soon they will heed *Her* call. Mightiest is She, all thy world shall be covered in sorrow." With these words, the shaggy priest stomped upon a toothlike gem that lay by his foot. A snarling construct of scales and talons leapt from the shattered stone onto Tertullion's breast. It scored grave wounds in the old man's flesh.

Tertullion's shaking hands met on the beast's head, holding the gnashing maw just shy of his throat. His eyes flashed, and his hands met in the middle. The creature's head and body were pulverized into gem dust. It glinted red in the moonlight as it settled.

Woobora drew forth an iron sickle that was pitted with corrosion yet crackled with menace as it soughed the air. Tertullion grasped for his absent staff and stumbled, nigh blinded with agony of burn and claw. Woobora cackled with glee. "Before you die, Magnus, know that shards of thy broken body will yield me many totems. Mighty magics 'gainst your crawling army will I make."

Tertullion gurgled in protest and swayed again, then righted his gaze on the advancing shaman. His voice grew resonant with righteous authority. "Your black wisdom fails you, Blauthauser, although you cannot see."

Woobora cocked his head, holding in check the sickle that strained with eager power. He sneered a pointed smile. "A last lesson ere death will I impart. See yon barrow fells?" His thin arm stretched to indicate a string of northern heights. "There slept sons and fathers of my people who battled the Steel Kings of old. For two nights' time have they lain empty! Even now, mighty liches in their hundreds and thousands march to the sea city of your master."

With a shout of defiance, Tertullion began an incantation. Woobora stepped forward and struck out with his scythe. Tertullion's head leapt to the side, his body silently slumping, frail in death.

Woobora took up the snow-bearded head in both hands, to hold it before his face in converse. "And so it ends, Tertullion of—"

The head's eyes snapped open, and lit the hill priest with a transfixing light that foamed white gold. Woobora gaped his mouth in agony, shaking his hands to release his deadly burden, but they obeyed him not. A crack sounded as the radiance burst through his skull, for an instant illuminating every particle of his being. Then all was dark on the Stonefist.

Below the Pleven Deep, adepts fell to their knees, ears covered against thrashing screams and granite-splitting bellows that welled from the depths of stone. The rock-face rivulet turned to steam and was no more. His fury expended, Grazmesnil withdrew into himself, healing the hurts the destruction of his dream weave caused. He would bide.

"*Soon,*" echoed an irresistible sending in his mind. "*Soon shall my sons be free.*"

Chapter 37

Fogleaf

Despite the joy of the reunion, the wayfarers did not linger past midmorning, for there was much broken country left to traverse before they approached the lowland forests, outliers to the Wyrnde. They lay a low cairn of stone over the body of the slain mage.

"Too good for the likes o' him," grumbled Henlee. Nonetheless he bent to join Apieron, followed by Jamello and finally Tallux. The wood elf hesitated. He had suffered much in the dungeons of the shaman's redoubt at the hands of the mage and his cruel companions. Completing their task in silence, the companions refilled water skins at the base of the ravine while Bump munched happily on tufted grasses and tender rushes he found there.

"I wish I were an ass," said Jamello.

That day and the next were spent navigating the pathless hill country. Evergreen oaks, ash, and beech now mingled with tough rock pines that had predominated the upper slopes. The sun was oft hid behind rocky crests or stands of foliage. Even so, they fared unerringly by skill of wood elf and King's ranger, and by the nose of the war hound. By evening of the third day from their reunion, they were well into the green flatlands east of the winged elves' grotto and encamped at the base of an enormous oak. It was a black forest giant, ancient but hale in gnarled and moss-festooned splendor. A ponderous monarch, it stood disdainful of clinging vines, themselves the girth of its nearest neighbors, and of the tall but short-lived pine and trembling alders that grew a respectful distance from its dense shade. The oak rose above its subjects and reached out in million-leaved glory to the sky. The little party rested while Tallux and Sut sought ahead for sign of the swamp elves.

Apieron bade Henlee kindle a small fire while he repeated a task he oft performed since their flight from the Duskbridge. He carefully incised and stripped small sheets of bark from the base of several pines so as not to leave a wound on any one tree too severe for it to overcome. As always, their female companion followed closely his every move with dark eyes, her face cast into shadow by her raven's hair. Of habit she stood apart, refusing any attempt to engage in conversation. Apieron pitied her.

When Apieron lifted a sufficient quantity of pine strips, he laid them out and bade Jamello scrape free the moist cambium under the bark. Apieron looked into the upper reaches of the old oak. Countless acorns hung there, too green to eat. Instead he rummaged through leaf mould in its shade for last year's leavings. There he found mostly shells emptied by delving beetle or greedy bird. Finally he was able to procure a hatful. These he split with a rock and added the nuts to the pile of meal Jamello had extricated from the pine strips. Water was added, the paste stirred with a poniard and formed into five small cakes and set upon a flat stone near the fire to bake.

Tallux returned, silent as a flitting shadow. The woman fixed the direction from whence he came a full minute before his arrival. He stepped into the camp, followed after a time by Sut. The elvin scout was clad in castoff garments and bore many wounds, yet his step was light and sure. The others noted how confidence returned in increments to the set of his shoulders and the glint in his emerald eyes.

"There is no sign of the kindred of your winged friend."

"You did not go far enough," said Henlee.

"Sut led me far, onto the very edge of their land where red forest giants make even this grandfather of oaks seem a spring sapling."

"That is odd," murmured Apieron. "Their sentries have keen eyes."

"And arrows," said Henlee. "Surely they would hail you, an elf, and they no doubt eager for news of the return of Sarc."

"Either they sleep or have retreated deep into the Wyrnde."

"Bah, I know elvin sentries do not sleep any more than dwarves," protested Henlee. "The winged ones would have halted you one way or the other. But come, Master! What have you brung us to eat?"

Tallux smiled. "I thought my task was to scout our trail for tomorrow, not to gather food for hungry dwarves."

"Why worry of tomorrow when today we hunger?" said Henlee. "Only this morn I had to drill a new hole in my belt, an' that going the wrong way."

"Sut had a dinner of squirrel on the way hither. Alas I brought you only these." Tallux produced a rag filled with pulpy red-black berries.

"Raspberries? Mulberries?" queried Jamello hopefully.

"Nay," said Apieron laughing, "chokecherries. A bit sour, perhaps, but an excellent topping for the mealcakes I've made you."

"Be thankful for these such as they are," said Tallux. "The poor tree was ill, and many birds tore at her, leaf and fruit alike. Tomorrow there will be nothing left."

Apieron pitted the small fruits and mashed them onto his

acorn bread. Before this was complete, Jamello managed to palm three or four from him and popped them into his mouth. He made a sour face but sucked and smacked, the juice staining his lips red. He thought of the green lamas he had eaten amidst the flowers of the vale of the Donna, so long ago.

"Do not chew the pits!" warned Tallux.

"Why? I'm hungry enough."

"Because," replied Tallux flatly, "they'll poison your blood."

"Cheery fellow," muttered Jamello, but he spit the stones far from him. Apieron gave out his cakes. Henlee and their female companion took theirs reluctantly. The woman bore her cake away to eat alone. Jamello looked at her retreating form and sighed. "She has eyes only for you, my friend." He nudged Apieron.

"I cannot discern her motive. Eat your food."

"The lass has the right idea," said Henlee, "always eating alone the way she does. If any of you blabbermouths breathe a word about these nut biscuits to King Redhand, I shall be exiled."

Jamello and Tallux smirked. Henlee glowered. "Then I shall come stay with you for a year!"

"Come, friend," said Tallux. "I'll make it up to you after you have finished your dinner." Two seconds later, he led Henlee to a wetland fir and inserted his long knife into a blistered knot on its bole. When he withdrew it, a resinous salve followed that he applied to the dwarf's wounds of foot and thigh. He repeated the procedure for Apieron's shoulder in turn before disappearing into the forest. They could hear him working a moment before returning with a handful of green birch shoots and a dozen squarish sheets of papery bark. He handed half of the shoots to Henlee and the remainder to Apieron.

"Chew on these tonight and tomorrow as we walk. Your pain will ease."

Apieron took one of the bark sheets as well and folded it into an open cone. "And tonight we have cups for our water. Who else but a wood elf?"

"Eating bark. Bathing in sap. Chewing branches and drinking water, what am I becoming?" groused the dwarf.

"Wise," assured Tallux.

The night passed without event, the woods uncommonly quiet save for a sighing wind that stirred the oak's upper reaches but did not reach the ground. Aperion banked their fire to let it die smokeless. At first light, Jamello went to find where the woman had bedded. Of her he found no sign, and her cake was on the forest floor, crushed into the leaves and covered with busy ants.

"What the—?" he exclaimed softly.

"What's keeping you, thief?" called Henlee. "Tonight we feast at the banquet of swamp elves."

Jamello hastened to the others, only to find her already with them. She did not look his way. "Women!" he mumbled. They set a good pace, stopping often for water, which was here in plenty as was grass and wetland clover for Bump. Swampbay and cottonwood joined sandpine and moss-draped cypress to line open waterways where broad-based mangroves crouched, knob-kneed like silent malformed sentries.

In a shady spot, they spied a stand of fleshy toscaras roots with their sickly sweet orange flowers, save these grew thick from the rotting corpse of a brown bat. Its four-foot body pierced by a dozen white shoots that, to Jamello, seemed to pulse slightly with a sickening, digestive peristalsis towards nodding plumes. Apieron pulled on his sleeve. "That is why one should not sleep under such growths."

Tallux mumbled a long word in elvish, surprisingly guttural. "What's that you say?" asked Henlee.

"The plant that eats children."

Little of fauna they saw save flitting birds. The sweet, sharp trill of a redwing called at times, and small, black birds dashed across the way whenever tall grasses were disturbed. Once, a covey of white-breasted quail burst from cover, chirping and drumming their wings in quick flight. Jamello felt a hand on his arm and lowered a stick he had fashioned for throwing. Tallux nodded to the stand of low shrubs where the birds had been feeding.

"Hemlock seeds. They taint the meat, paralysis."

"Curse this swamp and all the magics of clerics and demons above and beneath!" sobbed Jamello as he stomped off behind Apieron's ever-retreating form. "Are we lost?" moaned the thief. A black swan startled them as it fell, breaking the water. It folded its wings to fish, darting its orange beak below the Wyrnde's surface.

"We are not lost," answered Apieron.

In this wise they passed unchallenged beyond the first growths of the forest giants and soon deep into the domain of the winged elves. Water found channels and deep pools, leaving the mighty redwoods to their high, dry beds.

They came to the settlement of the Liflyne. There remained only their slight homes, abandoned and soon to be reabsorbed by the forest which gave them birth. Apieron leaned heavily on a pine stave. "In a year's passing, there will be no sign they have ever been."

The companions drifted singly, walking slowly about the giant boles, their steps making little sound on a soft carpet of countless generations of needle-fall from treetop heights. Without the presence of the swamp elves, the place was hush and desolate. Bump snorted disapprovingly, for here there was little undergrowth save a few grassy banks.

"Look!" called Tallux. They rushed to his voice to find him slipping into a man-high crevice within a tree. He poked his head out. "Come, there is room for all within."

"By Dangmar's twisted beard, what is he about?" demanded Henlee.

"It was marked," chuckled Apieron. "With this!" He bent to retrieve a tawny-haired feather from the loam. Its apex was north, toward the tree and the deepening forest.

"No, do not—" began Henlee, but too late as Apieron followed Tallux into the recesses of the giant redwood. Within he found a room-sized cyst, the living tree for walls and a fragrant floor of dusted bark beneath. Tallux squatted there, examining several items.

"A cache?" asked Apieron.

"We were meant to find this, a gifting from the friends you made here."

"Help me bear them out," said Apieron. "The dwarf will never enter such a cave."

"Then he should have to wait till last for a share," laughed Tallux.

Together they bore forth a skein of forest-green-and-gray cloth, three throwing javelins of heavy wood and bone, and a sheaf of arrows with a spare string for such a bow as Apieron had wielded. And much to Henlee's delight, more than a dozen sealed gourds whose sloshing weight suggested food and drink. These were broached immediately and found to contain a cooked porridge, quite unspoilt, of venison and tubers. Several of the containers were tall with curved stems and held an amber liquid, aromatic as wine but thick on the tongue. With little hesitation, each, save the woman, took a gusty swallow. Immediately they looked one to the other, expecting his comrade to notice the lively change he felt within.

The companions quickly finished the heady elixirs. In mere minutes, pain of wound, bruise, and burn ceased to bother. Eafora shook her head at the proffered drink and smiled thinly at Apieron. He saluted her with the flask and drank a second. Laughing, he flexed his wounded shoulder and placed the crooked bow of Sarc upright before him. He pulled its sinewy string from his pocket where he had long kept it, then secured it to the bottom of the weapon. With a fluid motion, he flexed the longbow and slipped the top loop of its string into its notch. He drew forth an arrow from the quiver, five hands long and feathered with the strange hair-feather quillions of the Liflyne. He bent the bow until the nock was at his chin and let fly a high-arching shot that swept out to disappear through the tree canopy.

"Long have I carried you, crooked bow. Fitting that you are whole again in the home of your master. I will name you Wracu, Woodwand of Revenge."

"Mighty guerdons from the winged people," called Henlee, who also procured a second potion. He shared it between Bump and Sut, with only an occasional swig for himself. All three smacked their lips once every drop was consumed. Henlee looked at Apieron, who rubbed his wounded shoulder.

Apieron smiled ruefully. "I should not have done that." He nodded to the gourd in Henlee's hand. "'Twas no Sangreal. The bow will have to wait."

"That your friends are completely gone, there is no doubt," said Tallux. "See how they hid the cache with no message or lingering herald."

"You call that hidden?" asked Henlee. "You've never been to my secret vaults in Saemid."

"It is a wide wood," said Tallux. "Could you have found it? Besides, the spirit of yon tree held it and called me to the feather."

Apieron nodded. "I agree, and deem by that token they fled northward. If we do not encounter them, at least we can walk the way they traveled before us."

"And shave a leg or two off the swamp, eh, Bump?" said Henlee.

"Yes," said Apieron. "We shall take the longer, but hopefully quicker route, and with good fortune come onto the king's lands from the east short days from now."

"Bump and myself vote for your plan," added Henlee. The burro allowed him to stroke his bristly mane. The donkey's ears stood straight up, and his eyes shined.

"He's drunk!" said Jamello.

"Bah, *you're* drunk. Bump has drank a keg of Old Dwarfroot by himself in his day."

"Elvin draughts are not intended for such as he," said Tallux, "yet it seems to suit Sut as well. Perhaps that is the way with all goodly beasts." They camped without fire at the base of the cache tree, setting watches as was their habit, although for the first time any could recall, there was little worry of danger. "Tell me of the Liflyne, people of the high-lofted tree bower," said Tallux. "Now that I have walked amongst their groves and breathed the airs of their homeland, I feel I can picture them in this place."

Jamello spoke slowly, as if finding the words, "They are ... noble."

"Aye," agreed Henlee, "to befriend a dwarf who owed weregild for a slaying. Would I could know dwarves act in similar wise."

A thought came to Apieron. It was a memory that had been driven from his mind by hunger, haste, pain of wounds, and the joy of friends reunited. He recalled the ambush; an image of the goblin cleric swam before him, the evil face grinning mockingly through pointed teeth. Atop the brutish shoulders had been cast an odd mantle. "Do you remember the orcish shaman who assailed us on the ledge?"

"Never will I forget him," said Tallux softly. "Bizaz."

"Saw you his garb? The short cloak he bore?"

"Only for a flashing moment, as he fled into the void."

"Good shot, elf," stated Henlee.

Apieron drew forth the feather token they found. "He wore a mantle fashioned of these."

A long moment's silence was broken by Henlee's growl. "If

that be true, I will return to that cursed vale and take vengeance for the winged ones. I swear it, even though it take a hundred years."

"Sarc of Fogleaf gave his life for us," said Jamello.

"Aye, thief," said Henlee, "when our business is done, come with me and we'll send the souls of those murderers to be his slaves in the afterlife."

Tallux spoke, his tones hushed and fierce. "Elves hold no such belief, but I will go with you if I may."

Apieron touched the crooked bow and living quiver that lay beside him, perhaps the only things on this earth left of Sarc. No other marked the gesture in the near dark. When he had strung the bow, he had felt as did the others. Now his grief left him exhausted in a way no elvin elixir could mend.

Apieron woke. He had been wrong. Though they had apparently fled, he knew the living presence of the tree folk would linger unseen in this place for years greater than those of his life, and perhaps a future wayfarer would sense here, amongst the red giants, the featherlike touch of their serene magic while trees called softly to one another down the ages. He lay back and looked to a gap in the canopy. Dusk yielded to night's soft encroach, and all at once many stars blazed forth in sparkling profusion as if some sky deity suddenly flung a handful of brilliant diamonds onto a blue-gray cloth.

As his eyes again grew heavy, the last sound Apieron heard was the muffled stamp of Bump's hooves on the loam. His dream took him like smoke amongst mighty boles and mossy stones of the eldritch forest. *Coming to a stream-side glade, he recognized the place of their sojourn long ago, save now it was strewn with pale flowers that mirrored the frosty stars. A shadow crossed the heavens. It was a flying steed of shimmering gold who came to him, silken mane and tail streaming.*

"*Ingold.*"

Apieron touched the horse's tapered nose and met her sapphire eyes. "Your master, Giliad of Amor, is dead." The pegasus tossed her head defiantly. "It is true."

Apieron felt warm tears upon his face and pushed words past a throat grown thick. "He fell in the Night Below. I was witness."

The winged mare arched her neck meaningfully toward her back. Apieron mounted, and in a flash they caromed away eastward, faster than any bird, and yet Apieron felt no wind on his face or sense of motion. Remnants of the wetlands folded into the treed reaches the companions recently quitted. Ingold did not slow, but overtopped the arid ring of the Haunted Vale before gliding over the stony covert where they had ensconced the horses so long ago.

Apieron dismounted. Ingold's clear orbs drew his own into a still blue sea. The pegasus snorted and blew her cool breath on his face. Then he saw …

"*Open!*" *commanded Bizaz. His jut-chinned face was split in triumphant grin as with a resounding crack, the shielding wall fell into a cloud of swirling dust. The protective sigil atop the entry flared up in a golden flash and was gone. Dranol Eserhaven emitted a high-pitched cackle.*

"*I understand not why you laugh, charlatan,*" *boomed Slysbeth. "You tried three times and got only scorched fingertips for your efforts." The gangly mage's mouth snapped shut, and he turned his malign glance onto the bounty hunter. Deuce chuckled evilly and produced a jagged poniard that he licked in anticipation. Within the covert, the alarmed whinnies of panicked horses came to their ears.*

"*In, you pissants!*" *screamed the shaman. "Slay them."*

The muscled bounty hunter and the ill-kempt dwarf thief leapt, eager blades leading. A mighty neighing cut the morning air as a mighty white destrier burst forth, scattering stony rubble in a shower of gravel. He was followed by an oddly striped equine that fixed

Dranol with a killing gaze. Behind trailed a wide-girthed burro, ears laid back and yellow teeth bared. Slysbeth aimed a cut at the charging stallion but was bowled aside, scoring only a glancing blow as the enraged beast bit and kicked in a one-ton fighting frenzy.

Bizaz stepped back and began an incantation of summoning that quickly coalesced into a pig-eyed, slaver-tusked monstrosity. It stole the very light from the day. The remaining ponies had made to follow Axylus, their leader, but when they beheld the cleric's horror, they shrank back into the recesses of the cave, shrieking in terror. The beast slouched in. No horse exited the grotto after that.

Cackling insanely, Dranol shot forth a sizzling black bolt that caught up the striped steed in midleap and brought it to the ground, kicking in agony. A hand-sized hole smoked in its broad chest. Wise in the ways of war, Xephard's stallion lashed out front and back at both half-goblin and the bounty hunter, scoring distracting hits on each.

"Don't let him escape!" screamed Bizaz as the warhorse already cantered westward.

"He will not," promised Slysbeth, sheathing his sword. He ran at full tilt after the wounded destrier. Axylus could have easily outdistanced his pursuit, yet lingered a tempting distance ahead, drawing shaman and human reaver into the chase.

Deuce faced off with Bump. They stood ten paces apart, the dwarf brandishing a rusted short sword and his crooked dagger. Bump clacked his teeth, hatred burning in his brown eyes. "Trifle with me, will you, ass? Think you better than I 'cause your master be a lord o' dwarves? I'll 'ave you for supper!" With this last, the dwarven thief lunged forward, hoping to cow the animal into turning flank in fear, thereby yielding an easy hit.

Instead Bump rushed forward, sharp hooves and sharper teeth pummeling and cutting the renegade dwarf in a dozen places before he could recover his wits. Whooping with fear, Deuce turned and scampered without grace down the southward slope, trailed a full mile by the vengeful Bump before he managed to slip into a badger hole. Snorting with disgust, Bump kicked the entrance full of debris and relieved himself. The burro's tall ears arched this way and that, searching for enemies or the sounds of other battles to join. Finding none, he lowered his head and ambled forlornly into the scrub, flanks heaving in a sheen of sweat on his dun gray pelt.

Two hundred yards to the northwest, Axylus fronted his pursuers in a naked bay dominated by a broken tree. Blades bared and grinning, Slysbeth and the evil cleric closed in …

"Enough," said Apieron. "You have shown me enough." *Ingold once again met his gaze.* Apieron felt as if he were falling inward.

He woke with a start. A half moon crested over their camp's high-sided clearing, filling the little dell with ghostly radiance. He had forgotten how bright the night sky was in this place—secret home of the Liflyne. Should he desire, he felt he could almost read by its silvery glow.

Apieron laid back his head. The elvin elixir overtook him again, and he heard beating wings. "Ingold," he said, yet knew as he spoke it he was wrong. The rhythmic sound was slow and deep, as if massive pinions displaced the very airs of the forest, calling to the trees and they to answer, to and fro it sounded, lulling him deep into a melody that whispered of silent, open spaces, and far-reaching vistas. *He beheld a gathering of winged creatures that flew under starlight, gigantic and moth-like they were. On their backs and in the space around them were many hundreds of Liflyne people, garbed for war.* Apieron opened his eyes. The moon had set, and no sound disturbed night's ending save the steady breathing of his companions and the mournful, blowing call of a dawn owl. He lay quiet until they woke, but the others seemed to have experienced no dream or vision, or if they had, made no mention of it. He kept his peace.

Morning's soft glow caught the dew-covered raiment of the

trees into an emerald-and-silver mass worn above reddish boles, like broad-shouldered gods in gleaming cloaks. The companions admired the view before striking camp. As they walked, the forest came to life to greet the new day, soft, spiny leaves shifted, insects chirped, day birds called and trilled, frogs barked, and small animals rustled unseen. "Do you hear the forest sigh?" asked Tallux of Jamello as they walked.

"I do," said Jamello. "At times it seems like, like the breathing of some mighty beast. I thought I was the only one to hear."

"You *are* the only one," declared Henlee. "The elf is teasing you, boy. He hears naught but wind stirring the treetops."

"Nay," said Tallux, "the ears of a dwarf are blocks of stone. The forest lives; her spirit calls to those who would listen."

A fox squirrel barked angrily at them for trespassing beneath his favorite limb. Henlee chuckled. "There's your wood sprite, boy, and he's mighty angry." Tallux put his finger to his lips and stared at the glowering squirrel. The little beast ran off the branch and into a hole in the trunk and was silent thereafter.

"Squirrel tamer," snickered Henlee. Sut licked his lips.

By day's end they had descended a low place so that the lands round them appeared a never-ending sea of green. Their way became difficult and strewn with standing water. From the bolt of elvin cloth, they had fashioned simple breeches and other garments that were light and cool. Jamello crafted a hood for his head, and its flopping cone fell to the small of his back. Yet even the silky material soon became soaked and cumbersome.

Tiny insects assailed the companions mercilessly. If one sat still or stopped walking for more than a few seconds, midge generals would mount swarming attacks to torment beast and man alike with a hundred small nips and a relentless, high-pitched whining in a vision-clouding dance of tiny dots. Worst of all, one sniffed in a dozen of the soft, black bodies with every breath.

So relentless was the torment that all efforts of wood elf and human forester failed to drive the swarming insects from their evening camp. At last resort, a smudge fire of wet greenwood emitted great clouds of milky smoke that only made the adventurers hack and cough but did not deter the midge legions. Rather than endure such a night, they pressed slowly forward in the darkness, reliant on Sut's keen nose for guidance. Their passing disturbed wild hogs that crashed noisily through cane and deadfalls in the darkness, but no mishap greater than grimed breeches and the relentless insects befell them. Dawn found them stumbling with exhaustion, although beyond the brunt of the swampland. Jamello's head swam in near delirium, having suffered worse than any and bearing half a thousand itching stings. He sat heavily against the deep crotch of a tall pine where, perhaps a half century ago, two saplings had fused to produce the twin tree, its many-layered bark stacked and peeling between dark grooves to create scales larger than his hand. Silvery red, they reminded him of the armor of a legionnaire he had once seen. That man had worn brigandine composed of hammered-bronze scales, riveted onto a leather jerkin.

Jamello molded his spine to the tree and watched the slow, practiced motions of the others as they prepared for rest. Even the woman seemed worn. Here the wind freshened such that the mosquitos and midges assailed him less, although the worst had been a long and tapered, brown fly that could bite through any cloth and always left a bloody divot in his skin that itched and galled him without cease. Sut and even Henlee's thick-hided burro had nipped and jumped when beset by these evil flies. Bump's surly nature had returned in spate, and no improvised halter could survive his chomping teeth and bucking neck. In the end, he was left free to follow as he might. During the night, Jamello's torment had been so bad that he smeared every inch of exposed skin with algae-covered mud, and he groaned at the recollection of its slimy feel and awful scent. Although dry and caked, its odor assailed him still.

Jamello did not know where he lost his pomander; it seemed too long ago to merit the effort of remembering. He *did* recall she who had given it to him. Ahh, Luciana's creamy arms and breasts, and thighs that jounced with her every motion in symphony of feminine allure.

"Come hither!" her jiggling breasts and taunting hips called to him, even when her smoky eyes flashed anger and she tossed her hair in disdain and named him a pig. He wondered where she was now. Probably *not* lying in a festering bog. No, he was quite sure she was flashing her angry eyes and jiggling her young, firm buttocks for some swaggering jack who no doubt was even more of a pig than he.

Only that morn, Jamello had killed a grouse with a stone cast. It had ruffled its haloed crest defiantly like a cornered dragon, flaring its patterned wings and tail. When it lay dead, its magic fled, the brilliant plumage but a pattern strewn like castoff art on the mould. He had not had the heart to touch it after that. It had rested but a moment over Henlee's small fire when the woman devoured it. They'd let her. And his bow, his mighty arbalest of Hel had developed a catch in its mechanism of folding, no doubt perpetrated by the filthy, wet atmosphere of the filthy, noisome bog. Jamello had carried or dragged it for uncounted miles, so powerful and well wrought it had been. He bit back a heart-wrenching sob at the injustice of it all.

"What's wrong, thief? You choke on something?" called Henlee sleepily.

It was midafternoon before they were rested enough to begin anew. The breeze had died, yet within a hundred paces, Apieron stopped as there came a sound, faintly discernible, which seemed to carry as much through the ground as in the air. A high tree sighed in the still. Apieron looked up, searching the sky all around, but the sound had faded. The forest was once again dreary and lifeless. It was then that he found the second token of the Liflyne. He bent to retrieve it, and like the other, its substance seemed a cross between hair and feather, like the poult of a young bird. It pointed along the dim game path they followed.

"I'm glad we ventured no farther in our fatigue, else we would have missed this."

"Would not the winged ones been flying instead of walking on this here varmint trail?" asked Henlee.

"It was placed for us," said Tallux. "A message of goodwill."

"Pretty subtle, elf," replied Henlee. "Good thing wind, rain, or beast did not find it before we."

"These are troubled times. War is come."

None ignored the words of the wood elf, and so they went swiftly but cautiously along such paths and shaded byways where rush-grown wetlands grudgingly gave way to open forest. That evening, Tallux loosed a quick shot from Farstriker to slay a feral pig that dashed across their trail, an immature female of sixty pounds. The meat was clean and tender. Unheedful of burned lips and tongues, they pulled gobbets of sizzling flesh from sticks placed over a fire, consuming them quickly. There was plenty for all. Even Sut's voracious appetite was sated, although in the morning, breakfast was again meager. Despite the excellence of the evening's feast, a lunch of river cabbage and a dinner of wind-scorched fruit soon had the dwarf grumbling again.

"This fruit is bitter," he said, flinging an empty skin aside. "You picked them too green."

"They are *orange*," retorted Jamello, though he did not appear to enjoy the fruits any more than did the dwarf. He pared one with his dagger, eating mincingly, a sour expression on his face.

"They are persimmons," laughed Apieron, "and mayhap taste no different to you summer or fall."

"I miss beer," said Henlee, "and smoked bacon."

"And sheets," added Jamello.

"I miss my children," said Apieron. "I wonder how much they've grown." It was with great excitement the next day, the fifteenth from the Hel Gate, when they came upon the farmer's croft.

WINDHOVER

Melónie had pouted and plead that a window be set overlooking her garden, for unlike other ladies of station in this strange northern land, hours would she spend in the kitchens. Finally and inevitably, as Apieron could not resist her long, a window was cut to face the garden, although it was less wide than she hoped and set with an iron grate anchored in the stonework by pins a foot long and twice a man's finger in diameter.

Below and in the cool shade of the keep's stone wall, she placed sweet-scented jasmine that climbed and twisted its curling tendrils around the casement. Blue pimpernel nestled in evergreen ryegrass like lavender stars set in a verdant sky. Bloodgrass colored the water's edge, bright as artists' colors under the sweeping boughs of swaying willows and tangled dogwood that shed flowers in a drifting blizzard of silken blooms of pink and white. Oft her happy voice lifted in a working song that wended its way past the garden and sloping turves to follow her chuckling stream in its serpentine course below deepening banks, where it dived under the curtain wall to find its way to Foslegen.

The day was done, and Melónie stood atop an embrasure on the wall with Duner. A scent wafted to her. The last of her lavender would soon be cut and dried for flavoring or cloth-wrapped for bouquets. Sun's setting blazed in a glimpse through the growing dusk, and Melónie took in her breath. She had never seen a sundown so bright. It burned like purest gold, fat and heavy in its descent. Then, like the closing of a door, it was gone. Night happened.

"It is said, Captain, that when one embarks on a journey such as my lord's, that one may take many steps but travel no distance. My Apieron may be only paces from us, yet *shifted* he once said, like a dance, such that we cannot see or hear him."

"My lady, I know not how a man may journey for weeks and not wind up far from whence he started, unless he walk in circles. My lord is not such a man."

"I know I saw him march off the southern borders of Windhover where we said good-byes. He charged me to guard you and the children, and hinted that he might first journey through wild Wyrnde fens where he would explore those untamed lands for the Candor Kings. From there, they would take their way upon the farther road."

"I suppose you are right," Melónie sighed. "The Duskbridge lays many leagues beyond our Foslegen, if my husband can find it."

Duner mumbled, "Mention it not, Lady. 'Tis ill luck."

"It is well I am wrong, for if such places share the same space with this world, then might not a *shifting* allow some foul beast here with us?"

Duner cleared his throat disapprovingly. "Thank the blessed gods it is not so, Mistress. Such creatures are prisoned beneath the world where their sins have sunk them." He fidgeted, apprehensive. "My lady, the air grows chill, p'raps 'twere better inside?"

"My dear Duner ..." Melónie smiled her true smile and gripped the warrior's thick arm. "You comfort me. I am glad my lord Apieron has such a man as you for captain and friend." Duner began to object. Melónie continued, "Tasking is it not, for the brave of heart to stay behind with household and women whilst his chief journeys into danger?"

In Duner's hard world, there had been scarce expression of tender sentiments, and the old soldier was quite overwhelmed. He knelt and took Melónie's slender hand in his calloused ones.

"Milady, when Apieron brought you hither from the uncouth East, he set me to assume your safekeeping beyond my duties to the troop. This has been by far my nobler task. My life is many times forfeit before harm comes within arm's reach of you and yours."

Melónie gazed into the old widower's face with its fiercely sweeping moustaches and eyes that held hers so intently. "I know." She smiled again and touched his face. She turned, silks swirling, to enter her balcony.

Duner raised himself and stepped to the wall where he resumed his post with renewed vigor. He knew adequate guards were stationed thereon, plus roving patrols with their random sweeps and alarm horns. They were good men, and none slept or shirked his duty. Nonetheless, he peered intently into the surrounding tree line, suddenly ominous after the lady's words. He shook his head. She, a delicate eastern princess, removed to this colder clime in a kingdom where threat of war was daily life.

He would not fail her, no matter when or if Apieron returned. The closing darkness hid from the eyes of his men the rim of moisture that lined the eyes of Duner, captain of the guard. He did not wipe it away.

Chapter 38

The Wyrnde

In a stand of larch, the companions discovered a foot-worn track and followed it over a small crest where it gave unto a cultivated plot. Lowering clouds stole the light from the day, and a cool wind got up, smelling of rain as the party crossed the small field. It was not a black-earthed, bottomland farm such as was coveted by the great country barons. Its stone border was fallen into disrepair, there were too many thistles grown into the harvest stubble, and no sound of lowing cow or clucking hen came to them. A wattle-and-thatch hovel crouched amid a yard of dirt and uncut wildgrass in the center of the croft, and behind it was a low-slung barn. Apieron stepped forward.

"Hallo the house! Travelers weary, seek shelter from the storm." Wind licking along the straw-bundled roof was his only answer. The structure's only window, a paneless hole cut in the wattle, remained dark and silent.

"If not a cup and welcoming word," said Jamello, "a house deserted at least offers roof and fire."

Apieron nodded thoughtfully, advancing to the rough-planed door. It was secured by a lockless latch. His tracker's eye noted bird droppings in the yard, old and dusty. He caught sight of thin brush marks in the soil. He smiled faintly and said aloud, "Do we enter? Or seek shelter elsewhere?"

"We must decide quickly," said Henlee, "though I daresay we will find no cot as good as this."

Large drops from scudding outriders of the storm spattered the dust. With a dagger, Apieron flipped the leathern catch and stepped into the darkened hut. Henlee and Jamello pushed in on his heels, eager to avoid the gathering rainfall. Brandishing an axe, a haggard figure gave a shout and leapt from the shadows. Apieron parried, his dagger yielding before the heavier weapon. Freeing Maul, Henlee cursed and bounded to the room's center.

Jamello felt a thud against the back of his skull and pulled a dull-tipped wooden quarrel from a fold in his soft hood. Incredulous, he threw it down and rushed back outside, looking up to the noise of scrabbling feet. A small head ducked behind the roof's peak as a shriek of rage echoed from the hovel's interior. The axe borne by the tattered man was a woodcutter's tool of black iron with a hammer-back on an oaken shaft. Its fresh-burred edge gleamed as it careened to where Apieron no longer was, embedding itself with a heavy thunk into a trestle. Apieron stood behind the man, his dagger sheathed and an arm looped about his attacker's chest.

"Desist, man! I am the king's servant," he spoke into the greasy locks about the man's ear. Henlee rested Maul.

Outside, the small figure reappeared. Jamello called, "Come down now, boy, before you hurt someone with that squirrel tamer." His eyes widened as a second quarrel took him full in the stomach. He groaned and sank to his knees and crawled toward the shelter of the overhanging eve, fearing another shot to his exposed back.

"Kids," he muttered, "and they ask me why I've none of my own!"

The peasant's thick shoulders slumped in defeat. He shrugged free of Apieron's grasp to advance to the table and his axe. Henlee stepped aside but tracked him closely. Apieron noted that the crude table and a few stick-and-hide stools were the only furniture to occupy the room. The floor was hard-packed earth, and the far wall boasted a fire pit with kettle brace and a smoke hole, obviously insufficient, as attested to by the soot-blackened ceiling. The man pulled free his axe and let it hang loosely, seemingly out of mind. They saw his other arm was bound in a crude sling. "Well, men of steel, if you be the king's men or more reavers, it matters little. All is waste anyway."

"Come forth, Fergi!" He dropped the axe wearily. A quilted hanging pulled aside, and his wife shuffled forth to stand under the protective arm of her man. Despite his words, the man pulled her close. His truculent gaze swept over Apieron and Henlee.

Jamello crawled over the lintel with an *umph*, trailed closely by a dirt-smudged lad of approximately eight who bore a crude hand-crossbow aimed at Jamello's hind end. The boy's eyes glowed with fierce pride.

"I caught me one o' those rascals, Papa!"

The farmwife put a hand to her mouth. "Oh."

Henlee burst out in loud guffaws, joined by Apieron. Tears started down the dwarf's face as he slapped his knees, roaring with helpless laughter. Tallux entered and bowed to the plowman and his wife. Eafora followed and stood quietly to the side. Sut bounded in with a shake and cocked his head quizzically at the strange tableau. The peasant began to chuckle and then hooted with the others. "Aye, ye 'ave at that, boy. Well done."

Jamello searched each face plaintively. His determined captor moved about, game-bow poised directly between his eyes. The wall hanging parted again, and a straw-headed girl of perhaps ten crept timidly into the room to join her mother. She voiced an identical startled, "Oh!"

"Leave off now, boy," said the farmer, his voice again robust. Apieron noted that the peasant was of fewer years than he originally guessed. The hair was more blond than gray, and the lines on his face were those wrought more by sun and wind than years. Apieron guessed him to be no more than forty winters.

"Not so fast, youngin'," Henlee managed to gasp between wheezes. "That one is a criminal, right enough, and wanted in several counties! Best tie him up for a few days until you're sure he's safe." Henlee nodded at some coiled rope on a hook. Jamello shot him an evil look. The boy spared a moment's glance to the rope but quickly snapped back to threaten Jamello's nose with the fowl gun.

The farmer ambled over to his son and gathered him by the shoulders. Apieron noted the corded muscles of his forearms and was thankful the peasant's strength was backed by little skill with weapons. The man stood with his son and wife, his daughter sheltered against the farm wife's bosom. He looked oppressed. Hoping to break the gathering silence, Apieron quickly spoke. "We truly are the king's men and have likewise been sorely pressed. We seek only shelter from the storm and will pay somehow for a loaf and a draught."

Indeed the rain no longer pattered but unfolded over the land in lashing sheets such that they were forced to raise their voices to be heard. "Rain's good," said the farmer. "Good fer next year's crop." In his eyes, Apieron read the quiet relief of a man who had feared muchly for the safety of his family.

"Yer mule—" began the man.

"Donkey," corrected Henlee. "Dwarven donkey."

"Is warm and dry in the barn," added Tallux.

The farmer eyed the companions. Tattered and wretched as the condition of their garments was, the original richness of the fabric remained discernible, and the soft sheen of the elvin weave cut into hood and pant had never been seen by any of his brood. His gaze fell on the body mail and skirt worn by the dwarf. Even in its present state, the perfect tiny links so formed as to be essentially steel cloth were but a rumor in such remote lands, and would be worth his entire steading a hundred times over.

"Ahem, good sir," said Jamello. "About the money. I have kept a coin or two and did not squander away my means as have my friends. Would these suffice?" Two circular objects flipped through the air to land without a quiver on the trestle, their faces gleaming a dull yellow.

"Gold pennies," exclaimed the goodwife.

"Aye, of the royal mint no less," answered the farmer. "And of true weight," he said, rolling them in thick fingers. Touching his diamondless beard, Henlee scowled at the thief, who seemed to truly enjoy the look. Apieron marveled at how Jamello could have preserved the soft coins when everything else had been so blasted.

Jamello was warming to the situation. "I'm sure the lad is handy with that bird stunner. Could he not perhaps rustle up something for evenmeal?"

"An' that 'e might," grinned the peasant. "Boy—"

The lad dashed out into the rain without a backward glance. The travelers sat at the trestle as the goodwife and young maiden bustled about the room. The axe was restored to its wall nook, and a merry fire was kindled under a kettle that soon filled the space with tasty aromas of garlic and onion, bay and mint. Hampers cleverly hidden under hatches in the floor were opened, and a clean linen was spread over the table and set with clay plates and mugs.

The dwarf's eyes widened as a small cask of beer materialized with two loaves not a day old. Apieron lowered his head and coughed to disguise quiet laughter. In lands on the fringe of the wilds and plagued by rumor of war, even simple folk learned subterfuge. Henlee banged down his mug and smacked loudly. Jamello joined his laughter when the farmer's son reappeared, bearing a wicker basket filled with four lop-ears and two forest hens. Apieron chuckled openly, for the lad had only been gone a few minutes.

The farmer stepped out to prepare the game on the edge of the rain. Within a quarter hour, he returned to sit at table with his guests while the meal simmered. He took a long, cleansing draught and cleared his throat many times in practice for the words he meant to speak. They waited politely.

"When the crop began to head up come springtime, I thought to take my extra west t'a earn a bit o' coin. You see, word was them city farms fell on hard times. That was afore the razin'."

The peasant paused and cleared his throat again, as if unused to so many words, or to speak his mind in such company. His craggy face was ruddy in the firelight. "Hard luck men, taken to banditry, came for the daughter o' me nearest neighbor. Her a lass o' sixteen or so and orphaned, an' them as adopted her past middle years. They be gone now, all gone." He took a pull from his cup while the fire popped under the copper kettle.

"Well, I know'd jes where to find 'em, jus as they knew where to find the lass. Shame was, I knew more than a few from hereabouts o'er the years. So I did. Find 'em, that is. Told 'em they done wrong by the ol' man, 'is wife, and the lass no more'n a whelp. Well, they beat me a bit an' broke me collar rider an' sent two o' their lads here—took the ox an' a few sacks o' grain. My flower here hid with the youngins in the forest where we keep a few things back." He winked at the boy, who stared with the awe of any eight-year-old who reveres his father above all other heroes, and grateful to hear the tale told in full for the first time.

"Thieves and villains," exclaimed Henlee, "where's their camp?"

"Gone," said the peasant. "Aught left to steal."

"Even lawful men," said Apieron, "if they be weak, will surrender to their baser natures in unlawful times." He wondered how pervasive the unrest in the uplands must be if it had reached to this remotest corner of settled lands.

"Aye, an' might 'ave been a light worser," said the farmer. "Me an' mine, we're yet hale and whole."

"And hungry!" said the boy.

With that, there was none but the sounds of a meal relished as the famished travelers and hearty farm folk sated their appetites. At last, plates and cloths were cleared. Pallets stuffed with cured grass and down were produced, and to the companions they seemed the beds of kings. The goodwife led her yawning children to the recess behind the hangings. The peasant added another log to the fire and refilled mugs all around. With a burning twig, he lit a clay-bowled pipe and stretched his legs, a rich and pleasant odor filling the little room.

The companions settled back to relax, bellies full and palates quenched. Their rescued captive was in her corner, alert but declining to participate in any conversation, as was her way. The flickering light glinted off her solemn face and night-black eyes. Her hair, broken and unkempt in the pit, already seemed to Apieron to have grown in length and luster. Truly, under ordinary circumstances, she would be an extraordinary beauty.

As if reading his mind, the farmer spoke. "How came a woman to be with four warriors on trek for th' King?"

For a long moment, Apieron did not at first reply and the rain rattled the thatch. Its sheaves were tightly bound and well angled such that few drops found their way within. Apieron stared at coals that sent sparks and liquid tendrils of blue and orange heat up to consume a fresh log. He sought his memories in the living depths of the fire. In more detail than he had intended, Apieron described how came the call of the land that somehow stirred his oldest blood memories. He spoke of the Oracle and her words, dire and hopeful. With minor additions from Jamello and Henlee, he recounted their journey to an evil place of fire and the friends who did not return. He told their names, and those of the noble beasts who accompanied them and who had also fallen.

Their host nodded, thoughtfully, expressing no surprise or disbelief at the traveler's tale. He said at last, "A hate has come to this place.

"P'raps from the first days when gods an' devils walked this land. Those what be close to root an' vine know this for truth." To his words, nobody had aught to add, so the companions gratefully sought their beds.

Apieron remained awake. The stiffness had returned to his shoulder and chest. His wounds had bled today, and they felt hot. Outside, the rain continued unabated while by the fire Sut cracked and swallowed the bones of rabbit and hen, leaving nothing to waste. The soft sounds of children breathing came to him from the alcove. Sounds he had not heard since … when?

Setie, Ilacus, and Sujita, my Jilly! Will you know your father when he returns?

To sleep indoors in comfort inevitably carried his spirit to Melónie in her soft bower. "I'm certain she has rearranged the place entirely by this time," he chuckled drowsily. The notion was soothing and buried him into a gentle sleep.

Once while exploring Foslegen, Apieron saw something. The light was low, and there was a mist. An apparition beckoned, a bow slung on its back. Transfixed, Apieron stared, then rushed forward.

"Father!"

He found only a seat of crumbling stone, pockmarked with lichen. Behind it was a crooked tree. Disjointed, Apieron wended home, missing twice his trail and spooking a forest pig, yet lowered his bow from an easy flanking shot as it grunted and trampled into cover. He did not know how he felt.

Morning came crisp and clean behind the departing rains. Apieron and the boy hitched Bump to the farmer's single-bladed plow. Together they turned wheat stubble back into the ground. Surprisingly, Bump warmed to his task, perhaps as a reprieve from their long journey. The freeholder began to object, but looking to his broken clavicle and empty barn, he grudgingly assented. Soon curiosity overcame pride as Tallux showed him an elfin way to sort the grain of his harvest into seeds for planting and those to grind for meal. When finished, Tallux intoned an open-hand blessing over the baskets to keep the kernels free from rot and invisible to hungry bird and quick-footed mouse. The wood elf then betook himself to the trees and brush about the croft, trimming and curing when able those beneficial to the farmer's family. Hawthorne and elm, honeysuckle and forest strawberry grew green and bountiful in that place for many years.

Henlee whetted and oiled a rusted spade found in the barn, then set about the low backgrinding work of recutting an irrigation ditch from a bordering pond, swollen with rain, onto the plowman's field. When he paused for the midmorning meal, he was smeared with black mud and dirt but smiled in his beard, satisfied with the drainworks he had made.

The farm wife and her daughter cried out in wonder as Jamello gifted her with a share of the elvin fabric carried from the forest bower. He took the boy aside and showed him the construction of a weighted throwing net, a common skill in the port city of Bestrand, though now crafted for fowl and small game rather than swimming fish. Shaking his head in painful memory, Jamello coaxed the young one into yielding up his hand-crossbow. After an hour's toil, the fowl gun shot farther and straighter than ever it had.

Even Sut joined the labors. Whilst others toiled at hut and

field, he ranged far into the surrounding forest and the wild, open lands beyond. From dawn's break until early afternoon, he sought out every predator and drove them forth. Badger and fox, wild cat and serpent fled the irresistible hound. Those that fought, he slew. Most left with eager will, not wishing to return, for he marked his territory well with paw and scent.

A shuffling black bear ambled away as quick as she might, bawling in protest yet not turning to face the fearsome war dog near as heavy as she. When Sut returned to the croft, the sun had begun her westward descent, and the companions were saying farewell to the peasant couple and their children. The woman drifted from somewhere to stand expectantly by Apieron.

The freeholder, his eyes blue as the arching sky, grasped Apieron's hand as an equal and gave a proud nod that spoke more eloquently than words might have. Men and dwarf, woman and elf departed the croft in better wise than they came. Jamello's gold and the goodwife's hospitality purchased homespun garments to supplement their tattered travel ware. What was lacking in fit and style went happily unnoticed as they walked across sodden fields and pasture. Henlee munched contentedly on cold rabbit and a coarse loaf. Best of all, the goodwife had pressed into his hands a round cheese, bound in twine, his burned and bewhiskered face cracking into a wide grin when she gave it over.

"That be a high lord o' the old King, is he not?" she asked, nodding her chin towards Apieron.

"Aye, 'tis so," he answered. "Apieron of Windhover, boon friend of the Prince, and captain of the king's scouts."

"Keep him well, Master. I read a doom on him."

"I will, Lady." The dwarf bowed low as she turned away. "So did his father," mumbled Henlee to no one. "Here now, Bump! This is one burden you won't have to carry." He pocketed his treasure and joined the others.

The travelers continued north from the peasant's garth, hoping to keep to open country, fearing the lowlands of Apieron's southern and easternmost holding would be nigh impassable from the heavy rains. "See how footsore we remain despite the gifts of elves and men. We are more in need of an easy trail than the caches I intended to visit on my own lands."

"Aye," added Henlee. "Had I another day at the barn, I would have fixed new shoes for Bump." He looked sadly at his own wrapped boot. "Guess we'll both have to wait."

Despite the late start, they traversed some miles of open forest and grassy glade before the sun reached the western tree line. A migration of gray-and-white clouds overhead coalesced and found their burdens too heavy to bear. The wind changed direction to blow in from the south, and soon fat drops were heard pattering on leaves and bracken. They found cover under a low-spreading hawthorne, its berries already red. Thus the day ended.

The rain grew more vigorous, slipping sideways into eyes and faces when the wind surged. A fortnight and more had passed since their escape from the Hel plane, yet after their fiery ordeal, the rain was prickingly cold. Lungs that had burned with each breath and coughed soot and blood-tinged sputum drew in the moisture-laden air like the sweetest of perfumes. The farm wife's cheese was broached. It was softly ripe and tasted of nuts deep within creamy depths. Jamello shook the wet from his hair and bound it back with a string. It had grown long. He fingered his goatee and regarded Apieron, whose chestnut hair was unkempt above an unruly beard that fell a hand's breath below his chin.

"Look at us," said Jamello, "happy as beggars in cast-off clothes, under a tree with bellies full of gifted food."

"Speak for yourself," said Henlee. "Dwarves do not beg."

Tallux released a hawthorne leaf, soft and tufted white. "We are come to the lands of men. Our journey is nearly ended." There was a quiet moment while each pondered the wood elf's words.

"Soon I will seek out the Prince and see how fares the kingdom. Also the fortunes of my own people."

"And I the dwarves," said Henlee. "If times are rough as everyone says, old Redhand probably has them holed up so deep they won't hear me knocking at the door." He winked at the others. "I shall knock loud."

"Ahh, Bestrand," added Jamello, "how your ladies have missed me."

"Where will you hie, lord?" asked the woman of Apieron. The others turned to regard her, startled at her ease of speech and the first words she had spoken in days.

"First to Windhover and she who holds my love. After, I don't know. I must bear news of Xephard to the Valley of the Goddess, where two women await the mighty grief I must gift them.

"Then perhaps to the Sybil. Or to the service of my prince such as I know Xephard wished to do." The woman did not answer. Her face was cast in shadow, and in the morning, she was gone.

"Should be easy to track in this wet," called Henlee to Apieron and Tallux, who ranged from the camp in expanding spirals once they wakened to find her missing.

"Her tread is light," said Tallux, pointing to a barely discernible print in the detritus of the forest floor a few feet from a low rise of rock.

They cast about a full hour before gathering at the spot of her only spoor. They did not call out, for the fear and suspicion of the arduous trek returned fully. "It is as if she made for the rock and disappeared," said Apieron.

"To her own purpose," added Tallux. "She was not carried thither by force or any great reluctance, else there would be more sign."

"And you saw nothing?" asked Apieron of Jamello, who stood last watch.

"Not a will-o'-the-wisp can stir unmarked by a thief of Bestrand when he watches," said Jamello. "I was in yonder tree, on the opposite side of our camp, and that woman can move as quiet as a night cat when she wills."

"She did so will," added Tallux. "Her path took her in the only direction you could not have marked."

"This grieves me," said Apieron. "I hoped to bring her to Melónie and then to the Matron. No doubt she suffered much in the abyss."

"And now?" asked Henlee.

"She knows what and where we intend, mayhap she will catch us up." Apieron took up some small pebbles and a rough stone. With marks scratched on the rocky shelf and ordered pebbles, he etched out a simple map.

"The path to Windhover?" Henlee grunted.

"More than this I durst not leave," replied Apieron. "We are yet in the wild."

"I do not fear for her," said Tallux. "She showed rare skill in the ambush fight, and passing strange, Sut lost her trail over the rocks."

"If we do not meet again, I wish her well," said Apieron.

"Women!" said Jamello, shaking his head. The companions departed immediately. The southern wind, persistent throughout the night, had pushed clouds into marching ranks across the heavens, orderly as any parade of the king's legions. Strips of blue sky were revealed between the drifting columns, calm and untroubled by any event of the surface world. To the north, a rainbow fell gently from the receding cloud-ranks onto a muted tree line.

Tallux pointed. "Bride of the Rain."

"A good omen and a sign of hope," agreed Apieron. "At least I will take it to be so."

Despite the loss of their quiet female companion, moods remained buoyant throughout an easy day's travel. The forest thinned out, and at one point they crossed a grassy meadow bound by a hedge of laurel, leathery leaved to the touch. There was no sign of those who had planted it or why. They harkened back to Tallux's words the night prior and knew they would soon turn west, hoping to strike one of the trade routes to Windhover from Wulfstane's lands in the north.

That night, Apieron reclined, feet up on a cloth satchel fashioned by Jamello. His chest and shoulder bled fresh blood whensoever the dressing was changed. Henlee would scowl and cluck his disapproval. Nonetheless, Apieron was comforted by the hope he heard rekindled in the voices of his friends. He laid back his head and was soon submerged in sleep. Deep and well he rested until later waking to a light caress and soft, tinkling laughter. The body that stirred next to his was warm and fully awake, mischievously playful under the bedclothes. By her scent and touch, he knew her asleep or waking after six years of marriage.

"Melónie, my chosen, your man needs his rest. And well deserved!"

"But Apieron, lord," she breathed wetly into the nape of his neck, "there really 'is' something you must see."

Apieron turned his head with lids half closed. Melónie smiled full into his face. She had no eyes. Blood trickling obscenely down her cheeks and from the corners of her smiling mouth. He yelled, starting up, left hand groping for the long dirk that hung above the bed. His right grasped her by the middle, bunching her nightshirt in his clenched fist. She shrieked in laughter and began to buck and jerk convulsively, her hair whipping against him, spattering black blood over his chest and staining the pure white garments she wore, a bridle gift.

A deep laughter joined hers. Apieron became aware of a horsed, ebon-steeled warrior towering over the bed. Melónie's hands grew monstrous talons that tore his hands from her bodice and clawed for his throat. Out of the corner of his vision, he saw the stallion rear high, neighing shrilly as a sulphurous reek filled the air. He heard the rasp of a greatsword clearing its sheath.

"Melónie!" Apieron shouted and plunged his dagger between her breasts. Her talons fell limp, and she was jerked suddenly into the air.

As if suspended by some gigantic puppeteer, she flailed weirdly, her back against the ceiling arch. Reaching with both claws, she yanked the dirk free and dropped it clanging, a gout of crimson ichor following in a cascade over bed and floor. Apieron knew he should turn to face the knight, but Melónie held him mesmerized. Her eyeless gaze met his with no doubt that she somehow saw him well. Rocking her head back, she shrieked wildly in wracking ecstasy.

The warrior bellowed. Apieron wheeled about—too late! The stallion screamed and crashed its mighty hooves onto his chest and neck. Apieron felt bones shatter. He found that he could not move his neck but rolled his eyes up in time to see that burning blade descend its fatal arc. Then there was only darkness.

Henlee's wiry beard pricked Apieron's face. Apieron opened his eyes. "What are you doing?"

"What am *I* doing?" said the dwarf. "You should ask, what were *you* doing."

"Me? I was sleeping."

"No, you were laying there sweating and shaking. Then you shouted a strange word. *Malesh.*"

"Oh."

"Far be it from me to know aught of the ways of men, an' yet where I come from, shouting is not sleeping."

Apieron eyed the camp, surprisingly quiet in the pale luminescence of predawn that colored the world in blues and grays. He rubbed his shoulder; the pain of his Hel wound reawakened such as had not bothered him since the healing draught of the winged elves. "Where are the others?"

"Elf and his dog are gone scouting. Thief's out gathering the sticks I told him I wanted for the fire." Apieron regarded the supply of kindling left stacked from the night before. Henlee sniggered, the stubble jutting from his chin, if anything, more fiercely than ever. "I told him I wanted some cuttings from that dead fir across the way."

A smile found its way to Apieron's bearded features. "And he believed that?"

Henlee barked a rumbling laugh. "Who cares?"

Apieron eyed the broad-shouldered dwarf; much of his hair either burned or rubbed off, his dark skin covered with darker scars or raw abrasions. His heavy Maul was at his side as he crouched on one knee, his punctured foot in its enormous wrap behind him. Even now, defeated and bruised, Apieron would put even money on Henlee versus any opponent, real or from the dream world.

Apieron laughed loud and long. Henlee joined him. The sound of it echoed in the trees, dispelling night's gloom. Bump heehawed. "I fear this Malesh, Henlee. It was he who routed us in the waelstow." The dwarf stirred at this but said nothing. "I fear him not in combat," Henlee visibly relaxed, "but rather the darkness he carries within. He reminds me, of *me* … grown evil and delighting in some malefic quickening."

Henlee clapped a hand like stone on Apieron's shoulder. "I'm a simple one, lad. When your father set me to watch over you, I groused for a year an' thought my ways too blunt for more subtle folk. He insisted, and the lords of earth know I've done my level best. So I say this: Dwarves have long memories, and when I next see this Malesh, he may not much like what happens. Then will your dreams be easy."

"I think Xistus was very wise."

"*Is* wise, boy."

Jamello crept silently back into the camp, arms full of fir cuttings. "Here you are, Master Dwarf!" He beheld the twain sipping from cups over a very adequate little blaze made from the prior night's tinder. The fir boughs clattered to the ground.

"You're too late," declared Henlee.

"What?" gasped Jamello.

Henlee nodded at the fir wood. "And that's the wrong tree." Jamello produced only strangled sounds from his working mouth. Henlee stood and unconcernedly tossed his dregs into the fire. He gathered his new pack, pieced together from castoff cloth and salvaged strips of leather. Apieron ignored them both and led Bump northward out of the camp. They would meet Tallux on the trail. Jamello scattered the wood he had gathered with a kick and turned to follow, speaking to himself of dwarves, the ancestry of dwarves, the progeny of dwarves—but softly so.

Two hours later, they found the cippus. Rough hewn and over ten feet in height, it dominated the center of an ancient forest clearing given over to weeds and new tree growth where young pine and elm competed with man-high grasses for the open sun. "This here grave marker reminds me," said Henlee, "Bump is the only living donkey with a tombstone, and a nice one too." Bump gave no heed to these words, chewing contentedly on tufted grass.

"'Tis no cairn," said Tallux. "The men of this country did not bury their dead so. It is a way stone."

"Its name is Afyld," said Apieron. "I've never seen it but have heard tell of it. Wulfstane claims all lands north of it to the door of his keep, but I understand it to be much older than he or even his grandsire."

"It looks like it should be a tomb marker," said Jamello in rare agreement with the dwarf. "See how cold it is despite the sun." He removed his hand from its age-worn story of queens and heroes, serpents and griffins that whorled their eternal dance.

"Would that I could have done so fine as this for the steeds," said Henlee. He gazed meditatively at Bump.

Apieron and Jamello thought of their own fine mounts, gifted by the matron. No more would Apieron's racer toss her aristocratic head in disdain of lesser beasts. Never again would Jamello's palfrey, barely an adult, lead a merry hunt or make nickers after the mares. They thought also of Turpin's fine horse and the strangely striped forest steed of the winged elf that he called Beg. Lastly, Axylus came to mind, over twenty hands and one hundred and fifty stone of argent splendor. He was the very embodiment of a paladin's warhorse if ever there was one. Like his master, he fell defending others, innately choosing honor before life.

"Ware the Baron and Buthard, his son," said Tallux. The elf's words broke their reverie. "You have long been away from Court, Apieron. With the King's death, there will be little to restrain them."

"Judge them not too harshly," said Apieron. "No doubt 'tis difficult, for them to accept the advent of an outlander of strange mien, risen to nobility in the king's favor. Surely with the coming threat of darkness, all the king's servants will put aside such feuds."

"Xistus earned his title, as did you your land," growled Henlee. "Unlike most of the man-lords I've ever met."

"In any case, we are fortunate to have found the dolmen, whether Wulfstane's or no. We came farther north than I reckoned and must here go due west, else we will be Buthard's guests for supper tomorrow."

"Then let us be gone," cried Jamello. "I could use a home-cooked meal. If you half elves and almost elves brew any more of that mugwort tea, I shall be ill."

"You were grateful enough when I first gathered it," laughed Apieron.

"That was two days ago. I've drunk a gallon since."

"I agree," said Henlee. "Stuff's only good in beer." He wagged his thick finger at Apieron. "And slip no more sweatroot in my drink. I'd rather die."

Apieron and Tallux laughed. They walked, and before day's end, they did not find a friendly farmstead, but rather an abandoned orchard. Fruit trees of an unknown sort lay blighted and consumed with wood rot. Hearty olive and grape persisted and yet bore fruit, though the vine was grown bushy and a flight of starlings rose in protest from their feeding spot. Tallux showed the companions how to gather first the most ripe and sweet fruit from the vines' side most exposed to the sun. Jamello claimed a stick from a broken citrus and climbed into the largest olive. He soon threshed a dusky harvest onto cloaks and garments the others spread below. Only Henlee and Bump ate the bitter raw olives, but the grapes were consumed by all. They enjoyed their repast against a tree's gray and gnarled bole while Tallux told of the great age of such plants, reaching even unto a millennium for the eldest scions of olives, and a thousand feet deep for the heartiest of grapevines. "I knew I liked them for a reason," quoth Henlee, munching happily and spitting pits.

On departure, the companions discovered an abandoned footpath, overgrown with weeds, that trailed away west and south. Putting in a good step before nightfall, they found it reliably skirted low places that smelled of fallow and avoided ancient tumbledown, such that it remained true to its original direction. The next morning's breeze brought to them the smells of familiar countryside. By the time the sun brushed aside night's lingering mist, they struck a road. No more than a wagon track it was. Even so, to the wilderness-weary wayfarers, it seemed the king's very highway. Upon it they turned south and soon passed isolated bourns.

Henlee nearly wept with joy when they traversed a field planted in hops, the cones bent heavily, neglected to the harvest. Despite the dwarf's enthusiasm, Apieron was troubled. The steadings seemed abandoned, or perhaps the peasants were wary and hidden. What plowmen or herd boys they drew nigh turned their charges away from the travelers in haste. By Apieron's thinking, they should have encountered a merchant or messenger or at least a farm wagon on the road. They did not. Nonetheless, on the outskirts of a nameless huddled village, they espied spring colts and kids of sheep, knock kneed and frisky. Young calves sported blunt horn-buds amongst swirled and matted hair, and gamboled and grunted, frolicked and sparred in mock battles. Villagers had few words and less hospitality for such outlandish wanderers. Only by surrendering the remainder of their elvin cloth were they able to obtain a string of eels and a dozen ears of busked corn with watery beer with which to wash it down. They ate as they walked, for no tavern or commonhouse beckoned with open doors and friendly lamplight. Breasting a low rise, they found the road widened to a well-worn and rutted byway that looked as if it had once born heavy traffic. It was there that they encountered the piebald mule.

Although he was a true mule, he was no larger than Bump, who was as mighty of stature among burros as his master was among dwarves. After the companions passed, the mule stalked toward Bump, who stood stock still in the middle of the road awaiting him. The piebald's ears were laid back and his long teeth bared as he ambled confidently over, nodding his brushy mane. He pulled up, muzzle mere inches from Bump's, and neighed aggressively.

Making no gesture or noise, Bump darted his neck forward

and bit the other on the lips. The piebald made as if to rear and plunge, but Bump shoulder-rushed at the apex of its jump. The mule was struck off its feet to roll twice before finally righting himself in a flurry of flying hooves and tail. He plunged away, braying his outrage and fear.

Henlee wagged his beard as his burro fell in nonchalantly behind him. "You ought to have been nicer to that young lad, Bump. For all you know, he might 'ave been your son." Bump snorted in derision and kicked a cloud of dust over the dwarf's legs before trotting past to rejoin the others. Two more days passed on the road with little adventure. The countryside grew more familiar with each step, yet an uneasy quietude remained on the land. What few travelers they encountered remained curt of word and hurried past with faces cowled and eyes downcast. With each rise or bend, Apieron hoped to catch sight of his home, although he knew it lay farther ahead.

Dawn of the third day on the road and the twenty-first from the Hel Gate came clear and bright. To the south, the scent of smoke and a pall hung on the air as the companions breasted a wooded rise and beheld the pink-white stone that was Windhover. The sky behind it was smudged brown, as if after a burning. Black specks wheeled and circled the tower, and to their ears came the raucous calls of carrion birds. Apieron was home.

Chapter 39

Tyrfang Over Körguz

A t his general's message, Iblis, Prince of Kör, laughed. A sound that caused no small apprehension in the breasts of those guards and principals who stood nigh the Dream Throne, its depths churning in concert with the exaltation of its master. Alcuin did not cower, nor even flicker an eyelash, as did even the stoutest demon-sired warrior in attendance of the Kör prince.

Iblis met the sightless gaze of the young human and wondered what strange vistas the strangeling beheld. It seemed a lingering shadow of crimson stained the pale cheek of his favorite savant. Well Iblis remembered that image, for it was he who ordered the ingots, ensorcelled from iron of the Starfall, be driven into the newborn orbs of the albino human. Pilaster had said such would sharpen the spaedom of the unusual child. And never before had the words of Pilaster, Faquir of Kör, proved false.

Iblis gathered the treasure placed before him, his claws grasping the gilt skull as they would a lover. Above the strong cheekbones, its shadowed sockets were set with Hel stones glowing with the ruddy fires that made them more precious than diamonds. He held aloft the skull of Bardhest Redhand, King of Uxellodoum.

Hands struck chests, and heavy feet drummed obsidian flags in acclaim. All save Alcuin. Iblis fixed him with a strange look as the applause faltered.

"What befalls, Seer? Like you not this gift of Iz'd Yar?"

The young man's pallid face was, as always, expressionless. He angled his head as if to behold the object with his sightless gaze. "Lord of Empires, the soul of the dwarf king hast departed this earthly shell. Thy servant was careless."

"Nonsense," hissed Pilaster through plate-like teeth. "What knows such as he of the trophies of conquest? No less a gift from thy very cousin?"

"Silence, fool!" roared Iblis, his glare shifting from Pilaster to settle dangerously on the young human.

"And do you, Savant, thusly deem this bauble useless?"

"Quite so, Slayer of Nations. As much so as that blood phile from the Candor king, tainted by the vomitus of Grazmesnil's assassin."

"Bastard human," threatened Pilaster. "Never should I have let you live beyond your birth." It was Pilaster who received the totem of the elder Candor from the very hand of his prince.

Iblis laughed again. "I had meant to punish you, slave. But I have not seen Pilaster unsettled so by word or deed in as many years as you have drawn breath."

"That can be amended." Pilaster drew a murderous-looking iron and advanced a step on the frail human.

"Nay." Iblis wagged one clawed finger, setting his pangyrist back into place. "Today I feel expansive, my noble cousin has gifted me with the death of this lord of dwarves." The gold skull was tossed lightly in the massive hand, then turned so that its crimson eyes regarded Iblis' own lambent yellow.

"King Bardhest Redhand, Gatekeeper of the West, thy troth is failed. Soon Snakes of Kör will gnaw the belly of thy burrow.

Alcuin, take thy reward!" The Kör king hurled the heavy skull, which struck the thin-robed human in the midriff, the force of it flinging him on his back to career across the slick stone to fetch up against a pillar. The assembly applauded.

Alcuin stood with creaking slowness, the skull clutched to him. Half those present narrowed their eyes at the puling human who survived a blow that could have splintered vertebrae or ruptured organs. At a nod from Iblis, Alcuin bowed painfully and took his way from the Dream Throne with measured steps.

Slender white hands caressed the heavyset brow of the skull. A *presence* tingled Alcuin's fingertips. Bereft of soul perhaps, yet possessed of a lingering contact—the spirit of the dwarf king remained accessible to he who was Savant of Kör.

WINDHOVER

Apieron passed into the great hall. Mechanically he stepped around the remains of his feasting board and many fine chairs and hangings that had adorned it. There was little sign of the bodies of those who fell in a brave but futile defense, the people of the garrison town having come since to claim brother and friend, father and son. Where each had lain, a small flower of chalk was inscribed on the floor. Apieron picked his way to the stairwell. Tallux and Jamello and Henlee followed gingerly. Their eyes were on him. His were fixed ahead. Back rigidly erect, Apieron took the steps in a slow cadence that echoed forlornly from the cold stone.

First he came to the nursery; torn bolsters and the splintered remnants of the delicately carved cribs told the story in a glance. His face blanched, but he uttered not a sound when he beheld a smear of blood, partially scrubbed, that had splashed the farther wall. A moment later, he passed to the room he had built for Melónie. The destruction was total, and lingering fumes of the burning stung his nostrils more than any stench of Hel.

When he returned to the lower entry, the priest Desolaix awaited him. "My lord Apieron … would that I could 'ave given my life for theirs." The man's words faltered, hands nervously plucking his garments.

A single tear, scintillant as a diamond, stood on Apieron's cheek, but his face was stiff as wood. When he spoke, his voice held its full power, although devoid of warmth as a sparkling river that is frozen into bleak waste by the sudden fury of a night storm.

"No white iris, Desolaix, for the children? Or their mother?"

The paunchy priest shook his head, shoulders shrugging helplessly. "We ne'er found any bodies, lord. None at all." Apieron nodded. He stared, unseeing. To what memory or dire hell his mind fled, those assembled could not begin to guess, for in a moment he was back. His gaze swept over them as if anew.

"My true friends." Apieron nodded his head in respect. A tattered beard touched his front, and brown hair fell past gray eyes to search each of theirs. He beheld the pathetic remnant of the settlers who clustered behind the priest. Noticeably absent were any males over twelve summers, save those wounded and not yet succumbed to blood loss or the nigh inevitable onset of battle rot.

Girls and women wailed for Melónie. Young boys stood with clenched fists and quivering lips, unsure whether to cry with the others. They remembered the many kind words and special treats she gave them. Such a one, no more than six, dashed from the gathering to come before Apieron. His hair was burned to the scalp. In his trembling hands, he proffered a scrap.

Apieron took it and touched the boy's head with a soothing word. He remembered the child as the only son of a gate warden.

A good man, handy with a crossbow. The boy's eyes were shiny, bright as polished glass. The fabric was old and soot begrimed. Apieron knew it well. Rich relief in cloth of gold-and-silver threads set off a design of speaker's stave held in gauntleted fist. Its base placed on a forested mountain, the top lost in clouds fretted with lightnings—his father's standard. It must have been borne on heated winds from the burning, for it had depended nigh ten feet long from the rafters of the great hall, a place of honor. Apieron ripped free the blazon of the king's rangers from his front and flung it down. With its clasp, he affixed his ancestral colors to his breast. The townsfolk watched in silence.

Apieron raised his head to address them, but his gaze spied a carved font set on the blackened threshold to his house. Perched on its supporting pillar, it was intact. Surprisingly, it yet held water, although blackened. "Touchstone of the gods. Guardians of my home?"

He jerked the basin free and raised it over his head. The people gave back as Apieron's face worked with passion, then a tremor seized him. He clumsily replaced the bowl, spilling its water over his hands. Henlee's firm grip at his elbow took him aside.

"No more today!" growled the dwarf to all. Tallux and Jamello made off to prepare a resting place, upwind from the burning that was Windhover.

Chapter 40

Lampus

The brief journey to the Lampus commenced without farewell. The bodies of Melónie and the children remained undiscovered, and no retainer or priest approached Apieron to make funeral. The four companions departed in the gray morning after their arrival at Windhover. Well past darkness and despite Henlee's protestations, Apieron had listened to tales of woe and loss as village folk approached singly or in clans to speak or simply gaze upon their lord. Not few were those who gave him some word of comfort or small gift of food or clothing or the war gear of slain kindred. These were gratefully accepted by Apieron's comrades who slept little, oft waking in the still to find him gazing into the flickering fire of the camp they had set by the broken culvert and scorched trees of Melónie's garden. No food or drink passed his lips as he listened to the folk. He heard much and said little.

The four walked in morning's silence, images of fire-scarred Windhover filling their waking vision. The stench of its burning stung in noses and would do so until miles fled beneath weary feet. For his part, Apieron marched woodenly, eyes fixed beyond the horizon. He took no note of the muted conversations of the others, and if he perceived the changes that befell his beloved countryside, he did not speak it. Before the Helquest, the subtleties of a broken cart rotting by the wayside or a weed-strewn crop tended by a sullen plowman would have seemed drastic indeed. The travelers passed them by without blinking. Jamello and Henlee reminded themselves that in the seeming few weeks they had been gone, a long season of unrest had stricken the very soul of the kingdom.

The forlorn grays of dawn departed, leaving the day bright and cool with whispered hints of fall on a wind that stirred in hair and treetops, yet rather than the festive orange and reds of the season's turning, the leaves of hedge and tree passed from summer's green to limpid yellow or brown husks that rattled on arthritic fingers of the weary growths. Crude cairns of piled stone they passed, no doubt marking the graves of unheralded peasant or strangers. Some of these were quite small, obviously the burial places of children.

"So many," muttered Jamello.

Henlee and Tallux were nearly as silent as Apieron as they walked behind and to the sides, responding to Jamello's comments with single words and noncommittal shrugs, their attentions fixed concernedly on their friend. As the day wore on, they shared between them a loaf of baked oats and a skin of watered wine. Apieron stared at their offerings as if he did not recognize the nature of what they held.

As the journey lengthened, Jamello found a malaise he had never considered. A fortnight ago, he felt that if he would ever again draw a breath not scorched with sulfuric fire or take a step not weighted by fluctuant gravities, he should then be forever content. A notion grew in his mind that the violation of one's own home was somehow worse than any atrocity witnessed in distant lands. Previously he had chafed at the iron-handed laws imposed by the Templars of the valley on the land surrounding their holy places and anywhere else they deemed fit. He felt now it had been less than it should. Amidst his shadowy haunts in Bestrand, often violent and unforgiving, there was nonetheless an order to the intricate weave between cutpurse and guardsman, harlot and merchant. Wasteful slaughter or senseless acts of destruction profiting no one were not tolerated, the perpetrators inevitably brought to the justice of a watery grave, as oft at the hands of the guild of thieves as by the law of the city's lords.

"Where are the paladins of the vale?"

"Gone off to the fighting by my guess," said Henlee. "Betwixt Apieron's absence and Buthard's treachery, hard times have befallen these simple people. Now we know traitor he is."

They crossed an apple orchard brutalized by torch and axe. Never again would the hacked stumps or blackened branches bear fruit for earnest farmer, playing children, or shying doe. Tallux's knuckles clenched white on the haft of Strumfyr. He said nothing. A pack of feral dogs, squealing and snapping, angled towards them. The lead animal, a great yellow cur, fixed his dog's eye on them, glazed and greedy. He caught a whiff of Apieron and wheeled as if stung. Suddenly silent, they filtered off to the shelter of the forest, unraveling amongst the trees. Sut and Bump beside him eyed them with scorn. "See how the wilds return to the very border of the valley itself," stated Henlee, shaking his head. "Men! They build quick as hares in sand. An' a heavy rain washes it all away."

Jamello wanted to say something in defense of his kind; instead he quickened his steps to catch Tallux and Apieron, whose pace had not slowed for sightseeing or conversations. To Jamello, Apieron's long strides were as ceaseless as those of an automaton. He wondered if his friend's mind would break. If so, what would they do? What would *he* do? For untold days, return to sunny Bestrand had been foremost in his thoughts. His ladies, his fineries, and, not least, thoughts of the revenge he owed

Procrius brought comfort to him. Now that life seemed somehow less glamorous, thoroughly unromantic, and pointless. Jamello kicked a rock in frustration. His toes stung through the worn tips of his once fine boots.

"Hey! This isn't a foot race." Nobody listened.

Noon of the fourth day saw them approach Hyllae. "Well, well," grunted Henlee appreciatively. "Templars keep to their steel."

They strode to what Jamello thought to be three bundles, dependent from the branches of a lob-leafed oak which stood athwart the road. As the companions drew near they saw them to be men, hung by the neck, the desiccated bodies swaying slightly in the wind. A small placard was nailed to each chest. Jamello spoke the several tongues of the polyglot city of Bestrand, yet these letters were of a sort unknown to him, although he had seen similar characters amongst the writings of priests and scholars.

"Their crimes were many," said Tallux, briefly reading the script as they strode beneath. "Bandits."

"*Criminals,*" declared Henlee, his eyes fixed smugly on the young thief.

The companions crested the wooden rim of the Vale of the Goddess. "Even here—" breathed Tallux.

Where there had been flowering groves and food plots bordered with orderly rows of piled stone and tall hedgerows, the ground was torn and rutted as with the passing to and fro of a thousand iron-shod feet. Many trees had been cut and drug into piles, then fired. The companions beheld the small figures of acolytes and husbandmen who labored to set the field boundaries anew or solemnly raked the ash piles. Jamello's keen eyes narrowed, he spied many burial urns stacked amidst tools and sacking on work carts.

"There," cried Tallux, pointing forward along the valley's primary road. "A rider. Nay, a knight on a proud steed!" Soon all marked the horseman who rapidly approached.

"Xephard?" said Jamello. "*Foolish,*" he muttered.

The paladin was girt with silver mail, a sword depended from his waist. He bore a lance of twenty hands on his right. He sat his steed in an easy gallop, and his visor was lifted. They knew that in a trice, it and the deadly lance could be lowered. "If yon horseman hails us not, elf," growled Henlee, "feather him with your dark bow."

Tallux slung an arrow upon Farstriker but did not raise it. Henlee unslung Maul for the first time in days. He swung it back and forth, weighing the odds of a strong throw versus twenty hundreds pounds of steel-clad knight and horse. He stepped before Apieron, who had not reacted.

Jamello ran his fingers over the assorted daggers he had acquired at Windhover, all poorly balanced. He wondered if he would so much as tickle the perfectly armored warrior and the equally impervious steed. Its barding flashed in the sun. The paladin advanced uphill without slowing, horse and rider possessed of fluid grace as if they were one creature. "Centaur," muttered Jamello. Small-wonder yokels and ignorant peasants contrived such a legend.

"He chooses battle!" said Henlee. The dwarf filled his lungs to shout a challenge before striking, yet before he could utter his war cry, the rider drew up three horse lengths' distant.

"Isander!" cried Jamello. The thief laughed nervously, hands falling away from his daggers.

"Hail, travelers!" called the temple warrior, eyeing their ragged forms closely. "The Donna bids you welcome. For my part, I apologize for our poor greeting, and not least, lack of page or pony for your comforts." He nodded to the laborers toiling downslope. "We have been busy of late."

"And?" said Henlee. The paladin's searching gaze and strong chin turned to study the dwarf, then fixed on Apieron.

"So much like Xephard," muttered Jamello, "and different."

"Apieron Farsinger knows well the way. Cynthia commands your presence as soon as you come to Temple."

Apieron's face remained hidden beneath his bowed head and veil of brown hair. When he did not acknowledge the paladin's words, Isander continued. "Others are known here as well." His gaze fell swiftly across the dwarf and elf to linger on Jamello.

"Paladins and clerics!" said Jamello. "Why did I come here?"

The temple knight saluted in midspin and spurred his stallion back whence he came. "Pretty," declared Henlee as he grasped Apieron by the arm to assist him onward.

"The knight speeds word of our coming to the mistress of the vale," said Tallux.

"She needs it not," said Jamello ruefully. "Our name and number she knew ere our feet touched her borders." He stood awhile fretting. "It's not too late to go elsewhere!" Their retreating backs did not turn.

The door to the rectory flew open, and Apieron's hand fell from the clasp. He swayed drunkenly on the step. Isolde drew back as she scanned their number. She gasped, hands flying to her lips. Cynthia pulled her gently but firmly aside. Apieron staggered to his knees. With a strength beyond her wasted form, the Donna lifted the man thrice her weight. Commanding the others follow, she guided him into the cool dark of the caldarium.

The End

Epilogue

The elf took his way along a path that would be both invisible to mortal eyes and perilous to mortal feet, but this was of little import since none had ever been there. The elf moved and breathed in harmony with the slow life of the forest floor and the soft whisperings of its canopy. Although he was close-wrapped in gray, the merest glimmer of golden hair and golden eyes flashed like sunlight that pierces a cloud. Birds displayed their best colors, singing sweetly while tree boughs lifted in salute to his passing, the breeze freshening with a hint of salt-air perfume. After months transformed into a golden beech, the elf lord rejoiced to walk his domain.

Away north, first-growth trees shaded their hoary secrets for many hundreds leagues. Past the eastward forest, an invisible keep stood vigil over tumbledown fells cast from the Arnost range that declined into boundary lands of scarp and tundra. To the west was a slender, white tower on the sunfall sea. There lay his course.

The freedom of his limbs in movement pleased the elf. Lengthy sleeps amongst trees had become more frequent in recent decades, and the elf smiled when he mused that his kingdom was wisely governed by a Ring of Six, chief of whom was his queen, the enchantress Dorclai Trazequintil. Under the rule of her wisdom were several thousands firstborn, plus the myriad allied peoples who named Amor as their home. Clever gnomes, singing forest elves clad in dun and green, and burrowing halflings dwelled in communities apart, albeit bonded by the wise sovereignty of their overlord.

Long ago were the days when the elf first beheld the time-forgotten port with its inland marshes and trackless woods. He had removed the dark spell that had lain on the land; now slender ships of white timber and silver spars plied trade and sport along the western coast. A great road pierced the forest through a southern gate for communication with the free kingdoms away south. The elf paused, for he perceived a small sound, as if the tinkling of a delicate bell. Under the arbor, his passage became a swift glide. If any eyes had seen, it would appear as if he would run straight into a given tree athwart his path only to emerge far distant from another.

The bell sounded again. The elf's thought called to a cloud, and he shot from the top of an ancient oak in a shower of golden mist to step-mount a new rainbow that arched forty leagues onto a balcony near the apex of a gleaming tower above Eufalla the Fair, chief city of Amor by the sea.

No expression played on the faces of the resplendent guard whose master they had not seen in half a year. Their captain bowed deeply. "Welcome, Lord Galor. You command aught?"

"I command ... a council of war."

The elf soldier's face beamed with delight. "It is done, lord!" He spoke a deep-voiced word and was gone.

Galor leaned upon the silver rail, his mind scanning the reaches of his wide domain. Unto his dreams had come mighty portents. The plight of friends and kin, a twisting within the earth, and grave danger to animal and plant, mountain and stream. The faces of men were cast in sorrow. Some grew fell of heart and allied with shapes of darkness, yet to the mind of the elf king their secrets were laid bare. For had he not known and battled those of old?

"My lord," said an elfin knight. "Champions await."

"My thanks, Drust. Too long have I slept."

Index of Names, Enter, Knight

Bizaz, half-orc cleric
Black Shirts, Uxellodoum's ready force
Bolechim, chamberlain of Hel
Bragen, leader of Liflyne folk
Briesis, Sybil of Western Lands, Oracle
Brockhorst, prefect of police at Sway
Bump the burro
Buthard of Wicklow, Xephard's mighty destrier
Captains' Hall, the Ca' D'Oro
Candice, Gault's mother
Celadon, site of river battle
Conrad, Gault's serving man
Cryse, Melónie's gentle goddess
Cynthia, Donna of Lampus at Hyllae, Wisdom's Perpetua
Denfirth, coastal garrison north of Sway
Deuce, renegade dwarf
Dexius, Minister of Sway
Dorclai, high priestess of Amor, married to Galor
Drannôk, knight of the Everfire
Dranol Eserhaven, mountebank magician
Dream Throne, Living Throne of Tyrfang
Dromlich, a menhir on Xambol the Stonefist
Drudges, under dwellers of Kör
Drust, champion of Amor
Duner, castellan of Windhover
Durmfere, rune maid of Nar
Duskbridge, the dark gate, Matog in the language of Kör
Eafora, rescued maiden, also called Scipflot
Eirec of Amber Hall
Eldûn, swamp forest near Sway
Erasmus, apprentice mage
Exeter the Hawk, Seneschal of Ilycrium

Farceps, chief municipality of Prebanks in the Saad Isles
Fafnir, Ring of the Dragon
Far Darter, brother to Wisdom, Archer and Healer
Findlán, Apieron's stream in Foslegen
Fogleaf, Liflyne home
Foslegen, forest nigh Windhover
Fuquit the Fat, merchant captain of Farceps
Galor Galdarion, the golden elf
Gault Candor, Prince of Ilycrium
Ghaddur, fiend of the Pit
Gilead Galdarion, warrior mage
Gor du Roc, Gault's birth father
Gorganj, high country above the Haunted Vale
Gorgon of Hel, manifestation of Ulfelion
Gray Ess, the Western Sea
Grazmesnil, eldest earthbound dragon
Gugnir, Sarc's twisted spear
Hardel, military governor of Sway
Haunted Vale, the Starfall Valley
Hel, plane of Tiamat's imprisonment
Henlee the black dwarf
Hills of Ulard
Holfstag, Acupundi fastness
Hyllae, Valley of the Twin Gods, the Holy Vale
Iblis, Emperor of Kör
Ilacus, second child of Apieron
Ilus, sword heirloom of house Candor
Ilycrium, land of the Sea Kings
Ingold, Gilead's Pegasus mare
Isander, paladin of the Vale
Isolde, warrior priestess
Ivanest, Bardhest Redhand's nephew

Iz'd Yar, Field Marshal of Kör
King Dryas, lord of the wood elf enclave, Malave
Khôsh, servants of the Gate
Kör, empire ruled by the Azgod
Körguz, capital city of Kör
Lampus, temple of Wisdom at Hyllae
Leitus, Xephard's great sword
Liflyne peoples, winged elves
Llund, Helfort
Lord Count Malchar, at Denfirth
Lysander, merchant of Sway
Malave, Greenwolde of Ilycrium's wood elves
Matog, the Duskbridge
Maul, Henlee's hand-glaive
Melónie, wife of Apieron
Mgesh, fierce nomad tribes of Kör
Mogush, slave city of Panj
Mylenscarp Range, mountains north of Sway
Nagwolfe, legendary wolf species, long and cat-like
Nessur, the fallen people
Palazzo of Farceps, chief municipality of Prebanks
Panj, land of theKhôsh, servants of the Gate
Pankapse, Hel's Westfort
Pilaster, Faquir of Kör
Pleven Deep, the Dragon Rift
Prebanks, the Saad Isles
Procrius of Bestrand, merchant prince
Quas, the Star People
Quk, Sarc's living quiver
Renault, chevalier of Ilycrium and First Knight
Rudolph Mellor, also known as Jamello, and Edshu the jongleur
Sadôk, demon-apes

Saemid, Henlee's secret redoubt
Sarc, Liflyne druid
Scaelp, the Bladenfex of Mylenscarp Range
Seamus, armsman
Seod, Western hillmen of Ilycrium
Setie, Apieon's eldest daughter
Sky, the Thunderer, father of Wisdom and the Archer
Skytop, castle in the clouds
Slysbeth, bounty hunter
Snake of Kör, military legion of approximately six thousand soldiers
Starfall Valley, the Haunted Vale
Strumfyr, also called Farstriker, Tallux's famous bow
Sujita, little Jilly, Apieron's youngest child
Sut, Tallux's Gelyfin war hound
Sway, capital of Ilycrium
Swaymeet, keep of the Candor kings
Swaywynde, Sway's harbor river
Tallux, archer of Greenwolde
Tartarus, the Hel of Tiamat's imprisonment
Tareg, orc tribe of the Dripping Eye
Telig Foesplitter, gnome gate warden
Telnus, ranger of Windhover
Templars, guardians of the Vale
Templemore, manufacturing village
Tensel, Apieron's bow, broken by Malesh
Tertullion, Magnus of Ilycrium
Tiamat, Mistress of Hel
Tizil, imp of darkness
Trakhner, General of Ilycrium
Turpin, Archbishop of Sway, high priest of Sky
Tyrfang, Iblis' palace in Körguz
Uglich, chieftain of Seod

Ulard, tribal region of western Ilycrium
Ulfelion, Prestidigitator of Hel
Ulrich of Bestrand, Regent
Uthos, Adestes' father
Uxellodoum, place of dwarves
Valente, Regent of Shipmasters' Congress
Vergessen, centaur chief in Foslegen
Vodrab the Foul, Makis of Kör's march
Wgend, race of the Sea Kings
White Throat, the Vigfil Stair to Kör
Windhover, Ilycrium's borderkeep south and east
Windstrong, Tallux's steed
Wisdom, Gray-Eyed Goddess of the Vale, War Goddess
Wondensteel
Woobora the Black Druid, Unggirat of ancient days
Wracu, Sarc's bow, Woodwand of Revenge
Wulfstane, Baron of Wicklow
X'fel the Accursed, named Serpent Fire by elves
Xambol, hill called Stonefist
Xeopolus, advisor at Lampus
Xephard Brighthelm, Wisdom's perfect warrior
Xistus Farsinger, father of Apieron
Yambol of the Rose, second traitor of Farceps
Zaddick, Capacian wagon merchant

Edwards Brothers Malloy
Oxnard, CA USA
February 16, 2016